DAVID NOBBS

The Second Life of
Sally Mottram

HARPER

Harper
An imprint of HarperCollins*Publishers*
77–85 Fulham Palace Road,
Hammersmith, London W6 8JB

www.harpercollins.co.uk

A Paperback Original 2014
1

A catalogue record for this book is
available from the British Library

ISBN: 978 0 00 744998 9

Set in Meridien by Palimpsest Book Production Limited,
Falkirk, Stirlingshire

Printed and bound in Great Britain by
Clays Ltd, St Ives plc

MIX
Paper from
responsible sources
FSC™ C007454
www.fsc.org

For Chris

ACKNOWLEDGEMENTS

Thanks to my wife Susan for her usual incredible patience, to my agents Ann Evans and Nemonie Craven at Jonathan Clowes Ltd for their support and wisdom, to Cassie Browne and everyone I know at Harper for their support and enthusiasm, and to Mary Chamberlain for another great editing job.

I'm also very grateful to my stepdaughter Kim and her husband John for inspiring me to write a book with the Transition movement at its heart. They are heavily involved in this in France and have played a big part in the creation of the film entitled *Transition Au Pays – Aventure Lotoise*.

I have also learnt a great deal about the Transition movement from two books by Rob Hopkins – *The Transition Handbook* and *The Transition Companion*, which Sally buys in Totnes, and I was also inspired in my choice of subject for this novel by reading *The Energy Glut: The Politics of Fatness in an Overheating World*, by Ian Roberts.

However, I have not witnessed or taken part in any of the Transition movement's initiatives. I wished my beloved Potherthwaite and its characters to remain entirey imaginary.

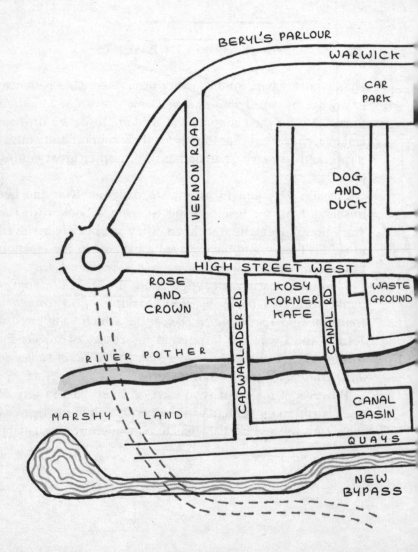

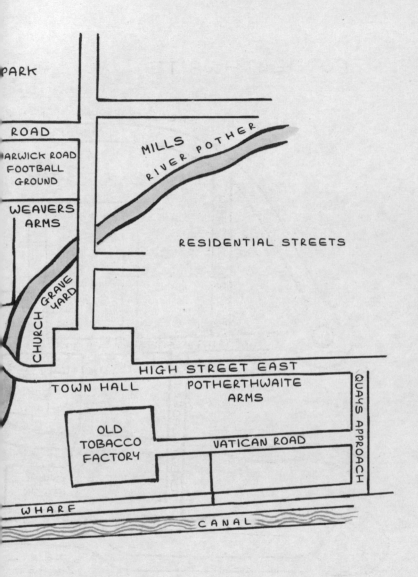

Contents

BOOK FOUR: Conrad

BOOK FIVE: Transition

BOOK SIX: The Last Day

BOOK ONE
The First Day

Of course they didn't know, on that day, that it *was* the first day.

ONE

Two nines and a six

Sally Mottram had never liked Potherthwaite. She had never even liked the North of England. She endured it because of Barry's business.

She liked it less than ever today. She had walked the length of the High Street, as part of her exercise routine, and because she wanted to call in at the bookshop on the Potherthwaite Quays – the plural was an exaggeration. There she had received the devastating news that the bookshop would close in three weeks, unable to match the special offers given elsewhere in a world where a book is expected to be a little cheaper than a starter in Pizza Express.

On the Quays there was a very basic café and an empty building with a rusting sign that stated '*The Terminus Bist o*'. The bistro had closed its doors – another exaggeration, its door – seven months ago. Soon 'The Canal Bookshop' would also be empty. One day a letter would drop off there too, and '*The anal Bookshop*' would fester among the floods for ever.

This was the scene at the end of the Potherthwaite Arm of the Rackstraw and Sladfield Canal, which the great Sir Norman Oldfield no less had once planned to turn into a rival for Wigan Pier. Sally stood and looked at the dereliction. Up the canal, three narrowboats lay moored. One had sunk, but the canal was so shallow that it was hard to notice this. The second was rotting, as was its occupant, a sculptor who had suffered from sculptor's block for seventeen years. The third was beautifully maintained, and lived in by a rather posh couple, who had once just managed to get to the Quays through the silt, only to find that there was no longer enough water in the cut for them to turn round and go home. They had lived there for eight and a half years now, getting slowly older and slower, but always offering generous noggins to their new friends.

Something had to be done about Potherthwaite, but who would do it?

She turned her back on the sad scene, and began to walk along the unimaginatively named Quays Approach towards the east end of the long High Street. Waddling complacently towards her was Linda Oughtibridge. Some people thought she did the flowers for the church quite beautifully. Others didn't. Linda Oughtibridge was in the former camp, Sally Mottram in the latter. Sally noticed something that afternoon that had never occurred to her before. Linda Oughtibridge was just about the squarest woman she had ever seen.

'Oh, good afternoon, Mrs Mottram,' said Linda Oughtibridge in a voice treacly with false enthusiasm. 'Not a bad day.'

Not a bad day! This was almost the final straw for Sally. It was a vile day. The lowering sky was uniformly grey. True, it was dry, but there was dampness in the chill air. True also that there was no wind, but the stillness was so complete that the air almost became solid; walking through it was hard work.

There's a certain kind of smile that demands to be wiped off a person's face, and there's a certain kind of face that demands to have the smile wiped off it. Linda Oughtibridge

4

possessed just such a face, and just such a smile, and she was smiling now. The words formed themselves irresistibly in Sally's brain.

'Oh, piss off!'

The shocking words hurtled from her brain towards her lips, where she clamped down on them just in time.

'Not so bad, Mrs Oughtibridge.'

In twenty-four years of meeting, neither Sally nor Linda had ever ventured into Christian-name territory.

The narrowness of her escape brought Sally Mottram's flesh out in goose pimples. She had nice flesh; she was an attractive woman in a slightly restrained way, but with an elegant shapely backside over which at least two men in the town fantasized furiously. She was forty-seven, and was experimenting, but not too boldly, with hair the colour of straw. She had a husband and two grown-up children, a boy and a girl. Her husband was a lawyer. She was not the sort of person who said 'Piss off' to esteemed arrangers of the church's flowers.

She walked slowly along High Street East, past two pubs, one of them boarded up, past two nearly-new dress shops, three charity shops and five empty buildings.

She passed a rash of tediously named enterprises – the Potherthwaite Café, the Potherthwaite Arms, the Potherthwaite and Rackstraw Building Society – and stepped into the Market Place, which was full of unlovely parked cars. The two best buildings were banks. The Town Hall, on the south side of the square, had architectural pretensions that it didn't quite justify. The George Hotel had once looked handsome, but was peeling badly. On the west side of the square was the Victorian church, stone, solid and almost as square as Linda Oughtibridge. The church had been built to look instantly old. Paradoxically, it looked less old with every year that passed.

A noticeboard outside the church announced: *'If you want to be saved, there's always a welcome here.'* Beneath it someone had scrawled: *'If you don't, call at 9 Canal Basin and ask for Sophie.'*

Beyond the church, the River Pother crossed under the High Street at an angle. Sally paused on the bridge, and looked down at the sullen stream. There had once been dippers, inappropriately lively and pretty, dipping eponymously on the little rocks in the middle of the river. There were no dippers now. Today there were only the two bipolar mallard, swimming listlessly against the sluggish waters.

She stopped to take in the scene. The river curved round the edge of the graveyard and ran north-east to the great textile mills, not a window unbroken now. Beyond the mills, rows of houses climbed the lower slopes of Baggit Moor as if turned to stone while striving to escape from the river's last flood. She shuddered. She had almost said 'Piss off' to Mrs Oughtibridge. It was time to take herself in hand. It was time to get a grip.

She walked across the square into High Street West. A large furniture van passed her in the slow traffic that was clogging the grim road. *'Barnard's Removals. Serving Chichester and the World'.*

Oh no. Marigold Boyce-Willoughby was walking towards her; she was a friend, and she couldn't snub her. Sally found sympathy easy to feel, yet very hard to express. But she would have to.

'Afternoon, Sally.'

'Afternoon, Marigold.'

'Better day today.'

The awful thing was that this was true.

'I suppose so. At least it's dry. Almost. Marigold, I . . . um . . .'

'Don't say it.'

'No, but I . . .'

'Don't say you're sorry. I'm not. I've had men up to here.'

Sally turned away, for fear that she would smile at this unfortunate phrase.

'I'll get by.'

'Of course you will, Marigold.'

'I have before.'

'I know.'

'I will again.'

'I know. Well . . . um . . . I must be on my way. Barry's a stickler for his tea.'

Oh God, why had she said that? What an awful picture of their life it painted, and their life was happy, wasn't it? Marigold made it worse by commenting on it. Well, she would. She liked Marigold, but it was small wonder that three husbands had walked out on her.

'Oh well,' said Marigold Boyce-Willoughby. 'You'd best be on your way. Mustn't keep a stickler waiting.'

She would forgive the sarcasm, under the circumstances. After all, she was a Christian . . . a long while ago.

She walked on, on on on, as it felt. She passed the post office, and the forbidden territory of William Hill, never been in, couldn't, imagine what folk would say! 'I saw Sally Mottram in William Hill's. She was pretending she didn't know how to fill in a betting slip. Didn't fool me. She's a secret gambler.'

There is no sense of an incline in Potherthwaite High Street when you walk from west to east, but Sally found her legs growing tense and weary as she climbed gently from east to west. Surely the incline that day was just a little steeper than usual? She found herself wondering if the High Street was a geological oddity, level in one direction, uphill in the other.

She crossed the road. It was an entirely negative move,

7

symbolic of Potherthwaite. She wanted to avoid walking on the edge of the waste ground, which stood like two missing front teeth in the unsmiling mouth of High Street West. The local department store, Willis and Frond, had failed seven years ago. The failure had been followed by several years of fierce lethargy, but now there were plans to pull down the adjoining delicatessen – yes, it *was* called 'The Potherthwaite Deli' – and build a large supermarket on the site. She shuddered. Potherthwaite already had a supermarket, tucked away at the head of the valley, beyond the allotments. It didn't need two.

She hated walking on the edge of that gaping pit, not because she might fall into it – a criss-cross of barriers had been erected by the Overkill Department of the Health and Safety Office – but because she wouldn't be able to resist looking down and seeing all the rubbish people had dumped there. Her neighbour referred to it as Condom and Coca-Cola Corner. It made her feel so angry that she could scarcely breathe.

Ahead of her, the removals van had its right-hand indicators on. It was going to turn in to the cul-de-sac. Some lucky people were going to move, escape from Potherthwaite, settle in or near Chichester. Hayling Island, perhaps, the gentle waves dappled with sunlight; the weather was different down south.

Luke Warburton, Johnny Blackstock and Digger Llewellyn were playing on the waste ground, idly kicking an empty Diet Coke tin around, bored out of their tiny minds in this tiny-minded town. Ben Wardle, that strange boy, appeared to be building a column of stones, placing a stone rather perilously on the top with infinite care. Johnny Blackstock, for whom the word 'unstrange' might have to be invented, strolled over and kicked the stones down. Luke Warburton and Digger Llewellyn thought this the funniest thing they had ever seen. Sally hurried on.

Mrs Oughtibridge – Sally was no longer religious, she didn't believe in miracles, but it was almost a miracle that there was a Mr Oughtibridge – condemned all youngsters as wastrels, pointing out that there was a perfectly good youth club to which they never went. Sally hadn't liked the little drama played out on the waste ground, but she had some sympathy for them. When she was their age she wouldn't have been seen dead in a youth club, particularly a perfectly good one. Sometimes, when she was young, she had been naughty. She hadn't been naughty now for twenty-five years. She didn't think she would ever be naughty again. She did have thoughts, she was still attractive and attracted, but she dismissed them. Barry might not be the most vibrant man in the world, or even in Potherthwaite, or even for that matter in Oxford Road, or even the south side of Oxford Road. He didn't go in for dramatic or romantic gestures. Men who are sticklers for their tea usually don't. But he was a good man. Suddenly she felt that she wanted to get home, hoped he'd be back early, loved him in her way.

She crossed the road again, deftly dodging the slow-moving traffic. The removals van had disappeared into the cul-de-sac.

She passed 'Hair Today, Gone Tomorrow' – how she hated attempts at funny names for small businesses. She passed 'The Kosy Korner Kafé', on the corner of Canal Road which led to Canal Basin, the town's minuscule red-light district.

She took a brief glance up the cul-de-sac, being mildly keen, in the dreary waste of that long, grey, almost motionless, late afternoon, to discover the identity of the lucky people who were leaving stony-faced Potherthwaite for the sunny environs of Chichester.

The big double doors at the back of the van were down, and the first items of furniture were being removed and taken into one of the semi-detached, Gothic-windowed old

9

Victorian town houses in Potherthwaite's Conservation Area. These were not lucky people at all. They were either deeply unfortunate people or really rather thick people. They were moving *from* the exciting creeks of Chichester Harbour *to* the cul-de-sac under Baggit Moor. Sally thought, from the position of the van, that they must be moving into number 9.

She should have realized that at five o'clock a furniture van would be delivering, not arriving to load up, but the sight of the van had set her thoughts rolling in a familiar direction, that of escape down south, and there had been no room for even the consideration of people moving to Potherthwaite from anywhere, let alone Sussex. As she stood staring at the furniture being removed, she was actually seeing that mythical day when *her* furniture van would set off, taking Barry and her down south, to glorious Godalming perhaps, or even cloistered Chichester.

But her fantasy didn't last long. Barry would never move; he had his solid little business, his valued clients. He wasn't one for grand gestures or for brave moves, and she could never leave him.

As she passed the turning into Cadwallader Road – how did they choose these street names? Cadwallader was absurd, it was a street of small terrace houses – she glanced at number 6 as usual. The curtains were closed in the front room. Sally always glanced at those curtains. It saddened her when they were closed, and cheered her when they were open, which was ridiculous, because Ellie Fazackerly was bedridden, had been for years – how many? Didn't bear thinking about – couldn't get up to see the view, not that you would want to see the view even if you could, but Sally was a humane person and she couldn't bear to think of poor Ellie Fazackerly, trapped in her bed, second after second, minute after minute, hour after hour, day after day, week after week, month after month, always. Of course a lot of people didn't feel sorry for Ellie. All her own fault. Brought it on herself. Saw her eat seven pies in half an hour once.

But Sally did feel sorry, and she thought of calling on Ellie, helping a few of those minutes to pass. But Barry was a stickler for his tea, however unwise it was to broadcast the fact, and he was a good man, on balance, and not every woman could say that about her husband.

She was coming to the edge of the town centre now, and High Street West was beginning to lose what little charm it had. To the right was Vernon Road, home to three adjacent Indian restaurants, the Old Bengal, the New Bengal (family feud) and the Taj Mahal. Already the smell of frying spices was drifting in the evening breeze. On the end wall of a Chinese takeaway, beneath a window beyond which rows of cheap pink clothes were hanging, someone had sprayed 'Immirgants Go Home' in angry black.

Now, at a confusing mini-roundabout, High Street West breathed its last. To the left were allotments, extensive, too extensive for these busy times, sadly. Many of them were badly cared for, and quite a few were unoccupied. Beyond them was only the supermarket and its huge car park, and then the bare inhospitable hills marked the head of the Pother Valley.

To the right, the moment you left the remnants of High Street West, you were suddenly in smarter territory. The houses were larger than anywhere else in the town, most of them were detached, and two or three even had swimming pools, which was ridiculous in that climate. Even the occasional solar panel spoke of wild optimism.

Now the road forked. Sally took the right-hand fork, along Oxford Road. Beyond the road, at the head of the valley, high above the rushing streams that formed the headwaters of the Pother, stood the nearest things to spires that Oxford Road afforded. Eight vast windmills stood guard on the tops of the hills, motionless and silent in the still air, neutered by nature.

Peter Sparling was walking towards her with his Labrador, and she knew the sort of thing he was going to say, and she dreaded it.

'Not a bad day.'

She thought of the shock there would be if she told Peter Sparling to piss off. Or worse. Something sarcastic was needed, though. She had to bleed this sudden overwhelming feeling of frustration.

'Yes, not bad at all,' she said. 'Very little thunder, the lightning scarcely forked, and not a tsunami in sight. Mustn't grumble, eh, Peter?'

Peter Sparling gave her a puzzled look, said 'Come on, Kenneth', as if urging his beloved dog out of the contaminated area surrounding this madwoman, and walked on.

Sally walked on up Oxford Road, past 'Windy Corner', the home of the town's only psychiatrist, the overworked Dr Mallet, and past the trim, neat, lifeless garden of 'Mount Teidi', where her neighbours the Hammonds were so silent that she often thought they must be in Tenerife when they were in fact at home.

Everything was silent today. The silence oppressed her.

She opened the gate into the immaculate garden of 'The Larches', just as lifeless at this early moment in the year, but full of the promise of bloom. She noticed a weed or two, and decided to let them live a little longer; she wasn't obsessive, she wasn't a Hammond.

She put her key in the lock, turned it, opened the door, entered the hall.

Inside the house it was silent too. She saw him straight away, and, that day, he was definitely not being a stickler

for his tea. That day he had done something that was definitely dramatic, and might even be considered by some
people to be brave. He was hanging from a beam at the
top of the stairs. There was a rope round his neck. He was
very, very dead.

TWO

In the cul-de-sac

'They're old,' said Arnold Buss in a low voice.

'And we aren't?' said Jill, also in a low voice, although it was absurd to feel the need to speak so quietly, as their new neighbours had only just pulled up behind the furniture van, and were busy getting things out of the ample boot of their silver VW Passat.

The Busses were standing a little back from the window, Arnold further back than Jill, in the cold spare front room on the first floor of number 11 Moor Brow, which was always referred to as 'The Cul-de-Sac', as if Potherthwaite was actually rather proud of having such a thing as a cul-de-sac. They didn't want to be caught peering out. Arnold had taught history, and Jill had been in the forefront of the world of the colonoscopy in the District Hospital. It wouldn't do to be seen to be curious about their new neighbours.

The man, now carrying two small suitcases, suddenly looked up to examine his new surroundings. Jill and Arnold hurriedly stepped back even further from the window.

'I don't like the look of their standard lamps,' said Arnold.

'What's wrong with them?'

'Ostentatious. They're going to be materialistic. I know the type.'

'And what did they do for a living?'

'I don't know. How could I possibly know that?'

'I'd have thought their occasional tables might tell you.'

'Oh, don't be silly, Jill. Where are you going?'

Jill Buss was striding towards the door with a sudden sense of purpose. It unnerved Arnold when she showed a sense of purpose.

'I'm going to tidy my make-up, if you must know.'

This was dreadful news. No good could come out of Jill tidying her make-up. Arnold was not sociable.

'And why might you be going to tidy your make-up at this moment?'

But Jill was far ahead, out of earshot. She had marched across the landing, now she burst through their large bedroom – the rooms were big in these old houses – strode into her en-suite – they had separate bathrooms, the en-suite was her stronghold – and shut the door in Arnold's face. She didn't like him in the room when she was doing her make-up; he could never resist sarcasm. 'We're going to the pub for the early bird, not Buckingham Palace.'

He hesitated, then plucked up his courage, opened the door, and went in.

'Arnold! I might have been on the toilet.'

'You aren't.'

'But I might have been, that's the point. You couldn't know I wasn't.'

'I'm surprised that . . .' He stopped. What he had been about to say wasn't wise, wasn't wise at all.

'You're surprised what?'

'Nothing.'

'No, come on, Arnold, what?'

He sighed. His sighs were deep and frequent.

15

'I'm surprised that a woman who earned her living giving people colonoscopies should be so ladylike about going to the toilet in front of a man who has known her and her body for forty-four years. Why are you touching up your face, Jill?'

'I'm going round to see them, if you must know.'

'See them? See who?'

'Arnold! You aren't stupid. Don't pretend to be. Them. Our new neighbours.'

Arnold's mouth dropped open. He looked as if he'd had a stroke. He could see his appalled face staring out at him from behind Jill's still-lovely face in the mirror. It was a bad moment. He was terrified of having a stroke, and ending up looking as he looked at this moment, and it was painful to see his face there, haggard, rigid and grey, just behind hers. She looked infuriatingly attractive still, the softness of her auburn hair, the strong curves of the nostrils, the elegance of the upper lip. Even the lines of her face, because they came from smiles more than from grimaces, enhanced her charm. He looked so much older than her. He was older, but only by a year, seventy-three to her seventy-two. No, the picture he saw in her mirror in her bathroom did not please him. But worse even than that was her announcement. Going round to see them!

'See them, Jill? Why?'

'Welcome them. See if they need anything. Don't you want to be friendly?'

'Of course I do. If they're the sort of people we want to be friendly with. But they might be Jehovah's Witnesses. They might be shoplifters. They might be Liberal Democrats. They might be Catholics. They might be vegetarians. They might be Welsh.'

'They might be Welsh vegetarian Liberal Democrat Catholic shoplifters.'

'Exactly. Now do you see why I don't want you to just charge round there?'

'So how do you propose that we find out if they're our sort of people? Do we send them a questionnaire?'

'Don't be silly. We observe them. We listen. Do they argue? Do they shout? What sort of music do they play? Does he put the box on when he mows the lawn? Do they hang out the washing in a seemly manner? What quality are their underclothes? Do they put the bins out properly? Do they have dogs?'

'How many times do they pee in the night?'

'You're not taking this seriously.'

Jill turned round, away from the mirror, to give him a sober look.

'I am, you know,' she said. 'We've been attached on to an empty house for more than two years. This means change, this could be the end of paradise, of course we're edgy, but we're human beings, and they'll be knackered, and they'll be edgy too, they'll need cheering up, I would think, coming to Potherthwaite from Chichester, I would be . . . so . . .'

'I wish you wouldn't keep running Potherthwaite down, Jill. It isn't Venice, but it's home. And you only run it down to rile me.'

Arnold was writing a history of Potherthwaite. It was called 'A Complete History of Potherthwaite'. It was very long already, because he was unable to leave anything out, now that he had described it as complete, but also because he was terrified of finishing it, which was in truth why he had described it as complete.

'They'll be stressed. They may not have anything to cook with. I'm going to invite them for supper.'

'Jill. This is recklessness personified.'

'Yes. Let's live a little.'

Arnold left the bathroom quietly, shut the door carefully,

left her to it. He had almost said 'I don't want to live a little, I'm seventy-three', but luckily he had thought better of it.

So twenty minutes later, having titivated herself to her satisfaction, and looking, she knew, rather stunning for a seventy-two-year-old, Jill called on the neighbours.

There were eight identical buildings in the cul-de-sac, four on each side of the road. Each building was divided into two identical residences, dignified and solemn in dark, stern stone, listed buildings on which no bright paint could be used. The new neighbours' house was joined to the Busses' on the southern side.

In the slowly fading light of a day that had never been fully light, Jill strode up the wilderness that was the neglected front garden of number 9.

She rang the doorbell, and wondered what Arnold would say if they were Muslims. She heard a key and then another key – what were these people frightened of? – and suddenly the front door was open.

The woman who was standing there was shorter than Jill, older than Jill, less attractive than Jill, but could have looked a great deal better than she did if she had made the best of herself. True, she had just endured a tiring journey, but Jill knew that this woman had long ago given up making the best of herself, and this irritated her.

They introduced themselves. The woman's name was Olive Patterson. Jill didn't waste time on small talk.

'I wondered . . . I expect you've had a long journey, you must be tired . . . I wondered . . . because I don't expect you'll have unpacked your cooking utensils and things, Arnold and I . . . that's my husband . . . we wondered . . . would you like to pop round for a bit of supper tonight?'

Confusion painted a faint red glow on to Olive Patterson's pallid cheeks.

'Oh, that's so kind of you,' said Olive. 'So kind. No, it is,

18

that is so kind, really, really kind, but really we're . . . we're fine, we're all right . . . and I mean we had a sandwich in the car, at a service station . . . well, we had it in the car because you don't want to both leave the car at the same time, with so much stuff in it, do you? I mean, who can you trust these days? You can't, can you? So, no, we're all right, but thank you, thank you again, we so appreciate . . . Harry . . . that's *my* husband . . . will really appreciate your offer . . . but we don't want to be a nuisance, and we really will be all right, honestly, but, as I say, that is so kind, thank you, but . . . as I say, another time.'

So Jill went back home, feeling strangely disappointed, but when Olive told Harry what she had said (though not at such great length) he exploded. He told her that in his opinion it was rude to refuse such a friendly offer, it was the first good thing that had happened all day, and he was going round to say they'd changed their minds. Olive pleaded with him – it would make her look silly. He told her that she was silly, and off he went.

A minute or two later, he met Jill's eyes for the first time, and they held each other's eyes a second or two longer than might have been expected at the door of a listed building in a cul-de-sac in Potherthwaite at the darkening death of a gloomy late winter's day. He told her that if the offer was still on they would be delighted. She told him that the offer was indeed still on, and he was indeed delighted.

Bang on half past seven – Olive hated to be late – Jill led the Pattersons into the lounge, which was a large, high-ceilinged room with a chandelier, furnished with a curious mix of Arnold's reticence and Jill's ebullience. Jill had dressed down, Olive had dressed up, but Jill still looked the smarter. Arnold looked formal and old-fashioned in jacket and tie and a pale blue shirt with silver cufflinks. Harry was in full 'they'll know we haven't had time to unpack' mode. How different the two men were: Arnold tall and slim and grizzled, with salt-and-pepper hair and a very obedient little salt-and-pepper moustache; Harry short, not fat but bursting at the seams of his casual clothes, and as bald as a balloon.

Harry glanced round the room, taking in the reticent chairs and the ebullient vases, and said, 'Nice gaff. Nice room. Just trying to guess, who bought what?'

'Harry!' said Olive.

'I embarrass her,' said Harry complacently. 'Sorry, doll.'

'This is so kind of you,' said Olive, forced into speech.

'What are neighbours for?' said Arnold gravely.

Jill was puzzled by a rather odd look that had passed between Olive and Arnold, almost an exchange of sign language. It was time to leap into action.

'Now, what would we all like to drink?' she asked.

'A small sherry, please,' said Olive shyly, half blushing at her boldness in asking for alcohol at all. I don't want to be beholden, said her blush.

'A gin and tonic, please,' said Harry with a huge grin. Large one please if poss, said his grin.

'Usual, Arnold?'

'Of course,' said Arnold complacently.

'Right. I'll just go and get them,' said Jill, looking meaningfully at Arnold, for whom the look clearly had no meaning.

'Let me help,' said Harry hastily.

'That's very kind,' said Jill, looking not at him but at Arnold.

When Jill and Harry had left the room, there was a moment's silence. Olive broke it.

'I thought, "Is it? It can't be." But it is, isn't it?'

'Oh, yes,' said Arnold. 'Oh yes, Olive. It is indeed.'

THREE

Purely routine

The policeman had explained to Sally that because there was no suicide note they had to make certain inquiries. It was purely routine. Had she any idea why Barry had killed himself?

She had shaken her head.

Strangely, she had felt nothing. 'Cry if you want to,' a female officer had said. 'Feel free.' But she hadn't been able to.

'I'm afraid nobody can go upstairs,' Inspector Pellet had explained. 'It's designated a crime scene. Purely routine.'

He had made gestures to the female officer to get Sally out of the way. He hadn't wanted her to be in the house while they examined the rope, tested for fingerprints, searched for minute traces of thread dropped from clothes, or earth brought in on shoes. It wouldn't be a thorough search, of course – there was really no doubt that he'd killed himself – but things had to be done by the book these days.

The female officer, PC Cartwright, had put her arm round Sally, to lead her towards the door of her own home. Inspector Pellet had turned and said, 'Thank you, Mrs Mottram. We don't need to bother you again tonight, and

we have no reason to think that this is anything but . . .'
He had hesitated. He hadn't wanted to say the word. He'd
been to a two-day seminar on Tact and Consideration in
the Isle of Wight in 2007, and it had stayed with him.
'. . . what it appears to be. However, an officer will want
to talk to you in the morning, when you've . . .' He had
been about to say 'had a good night's sleep' but had realized
that this was unlikely. He had abandoned that sentence and
had asked, uneasily, 'And . . . um . . . we . . . um . . . we
might have to ask to borrow your computer. So . . . um
. . . if you're needing to use it . . .' He had let that sentence
go unfinished too.

'I don't use the computer,' she had said.

'Ah!'

Inspector Pellet had winced. He had realized that the
emphasis he had put on that 'Ah!' might carry with it the
implication that, in the knowledge that she would never be
able to discover them, it was therefore possible that this
seemingly innocent lawyer had thought it safe to save large
numbers of horribly indecent photos of young children and
domestic pets, or of the wives of fellow lawyers caught in
flagrante. Or both. In truth the inspector was a nice, sensitive family man and had driven himself close to depression
due to his attempts to follow what he had learnt at the
seminar all those years ago.

Luckily Sally had been so shattered and so bewildered,
and also so innocent, that she had been completely incapable
of picking up any implications, let alone ones so extreme.
PC Cartwright had led her out of her own front door, pushing
her in such a direction that she would have risked dislocating
her neck if she had attempted to turn to take one last look
at her husband hanging there.

When they were outside, PC Cartwright had asked her,
'Have you any children you could go to?'

22

'Well, my daughter, I suppose,' she had said.

'Right. Good. And where does she live?'

'New Zealand. That's the only bugbear.'

PC Cartwright had looked at her in astonishment.

'I probably won't,' Sally had added.

'No. I meant . . . now. For a couple of hours like, while they . . . till you can return.'

'Oh. Of course. I'm sorry. I was being stupid.'

'No, not at all, lovey. You're in shock.'

'Yes. Yes, I am. No. No, I haven't. My son's in Barnet.'

'Neighbours?'

'Well . . . It's not the most . . . um . . .'

'. . . sociable street in Potherthwaite?'

'No. And my husband isn't . . . wasn't . . . oh God . . . oh God . . .'

'Now now. There there. There . . . um . . . surely there must be somebody?'

'Well, there's the Hammonds, but . . . I think they're in Tenerife. Peter Sparling's around, I saw him earlier with Kenneth. I could go to them, I suppose.'

'Oh. Right. Well. Good. I'll take you. Can you walk it?'

'Oh yes. It's only five houses.'

PC Cartwright had led Sally slowly along the road. If there had been any passers-by, they might have thought she was disabled.

'I'm sure they'll look after you,' she'd said, and then she'd lowered her voice, as if she hadn't wanted her progressive views to be overheard by any colleagues who might be lurking in the bushes. 'Gays can be very considerate and understanding. It's with the female hormones, I suppose.'

'Gays?'

'Peter and Kenneth.'

'Oh. No no. Kenneth's a Labrador.'

PC Cartwright had looked astonished, then shocked, then just bewildered. She had entirely forgotten that she had been to an afternoon seminar on Not Making Assumptions at a moated country house outside Droitwich in 2009. And if she had remembered that she had been, she would still have forgotten what she had learnt.

'P'r'aps you should just wait a moment at the gate, love,' PC Cartwright had said, when they arrived at the Sparlings' house. 'Best for me to explain, p'r'aps.'

So Sally had stood in the cold at the gate of 'Ambleside', and had endured the unpleasant experience of watching two people discussing her, and wondering what had been said when Peter Sparling had shaken his head, and when PC Cartwright had suddenly turned round to have a look at her by the gate.

Then they had shaken hands and Peter had come striding over the cut grass.

'Sally! Sally! I am so sorry,' he'd said.

'Thank you.'

'Come in. Come in.'

'Thank you. Thank you.'

'Will you be all right, lovey?' PC Cartwright had asked.

'I'll be fine. Thank you.'

Sally was going to be brave. She wasn't even going to be upset by this woman she had never met before calling her 'lovey'.

'We'll come and let you know when it's all right to go back.'

'Thank you.'

'Not long, I wouldn't think.'

'Thank you.'

'Purely routine, lovey.'

'Thank you.'

Myfanwy and Peter Sparling had made Sally comfortable

by the roaring fire, and had plied her with gin and tonic. Myfanwy, who talked like a mountain stream, had found more words for 'sorry' than most people even knew. Sally had told them of PC Cartwright's confusion over Kenneth. They'd had to laugh. In fact Sally had laughed too, and in that charged moment the laughter had become hysterical, and then, just as the laughter had died, Kenneth had farted, and none of them had been able to look at each other. They had controlled themselves heroically, and in the flat silence that always follows hysterics, Peter and Myfanwy had apologized for laughing, and Sally had said, 'No, please. I wanted you to laugh. That's why I told you. Life must go on.'

And she had thought, 'Must it?' Back home all alone now she recalled that moment and she thought, 'Must it? But how? How can it?'

After that, they had talked soberly. The Sparlings had raised Barry to something only just short of a saint, the question of why he had done it had been raised but not answered, and Sally had said, 'But why didn't he leave a note?' with such force that even Myfanwy had made no attempt to provide a facile answer. Sally had seen that Myfanwy was very close to tears, the easy yet genuine tears of South Wales. Myfanwy had lowered the emotional tension but only slightly by saying, 'I can't believe that only . . . what would it be? . . . four hours ago . . . Peter and you were talking quite casually having no idea what had happened. I can't get my head round it.' And then they had reminisced about a trip the four of them had made to Whitby for fish and chips at the Magpie, and they had agreed that they should have done that sort of thing more often, but you don't know what's going to happen, do you? That's right, you don't. Just as well, perhaps. And Peter had said, 'I can't get my head round it either, Sally.

25

There we were, you and I, talking about the weather . . .' a frown had passed across his face as he'd remembered Sally's strange comment about lightning and tsunamis '. . . and we had no idea what had happened,' and all the time Sally had been wondering, underneath the talk and the socializing and the memories and the gin and tonic and the log fire, how far they had got at 'The Larches', whether they had taken Barry down yet.

Father Time is a playful patriarch. Sally would have said that they had been sitting there for two hours at least, but it turned out that it had only been just over an hour before PC Cartwright had come to tell her that it was all right for her to go home.

She hadn't wanted to have to talk any more. There was nothing anybody could do. The rest of her life was up to her now, though of course she had no idea of the immense consequences of that thought. But she hadn't liked to leave straight away. Even at this dreadful moment that would have seemed like a betrayal of the social code here in the posh end of Potherthwaite.

At last she had decided that it would be all right to leave. The Sparlings had insisted on escorting her home, and she had been glad of that. The street lamps in Oxford Road were few and dim, and there was no chance of the moon breaking through the thick motionless clouds.

They had offered to come in. They had invited her to collect a few things and go back and stay with them for the night, and she had known that they had meant it most sincerely. It had been tempting, and she had very nearly agreed.

Now that she stood, all alone in her sitting room, all alone in the house, she felt hugely grateful to the Sparlings, but she would resist the temptation to go back. She could hardly bear to stay in the house on her own, though. Was there anywhere else she could go?

Of course there was.

There was even a place to which she wanted to go.

There was a place to which she must go.

FOUR

A lovely evening

Olive's heart sank at the sight of the dining table. Jill had laid it beautifully, and it was lit by two tall candles in handsome, gleaming candlesticks. The room was quite small, with pale green wallpaper. Smart red curtains covered the French windows that led to the back garden. There were six decanters on the sideboard. She would never match this.

She caught Arnold's glance and had an uneasy feeling that he could read her mind.

She didn't like the starter, which was a peach stuffed with a mixture of yoghourt and mild spices. She didn't like peaches or yoghourt, she didn't like mixtures, and she didn't like mild spices, although she didn't dislike them as much as she disliked spices that weren't mild. It crossed her mind that they would need to find a good doctor pretty quickly. She would miss Dr Renwick. She hoped Harry wouldn't ask them who their doctor was. They would have to go to him, if he did, and she didn't want the state of her kidneys to become public knowledge throughout the cul-de-sac.

'This is just something rustled up from the store cupboard,' said Jill.

'It's delicious,' said Olive. 'How clever of you to be able to rustle things up.'

Harry gave her his 'don't overdo the compliments, it's a form of running yourself down' frown, and of course, now that she had said it was delicious, she would have to eat every mouthful.

'I always eat slowly when I love things,' she said.

Harry gave her his 'when you're in a hole, don't dig' frown.

The others had finished. She could hardly get it down. To help herself get through it she thought back to that brief romance forty-eight years ago. Well, not so brief. A few months. But a few months in which they'd had so much shyness and ignorance to overcome, so many inhibitions to let out, that it had never reached its climax, or any climax. She wondered what her life would have been like if she had married Arnold. She wasn't attracted to him now. She couldn't imagine life with him. She felt that she ought to say something, and was on the point of asking him if he'd ever been back to Cheltenham, when she realized that this question would have let the cat well and truly out of the bag.

In their brief, urgent, almost whispered chat, back in the chandeliered lounge, while Harry had helped Jill fix the drinks, after consideration of the fact that it was a small world, after the horrified realization that they had last seen each other forty-eight years ago, after the lies about how kindly time had treated them, Arnold had made it clear that he didn't want to tell Jill and Harry about it. She had thought this unwise. There was nothing to hide, so why hide it? She would have been horrified if she had known his reason, which was partly mere laziness and dislike of emotion past, present or future, but also at least a touch of shame. Olive was not now a trophy about whom one would boast.

At last, in the chandeliered dining room, she had finished her starter. She smiled at the company. It was evident to them that the smile was hard work.

'Delicious,' she said.

'I'll get the main course.'

Harry and Olive both realized that Arnold wouldn't lift a finger. He'd been Head of History for twenty-nine years, after all. The fact that there had only ever been one other teacher in the department, and he had been either on work experience or a supply teacher, was of no account. Arnold had gone down in history as Head of History. He had thought it a great job in this modern world – to be paid to live in the past.

Harry waited a few seconds – he was not entirely insensitive, despite what people said – and called out, 'Can I help?'

'Thank you,' called out Jill from the kitchen.

Harry hurried off, and a curious thing happened. Both Arnold and Olive realized that they had nothing whatsoever to say to each other. They couldn't analyse their months of 'walking out' as it had been called in those distant days. It had been enjoyable, they had both felt romantic at times, but nothing worth recalling had happened. Do you remember the day we got the dates mixed up and went to the wrong film? Do you remember that French restaurant where we didn't know what globe artichokes were and had to be shown how to eat them? Do you remember when I snagged my stockings on the door of the taxi? It was not the stuff of rich reminiscence.

Nor was 'So what have you been up to?' likely to yield a great harvest.

When I qualified as a teacher I taught history in Hereford and then in Hartlepool, where I met Jill. Shortly after that I was appointed Head of Department here, and remained it till I retired. I'm writing the definitive book on the history of

Potherthwaite, which is also the only book on the history of Potherthwaite.

I was Harry's secretary. He was fun. He was good-looking. He had hair in those days. We married young, had three children, all of whom have done just about OK. I stayed as Harry's secretary. He was in and out of things, no one else could understand his affairs. His business affairs, I mean. He's never had the other kind. Well, as far as I know. No time. We've lived in nine houses. Harry has a boat. I hate boats.

None of that was worth going into, so they didn't go into it. But the curious part of it was that in not having anything to say they found common ground. They hoped Harry and Jill would take at least a few minutes; they were restful together.

And Arnold smiled. Olive could have had no idea just how rare his smiles had become – there hadn't been many in Cheltenham, but lately there had been very, very few. But when she saw that smile, just a little frisson of regret passed through her, and she understood for the first time what Jill had once seen in him.

The smile emboldened her to ask a question.

'Don't you think we should tell them? Wouldn't it be easier? Don't you think if we don't we'll be treading on eggshells?'

'Don't forget I was a history teacher, Olive,' he replied.

Somehow I don't think there's any danger of that, thought Olive.

'If we tell them, it becomes part of our shared knowledge, it lives on in all our memories and will become a part of our common experience. If we don't tell them it will remain a piece of history. It will fade.'

'Do you want it to fade?' Olive was surprised by her boldness.

Arnold paused, thinking carefully what to say.

'Yes, I do,' he said. 'It was good then, but there's no point in its being part of our lives now. It has no relevance.'

'I'm not good at secrets. I almost mentioned Cheltenham earlier.'

'It's fresh in our minds. It'll fade. The whole thing will be forgotten. Shh. They're coming.'

Harry was carrying a huge dish, which he plonked on a mat on the table. Jill brought a smaller bowl.

'That smells lovely,' said Olive.

'Just a casserole. The old standby,' said Jill.

'Lovely,' said Olive.

'Haven't you even poured more wine, Arnold?' said Jill.

'Sorry,' said Arnold, looking anything but sorry. 'The host fails in his duty yet again.'

He stood up, lifted the white wine bottle, poured a small amount into Olive's glass.

'Thank you,' said Olive. 'Lovely. I can't drink red, I'm afraid.'

Harry gave her his 'don't advertise your shortcomings' frown.

Arnold poured regrettably small amounts of red wine into Harry and Jill's glasses, and nothing into his own.

As she served the food, Jill told them that Harry had been chatting about his boat.

'What sort of boat?' asked Arnold.

'Oh, are you interested in boats?' said Harry.

'Not remotely,' said Arnold. 'I was trying to please Jill by being proactive in the conversation, as a good host should. It seems I've chalked up another failure.'

'Don't be disagreeable, darling,' said Jill. 'And you still haven't told us what sort of boat it is?'

'She's a thirty-foot yawl,' said Harry.

Arnold and Jill hadn't any idea what a thirty-foot yawl was.

'Tell Arnold what you said, Harry,' said Jill.

'I said that I've got to bring her round from Emsworth, that's where I keep her. Olive doesn't sail.'

'I tried,' interrupted Olive, 'but I got very sick.'

Harry gave her his 'I think you're forgetting the frown I gave you a few minutes ago' frown.

'So Harry suggested, because it's a big ask to do it on his own, that I help bring her round to somewhere nearer. That's all.'

'Quick work!' gleamed Arnold.

'Don't be stupid, Arnold,' said Jill. 'We're talking boats, not sex. I love you, God knows why sometimes.'

'This is lovely,' said Olive. 'Spicy.'

'I've told you you should put more herbs in your stews,' said Harry.

'I have to ask you this,' said Jill. 'Arnold's life has been here and we've grown to like it, in a funny sort of way, but what's brought you here from . . . where was it?'

'Emsworth. Chichester Harbour. Near Chichester, not surprisingly. Family.'

'Oh, you have family in Potherthwaite?'

'No. We have family in Emsworth.' Harry laughed. Jill tried to laugh. Olive smiled faintly. Arnold's face didn't flicker. 'Just joking. No, we have a son and two daughters within thirty or so miles of here, all in different directions. I got the old map and compass out and, believe it or not, the most equidistant place was right here in Potherthwaite, and I said to Olive, we've got to start somewhere, let's start there. And this house came up and, Bob's your uncle, here we are.'

'And how nice that is,' said Jill. 'Isn't it, Arnold?'

'It's providence,' said Arnold dryly.

'Well, don't expect too much,' said Jill. 'The town is in the doldrums, if I can put it that way to a sailing man.'

'Maybe we can help to take it out of the doldrums,' said Harry.

Jill gave him a look.

'Do you mean that?' she said.

Harry shrugged.

'Not really, I was just making conversation really,' he said, 'but no, if there are things going on, count us in. Eh, Olive? Mustn't let the grass grow under our feet.'

Olive didn't even bother to reply to this absurd suggestion. To imagine that she wanted to be counted in to anything! And the only thing to do with grass was to let it grow under your feet. That was the whole point of grass. She took another mouthful. It was far too spicy for her.

'I know you taught history, Arnold . . .' began Harry.

'Head of History for twenty-nine years.'

'Quite. But what was it you said you did at the hospital, Jill?'

'Jill was the big noise in the endoscopy department,' said Arnold.

Olive found herself crunching on a chilli. She wanted to spit it out. How could she?

'Some said she *was* the endoscopy department. What she doesn't know about the large intestine isn't worth knowing.'

Olive gasped, retched, put her hand over her mouth and rushed out of the room.

Harry jumped up.

'She won't know where it is,' he said. 'Where is it?'

'At the end of the corridor, last door on the right,' said Jill.

Harry rushed out, followed by Jill. There was no sign of Olive.

She emerged slowly from the last door on the left.

'Sorry,' she said. 'Wrong room. I'm afraid I've thrown up all over your vacuum cleaner.'

'Will you be all right,' said Jill, 'or should I ring Dr Parker? That's our doctor. Marvellous doctor.'

'No, no, I'll be all right now,' said Olive. 'I'm so sorry.'

'Dr Parker. We'll need a doctor. We must sign on with him, mustn't we, Olive?' said Harry.

'Her,' said Jill.

'What?'

'He's a her.'

'Better still. That's marvellous, isn't it, Olive?' said Harry.

'Lovely,' said Olive. 'I'm so sorry, Jill. It's a top-of-the-range Dyson too.'

FIVE

The Fazackerly sisters

It wasn't pleasant walking along Oxford Road in the dark – it was very inadequately lit – but she didn't trust herself to drive the car. She knew that she was still in shock. Besides, she'd had quite a lot of gin and tonic with the Sparlings.

She walked past 'Mount Teidi' – the Hammonds tried to live in Tenerife even when they were in Potherthwaite. Barry had joked that their house should have been named Mount Tidy.

Barry would never joke again.

She hesitated outside 'Ambleside'. It was tempting to call in, so tempting.

No, she must be strong.

Why? Why on earth should she be strong? She walked towards their gate, even reached out for the latch.

But she walked on. She hesitated in the pool of yellow light from each street lamp, then plunged on into the darkness of the Potherthwaite night.

A girl ran out of the drive of Dr Mallet's house and nearly collided with her. Sally's heart almost stopped. The girl looked terrified too, and the large vase she was carrying slipped out of her hands in her shock. She grabbed for the vase at incredible speed, got her arms round it, gained control of it just before it hit the ground, and ran off with it at a great pace. Sally had a vision of golden hair and a very slim body.

Sally's heartbeat had barely slowed when she heard a cough from the allotments on her right. Oxford Road had become a minefield that day. Her blood curdled. Her heart missed several beats. She hurried across the road, to walk alongside the houses that carried on right into town on that side.

She'd imagined it. She was in an acutely nervous state.

She hadn't imagined it. There had been a cough. A man's cough. The cough of a killer.

She walked fast now, listening all the time for footsteps. But there were no footsteps. It occurred to her that it was odd that she should be so frightened. A few minutes ago, in the house, she had felt that she wanted to die. Turn, Sally. Face your killer. Get stabbed.

But he might just rape her and leave her. Besides, there was no one there.

The curtains were drawn in the Rose and Crown. People said that would be the next pub to go. She didn't care if it did. Why should anybody be happy, with her Barry dead?

She crossed the street again, and turned into Cadwallader Road. The street lights were dim, and one of them was out. In her heightened state she could feel only hostility from the low stone terraces. Their very regularity, the total absence of decorative features, admired by purists, seemed comfortless now. Why on earth was she visiting number 6? Wasn't it absurd to call on Ellie Fazackerly at this hour?

She had to speak to somebody. She didn't know Jill Buss quite well enough to call so late. She couldn't go back to the Sparlings. There was nobody else.

Ellie would be glad to see her. Ellie would be glad to see anybody.

She rang the bell. The moment she had rung it she wished that she hadn't. Ellie would be watching her favourite television programme, her one way of escaping the prison she had built for herself.

You can't de-ring a bell.

Perhaps they wouldn't answer.

She heard footsteps. The door opened. It was Ali. She was the least obese of the three Fazackerly sisters. She was nineteen stone five.

'Is it . . .? I just thought I'd call and see Ellie. Is this a bad time?'

'Nooo! She's always pleased to see you, Mrs Mottram.'

It was no use trying to get any of the sisters to call her Sally. She was Mrs Mottram, a do-gooder who lived on a higher plane. She had first met the Fazackerly sisters when Ali had fallen in the street; she had rushed to help, and she had escorted her home. She'd known of Ellie's existence, and a few days later she had called round, to see if Ali was all right but partly also out of sheer curiosity, and she had stood at the doorstep for so long that in the end Ali had felt obliged to ask her in. She was still slightly ashamed of the origins of her concern for Ellie.

Ali led her along the corridor, her shoes squeaking on the lino – they were in a time warp – and took her into the tiny kitchen. Oli was seated at the table, watching television. She tried to get up, not easy. Ali and Oli had lived in the kitchen, in the tiny claustrophobic house, ever since the moment had come when Ellie could no longer go upstairs.

'No, no, Oli, it's all right. I've just come to have a word with Ellie. You keep watching. How are you?'

'Very well, thank you, Mrs Mottram.'

Oli was twenty-one stone three. It didn't help that she worked in the cake factory. Ali was a cleaner at the hospital, where cleaners moved slowly. They both worked antisocial hours, so arranged that one of them was always at home to care for Ellie. They were adamant that they didn't want any help from anyone else. They were proud people. Only Sally was welcome, and she felt now that she was almost on the verge of being considered a friend rather than a voluntary social worker.

'I'll tell her you're here,' said Ali.

Ali went through into the front room, which had once been the lounge when Ellie could still get upstairs. A thought occurred to Sally now, a thought that astonishingly had never struck her before. What would happen when first Oli and finally Ali could also not get upstairs? How would they sleep?

Sally heard the television set go off in the front room. Ellie had been watching something. She shouldn't have come.

There was always a very faint smell of festering humanity in the house, a sense that not enough windows were opened often enough, a feeling that rather too much air was being used up and not replaced fast enough. On the whole, though, it was clear that their standards of cleanliness were amazingly high, considering the circumstances. Sally never felt an overwhelming urge to leave, and now, sitting and waiting, she felt less traumatized than she had been all evening.

Ali came back in.

'Right,' she said. 'She's ready for you.'

Sally's heart sank slightly at Ali's words. She was still Ellie's voluntary social worker, calling not out of love but out of the goodness of her heart. Maybe there was further to go than she had hoped, before she became a friend.

She entered Ellie's room.

'Hello, Ellie,' she said.

'Hello, Mrs Mottram.'

Ellie's face was now so fat that it was hard to tell if she was smiling. Her huge body was hidden beneath the vast, specially made duvet. It stretched over the mounds of her fat like dunes in the desert. She hadn't been able to get out of bed for more than two years now. She was thirty-three years old. It didn't do to think about her weight. She was fat because she couldn't help it, not because she wanted to be in the *Guinness Book of Records*.

It also didn't do to think about the toilet and bed-linen arrangements. Ali and Oli looked after her brilliantly, did everything necessary with never a complaint. Easy to make fun of Ali, Oli and Ellie but beneath all the blubber there beat hearts of gold, and how many of those are there in this stony world of ours?

In fact it didn't do to think about Ellie's life at all, and Sally realized why she had needed to call here rather than anywhere else on this terrible night. She wasn't proud of her motive. She had needed to feel sorry for someone else, because she couldn't stand how sorry she felt for herself.

'I hope you weren't watching something,' she said.

'It were rubbish.'

'Oh dear.'

'It's all rubbish.'

'Oh dear.'

'I only watch it cos there's nowt else.'

'Oh, Ellie.'

'You'd think they'd put good things on, wouldn't you, for folk like me?'

'You certainly would.'

'They haven't a clue, have they?'

'They haven't. They haven't a clue.'

'None of them have. Politicians, clergy, doctors. None of them have a clue.'

'You tell them, Ellie.'

40

'I would, but they wouldn't listen.'

'So, how are you, Ellie?'

'Mustn't grumble, Mrs Mottram. Sit yourself down.'

'Thank you.'

'Make yourself comfortable.'

'Thank you.'

'And how are *you*, Mrs Mottram?'

'Well, I suppose I too shouldn't grumble, Ellie. I . . . um . . . something's happened, Ellie. Something terrible.'

'Oh, Mrs Mottram.'

'Yes. Terrible. I . . .' She swallowed. 'Barry's killed himself.'

'Oh, Mrs Mottram.'

'I know.'

She told Ellie the whole story of how she found him, of the police, of the Sparlings and Kenneth. Ellie was too upset even to laugh at the story about Kenneth.

Oli came in with plates of cake.

'Not just now, Oli,' said Ellie.

Oli looked at her sister in astonishment.

'Not just now?' she said.

'Not just now.'

'But it's cake.'

'Later, Oli. Oli, Mrs Mottram's husband has committed suicide.'

Sally still hadn't been able to use that word, and on Ellie's lips it came like a gunshot.

'Oh, Mrs Mottram. I'm so sorry,' said Oli. 'And so's Ali. Well, she will be. Can I tell her?'

'Please do.'

'Thank you. Um . . . was it . . .? How did he . . .? I mean . . .'

'Can I tell her, Mrs Mottram?' asked Ellie.

'Of course.'

'She found him hanged at the top of the stairs, Oli.'

'Oh my God. Oh my God, Mrs Mottram.'

'I know.'

Oli left the room.

'Thank you,' said Sally. 'It was nice of you to send the cake away.'

'Not appropriate, Mrs Mottram. Not appropriate at all.'

'I just couldn't stay in the house any longer on my own, Ellie.'

'No wonder.' Sally could sense that deep inside her big head Ellie was struggling with an immense thought. 'If you don't want to go back,' she said at last, 'you could stay here. There's my bed upstairs. Ali could go in with Oli. Gladly.'

The thought of Ali and Oli in the same bed was more than Sally could bear.

'Gladly.'

'I'm sure they would.'

'They're great, them girls. Angels. They're angels, Mrs Mottram.'

'They certainly are. No, that's very kind of you, but . . . no . . . I have to face it. Get it over. Get myself tired enough, I'll sleep.'

'You can stay as long as you like, Mrs Mottram. And come round any time.'

'Thank you.'

'I'll be here. I'm not going anywhere.'

And Sally talked about the fact that there was no note. She talked about why she thought he might have done it. She talked about her marriage and how happy she thought they had been – well, they'd had their ups and downs etc., 'as you do'. 'As you do,' repeated Ellie, who had no idea really. Ellie was a good listener and Sally could see that she was truly upset for her, but she could also see that the thought of cake was slowly growing; movement of that great neck was not easy but the eyes, deep in their folds

42

of fat, began to stray longingly towards the door, as if Ellie was an enormous Labrador, a giant Kenneth.

'I think, Ellie, that it might be appropriate to have that cake now,' she said.

'Are you sure? Only I don't want to . . . well, thank you,' said Ellie. Then 'Oli!' she bawled. 'Ali. Cake.'

The two angels entered with plates liberally piled with cake. Two angels killing themselves and their sister with their hearts of gold.

SIX

A very short chapter, but fear of a very long evening

At last it was over. Olive would never know how she got through the dessert. Very few people dislike treacle, but those who do find it a particularly difficult thing to eat.

Jill led them to the door. Arnold wasn't very good at goodbyes.

The damp, cold night air of the cul-de-sac was as welcome to Olive as the scent of oranges on a sunny Spanish morning.

'Thank you, that was lovely,' she said, kissing Jill on one cheek.

'Lovely,' said Harry, kissing Jill on both cheeks. 'We must do it again soon. Our turn next time.'

He was pleased that the street lights were so dim in that impoverished town. There was a chance that Jill couldn't see the horror on Olive's face.

SEVEN

Marigold goes to a party

Marigold Boyce-Willoughby was going to be very late. She was taking such a long time to get ready. It really wasn't that surprising. The party was her first outing into Potherthwaite society since Timothy Boyce-Willoughby had ditched her for a Venezuelan dentist and ex-beauty queen, leaving her with a house she hated, a name she loved, a few happy memories, rather more unhappy memories, and sixty-two pairs of shoes. 'Is it the shoes?' she had asked plaintively when she had pleaded with him not to go. 'I won't buy any more, if it's the shoes.' 'It's not the fucking shoes, Imelda,' he had exploded. 'It's that I can't stand the fucking sight of you.' And he was the man Potherthwaite regarded as a gentleman. Always such a gentleman. Always except at home. Thousands like him.

The party wasn't going to be easy. She was a social climber and she no longer had a rope. She had looked wonderful on her third wedding day, dressed from head to foot in ironic white and happily married in Potherthwaite church by a vicar desperate for money. Her long train had flowed magnificently behind her. Now her train had hit the buffers. She knew what people would be saying tonight in posh Potherthwaite,

45

that tiny enclave. Pity Marigold has such bad taste in men. Must be something wrong with her, to be ditched by three husbands. Maybe she was cold in bed. Cold in bed? Her! Or maybe she was too voracious. Wore them out. She had prided herself on being rather a good lover.

Maybe she hadn't been a good lover. Nobody actually knew what a good lover was. She had never seen any other woman make love. Potherthwaite wasn't Hebden Bridge.

Everyone would be thinking these sorts of things about her tonight. So why was she going? Because she couldn't admit defeat, not to Potherthwaite, not to herself.

But what should she wear? It boiled down to a simple choice, between humility and defiance.

She could present herself as being ashamed of having been carried away by her wealthy husband, her glamorous lifestyle (for Potherthwaite – she had once met Hockney for three whole minutes and had talked about it for three whole years). She could show that at last she had realized that deep down she was still what she had always been, a modest working-class girl.

No. Wouldn't do. Couldn't do it. She had been born Marigold Smith. She'd hated her name. Smith. So common. Marigold, hateful. Marigolds were among the coarsest flowers in the garden. They were also washing-up gloves. And here she was, coarse and washed up.

But the name had been saved by being attached to Boyce-Willoughby. There was every chance that she had been the first person from her road ever to become double-barrelled. She had ceased to be a Dalston girl. She had become a Boyce-Willoughby, one of the Somerset Boyce-Willoughbys, and she wasn't going to throw that away, husband or no husband. No, humility wouldn't work, not for her. It was defiance or destruction.

So it was a lavishly dressed ex-Mrs Stent who wandered

out to her waiting taxi in the cul-de-sac not much before ten o'clock on that chill Potherthwaite evening. It was a glamorous ex-Mrs Larsen who walked round on her high heels to the far side of the taxi, just in case somebody should be looking out, fusty old Arnold Buss, perhaps, who wanted to interview her for his history of Potherthwaite, or the new people whose furniture van had arrived earlier. The man had looked all right. Bald, but they said that was a sign of virility. She shuddered. That was the last thing she wanted.

It was a defiant Marigold Boyce-Willoughby who gazed out at the dreary High Street and told herself that there was now no reason why she should stay in Potherthwaite. We laugh. I know, and you suspect, that she will still be there in ten years' time.

The taxi took her the full length of the High Street. She could feel her defiance slipping away as it rattled past the church she only entered for the sake of appearances, past the nearly-new shops she wouldn't be seen dead in, past the end of Quays Approach. She hadn't approached the Quays for months.

The taxi turned right where the High Street became Valley Road, sped through the empty roads towards the hills, began to climb one of the hills, passed through grand but rusty gates, crossed a large gravel forecourt, circling a fountain topped by a statue of a wool magnate, and pulled up outside a pillared entrance. This was – you've guessed it – Potherthwaite Hall – and the party was being held – you may have guessed this too, for we are in the twenty-first century – in one of the eight apartments into which that great house had been split.

Suddenly Marigold Boyce-Willoughby, glamorous lady, defiant spirit, brave soul, owner of many shoes, wanted to turn round and go home.

Apartment 1 was the home of Councillor Frank Stratton,

owner and managing director of Stratton's, whose stationery shops can be found in many towns around the Pennines. Frank Stratton was big in bulk, big in appetite, big in stationery, and big in charity. He wasn't actually quite as big as he thought he was, which was why he only owned an eighth of this great house. However, Apartment 1 was the best. His lounge had been the drawing room. It was absurd to call this huge room the lounge, but he had to persuade the voters that he was still humble.

The event was his famous annual bash for those who had supported his cancer charity. His daughter had died of breast cancer in 2005 at the age of thirty-seven. Some said he had never fully recovered, and he and his wife Marian had devoted themselves to raising money for cancer ever since. The party was for those who had given during the past year, and for those who unaccountably hadn't but might with luck be persuaded to in the coming year.

It took courage to step into the great lounge. The bulky brown leather furniture had been pushed back to the walls; almost all the men were in suits and ties, while the women were in various stages of excess, although not quite so excessive as usual.

Frank and his wife Marian greeted Marigold warmly.

'So sorry about . . .' began Frank nervously.

Marigold waved her arms in a negative gesture.

'Good riddance,' she said. 'Past history.'

'Thank you anyway for all your support,' said Marian.

'I've no idea what'll happen this year,' said Marigold.

'No matter,' said Frank. 'You're always welcome here.'

'Nonsense, but nice to hear,' said Marigold. 'And I'm so sorry I'm so late.'

'You've missed my speech,' said Frank.

'She heard it last year,' said Marian. 'Only two words were different, Marigold.'

Marigold laughed dutifully.

'Go and get yourself a drink,' said Frank. It was an abrupt but attractive dismissal. She longed for a drink.

She accepted a glass of champagne and a mini Yorkshire pudding from smiling waitresses. One or two people were already leaving. She really was much too late. And it wasn't as crowded as usual. The town was on a slide. She wouldn't stay long – here at the party, or in Potherthwaite.

She looked around the room, searching for women she knew and liked. Searching particularly for Sally. There were women in the town whom she liked but didn't much trust, and there were women whom she trusted but didn't much like, but Sally was the only woman whom she liked and trusted, of those she knew well enough to approach.

She was lost, lost on her own, lost without her other half, lost in the world, and seeking comfort from other women, not from men. This was a huge shock.

She found herself walking past Terence and Felicity Porchester, who lived on the stranded narrowboat.

'Hello, Marigold,' said Terence Porchester in his posh, fruity tones. 'You grow more gorgeous with every passing month.'

'I'm green with envy,' said Felicity in her matching voice. In plain-speaking Potherthwaite their voices had been much mocked, but slowly people had begun to realize that there wasn't an evil bone in either of their bodies.

'Where is that naughty man of yours hiding tonight?' asked Felicity.

'I've no idea,' said Marigold. 'At the bottom of the canal, I hope.'

She strode on, realized that she had been rudely abrupt, began to turn to apologize, found herself facing Matt Winkle, the supermarket manager, sallow, callow, anxious, fractious.

'Bloody woman,' he said. 'Here. Now. Tonight. What a time. At a party.'

'What a time for what?' asked the bemused Marigold.

'Complaining our apples aren't ripe. Bloody woman. Linda Oughtibridge. Sorry.'

Marigold turned away, found herself approaching two more men she didn't want to speak to. Gunter Mulhausen was German and formal and not very exciting, and he pretended to be in love with her, in a rather heavy Teutonic way, and she wasn't sure she was up to the jovial little fantasy today. Bill Etching was a randy little tosser who was regrettably successful in business and generous in charity. He was a worm who wormed himself in with his money. Timothy had joked that his surname was unfortunate. No woman would want to go back to look at *his* etchings.

She couldn't cope. Where was Sally? She would have said, 'Excuse me, chaps, lovely to see you, but I have something to discuss with Sally.' She couldn't see any woman whose name she remembered, apart from Marian and Felicity, so there was no woman she could use as an excuse. She had always liked men. She had been a man's woman. Now all these men frightened her. Now she couldn't cope with men. She couldn't even remember their names. All names were fleeing from her. She began to perspire. She had never perspired. She hadn't even glistened.

She saw a man she recognized approaching Frank What's-his-name. Frank led him straight out of the room. He was a policeman. Inspector . . . Inspector . . . Punnet. Not Punnet but like Punnet. What had Inspector Not Punnet But Like Punnet wanted? She heard Tommy What's-it, landlord of the Dog and Duck, say to her, 'I hope you'll still come to the pub, Marigold. We'll look after you.'

'I'm sure you will,' she said. 'Yes, I'll come.' His name had gone too.

'Now maybe one day that dinner invitation may be meeting with success very possibly,' said Gunter Mulhausen.

The thought of dinner with the smiling Teuton appalled her.

Pellet. Inspector Pellet.

What did he want?

'I would love dinner some time,' she told Gunter Mulhausen.

Pork Scratching's filthy little hand touched her bum. She felt it distinctly. Not Pork Scratching. Not come and see my scratchings. Come and see my etchings. Bill Etching, that was it.

She had to move. She couldn't. She was stuck to the carpet. She couldn't be. Walk, woman.

'Are you all right?' asked Tommy Allsop, his name suddenly recalled.

'Hold my arm. Hold my arm,' said Gunter Mulhausen.

Bill Etching clutched her waist.

'Don't touch me,' she shouted.

Everyone looked round. Everyone was staring at her. Such a shout had never been heard at one of Councillor Stratton's parties.

The men let go rapidly. All three looked embarrassed, even Bill Etching.

Again she tried to walk. She couldn't balance on her high heels, she was falling, it was all going black, her head was whirring, she felt a hand on her, trying to break her fall, and then she felt nothing more.

All sorts of people rushed over. Gunter Mulhausen rang 999. Tommy Allsop hurried over to Marian Stratton and asked where Frank was. She pointed towards their kitchen.

Frank Stratton was sitting at the breakfast table. He was white with shock. He had just heard of Barry's suicide. Tommy approached but was surprised and shocked by Frank's appearance, and hesitated.

'Oh God,' Frank was saying. 'I didn't invite him. He didn't give or come to anything this year. Didn't even hear from him, which I have to say annoyed me, which is why I didn't invite him. A nice chap once, but he's gone off. He has. He's gone off. And now this. Oh God. Poor Sally. I've a lot of time for Sally. Tommy, what is it? If it's about Barry Mottram, we've heard.'

'It isn't. Barry Mottram? No, it's Marigold. She's fainted.'

'Oh God,' said Councillor Frank Stratton. 'What an evening. That puts the tin lid on it. You know, I think this town is in danger of being officially declared a disaster area.'

EIGHT

Ben arrives home late

Night was folding Potherthwaite in its grip. The girl with the golden hair and Dr Mallet's vase must hurry. Soon Inspector Pellet would be back from his function. To get on to the roof of the garage was child's play – and she had forgotten that she was still a child. It was easy too to shin up the drainpipe, even with that great big delicate vase in her hand. It was hard to imagine that she had the strength, this slip of a girl, to open still further the upstairs window that hadn't quite been closed (and him a policeman and involved in Neighbourhood Watch!). She didn't need to open the window very far. She was so slim. The rest was easy: slip in, place the vase in full, challenging view on the dressing table in the scene of the Pellet lovemaking, ugh, the thought, slip out, leave the window open, slide down, disappear into the night, he'd never trace her, the stupid clod, he'd look ridiculous, ha ha, job done.

It was not yet half past eleven when the driver employed part-time by the council took a very subdued Marigold Boyce-Willoughby home to the cul-de-sac. The lights were on in number 9, where unpacking was still taking place, and the cocoa had not yet even been put on. The lights were still on in number 11 too. Jill was taking off her make-up, and Arnold was just putting the finishing touches to chapter 77, 'The High Street Suffers in the Era of Rationing'.

It was in fact twenty-seven minutes past eleven when she arrived home, and there was still no sign of that strange boy Ben Wardle at the Wardle home in Pomfret Crescent.

Marigold had soon come round after her panic attack, but she had flatly refused to go to the hospital. Her remark, 'They come out of there feet first,' had not gone down well with the doctors and nurses who had been rewarded for their generosity by being invited to the party. Councillor Stratton had pointed out that it was obvious that Marigold was unwell and was spouting careless gibberish in her embarrassment and shame. He would see that the hospital got a written apology from her asap.

Marigold had said that she felt perfectly all right now – it was just the stress of recent days, coupled with the heat of the room, that had made her faint. The only place in the world she wanted to be was in her own home. Councillor Stratton's secretary, fairly high on champagne, had been forced to type a report stating that Marigold had been offered an ambulance to take her to the hospital, and had refused, and that she knowingly accepted responsibility for any unfortunate consequences that might possibly occur as a result of her decision. Marigold was hurt by this, contemplated refusing to sign the description of her refusal, then suddenly couldn't be bothered and signed without protest, at exactly the same moment that, in Ellie's bedroom, Sally Mottram stood up, making the first move in what might well be a lengthy departure.

Sally didn't want to leave. She was terrified of entering her empty house. Ellie didn't want her to leave. She dreaded every night. But there is a convention in social life. You just don't call round uninvited, and stay till two in the morning. Leave she must.

By twenty to twelve she had reached almost to the front door of Ellie's house, and the girl with the golden hair had arrived home, had slipped in silently, had tiptoed through the door of the lounge, where her mother had fallen asleep in her chair, as she did most nights, and was snoring her head off and inhaling the alcoholic fumes of her own breath. The girl was asleep within five minutes.

Ben's father felt far from sleep. He was sitting at the kitchen table in his dressing gown, scowling, when Ben arrived home at last.

'What time do you call this?' his father demanded.

'Eric,' said Ben.

'What?'

'I call this time Eric,' said Ben. 'Though of course time is moving on, and it's no longer Eric. Aren't you going to ask me what it is now?'

'No, I am not.'

'It's now Eric plus one.'

'Well, I call it late.'

'Pretty dull name, Dad, to be absolutely frank.'

'I do my best with you, Ben.'

'I agree. I think sometimes I'm infuriatingly infantile, to be honest. But I'll grow up, Dad, sadly. And I don't happen to think I'm remotely late. I *am* sixteen, you know. You're so out of touch, Dad.'

'It's school tomorrow.'

'School's crap.'

'So what have you been up to?'

'I don't see why I should tell you, but it's true, you do do your best with me, so I will. Nothing. Sod all. No clubs. No films. No alcohol. No drugs. Nothing to eat.'

'And where have you not done all this?'

'In the allotments.'

'The allotments?'

'Yeah. It's nice there.'

'It's cold.'

'Yeah. Cool. We're all obsessed with cool, aren't we?'

'Why is it nice in the allotments, Ben?'

'Because it's dark, so you can't see Potherthwaite.'

'You love running Potherthwaite down, don't you?'

'I don't actually. I don't enjoy it at all. I bitterly regret that I wasn't born in a beautiful cathedral city with lovely old houses, a thriving arts scene, a Premier League football team and a beautiful estuary leading out to a warm southern sea.'

'Better do something about it then, hadn't you?'

'Maybe I will. Maybe I just will.'

'So what *have* you done all evening in the allotments?'

'I've told you. Nothing.'

'You must have done something.'

'Well, yeah. Talked. About nothing, though.'

'So you weren't alone.'

'Sharp, Dad. Very sharp.'

'Don't patronize me. We feed you, we look after you. We don't deserve to be patronized.'

Ben actually looked shamefaced.

'Sorry.'

There was a brief pause. Tick-tock of the kitchen clock, which was slightly askew – the cleaner had been.

'Who were you with?'

'Tricksy.'

His father tried so hard not to make any noise, but the very faintest sigh emerged from his mouth. Or his nose. Ben wasn't quite sure where sighs did come from.

His parents didn't like Tricksy. He knew that they wondered if he and Tricksy . . . did things together. On allotments. At night. They believed in equal marriage, although they couldn't really think it was worth all the time and money the House of Commons had taken up with it when the sea would boil in twenty years and the oil would run out next Thursday and seven million illegal immigrants were arriving at Dover every three days – Ben's dad was given to exaggeration. Ben had once told his dad that he exaggerated 367 times a week, and his dad hadn't seen the joke.

They were enlightened people, but they didn't want Ben to be gay. For his own sake, you understand. Mind you, it wasn't just that. They didn't even know if he was gay. They didn't know if Tricksy was gay. They would just have been happier if their only child was showing signs of having more than one friend.

Ben had heard the sigh and it made him very angry. Earlier, when he'd been teasing his dad, it had been all right, but now, over Tricksy, he couldn't tease. He could explode, or go to bed. He made a surprisingly sensible choice.

'Right. I'm off. It's bedtime.'

'It's past bedtime.'

'Whose fault is that? You've kept me talking.'

'Point taken. Guilty as charged.'

His dad suddenly smiled. It was entirely unexpected, and it threw Ben. He turned at the door, and said something he hadn't said for several years, and had had no intention of saying that night.

'Love you, Dad.'

He wished he hadn't said this. Saying it shocked him. He realized that it was no longer true.

It was three minutes past twelve as Ben set off upstairs. Sally Mottram hadn't reached home yet. She didn't want to reach home. She was walking increasingly slowly along Oxford Road. There were no lights on in Dr Mallet's, no lights on at the Sparlings', no lights on at the Hammonds', no lights on in Oxford Road. The council had recently started to switch the lights off at midnight, perhaps so that murderers

57

couldn't see their victims well enough to stab them or shoot them accurately enough to kill them.

Sally opened the gate, walked slowly up the path beside the lawn, put her key in the lock, turned it, opened the door, went in, and closed the door carefully from long habit, so as not to wake anyone, although there was no longer anyone to wake.

She decided to go straight upstairs, get it over. She didn't know how she would find the courage to walk past where he had been. But she had to. She had to start.

She climbed the stairs at a steady pace, quaking but resolute. She tried not to look, but she had to take a quick peek, and there he . . . wasn't.

She crossed the landing, opened the bedroom door, went in, and closed it.

She thought back to the strange words that she had thought to herself at the bottom of the stairs. 'You have to start.' What had she meant? Start what? She had no idea what she had to start. Just to live the rest of her life? Just to survive?

Or something more?

BOOK TWO

Sally Makes a Journey, and a Decision

NINE

Going south

The taxi had been late, and she had arrived at Potherthwaite station just in time to see the 10.22 snaking round the corner towards a better world.

Six weeks had passed since Sally Mottram had made that horrendous discovery at the top of the stairs. For six weeks there had grown in her an overwhelming desire to leave Potherthwaite, to go back down south. At times her desire had been to leave not just Potherthwaite, but this world. She didn't see any point in her living any more. Her children were settled and didn't need her. Her life was pointless.

She wheeled her suitcases along platform 1, past baskets of dull, neglected flowers. She passed the steps that led on to the footbridge, and pressed for the lift. The lift arrived with a sigh, as if utterly tired of its tiny routine. The doors opened. It was quite a job to get her two cases into the lift. They were too large. She had brought too much stuff. She hadn't been capable of deciding what not to bring. She was no longer capable of making decisions.

'Going up,' said the voice of a surprisingly posh woman, bossily and unnecessarily since there was nowhere to go but up. The lift rose to footbridge level like an asthmatic old man on his last legs.

'Footbridge level,' thundered the bossy woman with just a hint of pride at the lift's achievement.

It was now quite a job to get the two cases out of the lift. Sally wheeled them halfway across the footbridge and stopped for breath.

The railway line runs along the bottom of Baggit Moor and is therefore slightly above the level of the valley floor. As she stood there, Sally could see the town spread out before her. Grey stone buildings, grey slate roofs. She could even see back to Oxford Road, though it was impossible from this distance to single out 'The Larches'. What a feeling it had been, that morning, to walk out of the front door and know that she wouldn't have to pass the top of the stairs for at least two weeks, maybe longer, depending on how she got on with Judith. And of course she was far too far away, here on the footbridge, to see the *'For Sale'* sign.

Everybody said it was good that she was selling. She would never quite get over the shock, if she stayed. Everybody also knew that she was *having* to sell. She had no money.

She'd overheard Gordon Hendrie, in the supermarket, near the rather sad fish counter – she hated fish counters, all those dead eyes – she'd heard him say, in his idea of a low voice, 'It'll have been because of sex or money. It always is.' She'd known that he had been talking about Barry.

She'd hoped that it had been because of money, which was absurd, because if it was money she would live the rest of her life in poverty. But if it was because of sex she would have shared her marital bed with a monster, kissed a pervert, been made love to by a dirty dirty man, and that would have been even worse than poverty.

It had been money. Mottram & Caldwell had been

struggling. There weren't so many people in Potherthwaite who had been able to afford lawyers' fees. Tom Caldwell had handled his money sensibly. Barry, that precise sober lawyer, had gambled, and gambled badly on both money and horses. A lad who was on the dole had been pleased enough to get a bit of pocket money to put his bets on for him. Barry Mottram himself had never been seen in William Hill.

Much of this had been revealed at the inquest. The truth had hurt her. The fact that she had known nothing about any of it had hurt her more.

Dr Mallet, who wished that he had changed his name to something more befitting a psychoanalyst – Bronovsky, perhaps – had been persuaded to give evidence too, reluctantly, because the fact that Barry had killed himself had not been a good advertisement for a psychiatrist who had been treating the man for depression. This news too had hurt Sally. The fact that she had also known nothing about this had hurt her more. Not only had she known nothing of these things, but no suicide note had ever been found. That hurt her most of all.

Despite the lack of a note, there had been no difficulty in reaching the verdict that Barry Mottram had killed himself.

She could just see the roof of the building that housed Mottram & Caldwell. Her eyes passed on, drawn instinctively towards the uniform rooftops of Cadwallader Road. She saw, vividly, Ellie Fazackerly stuck there in her great bed.

'Having a quiet moment?'

'Sorry?'

'I said, "Having a quiet moment?"'

'I was, yes.'

'Good for you.'

Sally stole a quick look at the speaker of these words. A

middle-aged man was standing close to her, too close to her. He had sunken eyes, hollow cheeks, receding hair and an ominous long raincoat.

'Does you good, sometimes, dun't it?' he said. 'Stop. Listen. Have a think. Does you good.'

'Yes. Yes. It does. Yes. A moment of reflection.'

'In this hectic world.'

'Quite.'

'I think we may have met before.'

'I don't think so.'

She backed away from the man ever so slightly. But he noticed and moved closer ever so slightly.

'Not a bad view, is it?'

Yes, it is. Can't say that. Can't be rude.

Why not be rude? He's invading my space.

'Not bad, no.'

'No, there's nowt like a spot of quiet thinking. Young folk don't know how to do it. That's what's wrong wi' t'world. Thinking. It's a lost art.'

For you it is.

Couldn't say it.

'Very true.'

Oh God, Sally.

'I'm on me own, you see. Me wife died twenty-two years ago.'

Suicide, was it? Sally! You are not nice.

'I still talk to her.'

Suddenly Sally felt a wave of sympathy for the man in the long raincoat.

'I can understand that.'

'You get lonely, you see.'

'Yes. Yes, I do see.'

There was silence for a moment. Sally found that she couldn't just leave, not after that information. Somehow, it

64

had become an important moment, here on the footbridge, teased by a playful easterly breeze.

'As I say . . . you don't mind my talking, do you? Cos I know I interrupted you thinking.'

'You can think too much.'

'I pride meself on knowing when to talk and when not to talk. I was a taxi driver, see. Tool of the trade, is that. Gauge when the passenger wants to talk, gauge when he wants to be quiet. Tool of the trade.'

I'm rather glad I never hired your taxi.

'I bet you're glad you never hired my taxi.'

'No!'

She didn't want to move on until he did. But he showed no sign of going. It was an impasse. Maybe they would stay on the footbridge for ever.

'I'm sorry.'

'What for?'

'Interrupting you. When you were thinking.'

'It doesn't matter.'

'It does. I've let meself down. I'll be off now.'

Don't say anything, Sally.

'Leave you with your thoughts. And the view.'

'Thank you.'

'Not a bad old place. Bit of a dump, I suppose, but what somebody could do with it! What somebody could do with it, eh?'

'Absolutely. Very true. Well, it's been nice talking to you.'

Even he should take that hint, but she held out her hand to make the point even more positively.

They shook hands. She'd have time to wash hers before she had anything to eat.

He moved off. She was ashamed of the depth of her relief.

He was coming back!

'I remember where I saw you.'

'Oh?'

'Coming out o' kirk t'other Wednesday. I know it was Wednesday cos it wasn't market day and I'd thought it was, silly me. You and your daughter. Pretty girl. I could see the resemblance. Lovely couple you made, if you don't mind my saying.'

'No. Not at all. Not at all. It was my husband's funeral.'

'Oh no. I've done it again. I'm so sorry.'

'It's all right, but . . .'

'You want to cry. I understand. And I agree. Don't hold it in. That's trouble wi' Potherthwaite. We hold too much in. Let it all out, I say.'

Long Raincoat moved away, and this time he didn't turn back. Sally looked out over the grey town, and thought about his words. 'Bit of a dump, I suppose, but what somebody could do with it!' She shook her head at the impossibility, the absurdity of the sudden thought.

She looked over at the church. She thought of herself and Alice as Long Raincoat must have seen them. A lovely couple. Yes, they must have looked a lovely couple.

She hadn't felt lovely, that day. She'd hardly slept. She'd felt that she looked haggard. The service had been a total embarrassment. So much was said. So much wasn't said. The Revd Dominic Otley had spoken without conviction. The funerals of people who have killed themselves are hell.

And Alice. She had been lovely. She had grown into a really lovely woman, a proud mother of two lovely little boys. It was lovely that she had such lovely photos of them, and if perhaps she showed them slightly too often, well, it was good at a funeral to dwell on things that cheered, it would be wrong to criticize her for that. No, the only thing that had disappointed her about Alice was the thing she hadn't said. She hadn't suggested that Sally move to New Zealand. She understood why, it made sense. She had her own life. She had the boys. She didn't know whether, if Alice *had* asked her, she would have gone. Some people said New Zealand was a paradise. Others said it was boring. Perhaps it was in the ineluctable nature of things that paradises were boring. No, she didn't know if she would have gone, but it would have been nice to have been asked.

Sam hadn't sung the praises of Barnet, either.

She took one more look at the roofs of her home town, at a faint sheen from the emerging sun on the one tiny glimpse she could get of the Potherthwaite Arm of the Rackstraw and Sladfield Canal.

Beyond and above the canal and the Quays, on the moor at the other side of the valley, Potherthwaite Hall stood arrogant guard over the town. It had only occurred to her well after Barry's death that this year they hadn't been invited to Councillor Stratton's party.

She set off at last, slowly wheeling her two suitcases to the northern end of the footbridge. She pressed for the lift. It arrived slowly. 'Footbridge level,' exclaimed the bossy lady. Sally manoeuvred her cases into the lift. 'Going down.' She went down.

She wheeled her cases towards the ramshackle buffet, then hesitated. She didn't want to go into the buffet, in case Long Raincoat would be there.

But there was another reason too. She didn't need a vat of tea or a cauldron of coffee. She didn't need a Danish pastry or a slice of fruit cake.

She didn't need anything. She was going south, to the Land of Plenty.

TEN

A small flat in Barnet

Beth's lasagne wasn't exactly bad. She was an inexperienced cook – they lived mainly on ready meals and takeaways – but it was clear to Sally that Sam had told her that his mother would expect real cooking. She wished he hadn't done that. She had quite lost her appetite since Barry's death, and she knew that she had to eat up all her lasagne. It was a neat reversal of her relationship with her son. She had spent hours getting him to eat up, in the happy years.

'The happy years'! What did she mean? Hadn't she been happy throughout her marriage? She had thought that Barry had been too, but . . . consulting a psychoanalyst? Killing himself? And why oh why had he not left her a suicide note? To go, to hurt her so, without a word.

This was awful. This was not why she had come to stay with Sam and Beth. She had come to begin to recover from her trauma. She had come, with Barry dead and Alice in New Zealand, to find some family feeling, some family warmth.

'Lovely.'

'Do you mean that?' asked Beth naively.

'It's very good.'

'It is, Beth,' said Sam. 'Really. Beth has no confidence, Mum.'

Beth gave Sam a glare, which she turned into a comedy glare to try to hide the fact that it was a real glare. She wasn't unattractive, but you couldn't say she was beautiful. She's a bit like her lasagne, thought Sally, and then she wished that she hadn't, but you can't unthink a thought.

She was ashamed of herself for wishing that her son had found somebody more glamorous. She was ashamed of herself for wishing that he had got a better degree from a better university and had a better job.

They were sitting on wooden chairs at a square, battered table in a corner of the small lounge/diner of their tiny rented flat in a street of small pre-war houses in Barnet. There were two round marks on the tabletop, where hot mugs had been put down without protection. Sally found herself wondering which of them had left the careless marks. She hoped it wasn't her son, he had been well brought up.

She calculated that she was now more than halfway through her lasagne. She could make it through to the end. And there came to her at that moment a sudden memory of Potherthwaite, the last thing she wanted to remember. Hadn't she in part come here to forget? Marigold had suggested, at the funeral wake of all places, that they go out to lunch together, damsels in distress, to cheer themselves up. There was a special Pensioners' Lunch Offer at the Weavers' Arms on Thursdays, and they had decided to cheer themselves up by going there and perhaps being the youngest people in the room.

Seated at the next table had been Jill and Arnold Buss, with their new neighbours, Olive and Harry Patterson. Jill, who knew Sally, had introduced Olive and Harry. At the end of the meal, Harry and Arnold had gone to the bar to dissect the bill, Jill had gone to the loo, and Sally and Olive had met at the coats, and as Sally had helped Olive on with her coat, she had praised the beef casserole, and Olive had told her about having to finish the beef casserole at Jill and Arnold's when it was too spicy for her. 'I shouldn't have told you. They were very kind. Please don't mention it,' Olive had said hastily as the men returned. Sally had thought this a very trivial story, but now she was beginning to sympathize with Olive.

Thinking back to Potherthwaite led her inexorably back to Barry. Oh God, she missed him. Had he not known, how could he not have known, how much she would miss him? How could he do it to her?

'Really lovely.'

It would have been better not to say that. It would draw their attention to the slow speed of her consumption, the almost desperate working of her jaw.

She felt guilty about wishing that Sam didn't look so pale and thin. It made him look too tall, a beanpole. It made his nose look too long and too serious. She felt uneasy about being so disappointed that Beth wasn't taller, and had such heavy breasts. She told herself that it was unreasonable of her to hope that they would soon move to somewhere more exciting than Barnet. Poor Barnet, how could it live up to her picture of 'The South', that mythical place she had missed so badly for twenty-four years? Every now and then she made some kind of reply to some kind of remark, but afterwards she couldn't remember what they had talked about, she could only remember what she had thought. It wasn't that Barnet was ugly exactly, it was just . . . commonplace. Ordinary. Rather like Beth and the lasagne, really.

Beth had left the lasagne in the oven too long, perhaps less than two minutes too long. But that was the trouble with pasta, leave it a smidgen too long and it went heavy, solid, stolid. As she chewed, she saw Olive chewing, and she was back in Potherthwaite again. This was terrible. Oh, why hadn't he left a note?

Each mouthful was a hurdle, but now she was in the final straight. Chomp chomp. Finished! Good girl! She's eaten all her dinner! Who's a clever Sally?

'Delicious.'

She longed for something sweet. How humiliating to long so much for something so unimportant.

Sam was clearing up, and soon Beth rose to help.

'I'm afraid we don't do desserts,' said Sam.

'We've turned our backs on sugar,' said Beth.

'That's fine,' lied Sally. 'I wouldn't have been able to eat another mouthful anyway.'

They refused to let her into the kitchen to help. It was too small.

'You go and sit down and relax,' said Sam.

Relax!

It wasn't only the kitchen that was too small. So was the lounge/diner, and her bedroom, and the bathroom. She longed to leave, and she was committed to staying for four whole days. She couldn't leave early. Sam was her son.

She felt at a loss, having no fire to sit by. There were just two armchairs, depressingly dark green and past their best. They were arranged facing the television set, the open fire of modern living. The central heating made the flat warm, almost stuffily so, but it wasn't the same as a fire. How spoilt she had been with her nice house in the best road in Potherthwaite. How could she not have fully appreciated it until she was on the point of losing it? She hadn't had a bad life, until Barry's death of course, but it had been . . . ordinary.

Rather like Barnet. And Beth. And the lasagne.

When they had washed up, Sam and Beth joined her. Sam plonked himself into the other armchair. Beth pulled a wooden chair over and sat between them. Sally wished she sat more gracefully. She also wished that her son had been more polite.

'Is there anything you want to watch?' asked Sam hopefully.

Yes. The movement of the hands of the carriage clock on the mantelpiece as it leads me slowly but reliably towards the moment in four days' time when I can leave this prison. Sally, that is not worthy of you. Pull yourself together – isn't that what this trip is all about?

'Not really, thank you. I'm not a great telly watcher.'

'I'll open another bottle of wine,' said Sam, standing up.

'I'll do it,' said Beth hastily.

Beth didn't want to be alone with her! Come on, Sally. Be bright and friendly. Let Beth in.

'Nice of you to bring all that wine, Mum.'

I brought it for myself, in case I needed it, but we don't need to go into motive, do we?

'I want us to be cheery, Sam. I want us to start to get over what's happened together. We need each other.'

Beth brought the wine and they all made an effort and really the conversation wasn't too bad at all, but all the time Sally was aware of Sam's anxiety.

Then Beth stood up.

'I'm a bit tired,' she said. 'I'm off to bed.'

She kissed Sam. Sally moved to stand up but Beth said 'Don't get up' and bent down and kissed her. Sally realized that Beth wanted to say something. What could it be? 'It's great to have you here'? 'Sam and I both hope you'll move down near us'? 'Let's have a lovely four days'?

'I've put you two towels and there's a glass of water by your bed,' said Beth.

When Beth had gone, Sally asked, 'Is she being tactful?'

'What?'

'Going to bed early. Leaving us alone together.'

'Ah. Oh, I see. No, no. Beth always goes to bed early.'

'Right. Well, anyway, Sam . . . um . . . we may as well kill this bottle.'

'Oh. Right. Yes.'

Sam poured and they clinked glasses.

'Good to have you here, Mum.'

'Thanks. Good to be here. Sam?'

'Yes?' said Sam warily.

'Um . . . I hope I'm not going to put my foot in it . . .'

'You couldn't, Mum.'

'No, but seriously, I must ask you . . . I know you, you can't hide things from me. Something's worrying you, and that worries me. Is there anything . . . is there something . . . on your mind?'

'Well . . . I mean . . . Mum, I'm twenty-three, you've had a terrible experience, I don't want to burden you with my worries.'

'I want you to burden me, Sam. It's what I'm for.'

'OK. OK. They say every problem is about sex or money.'

He paused.

'Go on.'

'You don't need to be Einstein to know that my problem's money. I'm sorry you've noticed, I've really tried not to show it, but . . . I'm scared shitless, Mum.'

'Right, so . . . why are you . . . scared shitless?'

'I'm a fairly junior accountant, Beth's a dentist's receptionist and she isn't the pushy type, so neither of us is very well paid, our degrees haven't been much of a passport to anything, and at this moment of time we owe between us a small matter of sixty-eight thousand pounds.'

'Oh my God. That's awful. You poor boy. Poor Beth.' She turned angry. 'It's a scandal that young people have this enormous pressure. Doesn't this nation value education?'

'Not enough, obviously. Beth knows two girls with violent anorexia because of their worries, and a bloke I knew at Keele topped . . . Oh God, I'm sorry, Mum. Mum, I'm so sorry.'

'Don't worry. I haven't forgotten, and I'm sorry too. Poor bloke.'

'No, but that phrase, it's . . .'

'It's what people say. Words don't hurt compared to . . . what's happened.'

'No. Sorry.'

'What did Beth take her degree in?'

Sam blushed slightly. He looked better when he had a bit of colour.

'Conservation.'

'I see.'

'Mum, this is going to sound awful, but . . . now that we've started . . . I don't know how to put it . . . I'm embarrassed.'

'Don't be.'

'Well . . . I mean, don't think Beth and I have ever been wildly extravagant.'

Sally couldn't avoid taking a little look around the room. The walls were bare except for two posters.

'I've never thought that.'

'Good. But . . . I hope in a way this is a compliment, but . . . we've regarded you as a kind of a safety net.'

'Always be here to help, you mean?'

'Well, yes. In a way. I mean, you seemed to have plenty of money. Dad a lawyer.'

'Sadly, not all lawyers are rich.'

'Not rich, but Dad's always been scrupulously fair about things, and you've always been very generous, you've been absolutely marvellous, and . . .'

'Could you repeat that?'

'What?'

'That I've been absolutely marvellous.'

'Well, of course you have. Didn't you know that?'

'Not really, no. So I'd like . . . it would just be nice to hear it again.'

'Right. Right. Mum, you've always . . . Sorry. I can't do it. Not . . . on request. I mean, of course I mean it, but it just slipped out, I can't just . . . sorry.'

'It doesn't matter.'

But it did.

'Beth is scared shitless too.'

'Well, at least I'll be able to use the lavatory whenever I want to.'

'What?'

'You won't need it. You're both scared shitless.'

'Mum!'

'Just trying to lighten things, Sam. Just trying to show I'm not a stuffy old has-been, failed utterly but so what? Is there a drop more?'

'Just a bit. You have it.'

'No, no.'

'I insist.'

'OK.'

Sam drained the bottle into Sally's glass. There were no dregs. The days of affording wines with dregs were over.

'You're trying to find out, very tactfully, how much I'm still going to be good for.'

'Mum!'

'No. You are. And I don't blame you. And nothing about your dad upsets me more than this. He's left me unable to help you. To any extent. Meaningfully.'

'I see. Well, I think I sort of knew.'

'It humiliates me.'

'No, Mum. It shouldn't. You shouldn't have to. Anyway, enough of that. We'll get by.'

There was silence for a couple of minutes. A bus roared by, then all was silence again. They stared into the non-existent fire.

'What exactly is your position, Mum?'

'Your father left me debts of roughly three hundred and fifty thousand, as far as we can ascertain, though it may change.'

'God!'

'The house is in joint ownership and is on the market for four hundred and fifty thousand, but we won't get it.'

'No? It's a nice house.'

'It's a nice house in Potherthwaite. I reckon that, by the time all fees are paid, I will be lucky to have fifty thousand.'

'What'll you do?'

'Don't know. Get by. I think . . . I actually think . . . something I didn't realize . . . deep down your mother's a pretty tough old bird.'

'I'll say.'

Sally reflected that the nearest Sam could get to a compliment was 'I'll say', and to say was exactly what he couldn't do.

She finished her drink and stood up.

'I'm glad I got that off my chest,' he said.

'Good. Sleep well.'

'I will. You too.'

'I will.'

Neither of them would. Sally didn't know what would keep Sam awake. He might have got that subject off his chest, but she could see that he was far from fully relieved.

There was something else, something that was worrying him even more than money.

Worrying about what it was would keep her awake.

ELEVEN

Sam's worry

She only found out what Sam's great worry was on the last evening, after Beth had gone to bed.

The days had passed pleasantly enough. They had made trips to Covent Garden, and St Albans, and the Great Bed of Ware, which had led Sally back to Potherthwaite yet again. How perfect it would have been for Ellie.

The evening meals had raised no problems. Sally had eaten sparingly during the day, so that she'd be hungry enough to manage, and even enjoy, Beth's cautious cooking.

It had been after Beth had gone to bed that things had got more difficult, as mother and son had sat in their dark green chairs, in front of the blank television, trying not very successfully to sip their wine more slowly as the evenings passed. Sally could see that there was still some subject that Sam was desperately wanting to broach. But he wasn't a broacher, and he had a haunted look, and she was haunted by his haunted look.

On the second evening, Sally had tested the ground over the question of where she intended to live. Was that the issue?

'It was good, despite the circumstances, having all that

time with Alice,' she had said. 'We got pretty close. It's a shame she lives so far away.'

This had prompted Sam to test the ground himself.

'Would you ever consider going to live in New Zealand?'

'I don't know if Alice would welcome that. She certainly didn't mention it. No, I don't think I'd want to go that far.'

'But would you consider coming back south?'

'I don't know. I might. They always say you shouldn't rush anything.'

'No. Well, there's no rush, is there?'

'Would you be happy if I came to live near you?'

'I think it would be great. And you could be very useful. You could babysit.'

'Oh, so you're planning to have children.'

'I presume so.'

'You presume you're planning. Surely you either are planning or you aren't?'

'I presume we'll have babies. We haven't planned anything. You're jumping the gun a bit, aren't you, Mum? We aren't even married or engaged or anything.'

There had been quite a long silence then. Sally had realized that where she might live wasn't Sam's great worry, but it still was a bit of a concern. When he next spoke it was warily.

'The only thing is, Mum . . . you know, about you coming to live near us . . . we aren't settled here, neither of us likes our job very much, we might move.'

'Well, I realize that. Sam, don't worry, I'm not coming to live near you. I might go and live near Judith, that's different.'

'Why is it different?'

'You're still discovering your way of life. You don't want your mother poking in. I'd be tempted to give advice all the time, and you'd come to hate me. My sister has her way of life. No advice. No hate.'

That second night she had slept better, but still not deeply. In the morning she had heard Sam and Beth talking earnestly, even urgently, in those ominous low voices.

On the third evening, over the wine, she had done a bit more broaching, while Beth washed up.

'Don't think I'm interfering, Sam . . .'

'I don't like the sound of that.'

'No, no, it's nothing, it's just . . . are you and Beth . . . you know . . .?'

'No, I don't know, Mum.'

'Is everything . . . you know . . . all right . . . between you? You know . . . in bed?'

'Mum!'

'I know. But . . . you know . . . well, no, you don't know, but . . . your father and I . . . in later years . . . it just stopped. You're young, and I shouldn't be saying this, but in this flat . . . it's so compact, the walls are so thin you hear everything.'

'What on earth can you possibly have heard, Mum?'

'Nothing. Nothing at all. That's what worried me.'

'Mum. You're right about the walls. The soundproofing is disgraceful. We've complained, but what can you do? We're helpless. But with these walls, Mum, and you right next to us, we wouldn't dream of making love while you're here. You'd hear every creak . . . every groan . . . every moan. Beth wouldn't even contemplate it. Basically she's quite shy about . . . those things. Her dad was a vicar.'

'But . . . um . . . no.'

'What?'

'No.'

'What do you mean, "no"? No what?'

'Well . . . no.'

'Oh, Mum. Now you've got me wondering what on earth you were going to say.'

'Well, all right. I suppose it's not that important, anyway. It's just . . . well. Beth goes to bed early and you said she's always asleep when you go to bed and I couldn't help wondering . . . you know . . . when you . . . you know . . . make love.'

'Right. Well basically, Mum, the timetable is as follows. We don't make love at night because our bedtimes are so different. We make love when we get home from work. On Mondays and Thursdays.'

Sally felt uneasy at what she took to be her son's mockery.

'I'm at night school on Tuesdays, and Beth is at night school on Wednesdays. It's a pity they're on different nights . . .'

Then she felt, if anything, even more uneasy. She realized that he wasn't mocking at all. He was deadly serious.

'. . . but it's the subjects. And on Fridays we meet some friends in a pub and go for – I know it's extravagant in view of the debt hanging over us, but you've got to live – a curry. Occasionally we just feel like it and might pop into bed at the weekend.'

'Oh, good. I'm glad there's some spontaneity.'

'Mum!'

'Sorry.'

'Young people lead busy, stressful lives. We live with the knowledge that if we lose our job there are probably more than a thousand people waiting to take it. Those carefree youthful days, Mum, they're a thing of the past.'

'Oh dear.'

'We're all right. So stop worrying.'

'I will. I will. Sorry. I won't drink so much tomorrow.'

'Good.'

'May as well finish the bottle now, though.'

It's amazing how quickly a little routine can set itself up, particularly when you know that you can afford to indulge the routine, because it will cease. Even in hospital, you can start to enjoy the routine, if you know that you're going to be discharged fairly soon. Sally had actually found that, despite the tension, she was looking forward to that last evening's chat with her son in the dark green armchairs with the wine bottle on a little severely distressed table between them. They might never have these little chats again.

One look at his face took away all the promise of enjoyment. He was even more severely distressed than the table.

Beth popped her head round the kitchen door.

'I know it's your last night, Sally,' she said awkwardly, 'but . . . I know it's pathetic, but I'm no use at all if I don't get my beau— my sleep, and I'm no use at work if I'm tired. It's been great having you, Sally, though of course we wish it hadn't been in these circumstances, and I'll be a better cook next time because I'm doing cookery at night school. So, anyway, I'll see you in the morning and I'll say goodbye properly then, and thanks for all the wine, and . . . well, I'll go along to bed then.'

'Thanks, Beth, it's all been great and I'll see you in the morning. Sleep well,' said Sally.

At the door, Beth turned and gave Sam a fierce stare. Sally's heart sank. Whatever it was, it was coming.

Sam sighed, and Sally waited.

She waited quite a while.

'Um . . .' he began.

He paused again.

'Mum?' he continued.

He paused again.

At last he managed a sentence.

'Beth has pleaded with me not to do this.'

'I've heard you talking in low voices.'

'Oh God, have you?'

He topped up both their glasses.

'Tonight, alcohol is definitely a crutch,' he said. 'Beth thinks what I'm about to do is wrong, and I have no idea if it's right.'

He looked so pale, his cheeks were so hollow, his eyes were so intense – the bags under them looked as if they had been waiting for years for him to slip into them. Sally was overwhelmed with love and pity. She reached out and pressed his hand. She could find no words.

He took a letter out of his pocket, held it with a shaking hand, tried to steady it by using both hands, failed.

'You've said so much about there not being a suicide note,' he said. 'It's worried you so much. You've told me so many times how you yearn for closure. I haven't slept properly since I got it. I've even taken advice about closure and its value from a psychiatrist. I've shown this letter to him, and told him all I know about you, how strong you are, how brave.'

Sally looked at him in amazement. She still didn't speak.

'He advised me, very cautiously, covering himself in caveats, to show it to you. This is Dad's suicide note, Mum. He sent it to me.'

'Oh God.'

It was barely a whisper. Sally could scarcely breathe.

'Read it,' she whispered. 'Read it, Sam, please. I don't think I could bear to see his handwriting just now.'

'Right. I'll read it. I wondered if you might prefer that.'

He cleared his throat.

'"Dear Sam,

'"This is a letter that I never expected to have to write, and it is one that I wish with all my heart that I did not have to write now. In one hour's time I will walk out of my office for the last time, and drive home, stopping only to post this letter. When I get home I will hang myself. In posting this letter I am, in a way, committing myself to the act. I am very frightened, but I am also extremely vain – see how carefully I compose this letter, taking care to put 'extremely' in place of a second lazy 'very'!" He puts an exclamation mark there.'

Sally, the blood draining from her face, made an impatient gesture, which said, Never mind the punctuation. Get on with it.

'"I'm very scared, but I'm much too conceited to allow even my son to see how weak I am.

'"The obvious reason for my killing myself is very simple. I'm losing money hand over fist and will soon have to declare myself bankrupt if I live. I cannot bear the disgrace. I cannot bear the thought of meeting our wealthy friends at the Rotary lunch and the golf club after such a disgrace. I dread the thought of even facing you, and Alice, after such a disgrace."'

Sally listened with a stony face. It would have been impossible for even the cleverest psychiatrist in the world, who undoubtedly was *not* Dr Mallet, to see what she was thinking. Was she turned to stone by the horror, by sympathy, by disgust, by simple pique at her children being mentioned in the letter before her?

'"But there is another reason, sadly also not very original. In death, fittingly, I reveal the reason that my life has failed. I am indescribably ordinary, a lawyer of no great talent or imagination, a husband with no real tenderness or warmth or understanding, a father bringing up his children as if from the pages of a manual.

'"I look at myself in a mirror and I see a little man, a dull man. I hate myself. I don't fear not existing. I look forward to it. I will be glad to be gone."'

Sam paused. He looked up at his mother. His hands were shaking as much as ever, the paper trembling as if being held in half a gale.

A single tear, a harbinger of floods to come, ran slowly down his mother's face.

'It gets worse, Mum. Can you take it?'

She nodded fiercely, almost angrily.

'"The one unusual thing that I am doing in this last act of my unmemorable life is sending this, my suicide note, to you and not to your mother. I feel a tiny, ridiculous, entirely callous twinge of pride at doing this. It will mean an inquest. My little life can entertain Potherthwaite just for a moment at the last. Potherthwaite, dear God, how did I end up there?

'"But no. The main reason for my sending you this letter is that I cannot send it to your mother. There are things I find I cannot die without saying. I want to say them. I want to tell you, which is very unfair on you, but you see my hatred of myself has made me a very unpleasant man. I . . ." I don't think I can go on, Mum. I think I've made a dreadful mistake.'

'Go on!' She tried to keep the sudden irritation out of her voice. 'You can't stop now.'

'No. No.'

He gasped. The simple, naked words came out very fast, as if he feared his voice would break.

'"I haven't said anything truly meaningful, or meaningfully true, to your mother for about ten years."'

He couldn't look at her now.

'"It's just . . . it's become . . . as if neither of us are real when we're together. It's as if we were holograms. There is no connection. It has turned into a dead, dull drama, a dismal fiction. I tried to write this to her, I just couldn't think of any words. I couldn't move my hands. The last few times . . ."

'I can't read this bit, Mum.'

'You must. You can't stop now.'

'Oh God.'

He went bright red. He was shaking. He came out with the words very fast.

'"The last few times we made love, I pretended that she was somebody else. Who, you may well ask. Sam, I can't tell even you that. That must remain my sad little secret shame.

'"There is no need to reveal the existence of the letter at the inquest. I haven't a shred of respect left for the law."' Sam was beginning to cry. '"And please don't tell your mother. She hasn't the character to survive this letter. Lies are almost always so much better than the truth.

'"This letter comes to you, Sam, with, if not love, the nearest perhaps that I can come to love."'

He was rushing now. The tears were coming. She could hear them approaching.

'"Do better in life than I have, Sam.

'"Your wretched, late father."'

As he read the last words Sam dissolved into tears.

'Have I done wrong?' he wailed. 'Mum, have I done wrong?'

She was crying too. She shook her head.

'You see, Mum, I don't think lies *are* better than the truth.'

Sally tried to smile.

'You see, Mum, I think you do have the character. I think you're marvellous.'

They clutched each other, then, mother and son, both with tears streaming down their faces.

'Beth'll kill me,' he said.

TWELVE

In which Totnes is mentioned many times

Sally woke up to find herself in a dream world. She was on a train, which was running right along the coast. The sea was sparkling under a southern sun. A few bathers were braving the chill waters.

She had no idea why she was on a train. She had no knowledge of where she was. For a moment she thought she was sixteen and travelling along the Côte d'Azur to meet up with her family.

Then Barry's letter, read by Sam only last night, fluttered from the luggage rack, turned into stone and crashed on to her forehead.

The sun went in, abruptly, terrifyingly. All colour drained from the sea. For a moment it seemed like a supernatural event. Sally shivered, even though the temperature on the train hadn't changed. Then the sun came out again, with startling suddenness, as if switched back on by a playful God, and she realized that a cloud had passed across it, a cloud so small and so fluffy that it seemed utterly incapable of hiding a whole burning planet even for a few seconds.

Now it all came back to her, the dreadful letter, the sleepless night, made all the worse because she had been separated only by an absurdly thin wall from her son's sleepless night, and worse still because beside her son had lain Beth, and beside Sally had lain nobody, yet that could no longer be regarded as sad, for it was far better to lie beside nobody than to lie beside someone who didn't love you.

And still the sun shone and the bathers swam. How could these things exist in the same world?

Then a more trivial, yet also more urgent, worry assailed her. She was travelling to Totnes, to stay with her sister Judith. But where was she? Had she passed Totnes? She had certainly been in a deep sleep. She had been peering determinedly at the countryside, trying to take an interest in every house, every tree, every cow, rather than brood over her misfortune, and she had fallen asleep, fast asleep on a fast train. She might have been undisturbed by many stops at many stations. Had one of them been Totnes?

She had endured an unhappy marriage and she had thought that she was happy. How stupid was that? She looked out of the window hurriedly, searching for happiness. The train was still passing the coastline, but it was turning inland, alongside an estuary. There was a pretty little town on the other side of the estuary. What town? What river? Before Totnes or beyond Totnes? Ask!! Don't be stupid, Sally. You may have been stupid for twenty-four years of marriage – it occurred to her for the first time that she would never have her twenty-fifth wedding anniversary, she had missed it by . . . quick calculation, absurd to be bothering to calculate at this moment, but there we are, you are absurd, Sally . . . twenty-three days . . . they were slowing down, they were approaching a station, ask!

She couldn't. At Totnes she would see Judith, and be able to communicate with a human being again – unless Judith was furious because she had sailed past her on the train in a mixed metaphor and fast asleep. Judith could get quietly furious if things didn't suit her, oh God, she had wondered if she could stand two weeks with her – now one week felt like a mistake. Perhaps she had passed Totnes and she'd just go on and on and jump off a cliff at Land's End. Don't even think like that, ask ask ask, you fool, she *had* to stand a week with Judith, Judith was her only hope.

The train had picked up speed again, but now it really was slowing down, and she couldn't ask, not these three people, two men and a woman, seated round the same table as her. It occurred to her that the human race looked absurd. The heads were so tiny, the arms and legs so long, the stomachs so large, all that body, all those bones and muscles with no thoughts whatsoever, no personality whatsoever, all the personality and character stored in a little mechanism in the middle of the tiny heads – no wonder the human race was making such a mess of things. No, there would be no point in seeking help from people, from any people, let alone these people, who were probably foreigners anyway. 'I not know this Totnes.'

They were sliding in to a platform. She heard a voice saying 'Newtnarbt. Newtnarbt'. It meant nothing to her, but it didn't sound like Totnes. She calmed down, searched the platform for the station's name, and there it was, clear on a large board. Newton Abbot.

It wasn't Totnes. She broke into a slight sweat of relief. Then she realized that nothing had been solved for her. She didn't know whether Newton Abbot was before Totnes or after Totnes. She was shamefully ignorant of her nation's geography. She would put that right if she ever recovered her sanity.

There was an announcement. Shut up, everybody. This is the quiet coach. I want to listen. 'The brain standing at platform . . .' Shut up with your trivia, you wankers. Oh, Sally, language. '. . . four twenty-seven for Penzance . . .'

Silence, pleeeeese! '. . . Totnes, Plymouth . . .' Oh, the relief. The tension drained from her, taking all her energy with it. She sank into exhaustion.

The relief didn't last long either

She realized why she had found it impossible to ask the other passengers at her table. She was terrified of them. She was terrified of them because she hadn't the faintest idea what they were thinking. That was the terrible legacy Barry had left her, not debt, not poverty, not loneliness – they were nothing compared to his legacy. He had left her mistrust. He had left her not daring to believe that anybody at any time was speaking the truth about anything.

The train was slowing down again. Was it approaching Totnes? She hadn't been able to hear the announcement on the tannoy at Newton Abbot well enough to be sure that she hadn't failed to hear the name of another stop *between* Newton Abbot and Totnes.

Luckily, at that moment, the woman at her table asked, 'Is this Totnes?'

'Yes, Totnes,' said one of the men.

'They usually announce it,' said the woman. 'They usually announce everything several times all the time. But I've had this one before, and he's lazy.'

'I'll do it for him,' said the other man wryly, dryly. 'This is Totnes. Please remember to take all your personal belongings with you. And mind the gap between the train and the platform edge on leaving the train.'

'Remember to put one leg in front of the other when walking along the platform,' said the other man.

The three of them laughed. Sally wondered if she would ever be able to laugh again.

She stood up, and busied herself remembering to take all her personal belongings with her.

The train drew to a slightly abrupt halt. Black mark, driver.

'Totnes,' called out a rather pleasant, reassuring, West Country voice. 'Totnes. This is Totnes.'

A kind man – was he really kind or was this all fake? – helped Sally with her cases. She minded the gap between the train and the platform edge, and stepped carefully out into the rest of her life, whatever that might turn out to be.

She walked along the platform, remembering to put one leg in front of the other.

Judith was standing there, elegant as ever. It was surprisingly cool on the platform; the swimmers she had seen from the train really had been pretty brave. Judith was wearing a light coat in spectacular pink. It was trimmed with fur. Sally wondered if the fur was real or fake.

Judith didn't move towards Sally. She let Sally move towards her. That was characteristic. But she was smiling. Sally wondered if her smile was genuine or fake. If she'd been a betting woman – oh God, Barry, William Hill – she'd have said that the fur was real, but that she wasn't so sure about the smile.

'Welcome to Totnes,' said her sister.

They hugged. How they hugged.

Was Judith's hug real or fake?

THIRTEEN

Uncharacteristic behaviour

Sally stood on the edge of a cliff. The sun was shining, but the breeze was cold. White horses took the edge off the loveliness of the sea, stifled its cry of 'Come in. Come in. The water's lovely.' Behind her, the fields sloped sharply to the very edge of the land. Awfully tempting for a farmer with money problems to just drive the tractor over the edge. Awfully tempting for Sally to just jump. Wouldn't reach the white horses. Would be splattered to death on the rocks below.

Did she want to be splattered to death? She didn't know. God, that was terrifying. It would be pretty terrifying if she had known that she did. But simpler. If she'd had the courage. To want to jump, and not be brave enough, that would be bad, but to be unable to decide, to make the wrong decision, and then, halfway down, have as your last thought, 'No! Wrong! This is a mistake' – that had to be the most frightening thing of all.

You might think, 'Well, if she has such doubts, she won't jump, in the end,' but the situation wasn't as simple as that. There was the pull of the sea, never to be underestimated. There was the obvious fact that the state of her mind was unbalanced. There was the knowledge that only by jumping could she absolutely settle the matter. If she didn't jump it would still be inconclusive. It would leave the possibility that later she would change her mind, and jump.

'Come come,' cried the sea. 'Come and join those who have ended their days with me. You will find many friends in the deep.'

She moved away, hurriedly.

She didn't go far. She knew that she hadn't made up her mind, she might be back. She found a small area of grass that seemed to be free of rabbit droppings, and she sat down. She shivered. It was cold. She hadn't enough clothes.

Four days had passed since she had hugged her sister Judith on the station platform. They'd spent much of it just wandering round Totnes. It was a delightful little town. They'd had coffees and teas and lunches and everywhere the food had been fresh and light and healthy. Judith had talked about the Transition movement, a movement which had begun there and had spread to all sorts of places, including Lewis, Whitstable and Brixton, the Valley of the River Lot in France, Monteveglio in Italy, even Los Angeles. Every bloody self-satisfied word seemed to Sally to be directed at her. Totnes is wonderful. Potherthwaite sucks. Later she would realize that Judith hadn't meant to have that effect. It was simple pride, marbled with massive insensitivity.

Judith and Sally hadn't exactly got on badly over the years, it was just that they had never been close. It was the age gap. Judith was eleven years older than Sally. Sally had been a mistake. In every way, she now thought. Judith, selfish though she was, had never been nasty enough to think that. She had regarded Sally as a tolerable nuisance, to be indulged and played with occasionally, but only when it suited her. Sally had regarded Judith as an extension built on to her mother. Life would have been better without the extension, but there were plenty of parts of the house in which it could be ignored. This was their first real attempt to be true, loving friends. Neither of them wanted the attempt to fail, but both of them were aware how fragile it was.

Judith had assumed that Sally's other purpose in visiting, apart from the need for sisterly friendship in a family rather short of relatives, was to sound out the possibility of coming to live near her. But not too near. Unfortunately, though, she didn't know of Sally's straitened circumstances. She hadn't been to the inquest – 'Things may come out that it would be better for our future together if I didn't know' had been her ingenious excuse – or to the funeral – 'Unfortunately it clashes with our half-marathon and I've promised to do it, it's for the air ambulance which I approve of totally and I'm quite heavily sponsored and honestly, darling, there'll be such a crowd at the funeral, all Potherthwaite will be there, I won't be missed and I would be missed very badly here, darling, and so, difficult though it was, I've made my decision, and, sweetheart, I do hope we won't fall out over it, and you know you're welcome here any time, any time, literally *any* time, except for Henley week of course, but otherwise *any* time' had been her almost as ingenious and considerably longer excuse.

So Judith had been very bold and very Judith and had booked with estate agents to visit four houses of different kinds near Totnes – but not too near – carefully chosen, exquisite houses, all good value, but all now hopelessly out of Sally's reach. And Sally hadn't mentioned her financial straits and had found that she couldn't bring herself to tell Judith about them. She despised herself for her weakness, but then she was also despising herself for her lack of love towards Barry, her lack of understanding of him, the complete failure of her life, so her weakness at that moment was hardly surprising.

So she had been forced to agree to visit all four houses. She had already been to three of them. Judith had extremely good taste, and good judgement of other people's taste. Sally had adored all three, and in coming up with reasons not to make an offer for any of them she had been scraping the barrel – once almost literally, when she had said that she didn't think she'd be able to reverse out of the garage without hitting the water butt.

Now, seated uncomfortably on a sloping field, in the only patch of grass not covered in rabbit droppings, on a cold evening against which she was inadequately protected, Sally thought about those absurd moments and what a waste of time they had been. And there was still one house to see.

She thought about the emotions that her time in Judith's bungalow had engendered in her. She had never liked bungalows, but this one was large, airy, tasteful, comfortable, she had privacy, it was perfect. Under the circumstances, after that letter the night before, the perfection had been unbearable. Judith had everything. A villa in Portugal. A flat in London. No man, but then she didn't want a man. She played golf. She played tennis. She played bridge. She visited lovely restaurants. Sally couldn't keep up, didn't play golf, didn't play tennis, didn't play bridge, didn't play life, wasn't a fun person. Even lovely restaurants palled when you could go every night. In the evenings, after dinner (exquisite) they had been able to watch any film they wanted. To be able to watch any film you wanted, and to want to watch none of them, that was hard to deal with. To have survived six weeks of anguish alone in her home in Potherthwaite, followed by four days of tension in a tiny flat in Barnet, and then to have all the air and all the space you wanted in a superb bungalow in beautiful Totnes, and still to feel claustrophobic, that was difficult to bear.

On the fifth morning, she had desperately needed to go

out. Judith was playing something called duplicate, which was a form of bridge apparently, and she'd had to go because her partner could be awkward, she'd had a trauma. Her tortoise had died, and she'd been attached to it. Sally had commented that this must have meant that she had to go around very slowly. The joke had not been a success. But the reason Judith had given had not fooled Sally. Judith had gone because she wanted to, as she had done everything in her life, including retiring with a huge pay-off from a successful distribution company at exactly the time that suited her best.

Sally'd had the house to herself, all that space, and she had felt trapped. She could walk through the conservatory on to the patio, stare at a utopia of conservatories and patios, feel the fresh, unpolluted West Country air on her face, but to her it wasn't *the* air, the open air, it was Judith's air, the enclosed air, the air within the boundaries so carefully drawn up in the documents of sale.

She had walked out, shut the door, not given a thought to keys, had walked through the trim streets, and past the perfect residences towards the river. The River Dart was a rebuke to the River Pother. The quay was an elegant two fingers to the Potherthwaite Quays.

She had taken a boat trip, on impulse. Down the elegant Dart to historic Dartmouth. Beautiful, searingly beautiful, a permanent, living satire on every yard of the Rackstraw and Sladfield Canal.

She had disembarked at Dartmouth, one among trippers, indistinguishable on the outside from the trippers, but not thinking the thoughts of trippers. Not thinking about food either. She had walked through Dartmouth, picturesque Dartmouth, as if it wasn't there. On on on. Away away away. Destination – none. She had kept thinking that she would stop, turn round, wander back, relish the sunshine. But she was in a place beyond relish, and she must walk, stride, walk energetically from nowhere to nowhere else. She thought of her sister's lean, taut, tight, sexless body, in the vanguard at fifty-eight in half-marathons, longest drive of all the women in the golf club, away away away. After quite a while, already she was a few miles from Dartmouth. She considered turning round and thought, 'No. Let her search for me. Let her worry about me. Let her know what anxiety is.'

And so she had come to her cliff edge, far from Totnes. She had been sitting for a long time now, almost nodded off once or twice, to her amazement. Unnoticed by her, afternoon had turned into evening.

She suddenly realized how cold she was. She would need to move around. She stood up, and found herself walking back to the edge. The memory of those ridiculous visits to houses she didn't want to buy swept over her. Disgust swept over her. She was weak, weak, weak.

She'd show them all that she wasn't weak. She'd show them how strong she was. She began to stride to the edge, resolute, almost exalted, nearer and nearer.

And then a rather extraordinary coincidence occurred. Except that it might not have been a coincidence, and in that case it wouldn't have been extraordinary at all. Sally saw a small yacht, beating up the Channel towards Torbay.

She wondered. Could it be? Why not?

She stopped hurriedly. She was only about two feet from the edge. Two feet. Twenty-four inches. The realization of how close she'd been to death sent an electric shock through her.

Would she have wanted to stop if she had not seen the boat? Would she have been able to stop if she had not seen the boat? She didn't know. And she never would know, that was what was so disturbing. In days to come she would relive the moment, and – it was unnerving – she still wouldn't be certain that this time she would stop.

She went back to her Droppings Free Zone. She sat down.

Her heart began to slow. She took the letter out of her pocket, opened it, pulled at the sheets of paper to get the worst of the creases out.

She read it.

Dear dear Sally . . .

You don't necessarily increase the power of your words by repeating them, but at this moment in her emotional life she was grateful for that word – 'dear' – and for its repetition.

I know you gave me this address for emergencies, and this is'nt an emergency, but we take each other for granted, and then when you are'nt there we miss you. I am missing you so much. Potherthwaite is missing you. I am also dreadfully worried that you will be so tempted by the southern zeffirs . . .

She smiled at Marigold's mistake. She did. She actually smiled. It wasn't much of a smile, but still, it was a smile. There was something about Marigold.

. . . that you won't come back. Please let me know that you will come back . . .

Could she believe any of this?

Anyway, you said that you were coming back next Tuesday, and I wondered if when you get back we could have lunch at the Weavers' one Thursday, when all the oldie's gather for their Pensioner's Offer's and we can feel like youngsters again.

What did a few apostrophes matter compared to a warm heart, but had Marigold really got a warm heart? Could she still believe of anybody that they had a warm heart? Could she believe it of herself?

I wondered if you'd mind if we invited Olive and Arnold to join us. Its a funny thing, and people will talk, but I don't

*think there's anything in it, but I may be wrong, but I
don't think so, well I suppose I wouldn't, would I, but
Harry and Jill have gone off together all the way to
Fowlmouth in Cornwall to collect his boat, which is a yawl,
whatever that is, and sail it back north somewhere so he
can use it. He keeps it at somewhere called Emworth or
something in Dorset or somewhere, but last back end he got
stuck with a bad gale going the wrong way as they do, and
no time to bring it back, so its been at Fowlmouth all
winter, which has cost a packet, so he's not keen on paying
out to bring it back. Jill's game for anything, and is very
strong, I've seen her in the shower's at the tennis club and
I'd put her in the second row if she did rugby she'll be
great with the close-hawling or whatever it is. I think its
just convenience and saving money, and no funny stuff, but
you know what people are.*

*I hope you don't mind, but I know you won't, you aren't
like that, but I called on Ellie, I hope you don't think I'm
butting in on your parade but I was very moved by what you
said about seeing her. She talked of your visits and how they
cheer her up.*

*Laugh of the week. Someone stole a big old illustrated Bible
from the church and broke into Sophie Partingtons' in Canal
Basin, you know, the prostitute who's so active they sometimes
say she's the red-light district on her own, and left the Bible
there. Someone with a sense of humour!*

Looking forward to next week,
Your fellow damsel in distress.
Marigold xxx

Sally stood up, put the letter back almost lovingly into
her pocket, and walked more slowly towards the edge. She
looked at the little boat, so bravely mounting the waves on
that windy evening. Was it a yawl? What was a yawl? It

had two masts, a big one in the front, a smaller one at the back. Was that a yawl?

She wanted to know if this was Harry's boat. She liked Jill and had taken to Harry instantly, and she so hoped that her life had been saved by them. Oh, it must be them. It just must be.

And then she realized that it didn't really matter. Even if it wasn't them, the thought that it might have been them had stopped her, and so they had saved her life anyway.

She waved. She waved frantically. But they were too far away, they didn't see her, they didn't wave back. She called 'Ahoy'. She knew enough about sailing to know that that was what you shouted. She didn't know what you shouted to fishmongers or solicitors but sailors were easy. You shouted 'Ahoy'. 'Ahoy,' she shouted. 'Ahoy there.' But it was no use. They didn't hear. They didn't see.

Quite soon they were past her, moving well in the evening wind. She felt flat now. The excitement was over. She began to wonder if they had really saved her life. Or had they only saved it *for today*?

There wasn't much point in saving her life if it was just going to be more of the same. There wasn't much point in saving her life if she was just going to exist, not trusting anybody.

It was an awful thought – she was ashamed of it even as she thought it – but if Judith was drowning and somebody saved her life, it would only be of real importance to Judith herself.

Gradually, then, she began to notice her surroundings. She saw for the first time that it was evening, late evening. The very last narrow arc of the sun had disappeared, in its rush to warm Alice at her breakfast in New Zealand. It was late, the wind had dropped but the air had gone very cold with the setting of the sun. There wasn't a soul in sight, she had no warm clothes, she hadn't brought her mobile, she hadn't eaten or drunk a thing since breakfast.

She was frightened. This struck her as pathetic too. She had been contemplating death, almost welcoming it, and now she was frightened of the cold and the dark and the loneliness.

Where should she walk? Inland. Nothing else made sense.

She found a hedge. She couldn't clamber through it. She walked along it and found a gate. She couldn't open it. She tried and tried. She tried to clamber over it. She tripped and fell in a heap, hurting her knees and an elbow. At least she had fallen into the next field. She couldn't get up. She hadn't the energy. She was starving and dehydrated.

Fight, Sally. This is all your stupid fault. Show your mettle.

Increasingly, we live in a virtual world. Have some virtual food, Sally. You need some virtual calories.

She ate two virtual bananas liberally heaped with virtual sugar and virtual double cream. It was virtually useless.

Or was it? She was still starving, but at least she found the energy to stand up. She tested her arm and her legs. Pain, but bearable, and nothing broken.

By this time it was completely dark. She was alone in a field on a dark night in the middle of nowhere, and she was very, very cold. A mist was forming in the fields, and through the mist she saw them. Cows. She was terrified of cows. Most people were terrified of bulls, but with her it was cows too.

For a moment, in the mist, they looked unreal. She had a brief hope that they were virtual cows. In her state of mind they could well have been. But they weren't, they were solid, huge, and emitting clouds of hot, foggy breath to thicken the mist.

She knew that she should be calm, must be calm, but she couldn't be. She ran for it, ran as fast as she could, on bruised legs with no strength in them.

The cows ran too. At the time she thought they wanted to kill her to protect their calves; it was spring, she imagined it was the calving time. Later she thought that they had probably been thinking, 'Hey up, this is the best night we've had in our unbelievably tedious lives since our mummies licked the placenta off us when we were born.'

She hurtled across the field towards the corner, some obscure instinct telling her there was more likely to be a gate at the corner. The moon shone briefly through the mist, giving a white ethereal light. There was no gate, but there was a stile. She clambered over it, feeling the warm breath of the cows. She fell into a mess of mud and water left over from the wet winter. Behind her the cows snuffled in disappointment. She had more bruises, and there was mud all over her face.

There didn't seem to be a house anywhere. Or a farm. Britain was an overcrowded, overpopulated island. There were new housing estates everywhere. Everywhere there were milling crowds of lost Hungarians, disillusioned Poles and Muslim women who couldn't see where they were going. How could there be nobody here at all?

And what a disgusting place the countryside was.

On the other side of the stile, beyond the mud and filth, there was a lane. Which way to go? She chose the right. It seemed right. That way, it felt, was civilization. That way, it felt, was Totnes. That way, it felt, was Judith. She almost turned round. She didn't want to face Judith. Judith would be livid.

She didn't know how long she walked. Maybe an hour, maybe two. She was weary, she was stumbling, she leant for a minute or two against a telegraph pole. She was shivering helplessly now. Her hands and feet were blocks of ice. She would die of hypothermia.

The lane ended in a T-junction, not with a main road, but with a slightly larger lane. She felt the sea to the right, so she turned left. She had no idea whether that was right, but if she turned left and right alternately she felt that she would run less risk of going wrong, if that made sense. Something must lie somewhere, if she went reasonably straight.

She heard it first. A growl. The growl of an angry, neglected lorry. Then she saw the headlight. One. Not promising.

She didn't know whether to wave or hide. She felt that the latter might be the wiser, but there wasn't time.

The lorry pulled up with a prolonged squeal of brakes. It was filthy. Sally, suddenly alert, noticed that the number plates were covered in the mud of a whole winter. That wasn't good, in fact it was very bad, but what alternative had she? If she refused to get in, he could rape her here, in perfect safety.

The driver switched off the engine. The sudden silence was unexpected and seemed laden with menace.

He clambered out of the cab, came round to her where she shivered. He was tall. He was muscular. In the headlight, just for a moment, she saw that his long, thick hair was matted with sweat, his broad, unshaven face streaked with mud. As he got closer, she smelt farmyard smells, smells she was unfamiliar with – slurry and pig shit. She was very frightened.

He put out his great hands as if to pick her up, saw her flinch, thought better of it. He had to help her up into the seat though, and inevitably, in the process of doing that, he had his hands round her buttocks, her much admired buttocks, her generous buttocks, though they weren't feeling generous now. He clambered into the driver's seat, glanced at her, smiled, but said nothing.

As she settled herself she reached in behind her anxious buttocks to remove a pamphlet that she was now sitting on. It might come in handy as evidence later. God, she tingled with terror at the thought of evidence. It was an advert for Storth Pumps and Stirrers. That didn't help much. She had no idea what they were.

He started up, and they roared off, the noise of the badly maintained diesel engine shattering the silence of the night and giving tawny owls paroxysms.

'Where to?' he asked.

'Totnes, please.'

'Right.'

'My sister's.'

She got that in quick, hoping the knowledge of a sister's existence might frighten him.

'Right.'

He was silent for a moment as he planned his route. Then he spoke softly, in a kindly tone. Even in her weary condition this made her suspicious. Oh dear, she thought, he's trying to put me at my ease before the attack.

'So what were you doing wandering around in this terrible state?'

His voice didn't match the lorry. It was not a voice covered in mud. It was not a voice on its last legs. He didn't growl. In fact he sounded, in the word she used later to describe him . . . couth.

She told him her story, very briefly, and not without tears.

He made no comment, no comment at all, no criticism, no sympathy, nothing. She realized, much later, that he knew that she was too tired for anything more.

She felt a strange compulsion to steal a quick look at him. His face was set firmly on the road. His profile was almost classical, apart from the mud. He looked tense. The mist was getting even thicker now, and he clearly had no confidence in the lorry.

Headlines from the tabloids filled the night sky, swirled in the gathering mist: *Police Hunt for the One-Headlight Rapist.*

Murder in the Mud. Dirty Secrets of 'The Good Samaritan'. Even Our Lanes Aren't Safe Any More. Where Is the Storth Pump Killer?

It was quite a long journey. She slept for a while, her head repeatedly lolling towards him. Then she woke and their eyes met. He tried to smile. It went horribly wrong. She almost cried out.

'Totnes soon,' he said, and then he pulled up.

She was terrified now.

He reached into his pocket. She almost stopped breathing. Was he going to shoot her first? Was he a necrophiliac?

He got out a hairbrush and began to brush his hair.

'Don't want to frighten that sister of yours,' he said with a grin.

He had a surprisingly boyish grin.

FOURTEEN

A surprise

Sally woke to find the sun streaming in through elegant curtains that Judith had bought because they were beautiful not because they kept the light out. The tulips on the elegant dressing table were as fresh as the day they'd been picked. The elegant glass of water at her bedside was untouched. She couldn't remember when she had slept so well. She glanced at the elegant little bedside clock and was shocked to find that it was twenty-five past eleven. They were due at house number four at eleven. Judith would be livid.

She didn't mind! She could face Judith's lividity. She had survived yesterday's ordeal. She felt stronger for it.

She practically leapt out of bed. Her legs buckled, her head swam. A moment ago she had felt strong. Now she felt weaker than she had ever been.

She sat on the bed.

The door opened and Judith came in. She looked as if she was dressed for lunch at the Ritz. She didn't look livid, but she didn't look exactly pleased either.

'We've missed our appointment,' she said. 'I'd cancelled a golf match because of that appointment.'

'I'm really sorry.'

'It's all right. I've rearranged it for three o'clock.'

'I hope you win.'

'Not the golf match. The viewing.'

Oh God. Could she face it?

No. No more lies.

'You're covered in bruises.'

'Am I? Sorry.'

'Don't be silly. Look at you. What did he do to you?'

Sally examined her body. She had slept in the nude since Barry had died, whereas she never had when she had been sleeping with him. This morning, when her nudity was witnessed by her sister, that suddenly struck her as odd.

Judith was right. She was black and blue.

'He didn't do anything.'

She could see that Judith didn't believe her. Mysteriously, she needed to make Judith believe her.

'He didn't, Judith. He really didn't.'

'All right. I believe you.'

But she didn't.

'How much did I tell you last night?'

'Not a lot. That dreadful man told me to give you a hot bath, something solid to eat and a hot drink. You kept falling asleep. You were like a very big baby. I virtually had to bath you and feed you. And I just couldn't stop you shivering.'

'He wasn't a dreadful man. He was very nice.'

'He didn't look very nice to me.'

'Nor to me. I thought he was awful. I feel bad about that now. I should have got his name. Did *you*?'

'Of course I didn't.'

'I want to thank him. He saved my life.'

'Don't exaggerate.'

'I'm not. Seriously, I think I might have died of hypothermia. It was very cold, and I only had thin clothes.'

'You're an idiot, Sally.'

'I know. And you aren't. It's nice to be so different. It's why we get on so well.'

'Do we?'

'I don't even have his number plate. It was covered in mud.'

'Exactly. He's not to be trusted. I knew the moment I saw him there was something odd about him.'

'In a way, what was odd was that he wasn't odd.'

'What on earth do you mean?'

'He didn't match the lorry. It had one headlight and . . .'

'. . . he should have only had one eye?'

'Exactly. Well, not that exactly. But he should have been . . . dishevelled.'

'He was dishevelled.'

'I thought so last night. But now I think he was trying to look dishevelled. That's a funny word, isn't it? I mean there isn't a word "shevelled". "I won't be long, darling, I'm just trying to get myself shevelled."'

Judith showed no response to that. She had no interest in words per se, only as useful social tools.

'He shouted at me,' she said. 'It was horrid. I'm not used to being shouted at by odd, strange men.'

The scene came back to Sally vividly. Judith speaking to her in a kind of whispered shout, furious with her for scaring her by disappearing, furious that she had needed to call the police, but also very anxious not to wake the neighbours. The man had shouted, 'Shut up. Fuck the neighbours. Give her a bath, some solid food and a hot drink – fast.'

'He shouted at you because he cared.'

'Rubbish.'

Sally stood up very gingerly. Her thighs protested hugely. Her head swam again. She put her left hand on the bed to support herself.

'I need food, Judith, and quickly. I'm weak.'

107

'Of course you do. I'm an idiot too.'

'Can I have it in my dressing gown?'

'Well, of course you can. What do you think I am?'

'You're very correct, Judith. Everything is always done very correctly.'

'Has it occurred to you that maybe that's because I lack the confidence to do it any other way?'

'You?'

'Me.'

'How about that breakfast?'

'You see. I am an idiot.'

Judith brought her dressing gown over, helped her put it on, and walked her through to the dining room where an elegant table was elegantly laid for one.

Sally sat there, bathed in elegance, but her face immobile. She was thinking hard. The sun beamed. The picture windows were spotless. Not a crumb sullied the carpet. Her future lay before her. She was thinking about what to do with the rest of her life. Big stuff when you were starving.

Judith brought orange juice from real oranges, perfect buttery peppery scrambled eggs, and good strong coffee. She left Sally to it. Sally resisted the temptation to gulp it all down. This was one of the great moments of her life, to be able to enjoy a good breakfast barely eighteen hours after she had almost thrown herself over a cliff and ended that life.

When she had finished eating, Judith brought more strong coffee, and joined her.

'You look as though you'll live,' said Judith.

'I think so.'

Something in the way Sally said it caused Judith to look at her with an expression she had never seen from her before. She suddenly realized what was different. Judith was taking her younger sister seriously.

108

Sally took a gulp of coffee and braced herself.

'You're not angry with me any more?' she began.

'I rang my doctor to discuss you. I had to. I was worried. He took it all very seriously. He told me to be very careful, and I do what doctors tell me, Sally. I think you ought to see him and get yourself checked.'

'I'm all right.'

'You should see him.'

Sally decided to give way on that one. The next few minutes were going to be hard enough, without an added disagreement over the doctor.

She forced herself to say what had to be said. She felt very nervous. She wasn't yet quite as strong as she had thought. 'I . . . I've a lot to tell you, Judith. Yesterday, I began to realize, without really realizing it, if that makes sense, that – this'll sound trite, but to me it's massive – that I have only two ways I can go. Up or down. I decided to go up. Again, I didn't really realize I *had* decided.'

Judith didn't speak. Sally had the distinct impression that she was listening properly to her, with all her being, for the first time in her life.

She told Judith about the cliff edge, about how she strode towards it before she saw the boat. If Judith had been silent before, she was now very silent. Sally was grateful for that. She sensed that if she didn't tell the whole story now, she never would.

She told her next about her financial situation.

'You mean . . .' said Judith. 'No. Carry on.'

'You're right,' said Sally. 'Doing those three viewings was a farce.'

'You could have told me.'

'No. I couldn't.'

'But you can today?'

'Yes.'

And then she told Judith about the letter to her son. She had an awful feeling that she was going to cry. She didn't want to. She hoped that she had cried herself out. If she cried again, she felt that she might let it destroy her, that she would cry and cry and crawl away to die like a sick rabbit.

She had an awful feeling, also, that Judith was going to cry. She had never seen her sister cry. She wondered if she ever had cried. She didn't cry now, but Sally believed that she had come close to it, that she had been truly moved. But the memory of how utterly she had failed to recognize what was going on in Barry's head was too recent; understanding Judith was a hope, an objective, but not yet, if ever, a reality.

Even when Sally had finished speaking, Judith said nothing. Sally had the impression that she had hunted for the correct words and not found them.

'Well, Judith,' she said. 'We'd better cancel that viewing.'

Judith looked shocked, almost as shocked as at anything in Sally's tale.

'Do we need to? Can't we just go?'

'Why?'

'I've already rearranged it. Difficult now to cancel it.'

'They'd rather that than waste their time.'

'Yes, but they wouldn't know they were wasting their time. That's the point.'

'Well, I think we should cancel.'

Judith looked very embarrassed.

'I'm sorry, Sally,' she said. 'I can't do it. I was so embarrassed postponing. I can't speak to them again.'

'I'll do it.'

'Are you sure?'

'Yes, it's no problem.'

'Well, thank you. I'm grateful.' Judith paused, hesitated,

at last spoke. 'This is going to sound awful, Sally, but would you . . . you know . . . sort of . . . take the blame?'

Sally looked at her sister in astonishment.

'Well . . . OK. Yes. Yes, of course.'

'It's just that you don't live here, I do. And you see, I just don't do that sort of thing. Cancel. Mess people around. I'm probably the only woman in Totnes who has never cancelled a hair appointment. It's the way I am, Sally.'

'Right. OK. Right.'

'Thanks, Sal. I really appreciate that. I'll dial it for you.'

As Judith dialled, Sally tried to remember if she had ever called her Sal before.

Judith handed the phone to her.

'Oh, hello,' said Sally. 'My name's Sally Mottram. I'm Judith Carpenter's sister. We have an appointment for three o'clock this afternoon . . . That's right . . . yes, that's right, we postponed it from this morning. Well, I'm very sorry, but we're going to have to cancel . . . no, not postpone again, cancel. I'm very sorry to mess you about, but, you see, I . . .'

She gave Judith an apologetic look.

'I find that I won't be coming to Devon after all.'

Judith's mouth dropped open. For the first time in her adult life she didn't look elegant. She must have caught sight of herself in the mirror, because she snapped her mouth shut very quickly.

'. . . Thank you. Yes, I find . . .' She glanced at Judith again. 'I find that I'm needed in my own home town . . . Thank you. That's very kind of you. As I say, I'm sorry, but I thought it better to let you know and not waste your time . . . I thought you would. Thank you.'

She put the phone down and looked across at her sister.

'You sounded as if you meant that,' said Judith.

'I did, Judith. I'm terribly sorry. You wouldn't want me

111

here anyway, when you'd got me. I'd interfere with your routine. And I wouldn't be able to stand your sort of life. What would I do in Totnes? Soak up the sun? Learn bridge? Learn golf? Meet people for coffee? Become friends with ladies who lunch? Live through my children's children? Join a rambling club? I don't see redemption that way.'

Redemption? Who said anything about redemption?

I did.

Sally didn't actually say any of that. All she said was, 'I think I must have.' She didn't want to fall out with Judith. There was no need. There was no point. They were inhabitants of different planets.

Judith shook her head.

'"Needed in your own home town"?'

'So it seems. Did it sound terribly pompous?'

'Well . . . a bit, perhaps. Yes.'

'Sorry.'

'No, I . . . it's just . . . I was surprised.'

'I'm not surprised. I was more than surprised. I was astonished.'

BOOK THREE

The Work Begins

FIFTEEN

A Tuesday in spring

It's Tuesday, a very English Tuesday in spring. It's coming to the end of daffodil time, and the beginning of tulip time. Showers are passing from west to east across the bursting, fertile fields. The sunshine between the showers is all the more glorious because of its fragility.

In exploring Sally's reactions to the great traumas that had so abruptly changed her life, it has been necessary to rather neglect some of our new friends from Potherthwaite. It has been unavoidable, for without some understanding of why and how she had come to take on the great role that she was soon to play in the transformation of the town, it would be difficult to appreciate where her great strength came from.

But on this particular Tuesday, we can perhaps dare to leave her to her own devices. She's travelling back from Totnes to Potherthwaite by train. Surely nothing untoward can happen to her today?

On second thoughts, maybe we should see her safely on to her train first. An apology has been broadcast over the tannoy at Totnes. The train is eleven minutes late, due to badgers on the line between St Austell and Lostwithiel. On the platform, Judith and Sally stand side by side, all smiles, touching each other affectionately every now and then, in a very public display of devotion, but from time to time each of them turns to stare down the lifeless, trainless line, imploring the train to appear. Sally is anxious because they have run out of conversation. Everything that could be said has been said, perhaps there will never be anything to be said between them ever again. What can they speak about now, to avoid the void between them becoming obvious to them both? For Judith the anxiety is both deeper and more shallow. She has booked a hair appointment, knowing that the wind on the platform will disturb her immaculate curls. Should the delay increase to fourteen minutes or more, should this be a day of unexpected badger activity in Devon as well as in Cornwall, she will be late for her appointment, and, as we have seen, she doesn't do lateness.

'Don't forget, Sal,' says Judith, 'you are welcome here any time.'

'Except Henley week,' says Sal, as she seems to be becoming, dryly.

Judith doesn't pick up on the dryness.

'Except Henley week,' she says, 'and Wimbledon. I'm not good company during Wimbledon.'

The train arrives, blessed lovely friend, but etiquette demands that Judith stand there on the platform, smiling an 'oh good, you've found your seat' smile and a 'your fellow passengers don't look too bad' smile. The train starts to move, Judith waves, but at least she doesn't walk along with the train and break into a run as it increases its speed. Sally cannot see her sister now and it is by no means clear that she will ever see her again.

Now we really can leave Sally to her journey. Nothing will happen to her now. Her travelling companions have received Judith's seal of approval. She is safe, and she is already feeling, we sense, a great wave of relief. It's a long journey, eight hours at least even if both the connections work. Each change will involve moving on to a smaller train, a dirtier train, but this will not upset her. She has discovered, to her great surprise, that she has real affection for the town that has been her home for almost a quarter of a century. She is looking forward to coming home, even though that entails walking past, every evening, the spot where she saw her husband hanging, not eight weeks ago.

But wait. She is standing up. Why?

She goes to the luggage racks at the end of the carriage, opens one of her cases, and removes two books from it. She bought them in Totnes. They are both by a man called Rob Hopkins. They are called *The Transition Companion* and *The Transition Handbook*. She knows what the word 'transition' means, but she had never heard of the concept of Transition until this visit and Judith's obvious pride at what the concept has done for her beloved Totnes, and later, it seems, for a lot of other places.

On the phone to the estate agent's in Totnes, Sally had said, 'I find that I'm needed in my own home town.' Don't deduce that she has already decided on her great plan, her destiny. Nothing of the sort. She was actually thinking of Ellie, poor obese Ellie, about whom she was actually quite obsessive. If she could save Ellie from her obesity, her life would not have been in vain, and, if her life turned out not to be in vain, then she had been justified in not hurling herself on to the rocks below just three days ago. Her logic was as simple as that. It explained why she was so keen to get home, why that strange interlude of lovely houses, excited cows and a rather unusual lorry driver had meant so little to her.

And yet, she has bought these books. The seed of the idea must have been planted. She begins to read. The books are

117

full of small details of little things that have been done to change and improve many places, mostly quite small places, but their underlying subject matter is not small. It is, simply, the saving of our planet. Implicit in Rob Hopkins's writings and actions is that big things come out of little things, that out of a thousand tiny acts, if they can be joined up, one mighty act may emerge. There are two great strands to his writings, two great hazards that he sees looming. They are peak oil and climate change. Sally knows a bit about climate change, nothing about peak oil. She settles down to read. As the train slides joyously alongside the Devon coastline, she puts the books down and watches the scenery. It's beautiful, but a great shudder passes through her. She is thinking of the rocks on to which she might have fallen. She is thinking of the sea that would not now claim her. She is thinking of a small boat, something called a yawl, that had saved her life.

The train moves inland, following the estuary of the River Exe. Soon the scenery, while still lovely, will be a little more ordinary. Sally turns back to Transition. Perhaps she is just getting the first, faint inkling of what her future will hold. If so, this is the beginning of her times of revelation. If so, it is a very personal time and a very exciting time. It would be polite now, perhaps, to leave her in peace, and to visit our new friends.

Where shall we start? The obvious place would be with Harry Patterson and Jill Buss. We have just mentioned the yawl in which they are travelling. For, yes, the happy news is that the little boat that saved Sally's life *was* the boat in which her good friend Jill Buss was travelling. It wouldn't have made much difference, to be honest, if it wasn't, and possibly it would have been wiser of Sally just to dream that it was than to risk disappointment. But Sally has a romantic streak, a streak that has long been dormant due to lack of opportunity, and, eventually, she will ask Harry if he kept a log of the trip, he will tell her that he did, and the log will prove, beyond doubt, that the yawl at which she had waved in vain had indeed been his yawl, that he had literally, though unknowingly, saved her life.

Harry and Jill are in crowded waters that morning. They are approaching the Straits of Dover. They can see the English and the French coasts clearly. They can see the towns where ordinary people are going about their tedious business. That's what a boat does to you. It makes you instantly superior. It turns you into kings and queens of the water. It turns land-lubbers into serfs.

Jill has told Harry, after her first night alone on watch at the helm, as the sun has slowly risen over an empty sea, that she has never seen anything so inspiring in her life. The night has been cold, and long, and uneventful, though frightening. She has never felt quite such responsibility as she has for Harry's lovely thirty-foot yawl, the sails on her great mainmast amidships and her smaller mizzenmast aft billowing strongly in the stiff breeze. Now she is at the helm again, the sea is distinctly choppy and this time it is not empty, there's a confusion of boats, a long long tanker, a bulky, ugly ferry, two other sailing boats. Suddenly it's all very confusing and very nasty.

But Harry seems oblivious of everything. He isn't, actually, he's oblivious only of the sea, of the sky, of the boat, of the ferry, of the tanker, of the other two sailing boats, of the danger. He's oblivious of everything except Jill. He adores her. He loves her. She is the soulmate he never quite had in Olive. He touched her as she brought him a cup of tea at the end of his watch that morning, and he'd gone stiffer than he had been for years, suddenly splendidly stiff, stiffer than the breeze, as stiff as the mainmast and the mizzenmast put together, gloriously, disastrously stiff. He was stiff again now.

How beautiful she is, how she defies her age, mocks it, laughs in the face of it as she now laughs in the face of the wind. But then he realizes that she isn't laughing. She's screaming. 'Harry! Harry!' Harry looks around and sees instantly that it's a disaster, there's no escape, he's done what no good sailor ever does – he's taken his eye off the other ships.

He grabs the helm, pushes Jill roughly out of the way, she falls, he should have used the engine, his pride in manoeuvring through these crowded waters under sail alone has been arrogance, he just manages to avoid one of the other sailing boats but he has gone too close to the wind, there's no wind in his sails, he's drifting, drifting towards the great bulk of the ferry, which is hooting messages that in his panic he can't interpret. He keeps his eyes on the sails, he's going to have to go about, right under the ferry, Jill has scrambled out of the way and is looking like a ghost, he is hardly aware of her, they are going, this is it, goodbye Jill, it would have been great, goodbye Olive, I'm so sorry, most of what we had was good, my darling. Somehow, as if of her own accord his faithful, hungry yawl finds some wind, the sails fill, she has a bit of way on her again, she's moving, still towards the ferry but at a lesser angle now, he can see the stern of the ferry, they'll still catch it, he wrestles with the helm, they may not hit, they will, they won't, they don't, they slide inches rather than feet past the stern of the ferry, they wallow horribly in its wake, but it has gone gone gone, they are alive, alive alive, the wind is still stiff, but Harry isn't, he will never be stiff again, that was criminal. He's the sailor, she is his responsibility, he has almost killed her, there is nothing between them, he is married, she is

120

married, he had promised Olive, she had promised Arnold, what had he been thinking of?

'Are you all right?' he says. 'I can't leave the helm to help you.'

'I'm all right. Bruised, that's all.'

They're silent then, and grim-faced, as the boat slides away from trouble. Their hearts beat more slowly. Breath returns. Harry's prick is a tiny thing now, it's shrivelled by the cold, his manhood is a frightened little boy, ashamed. He hopes that Jill is unaware of this, but also, and much more urgently, he hopes she didn't feel, as the waves brought them briefly together that morning at the top of the companion-way, that it wasn't a tiny thing at all, that it had been a stupendous thing, in a way that it must never be again.

It's ironic, really. At the exact moment when a collision is being narrowly avoided in the English Channel, a collision actually occurs in the far calmer environment of the cul-de-sac in Potherthwaite's Conservation Area. Arnold has gone round to Olive's for a cup of coffee, taken with a squirt of the sweetener that he has brought with him in order that he may avoid being killed by Olive's reckless use of sugar. As a direct result of the intake of liquid resultant upon his consumption of said drink, he has needed to use the smallest room. He returns in rather excited mood – he has examined his urine for blood, and found none. Olive, meanwhile, has decided to clear the occasional table of its contents, two dirty cups, two dirty plates, one containing crumbs, the other still holding a complete piece of her famous – nay, legendary – lemon drizzle cake. She is not in the very best of moods, truth to tell. She has baked the cake specially, only to find Arnold refusing to eat it. He has a good reason. He has tested his blood pressure that morning, and it's up. But Olive cannot accept this reason. She doesn't believe that, if he consumes a slice of her cake, he will drop dead, or worse, far worse, have a stroke and survive helpless and needing to be fed his cake for the next eleven years.

It's even more ironic really. Irritation causes Olive to walk out of the lounge faster than usual just as the opposite emotion, satisfaction, causes Arnold to walk *into* the lounge faster than usual. The resultant collision is dreadful to behold. Luckily, perhaps, there is nobody there to behold it.

The tray hits Arnold's stomach like a heavyweight boxer's low punch, winding him utterly, and the impact pushes the other end of the tray into Olive's stomach, winding her utterly. The tray slips to the ground between them. They both instinctively lean forward in their search for breath, and there is a clash of heads. They both end up on the floor, seriously shocked.

Slowly, carefully, they try to stand, and find to their surprise that they can. They move their arms and legs about, testing them gingerly, and it seems as if nothing is broken, though there will be bruising on both their bodies, and there are squashed pieces of lemon drizzle cake and dregs of coffee on Olive's new carpet.

Arnold now decides to be gallant and help clean Olive's new carpet. Unfortunately Olive decides to clean the carpet at the same moment, and their heads clash again. They reel away. This time neither actually falls. They bend, more carefully, and busy themselves removing the lemon drizzle cake and broken china. Olive will clean the coffee stains in a moment.

As they finish removing the bits, they find themselves kneeling with their faces in close proximity, in a proximity greater than they have been since a memorable kiss inspired on a fine summer's day almost fifty years ago by the superb views from the top of the Malvern Hills. Today there is no such inspiration. A kiss close to a new carpet that still smells of newness in a rather ordinary lounge to the noise of an April shower containing not a little hail banging against the immaculate Gothic windows of a semi-detached house in a cul-de-sac in the Pennines cannot be compared to the charms of the Malvern Hills, which once inspired Edward Elgar no less. Had Elgar lived in the cul-de-sac, what a loss it would have been to British music.

We have observed how easily cosy little routines can develop between people under unusual and temporary circumstances. Olive and Arnold have got into quite such a cosy little routine since Harry and Jill have gone away. Olive has invited Arnold round for coffee every morning at around eleven o'clock, and afterwards has said, 'Won't you stay for a spot of lunch now you're here?' Arnold has replied, invariably, 'Well, I won't say no.' Olive hasn't thought she was being at all forward in interpreting this as a yes, and there have followed meal after meal of a pleasant and traditional nature. You will be relieved – perhaps even mightily relieved – to learn that in his comments on Olive's efforts, Arnold has shown a little more inventiveness than he had in accepting the offer of lunch in the first place. His responses have included 'That's my kind of food, Olive,' 'Thank you. Most palatable,' 'Thank you. I won't need to eat again until this evening,' and 'That's what I call a lunch.' Not all his comments have reached those heights, but you get the idea.

This morning is no exception. The unfortunate collision makes no difference. The offer comes as usual, and is accepted as usual. One needn't read too much into this routine. Arnold was utterly unable to feed himself, having never lifted a finger to do so in his life, and Olive was happy to be able to satisfy a man with her cooking as opposed to thinking that every day her husband was wishing that she was a more adventurous cook. On none of those occasions had any physical contact whatsoever taken place between them, not a kiss, not a hug, not even a handshake. Now all that has changed. They still haven't kissed, nobody has ever called them fast workers. But a moment has occurred, they have come very close indeed to a kiss, and it seems reasonable to assume that it has led them to remembering past kisses and to thinking of the possibility of future embraces.

Certainly, at the end of this meal, if Harry and Jill were to hear the final exchange between Arnold and Olive, they might have been at least a little bit alarmed.

Arnold sighs, and says, 'Well, I must get back to my book. I'm writing about how changes in the pattern of national tastes affected the cake factory, and it's proving a bit sticky.'

'You'll sort it out, clever old you,' says Olive.

'Less of the "old" if you don't mind,' is Arnold's light-hearted riposte, and then he stands up. 'Thank you, Olive,' he says. 'That was delicious.'

Olive is amazed, almost overwhelmed, by his uncharacteristically enthusiastic adjective.

It's perhaps fortunate that Harry and Jill will soon be home.

It's twenty-five past one. Sunshine floods Marigold Boyce-Willoughby's large modern kitchen, so at odds with the early Victorian elegance of the cul-de-sac. She looks up from the fridge, where she has been hunting for something that she would like to eat, and failing to find anything. She goes to the window, and looks out. She sees that there is quite an extent of blue sky. She realizes how lonely she is without a man. But a man is the last thing she wants. She has, in that unfortunate phrase of hers, had men up to here. She checks on the sky once more. There might just be time for her to get to the pub on time before the next shower. She needs the pub. She's a social animal.

She adjusts her make-up hastily, and steps out into the cul-de-sac. It's colder than she expected. Somehow it is always colder than she expects, in Potherthwaite.

Arnold Buss emerges from the Pattersons' house, and raises his hat to her. He's the only man in Potherthwaite who ever raises his hat. This isn't because he's more polite than other men. He's the only man in Potherthwaite who wears a hat.

'Good afternoon, Marigold,' he calls. 'Just popped in to Olive's for an early lunch. Can't boil an egg. She's seeing me through till Jill gets back. Can't wait. Good to see you. Are you well?'

'Very,' says Marigold. 'While you and Olive are on your own, as it were, Arnold, how about a lunch with me and Sally at the Weavers' on Thursday, when it's the Pensioners' Offer? Not that I'm a pensioner, of course.'

'I'll say you aren't,' 'Marigold, the very thought, you won't be a pensioner for decades,' 'You'll never be a pensioner, in my book,' and 'You'll look as lovely as you do today when you are one' are just four of the things that Arnold doesn't say. What he does say is, 'You should try Olive's plum chutney some time.'

Marigold is not detained by any urge to discuss Olive's plum chutney. She can see a cloud on the horizon. She marches on, resolving to get to the pub before the next shower, resolving also to leave this town sooner rather than later. She speeds up. The Weavers' serves till two, they say, but they have a way of making you feel rather guilty if you order after one forty-five.

She approaches the Weavers' and suddenly she can't go in. She can't face the ladies who lunch. She can't face the way they'll smile, seeing her lunching on her own. No, she'll go to the Dog and Duck. That's a proper pub. That was where she used to go to drag Timothy home for his tea. He loathed her calling it 'tea', which of course was why she did it.

She enters the pub, and it's like walking into a time warp. They're all still there. The landlord calls them 'The Lunchtime Heroes', henpecked at home, giants in the pub at lunchtime. There's David Fenton, the estate agent and the nearest thing Potherthwaite has to a really attractive man, which, to be brutally honest, is not very near, this isn't Italy. There's Ian Mallet, who ascribes his relative lack of success as an analyst to that chunky, plain, aggressive, physical, British name – Mallet – and whose wife's nerves were such a very bad advertisement for his psychiatric skills. There's Mick Webster from the travel agency 'Unravel Your Travel'. Good place to have a travel business, Potherthwaite. Everyone wanted to get out.

There's even a detectable gap where Timothy used to stand, as if her husband is still present even in his absence.

There's a little chorus of greetings from the bored trio. All the words come out to her as if just one person is speaking. All the voices sound the same. 'Well, hello stranger where have you been good to see you we've missed you look we're all still here what's it to be the usual G and T ice and a slice?'

The usual. G and T. Ice and a slice. Or the Pinot Grigio that wasn't quite good enough. She can't bear the thought. She can't even be bothered to have a little private bet on which man will touch her first.

She can't join them.

She can't sit on her own, they would be furious. She would never live it down.

She does something that she has never felt comfortable about.

'Sorry. No time,' she says. 'Just taken short. Chris, can I use the loo?'

'Course you can, Marigold. You know where it is, do you?'

Laughter.

She hurries through to the loo. She doesn't need it but she feels foolish just standing up in the cubicle so she sits down, counts thirty seconds, pulls the chain, leaves the cubicle, washes the hands that she hasn't dirtied, dries the hands that she hasn't dirtied with the new hand dryer which makes a noise like a jumbo jet taking off, goes back into the bar, and to her horror hears herself say, 'That's better.'

She waves at the terrible trio, says 'Cheerio, chaps' and hurries out of the pub. It's pouring. She can't walk in this. She enters the first place she can find. It's Pizza Express. The schools have broken up and it's full of children. It smells, not surprisingly, of pizza and of children. She has never had any children. After failure with three men the problem must be hers. She's never had a pizza either. She doesn't like them. 'How do you know you don't like them if you've never had one?' That's her husband speaking out of the past. One of her husbands. Take your pick. The waitress leads her to a seat that she doesn't want, in a corner that she doesn't like, near the loo that she is definitely not going to use. There are umbrellas everywhere. She hates umbrellas.

She feels as lonely in this crowded place as she has felt in her life. She longs to get up and walk out. But she's a fighter, and she stays.

She orders the first pizza of her life.

Ben Wardle is eating his pizza in a strange manner, as befits a strange boy. He has chosen a capricciosa. It's his favourite. A few years ago it disappeared from the menu of Pizza Express. The things he likes always disappear. T-shirts, shoes, clothes, toothpaste, fizzy drinks, TV programmes, pizzas. If he likes them, nobody else does. But pizza capricciosa has returned. His parents are worried by the way he doesn't speak to people, except to Tricksy, of course, and with Tricksy they worry that he speaks too much, so that's just as bad. His father, whom he no longer loves, feared he has a CSD, a Compulsive Speaking Disorder, causing him to speak torrents to Tricksy and not at all to anybody else. Later, his father redefined the acronym. It was still CSD, but now it stood for Conversational Selection Dysfunction. Ben once said that his father had SAD – Servile Acronym Dependency. Whatever Ben may be, thick he is not. His father often cites the fact that STD once meant Standard Trunk Dialcodes and now means Sexually Transmitted Diseases as evidence of the world's CMD – Catastrophic Moral Decline.

'I'll have the pizza capricciosa,' says Ben. 'I'm glad to see it back. It was my favourite and it disappeared and now I see it's back.'

His parents beam. He's talking to the waitress, and talking like an adult. What a good idea this lunch was.

'That's right,' says the waitress, who, miraculously, is British. 'They took it off and they got more complaints about that than about anything else, so they brought it back,' adds the waitress, who, miraculously, is intelligent and well-informed as well as being British.

'That's great,' says Ben. 'It's good to know they take note of our preferences. It restores one's faith.'

A slightly uneasy look passes between Ben's mum and Ben's dad. Is he being a bit TGTBT – Too Good to be True? Is he mocking? There's always a risk, with Ben, when he *does* speak, that he's mocking.

'There is one thing, though,' says Ben. 'It says "NEW" on the menu in capital letters. But it isn't new.'

'Well spotted,' says the waitress. 'I don't think they could admit that they'd taken notice of the public. They'd be inundated with suggestions. So they've changed it slightly. It's ham hock instead of just ham. I think it's better, actually, more fully flavoured.'

'Thanks,' says Ben, and he exchanges a smile with the waitress. His parents are very happy to see this. Maybe he does fancy girls after all.

Ben sees that his parents are happy. He knows why. They are decidedly homophobic. His father is xenophobic. And noiseophobic, particularly popophobic, and, in the world of pop, strongly rapophobic. Well, to be honest, he's just phobic, really.

'If you don't mind my saying this,' says Ben's dad to the waitress, 'you're extremely knowledgeable and bright, for a waitress.'

Add 'waitressophobic'.

'I have a degree,' says the waitress. 'Couldn't get a job. There were eleven thousand applications for this job.'

A realistic silence casts a shroud over the table for just a moment. Hail is battering the windows again. It's England in springtime. A waitress drops a tray and several glasses break. Lots of people cheer. Ben wonders if foreigners do that.

When the pizza capricciosa comes, Ben starts to eat it from the outside in. It's one way of doing it, and his parents aren't worried by that. But when he starts to move slices of hard-boiled egg, olives, lumps of ham hock, pieces of anchovy, little capers, all the toppings in fact, from the edge into the middle, his parents look slightly concerned. He is now taking mouthfuls of a crust from which all toppings have been removed, leaving only tomato and cheese on it,

129

while in the centre of the crust, the toppings are piling up, egg cheek by jowl with ham, anchovy and caper struggling to find space on the crowded base.

His mother is crippled by worry. Is he suffering from one of these syndromes, she is asking herself. One of those puzzling things beginning with the letter A that are cropping up all over the place?

His father's mind is simpler, more direct, and more aggressive. He can stand it no longer.

'Why are you eating it like that, Ben?' he asks.

'Because I want to.'

Ben is pleased to have forced his father to speak, and now he continues to eat in the same manner, forcing his father to speak again. He can be very annoying, as an offspring, even though we deduce that in the past he has often told his father that he loves him. But then we know that he will never tell him that again.

'Why did you order it if you don't like all the things on it?' his father feels forced to ask.

'I do. I love them. That's why I'm saving them.'

'Please, Ben, don't get your father irritated. We don't go out often and we're having a lovely day,' says his mother.

Ben considers this, and suddenly smiles. 'Yeah,' he says. 'OK. I'm just having a bit of fun which will sound very silly and juvenile when I tell you, but you should be pleased about that because you always complain that kids grow up too quickly these days. What it is is, the base's an island, and all the things on it are creatures, and there's a tsunami, well, a very high tide anyway, and I'm saving the eggs and capers etcetera from the encroaching waters of the lagoon. And now comes the moment when I realize that I can't save them, the island's doomed, so I'm going to eat them, give them a quick death rather than a slow drowning. I'm a very compassionate boy.'

He grins. There's a moment's silence.

'You have too much imagination,' says his father.

Ben considers this, then smiles again.

'Not at all,' he says. 'It's just such a bugger that imagination is so little use in Potherthwaite. Somebody should come and change it.'

A pretty girl with flaxen hair, blue eyes and slim legs walks along the pavement of High Street West. She looks angry, and full of purpose. We have of course seen this girl before. She was carrying a vase.

She looks across the street and her eye is taken by a boy emerging from Pizza Express with two people who have the unmistakable depressing look of being parents. She has seen this boy around. He's strange. Sometimes she's seen him walking along the towpath as if in a dream, or, at least, a world of his own.

She sees that he is gazing at her, transfixed. Her heart leaps. She walks more slowly, as slowly as she feels that she can without losing her anger. She can feel his look on her back.

In their excessive desire that he should grow up normal, and their excessive worry that he won't, which is in danger of being what his father calls an SFP and the rest of us call a Self-Fulfilling Prophecy, Ben's parents notice the girl and Ben's longing look and have mixed feelings. They are pleased that he is showing signs of sexual attraction towards a girl, but they are upset that the girl he has chosen to be obsessed by has a ring in her nose, a stud on her chin, holes in her jeans, garish red streaks in her hair, bare feet, bare flesh between her jeans and her T-shirt, and the message 'Fuck You All' on that T-shirt. Apart from that, she looks a model of a young British schoolgirl.

*   *   *

131

Sally's train is eleven minutes late, due to the knock-on effect of rolling stock being delayed after somebody stole the points outside Pontefract. The light is beginning to fade, but she can still see the scenery of the Pother Valley clearly and she is, amazingly, looking forward eagerly to the first appearance of the outskirts of Potherthwaite.

She has enjoyed the journey, although she has noticed nothing. She has been buried in her two books, with their description of the purposes and the achievements of the Transition movement.

Of all the people in the world, who would she least like to come and sit next to her on the last few miles of her return to the town she had never loved until this day? Sadly for the future of our democracy, David Cameron, Nick Clegg and Ed Miliband are high on the list. But at the top, towering above them all, is Linda Oughtibridge. She looks squarer than ever as she asks, 'Is that seat taken?' and replies to her question so swiftly that Sally has no opportunity to speak, says, 'No? Splendid,' and plonks herself down on three-quarters of the seat, 'plonks' being the operative word.

'Train's late, isn't it?' she bellows.

'Yes. Cake on the line at Pontefract.'

There's something about Linda Oughtibridge that leads one irresistibly to frivolity.

'That's a new one,' she says, taking it seriously. 'You been away? I heard you had. Now, let me see, what's happened? Let me fill you in.'

I'd like to fill you in. Sally! Don't be nasty.

'Nothing much really. The vicar's had another cold. I think he's run down. I said to him, "Vicar . . ."'

Sally has found that she can switch Linda Oughtibridge off almost entirely, only half listening, and she can venture an occasional 'oh dear' in perfect safety. In twenty-four years she has never heard Linda Oughtibridge say anything to which 'oh dear' is an unsuitable response. She resorts to it now.

'. . . lots of people got the same.'

'Oh dear.'

She peers out of the window, noticing with pleasure all the ordinary little streets, noticing also . . .

'. . . awful lot of mucus with this one.'

'Oh dear.'

. . . the way the town had spread over the hills in its heyday.

'. . . late spring. Hard work for flower arrangers.'

'Oh dear.'

The train is slowing down. The arrival is spoilt. But no, nothing can spoil this astonishing joy. She is back, back in the town she has never known she loved.

'It's been really nice to have you to talk to.'

'Oh dear.'

'I beg your pardon?'

'Oh dear, we're there. And we've hardly begun to talk.'

'Oh, I see. Yes. Yes. Shame.'

She has to wait for a taxi. She doesn't mind. Mrs Oughtibridge has gone. Sally had taken a good look at Mr Oughtibridge's face, to see how much his suffering showed. Disappointingly little. Sally! You used to be a Christian.

No. She doesn't mind waiting. She drinks the air. It smells of stone walls and distant shit.

And there is the town, spread out before her in its narrow valley, its slate roofs hiding its dark secrets. So much dereliction. So much to save.

There are very few people in the streets. All that will change. What's that wonderful thing the Italians have in the early evening, where they all go out and walk? Perhaps they don't have any equivalent of *The One Show*. The Passeggiata,

133

is it, or is that a kind of tomato sauce? That thing where they dress so smartly and parade round the streets, anyway. Will they one day have the Passeggiata of Potherthwaite?

Oxford Road is deserted. No Sparlings, no Kenneth, no Hammonds. There are no lights on, of course, in 'The Larches', and the grass has grown terribly long and unsightly. She should have asked the estate agents to arrange for the lawn to be cut. It'll never sell in this state.

Her heart is beating ridiculously fast as she opens the front door. The air in the house smells of emptiness. It has been in the house too long.

She carries her two suitcases upstairs one at a time. It's hard work. Four times, twice going up, twice coming down, she has to pass the spot where he had been hanging. The first time isn't easy, but by the fourth time she's feeling almost nothing. This is an unwelcome relief.

She can't stay in. She just can't, not all alone, not tonight. She almost rings Judith.

She dresses up in hat, coat and gloves. It's going to be cold, after Devon.

She walks down Oxford Road. There's no sign of life at 'Mount Teidi'. The Hammonds must be in Tenerife again. Their carbon footprints could melt glaciers.

From inside 'Ambleside' there comes one short bark. A message from Kenneth? Does he know she's back? It's tempting to think so, and nothing would surprise her about that dog.

There's no sign that any of the mentally challenged of Potherthwaite are visiting Dr Mallet this evening.

The air is hard and chill and fresh. None of that warm Devonian mush.

She turns left out of Oxford Road on to the beginning of High Street West. There are no coughs from the allotments tonight.

The Rose and Crown has gone. It's boarded up. If only it could have hung on a few more weeks, till . . . till what? A cold gust of doubt rides towards her on the evening breeze. Hasn't she just been dreaming in her seat in the train's warm mouth? Can she really make a difference here, in this harshest of realities?

She hesitates slightly before turning into Cadwallader Road. A disturbing truth has struck her. She needs Ellie as much as she thought Ellie needed her.

She climbs the spotless step to the front door of number 6. She rings the bell. The moment she has rung it she wishes that she hasn't. Ellie will be watching her favourite television programme, her one way of escaping the prison she has built for herself.

You can't de-ring a bell.

She hears footsteps. The door opens. It's Ali.

'You're back.'

It's amazing how often people tell you things that you obviously already know.

'Yes, I'm back.'

It's amazing how often you give an unnecessary reply to the unnecessary observation.

'Is it a bad time?'

'Noooo! She's always pleased to see you, Mrs Mottram.'

Ali leads her along the corridor into the tiny kitchen. Oli is seated at the table, watching the television. This time she makes no effort to get up.

'You're back,' she says.

'Yes, I'm back. How are you?'

'Very well, thank you, Mrs Mottram.'

'I'll tell her you're here,' says Ali.

Ali goes through into the front room. A few moments later, Sally hears Ellie's television being switched off. She shouldn't have come.

There's the same very faint smell of festering humanity throughout the house. It's never any better, but then it's also never any worse, whatever time she comes.

'I have a plan,' Sally tells Oli. 'It's too late to tell you tonight, but it's very exciting.'

'That sounds exciting,' says Oli.

Ali comes back in.

'Right,' she says. 'She's ready for you.'

Sally enters Ellie's bedroom. Ellie is lying in the bed, exactly as usual.

'You're back,' says Ellie.

'Yes, I'm back,' says Sally. 'Ellie, I have a plan for you.'

'Oh.'

'For Ali and Oli too.'

'Oh.'

'Yes. It's too late to tell you tonight, but it's very exciting.'

'That sounds exciting,' says Ellie.

Sally realizes that she is more tired than she had thought. How stupid to announce that she has a plan when she knows that she hasn't the energy to reveal her plan.

'I shouldn't have told you,' she says. 'I've made you excited for no reason.'

She's made things worse still. She feels that she needs to explain.

'But I just had to tell you,' she says, 'because if it works, your lives will be transformed for the better.'

Now I've really done it, she thinks.

At least Ellie has company. When Sally gets home she has no company. She walks around the house, looking in the various rooms: the sitting room, the dining room, the kitchen, Barry's study, their bedroom. Everything is neat. Everything is tidy. In each room she remembers some moment or other that, at the time, seemed happy. Now she has to reinterpret these moments from a different historical perspective. In every memory, now, and in every photograph in every silver frame, there is an extra dimension. Barry was playing a part. He felt nothing for her.

It will be a long night. It will not be an easy night.

The girl with the garish red streak in her once glorious golden hair, in her fifteenth year of explosive life, looks up and down the street. It is past midnight and there is nobody about. The wall at the side of the police station is high and smooth; there would be nothing to grab hold of even for somebody who wasn't carrying a spray gun in her left hand.

There is one tree which might serve her purpose. She eyed it up a couple of days ago, on her reconnaissance. This girl is thorough. If she paid as much attention to her lessons as she does to her graffitist activities she would get good exam results.

She climbs the tree with astonishing ease, and virtually one-handed too, for she is still holding her spray gun in a duster in her left hand. Now she is above the level of the wall. Beyond the wall, in the bare side garden of the police station, there is a row of bushes. She has achieved far more demanding feats of balance, though of course she had a safety net in those days. As these thoughts pass through her agile mind, she feels a sudden pang of loss. She wonders where her father is now. The thought horrifies her. She needs to concentrate on the job in hand. This is no time for emotion.

She jumps on to a magnolia and clings to it. The branch sways but she is so light that it does not break. She is breathing hard, her heart hammering at her ribcage. This is so exciting. One cause of fear is eliminated. The security lights have not come on. Nobody has expected any threat from the side.

She crawls over the branches of the magnolia. She will have to stretch to deliver her message, but she can do it.

She reaches forward, points the spray gun, sprays the black letters on to the bare stucco on the side of the police station. This will not be a beautifully written graffito. Twice she almost falls forward off the slender, swaying branch of the magnolia, but she manages to cling on. There aren't many words – two, in fact – and the job is soon done. She can't see the letters in the dark, the writing won't be level, it will be a regrettably sloppy job, but that can't be helped.

Her eyes have adjusted to the darkness. It is never fully dark in a town centre. She can distinguish where the flower bed ends and the concrete path begins. She doesn't want to drop the gun on to the concrete. The noise would be very dangerous. She pulls the duster off the spray gun and drops the gun to the ground. There's a faint thud that nobody passing would notice. But she almost falls as she stuffs the duster down the front of her jeans. She will need two free hands on her journey back.

She slithers easily back over the magnolia. Now she has to jump up and grab the wall. It looks impossible. But it has only been five years. She won't have lost the knack. Will she?

She hesitates. Five years is a long time. Suddenly it dawns on her how stupid this is. She's tempted to just drop down to the ground and give herself up. But no. She could never give up. She calms herself down, balances herself, crouches, tenses, jumps, manages to cling to the wall, folds her arms over the far edge of the wall, pulls herself up on to the wall, hears the cheers of the crowd – where was that last performance? Harrogate, the Stray. The flash of memory takes her away from the present danger. She was an infant prodigy. Fame beckoned. Nothing is beckoning now. She's lying on top of the wall. She has to get to her feet with nothing to cling on to. Her legs don't have that old strength. She's gone flabby. Ugh! She starts to pull herself to her feet, the old balance isn't there, the legs are throbbing, she makes a supreme effort, she's standing, she's done it, but she's swaying, she's going to fall, she just manages to hold herself upright, she's going to fall, she has to jump before she's ready, before she's composed, before she's balanced. She crashes into the fork of the tree rather than landing on it, but she's there, and now it's a simple drop down to the road, she's in control again, but that was too much, too perilous even for her. She's badly bruised and cut – that will need some explaining – but she's safe again.

She looks to left and right. There is nobody about.

But, unbeknown to her, there was a witness to her activities, and he told the police what he had seen through the gates at the front. He hadn't been able to see very clearly – it had been very dark down the side of the police station, and he had consumed several pints in the Baggit Arms – but what he saw was unmistakable. A monkey had jumped from a bush on to the wall and then on to a tree outside the wall.

The police didn't believe him. They were aware of the fact that even if twenty thousand monkeys sprayed graffiti for fourteen years, the chances of any of them producing the words 'FACSIST PIGS' were infinitesimal, and who had ever heard of a dyslexic monkey?

SIXTEEN

The Great Bruise Special

It was supposed to be a wonderful and very important evening, the first of many wonderful and very important evenings. It was not supposed to be a farce.

The Weavers' Arms had an Early Bird menu every evening from Monday to Thursday. If you placed your order any time between 5.30 and 7.15, you got two courses for £10.95, or three courses for £12.95. This was considered, even by Arnold Buss, to be good value.

On this particular Tuesday evening, just a week after Sally's return to Potherthwaite, the Early Bird dinner at the middle of the five tables that ran alongside the windows of the pub was transformed into something that may possibly be unique in the annals of British dining out. A further reduction was made to the bill on account of the extraordinary fact that all six diners had suffered nasty bruising in various unpleasant accidents. The meal became known, to the diners and to the management of the Weavers', as 'The Great Bruise Special'.

There was also an element of thanksgiving. It was extremely fortunate that not one of the six had suffered anything more than bruising. There could easily have been broken bones.

The meal had been arranged by Sally, who had great things to tell them and great things to ask of them. None of her five guests knew that, while she looked like the same attractive, intelligent but unremarkable Sally, she had spent the week since her return full of thought, lit up by ambition. How could they possibly have known that this simple meal was actually the first great step in her campaign for the Transition of Potherthwaite?

The subject of the bruising came up over their pre-deal drinks at the bar. Rog liked to pretend that his pub was a real drinking pub, which wasn't true – he was only truly welcoming to diners – but he did like it if some of them spent a bit of time at the bar, giving the illusion of a pubby atmosphere.

Rog was out that night, as he was most nights, and when Rog wasn't there Sue, his manageress, made sure that she heard every bit of the tittle-tattle around the counter. The fact that they all had bruises came out in the course of the conversation. How, you might well ask? Did a researcher approach them and say, 'Excuse me, you guys, sorry to bother you, won't take three minutes, but we're doing a survey about the extent of bruising in Britain. We want to know how many people in Potherthwaite had any bruising on their bodies at seven o'clock this evening. Hands up, please, guys. What, all of you??!! That's incredible.' No. It came up quite naturally, because several of the people knew that others among them had been involved in accidents. Olive and Arnold had been too shy with each other ever to mention the location of their bruising, but little references to the colour – 'mainly orange now', 'quite a lot of purple' – provided a mild frisson over their subsequent lunches. When Harry and Jill got home after safely depositing the yawl in their chosen marina, they had heard – with just a touch of suspicion? – about Olive and Arnold's bruises and had mentioned, in amazement, that *they both* had bruises too – was there a touch of suspicion there from Arnold and Olive? – and it was natural, that evening, for them to mention to the other two diners that they were similarly inflicted, at which point the other two exclaimed in amazement that they had bruises too, and in the general astonishment, Sue announced that an Early Bird dinner in which all six diners had substantial bruises was such an unlikely event statistically that she would further reduce their bills by no less than £2.00 *per person*. Rog wouldn't approve, but Rog had no vision, and she, who had once been in PR, could see that 'The Bruise Special' would make a nice little piece in the *Chronicle*, and the news of her generosity would do the pub much good.

We know how Sally got her bruises. She fell more than once during her nightmare night in the muddy, cow-rich countryside of Devon. We know how Olive and Arnold picked up theirs. They crashed into each other, and both fell, in Olive's lounge. We know where Jill suffered her purler. She fell in panic in crowded waters in the Channel.

We have not yet revealed what caused the bruising of the other two members of the party. Harry's accident will be no surprise to you. Like Jill's, it was a misfortune at sea. A series of waves of foaming grey North Sea water caught his beloved yawl by surprise a few miles off Cleethorpes, and sent her lurching and wallowing helplessly in their peaks and troughs. As the first wave struck, Harry was propelled head first down the companion-way, where he crashed on to the cabin floor. He was still limping badly. All this had happened on a cold, wet, wretched day quite close to the mouth of the Humber, but the wind wasn't strong enough to cause those waves. Harry was convinced that they had been caught in the wash of a ferry that was going too fast. He hated ferries.

You will also not be surprised to learn that the sixth

member of that historic party was Marigold Boyce-Willoughby. In all provincial towns there is at least one woman who turns up everywhere, often for perfectly good reasons. Marigold was one such woman, and in her case the good reason was that Sally believed that, if she could help Marigold recover from the humiliation of Timothy's behaviour, her energy and enthusiasm would make her a first-rate right-hand man. Right-hand woman? Right-hand person? First-rate, anyway.

Marigold's accident had occurred in the Market Place, and had been caused by a wave not of foaming North Sea water, but of tenderness. She had been crossing the cobbles, bound for one of the nearly-new shops where she planned to buy at least three things in her effort to cheer herself up. We have mentioned that she had always despised such shops, but after the departure of Timothy she had quite cheerfully and frankly admitted that she couldn't afford to despise them any longer.

She had seen Sally coming out of the bank. Sally's face had been white, as many a woman's is after facing her bank manager. It had been the first time she had seen Sally since her return, and she had felt a great impulse to rush over to embrace her and offer her comfort. She had turned too quickly, and had crashed heavily over a bollard. She had been taken to Potherthwaite District Hospital in an ambulance. At the hospital she had been told that amazingly nothing had been broken, but she was still in pain and she still believed that the bill of good health had been given through a mixture of incompetence and the extreme age of the X-ray machine. Potherthwaite Hospital did not receive much respect from the average Potherthwaitian.

'Your starters are ready,' announced Sue.

They moved to their table, and they moved slowly. This was yet another bad setback for Sally. That evening, seated round that table with her friends, was to be the key first moment in the great project to which she was moving. But no less than four of them were limping, and three had bruising on their faces. The place was already full – give a Potherthwaitian a special offer and he'll be there, and this was Potherthwaite in recession. What must they look like to all these Early Birders? She knew the answer. Like soldiers getting on a train at Waterloo to go to war, and they were all injured already. She felt tiny and wretched and stupid. She wished she could abort the whole project.

Marigold, on the other hand, was much given to romanticism, and believed that the fact that they had all suffered accidents in which there were no broken bones was a 'miracle', even a 'sign' and perhaps also an 'omen'.

Sally stirred herself sufficiently to ensure that people sat where she wanted them to be. She at one end of the table, Marigold at the other, the Busses at one side, the Pattersons at the other. The evening had a subsidiary purpose for Sally. If it achieved nothing else, she hoped that it would have at least a minor influence by nipping in the bud anything there might be between Jill and Harry. Like everyone else, she saw little danger from Arnold and Olive.

Arnold didn't have a starter. He never did when he was paying, and he wasn't to be cajoled out of his economical ways even by Sue's generous offer. Olive had asked what the soup was, and on being told 'leek and potato', she had said, 'Oh good. I can eat that.' Jill had chosen mussels and Olive had said 'Ugh!' and Harry had given her a look. He had looked at Olive defiantly, and ordered the kidneys in mustard sauce. She had raised her eyebrows as if to say, 'He's showing off to annoy me.' Marigold ordered prawns with sweet chilli jam, saying, 'I can't resist hot things.' It was cosy with the curtains drawn behind the table, and the radiator full on. On every available space on the walls of the pub were photographs and paintings and mementoes of the great days of textiles, the halcyon years of the Potherthwaite mills. Rog and Sue argued regularly and fiercely about their choice, Rog believing it to be a moving tribute to a great era, Sue regarding it as a depressing little song entitled 'Look How Great We Once Were'.

Sally struggled with her food. She felt sick with nerves, but she had to eat up, she mustn't show weakness. She heard, yet didn't hear, Arnold describing, briefly but not quite briefly enough, the medical reasons why he never had rich sauces at his age. She heard, but didn't hear, Marigold saying that each husband had been worse than the one before, her judgement was getting worse with experience.

The main courses arrived. Lamb shank for Arnold, belly pork for Harry, chicken supreme for Olive, beef curry for Marigold, fish pie for Jill. Sally had chosen risotto as being likely to be the smallest. She didn't want her nerves to cause her to struggle to finish her food. She wished she was anywhere but here, wide awake in her tiny guest bedroom in Barnet even, or learning bridge from Judith, in lovely Totnes, going back to retrace her steps and find the dishevelled driver of that awful lorry, to thank him . . . for what? For not raping her? Had life in Britain come to that?

Her troops, who didn't know that they were her troops, had been dismayingly indecisive even over what water to choose. One wanted still, one sparkling, one tap (Arnold never paid for water), one wanted lemon but no ice, one wanted ice but no lemon, the waitress hated them already, what kind of PR was that, how could these people be her trusty lieutenants in a great project, when they argued so much about such trivia? All the things she had read on the train, all the achievements of Transition in other places, all the things that had inspired her these last few days to attempt something similar here, now seemed impossible. This was

Potherthwaite, forget it, Sally, forget it, deluded little woman who couldn't even make your husband happy.

With the desserts it was the same palaver all over again. With ice cream. With cream. With ice cream and cream. With neither ice cream nor cream. Nor was it any easier with the coffee. With milk. With cream. With neither milk nor cream. With both milk and cream. And still they all seemed to be making rather frequent visits to the loo, and still the majority of them were limping. Perhaps she should have told them that this evening was the start of a great movement, a movement that was beginning quietly with six friends but would grow to subsume a whole town. Their town.

At last they all had their coffee. She must start.

The pub was much less full now. Potherthwaitians were early eaters, and, besides, the Early Bird offer finished at 7.15. But two tables nearby were still occupied, and she didn't want anyone else to hear. If you didn't want anyone else to hear, Sally, why did you arrange to do it here? Because you are totally incompetent. And may I say something, Sally? Certainly, Sally. Don't you think it's silly, Sally, to be frightened of being overheard when you have booked the church hall in a month's time so that you can shout your message to the world? Well, not to the world exactly. To Potherthwaite. Yes, but it's too late to give up now. No, it isn't. Nobody knows what you are about to say. Just say nothing, and it will all never happen.

She couldn't give up. Her life must mean something. And she loved Potherthwaite. She couldn't just let it die.

She started, quietly. Too quietly. Her troops weren't deaf, of course they weren't, but some of them weren't exactly in the first flush of youth and they were, let's say, just a little bit hard of hearing when there's a lot of talking in a room. She had to speak up. But she didn't really want to speak up because she didn't want the people at the two other tables to hear what she had to say. Some leader, this.

She told them how she had first heard of the Transition movement, in Totnes. She told them what she knew of the movement. She told them what it had achieved. They listened. They seemed interested, even impressed. She grew in confidence. Her voice grew stronger. She was quite unaware that the people at the other tables were beginning to listen.

'This evening is just the start, a small start, an intimate start. I have invited you because I want you to help me, because you are my friends, and I love you. I want you to take this message I am giving you tonight, and take it to the people of this town.

'The great thing about this is that it can work on two levels. At the national and international level, we will be trying to deal with two major threats – global warming and peak oil. You may be less familiar with peak oil, but we are going to reach, or already have reached the moment when the world's oil resources are beginning to be used up, and one day, unless we act on an incredibly large and fast scale, a civilization built on cheap oil will collapse. It's as simple as that.

'However, their contribution to the global solution is based on small-scale local initiatives, and it so happens that I can see that the solutions for Potherthwaite can help the global solution while also helping to create an infinitely better Potherthwaite. So, we will be able to deal at the same time with world issues and with our problems here, with our town, its decline, its ugliness, its quiet daily despair. We will bring the canal back to life, we will bring the Quays back to life, we will bring the High Street back to life. Is this pie in the sky? No, because I have plans. Yes, me, a little widowed woman, a sad little failure, I have plans for Potherthwaite.

I am reborn as a town planner. Ridiculous? Yes, but what is happening now is ridiculous. It's ridiculous that we let our town die around us and do nothing about it. It has been ridiculous here tonight, all of us injured, all of us bruised – I thought it was not a good start, but as I talk I see that it is the perfect start. Our town is bruised, it bears the scars of decline in every street, but the greatest bruise of all is that to our souls, and our spirits, because we haven't cared – and I'll tell you this, it will happen, and it will succeed. Shall I tell you why it will succeed?'

She hurried on to answer her own question before anyone could shout, 'No. Shut up.'

'It will succeed not because I'm clever, or a great leader, or have any great ability whatsoever. It will succeed because it has to succeed.'

She stopped. There was a moment of silence, and then applause rang out, not just at her table but at both the tables where there were still people. A group of four, who had been putting their coats on to go out into the cold night, had stopped at the door, as if sensing that something was going to happen. They were clapping too. Sue Foreshaw, the manageress, was clapping. Even their grumpy young waitress was clapping, all grumpiness forgotten.

She had said so little, but an enormous energy had been released, even from these few people. Sally was deeply moved, and horribly scared. This thing was bigger than she had dreamt.

And the evening, due to her inexperience, had been badly constructed. She now had to explain, quietly and only to her table, what she wanted from them.

'In a month's time, I will be speaking in the church hall, setting out my ideas for Potherthwaite, my plans for Potherthwaite. I want you all to take an area of the town and visit it, calling at the doors, asking people to come to the meeting, explaining why it's important that they should come.'

'I'm up for that,' said Marigold, so excited that she started talking the English of a younger generation. 'I am so up for that. I'm, like, this is fantastic. I'm, like, count me in. I'm, like, "Sally, wow!"'

'Fantastic idea, Sally. Count me in too,' said Jill.

'Oh, Jill, that's great,' said Sally. 'I was relying on you, to be honest. You've got such energy. We've been friends for so long. Real friends. Oh, Jill, thanks. Hey, I think this calls for one last bottle.' She called the waitress over. 'Could we have one last bottle?' she said. 'We won't keep you too long.'

The waitress blushed.

'You can keep me as long as you like,' she said.

'You see!' said Harry, when the waitress had gone to get the wine.

'What?'

'It'll work. She's had a Transition already.'

'So . . . um . . . are you in, then, Harry?'

'Certainly am. It's a funny old place, this, but I have been warmly welcomed in this funny old place, and I would like to give something back to it.'

'That's marvellous, Harry,' said Sally.

'Give me a tough part of town,' said Harry. 'I love a challenge.'

'Good. You can do the Baggit Estate. You were too young to do National Service, weren't you?'

'Certainly was, why?'

'How would you like to be our sergeant major?'

'What does that involve?' asked Harry cautiously.

'Keeping everyone in order. Saving Marigold and me from our wildest dreams. Having the courage to take the unpopular decisions. Doing by force what cannot be done by persuasion. Being strong.'

'Harry! Blood pressure!' whispered Olive.

'Thank you, Sally,' said Harry. 'I'm flattered.'

Yes, you were meant to be.

Olive mouthed the word 'cholesterol' at him.

'That sounds right up my street,' said Harry.

'So, how about you, Arnold?' asked Sally.

'I don't think so, Sally,' said Arnold. 'I'm too old. Besides—'

He stopped abruptly.

The waitress brought the wine. Arnold and Olive declined it. Harry, Jill and Marigold raised their glasses and reached out to clink them with each other and with Sally, but not with Olive or Arnold.

'"Besides . . ."?' asked Jill remorselessly.

Arnold sighed.

'I thought I'd got away with it,' he said. 'Besides, I have my book.'

'But think how much more successful it will be,' said Marigold, 'when Potherthwaite is news.'

'Yes, but you don't know what my book is,' said Arnold.

'We do,' said Jill. 'It's a history of Potherthwaite.'

'Yes, but it's the rise and fall of Potherthwaite. I'm Potherthwaite's Gibbon. I'm writing a weighty tome about the reasons why it succeeded and why it couldn't continue to succeed, why it couldn't fail to fail, if you like. It's a historical interpretation over the decades and centuries. You are going to ruin my thesis.'

'But if your thesis is wrong, what can we do about it?' asked Sally as gently as she could.

'Nothing,' said Arnold petulantly, 'but do you think that's any consolation to me? To you all it's a joke. Oh yes, I know that. To me it's my life's work. It's my *raison d'être*.'

Sally turned to Olive.

'Olive, you haven't . . .' she began.

But Arnold hadn't finished.

'There's another thing,' he said.

Nobody spoke, but their eyes groaned.

'I'm not catching up fast enough,' said Arnold. 'At this rate I'll be dead before I finish it. And now you're going to have plans and suggestions and changes. I know what's going to happen. Do you know what's going to happen? I'll tell you what's going to happen. Lots. Lots and lots. That's what's going to happen. Lots and lots of happenings. Transmission. Transformation. None of you thinking of me. I won't catch up at all. I'll drop further and further behind. I wouldn't mind, but you're all so smug. Leave me out of your precious Transmission, please.'

'Transition,' said Sally.

'Arnold, darling,' said Jill, and in her anger her voice took on a rather unpleasant tone, a parody of sweetness. 'Perhaps you should consider making your book not quite so sodding long.'

'Thank you,' said Arnold bitterly. 'Thank you, darling, for your sympathetic comment, and your learned and constructive criticism of my great work. It's so sad that, with an analytical brain of that calibre, you wasted so much of your life peering up people's badly washed, spotty, polyp-ridden arses.'

There was silence. Sally felt that she had to break it.

'Olive,' she said. 'Can we count you in?'

Olive hesitated.

'I haven't said much,' she said. 'I don't. I only speak when I have something worthwhile to say.'

She paused, as if daring somebody, Harry perhaps, to say something devastatingly sarcastic. Nobody did.

'I agree with what Harry said about ceasing to feel an outsider here so quickly, yes, I do, and I appreciate it,' said Olive. 'I really do. But I still don't think I feel that I want to get involved in anything as ambitious as this. I have my

151

health issues, I have to be careful, I'm not overflowing with stamina, I never have been, can't help that, it's my metabolism. But it's not just that. You aren't going to like what I'm going to say, but it's how I feel. I'm not a very brave person, but I'm going to say what I really think for once. I can't see the point of getting involved at my age and in my state of health. If there's going to be an end of the world, why should I care? I won't be here to see it.'

'I think that's the most selfish thing I've heard in my life,' said Harry. 'I'm deeply ashamed to hear *my wife* say something as selfish as that. What about our children? What about our children's children? Are you alive, Olive? Are you?'

Sally Mottram, in her new role as a great local leader, learnt an important lesson that night at the Bruise Special Offer Dinner at the Weavers' Arms.

She had gone to the pub with two objectives. In the more important one, the introduction of her plans to potential supporters, she had succeeded beyond her wildest dreams. Not only at her table, but at other tables. She had learnt that she had underestimated the power of her ideals.

Her subsidiary aim, less important but still of real consequence, had been to deal with her concern over the two neighbouring couples in the cul-de-sac. She had wanted to bring Harry and Olive closer together on the one side, and Arnold and Jill closer together on the other.

It had been an abysmal failure. Jill and Arnold had shouted at each other. Harry and Olive had disagreed completely. Neither couple was now speaking to the other. Sally had hoped to have five reliable friends to carry out and inspire the next stage of the work, that of filling the church hall within a month. Already she was left with only three.

She had learnt that it is a big mistake to have a subsidiary aim. Having an aim at all was difficult enough.

SEVENTEEN

Sally breaks new ground

'What did you have for breakfast this morning?' asked Nick Podger, the burly, unshaven technician.

It's the standard question at sound checks, and it's hoped that the answer will contain the word 'porridge', which is, apparently, the most helpful word for a burly, unshaven technician to hear in a sound check.

Sally did not say 'porridge'.

'. . . Um . . . let me think . . .'

'You can say what you like. Dun't have to be true.'

But it did. She was too nervous even to be able to think up a fictional breakfast.

'Oh yes. I had muesli. With raspberries and blueberries.'

'Thank you. That's fine. Just getting a level.'

The memory of breakfast with Barry flashed through her mind. He'd been grumpy in the mornings, and very conservative. She wouldn't have dared have muesli with raspberries and blueberries and face his sarcasm, his hunger for 'a real breakfast', as if muesli was just a story. And she'd gone along with it! She'd been a mouse. How could she think she could carry this off tonight? The thought of his being there, listening, almost knocked her off her feet, and then she had a very strange thought. She wished the driver of that dreadful lorry, the man who hadn't raped her, could see her now, in all her . . . in all her what? Her glory? Come off it, Sally. But she so wished that she had thanked him. Not for not raping her. For saving her life. She really believed that was what he had done. She should have tried to find him, to thank him and apologize for thinking such awful thoughts about him. She should have trusted him. She would be helping, starting here tonight, to build a more trustworthy world. World? No, Sally, don't get carried away. A more trustworthy Potherthwaite.

Even that was hubris. The unlovely room with its high windows stared back at her without expression. There were rows and rows of empty chairs, ugly chairs which would, she was certain, remain empty. How could she ever have thought that she, the lawyer's widow, could command a stage of this size?

Her triumph at the Weavers' Arms meant nothing now. She realized that each triumph would simply make the next speech harder.

There had been notices about the meeting in every public place. 'The FUTURE of YOUR Town is in YOUR Hands'. Sally, Marigold, Harry and Jill had called on virtually every house, asking people to come and debate the town's future. Sally had found it hard going, although most people had been reasonably courteous. But almost everybody asked who they were doing it for – which political party, which think tank, what special-interest group – and where the money would be coming from. It seemed impossible for people to believe that they were ordinary unpaid citizens who simply cared about the future of their town and, almost incidentally, of the world. If everyone who had expressed an interest turned up, there wouldn't be room, but Sally felt in her quivering heart that there would be room and chairs to spare.

Marigold was the first to arrive. She was wearing a black dress patterned with scarlet roses. Her spectacular jade earrings had been a birthday present from Timothy in the early, generous years. She was showing far too much cleavage for a church hall. Sally liked her and needed her, but she felt a spasm of irritation now. It was her evening, not Marigold's. Nor did Marigold's opening remark please her.

'Nobody here yet, then?'

'Thank you, Marigold.'

'Oh, Sally, don't worry. I've had heaps of promises.'

'Promises!'

Marigold hugged her. Five different scents wafted around Sally. She must have been a little allergic to one of them, and had a coughing fit, choked, thought she was going to die, almost wished she could. Marigold banged her on the back and said, 'Take short breaths. Short breaths.' Desperately she took short breaths. The moment passed.

The next to arrive was the Revd Dominic Otley. He always carried his head to the left, as if there was somebody shorter there whose pearls of wisdom he needed to hear. He looked around the unlovely room and said, 'To think that this room is where it's all starting.'

Sally looked at him in astonishment.

'What's all starting?'

'My dear lady! This! All this! You! Transition. The Transition of Potherthwaite. Not nervous, are you? Well, I suppose you're bound to be.' He lowered his voice. 'I threw up before my first sermon.'

That makes a change, thought Sally uncharitably. I feel like throwing up *during* your sermons. The sermon was not the strongest part of a Revd Otley service.

Arthur and Jessica Frond entered, and looked round the hall uncertainly. Sally had a fear that when they saw that there were only two other people they would leave. Arthur had aged. He had never been the same man after Willis & Frond folded. He shouldn't have stayed on in the town that had once looked up to him.

But they didn't leave. They stood, in the chronic indecision of age, for quite a while, unable to decide which of two hundred and forty-six chairs to sit in. At last they chose two chairs right on the edge, in case they needed the lavatory or were utterly bored.

Nobody came in for another two or three dreadful, endless minutes. Arthur and Jessica Frond smiled bravely, covering their embarrassment.

Then Peter and Myfanwy Sparling entered. Sally was pleased and touched to see them. They came over to her, smiling, and both kissed her.

'That evening, Sally, when it . . . you know . . . happened . . .' said Peter Sparling.

'Don't remind her, Peter,' said Myfanwy. 'She won't want to be reminded, not tonight.'

'No, but I mean, that evening, and this, who'd have thought it? Marvellous. Marvellous, Sally.'

Peter Sparling pumped her hand, and she suddenly wanted to cry, had to fight the tears off. Waves of emotion came over her – she didn't know what half of them were about, and she fought them off desperately.

The Hammonds had sent a note. *'Good luck, will raise a glass to you in Tenerife.'* That was nice of them.

A few more people entered. Jill and Harry as expected. 'Couldn't persuade the others. Silly sods.' Rog and Sue from the Weavers' Arms. 'We'll never forget it started in our pub.' Sophie Partington, the town's one-woman red-light district. Dr Ian Mallet. 'My wife is uneasy in crowds. Claustrophobia, you know.' Then analyse her and cure her, man. Councillor Frank Stratton – good! good! – with his wife Marian. Gordon Hendrie and his wife Jenny, parents of Potherthwaite's most famous daughter, Potherthwaite's only famous daughter, Arabella Kate Hendrie, the opera star.

'Arabella is singing at La Scala tonight,' said Gordon in a low boom.

'Singing for you,' squeaked Jenny in her tiny voice.

Sally reflected on the improbability of Gordon and Jenny's voices having combined to produce the voice of a young woman sometimes referred to as 'the Yorkshire Callas'.

'For me?' she asked.

'For you.'

'For Potherthwaite. She asked us to tell you.'

'She'll be singing at La Scala, for Potherthwaite.'

'Well, that's . . . that's amazing.'

And it was. Sally felt really moved.

Gloria Wells from the better of the nearly-new shops, but there was nothing even nearly new about her. That strange boy Ben with his friend Tricksy. How wonderful to have youngsters there. Jill was talking to Harry and he was laughing. Sally wondered what she was saying to amuse him so. Actually, it was perhaps as well that she didn't know. Jill was saying, 'You see the man on my left. I've given him two endoscopies, a colonoscopy and a sigmoidoscopy. I know his intestines better than I know the Pennines.'

Now they were pouring in. Quite a few people had been wandering around in the Market Place, looking round to see if enough people were coming to make it worth coming. Now they too came in. Four of the people who had heard Sally speak in the Weavers' Arms were there, plus representatives of groups with special interests. There were people whose names she didn't know and people whose names she had forgotten, including Long Raincoat – where had she met him?

There weren't even going to be enough seats. Extra chairs were being fetched. This was massive.

Sally was surprised to see Matt Winkle, the supermarket manager, accompanied by his gaunt wife, Nicola, who was from a good family and embarrassed Matt by buying her food at the butcher's and the deli. He was about to sit next to Sophie Partington, but Nicola pulled him away and led him to the other side of the central gangway. Every choice of seat has significance in a small community. Every choice of seat is a little drama in itself.

At last it was time to start. The vicar had offered to introduce Sally, 'it being the church hall', and nobody had known how to refuse.

He strode to the lectern placed in the middle of the stage. Sally hovered at the back of the stage, her heart pumping.

'Good evening,' he began. 'How I wish that I could get an audience like this for . . .'

He paused. Sally's stomach muscles tightened and she cringed. That would have been better left unsaid, like much that the Revd Dominic Otley said.

'. . . my little events next door.'

Sally feared that the vicar expected at least a titter here.

'We all know why we're here . . .'

So don't tell us, please.

'We are here to listen to Sally Mottram, a . . . um . . . a most remarkable woman . . .'

Please. Don't.

'. . . a quite extraordinary woman . . .'

All eyes on her. How could she react? Agreement was impossible, denial would be ridiculous.

'. . . who has faced . . . um . . . misfortune with . . . um . . . courage and fortitude.'

The unnecessary nouns thudded round the hall like gunshot.

'We all know, I think, that Sally is proposing huge changes here in our little town. I believe in tradition, as I'm sure many of you know, but with tradition there must come change.'

He was in full sermon mode. Sally had a terrible fear that he would do his usual seventeen or so minutes.

'Change and tradition are the . . . um . . . the . . . um . . . the . . . um . . . the bedrock . . . um . . .'

Suddenly the Revd Otley realized what he was doing, and stopped.

'But you haven't come here to hear me,' he said. 'Ladies and gentlemen, it's time to introduce a lady many of us know and all of us admire, Mrs Sally Mottram.'

Sally stepped forward. There was loud applause. She was shaking. She wouldn't be able to use her notes until she stopped shaking. All afternoon she had been reminding herself to remind herself tonight of the advice she had been given by Councillor Frank Stratton. She remembered to remind herself of it now. 'Your whole being will urge you to hurry. Resist it. Slow down. If ever you feel the urge to hurry, slow down.'

She waited, and waited, until there was total silence. This gave at least the illusion that she was in control.

'Ladies and gentlemen . . .'

Her voice didn't sound as nervous as she had feared, and suddenly she was thinking not of herself, but of Potherthwaite.

'Ladies and gentlemen, I am so thrilled to see so many of you here this evening. Thank you so much for coming.'

She paused, raised her voice.

'I have a vision for this town.'

The word 'vision' had come from nowhere, fought its way in. It frightened her.

'Not that I have any intention of forcing any vision of mine on you. Regard it as just a starting point.'

No, Sally. Too negative. Too modest. She needed her notes. If only her hands weren't shaking.

159

'My house is up for sale, and I fully intended, when I found a buyer, to go back south. I found that I couldn't. I found that I love this town. I believe it has enormous potential.'

She was trying not to notice anybody in particular in the audience. She was trying to see them as a blur. But she caught sight of Katherine Kavanagh, from the Kosy Korner Kafé, and found herself thinking how good it was of her to come. No, Sally. Fatal. Concentrate.

She started to talk about climate change.

'Some people argue that the case for climate change is unproven. Others say that while the case is proven, it is not necessarily man-made.'

Her voice was quivering. She caught sight of Terence and Felicity Porchester, trapped on their narrowboat at the silted Quays. What she said could help to release them. They were lovely people. She wanted to release them. She had paused for too long, but now she had a sense of purpose and suddenly her hands weren't shaking. She also realized that she didn't need her notes any more. It was a miracle. She had been silent for too long. Say something, Sally, quickly. But say what?

Say that, Sally. Be human.

'I have my notes here. I haven't been able to use them, because my hands have been shaking too much, and I didn't want you to see how nervous I am. And, do you know, I find I don't even need those notes. I will speak from the heart.'

A few people clapped and on hearing them clapping a few others joined in. It wasn't much, but it was encouraging.

'I say that most if not all of the things man needs to do to combat climate change are things that are good in themselves, so let's stop arguing and start acting. To wait for incontrovertible proof would be the most ludicrous risk.

'Just as important as climate change is peak oil, yet this is an issue that is hardly mentioned in our petrol-guzzling world, because we are so terrified of it. What does it mean? It is a name for the moment when the amount of oil available in the world becomes less by the day rather than more. Oil is finite. It will run out, unless we use less. A lot less. A whole lot less. Or find alternative sources of energy. But we cannot rely on that. We must use less oil.'

These were powerful words. Sally paused, calming herself down. From the corner of her eye she caught sight of one of the doctors from the Baggit View Surgery whispering to a colleague. She imagined that he was making some highly intelligent, pertinent comment. Luckily she couldn't hear him. He was actually saying, 'Look at that Boyce-Willoughby woman's tits. How could three husbands have walked out on her? Where did she find them? St Dunstan's?'

'There are people in Oxford Road, where I live, thoroughly nice people,' continued Sally, 'who take their families to Portugal four times a year. They are helping to poison the world. There may still be fuel for their children and their children's children to take their families to Portugal, but will there be fuel for their grandchildren's children? I think not . . . unless we change.'

Sally had almost shouted those last three words.

'This is where I turn to our own little world,' she said in a softer voice. 'We in our little way here cannot act on a world stage, but as it happens there are plans afoot for Potherthwaite's future and there are alternatives which will help us to fight these great threats to the world and also improve our town. This is where the global and the local come together. I will tell you how I hope to persuade you to fight these plans.'

Her eyes swung towards Councillor Frank Stratton. She couldn't stop them. He was tense, and he was frowning.

161

She didn't mind that she had caught his eye. In that moment she felt strong enough, with the town behind her, to fight.

'I said, when I spoke to a few of you at the Weavers' Arms – and I'm happy to see that one or two of the people who heard me then at the neighbouring tables didn't feel I'd ruined their meal, they're here tonight.'

There was applause. She smiled. She was beginning to enjoy herself, she really was.

'I said then that I have a plan. I'd better tell you what it is. I've spotted two or three councillors here tonight, and you'll think, What a cheek, is this woman a town planner? No, I'm not, but I find that I'm something perhaps even more important than a town planner. I'm a town dreamer. I'm a dream maker, and my dream is this. There is a plan for a second supermarket in the town, on the waste ground in the High Street, and this plan involves destroying the Potherthwaite deli. I'm not against destroying the deli . . .'

There were murmurs of surprise. She held her hand up.

'. . . because we don't use it enough. But of course I have a solution for that. Use it. Use it or lose it.'

Her eyes strayed to Matt and Nicola, Nicola giving Matt a smile with cold triumph but no humour in it. Look away, Sally. Don't let your concentration be broken again.

'And with my plan you will not need to lose it. Keep the deli and all the other small shops and use them.'

There was loud applause.

'Applause is not enough.'

She dared to glare at them for a moment, and she felt, for the first time, something that she knew to be very dangerous indeed. She felt, in a small but deeply beguiling way, the excitement of power.

'Now, my plan. I turn to the roads. We have a plan for a

new road to the south of the town, turning right to feed the new supermarket. I suggest that it won't cost a great deal more if this road doesn't turn right, that there is no second supermarket, that it goes straight on and joins the existing road at the roundabout before the allotments. What will we have produced then? A bypass.'

There was more applause.

'Imagine if the High Street was pedestrianized.'

There was yet more applause.

'Yes, ladies and gentlemen of the council, I know I am not a member of the Highways Department or the Highways Committee, but my plan makes sense. The only thing I haven't mentioned is the open space. I know that we have a park, a rather large but also rather featureless park, on the outskirts of town. What about another park here, small but elegant, right in the middle of town. I even have a name for it. Central Park.'

Again, the audience applauded.

'Potherthwaite, the New York of the Pennines.'

Don't get carried away, Sally, or you will be carried away.

She paused, calming herself down. When she had calmed herself down, when she felt certain that she wouldn't make grandiose promises that she couldn't fulfil, Sally spoke in a lower, softer voice.

'I don't want this to be a one-person campaign. I just want to set it in motion and let you, the people of Potherthwaite, take it from there. I can only do so much, but I make you one promise. I'm not a miracle worker, I leave that side of things to the vicar . . .'

There was some laughter at the thought of the Revd Dominic Otley performing any kind of miracle. The vicar himself smiled rather grimly.

'. . . but some of you may know that I am friendly with a lady in the town who is well known for all the wrong reasons.

My plans for her are also my plans for all of us. With our marvellous allotments fully used, with local food shops in the High Street, Potherthwaite can eat locally and healthily. I didn't know what permaculture meant until I read the Transition books. It's an ugly word for a beautiful concept, the development of agricultural ecosystems that are sustainable and self-sufficient. We will set up our permaculture here, and its symbol will be the lady of whom I speak. It has been said, though it has not been confirmed, that she is the fattest woman in Yorkshire. I refer of course to Ellie Fazackerly. I have a dream for Ellie. She knows of it and she knows that I am telling you this tonight and at this very moment, trapped in her great bed, she will be dreaming of it too. My dream is that one summer's day, in the not-too-distant future, when the canal has been dredged by volunteers – and that means us. I have to tell you that none of you are just here to applaud. Sorry about that . . .'

She smiled with just a touch of relish.

'. . . I dream that when the Potherthwaite Arm of the Rackstraw and Sladfield Canal is perhaps officially reopened, Ellie Fazackerly will walk from her home in Cadwallader Road, down the pedestrianized High Street, turn right into Quays Approach, and witness the grand opening ceremony. Maybe – is it too fanciful to think? – right here in Potherthwaite we will create a symbol of hope and encouragement for all the obese of the land.'

There was thunderous applause.

She realized that already she was getting carried away again.

'But let's not get carried away,' she said to her audience, and also to herself. 'There's a lot of work to be done, and it'll be hard work and sometimes very boring work. I believe we can do it. I believe we can persuade the good people on our council to support our dream and help us make it happen. I believe that it is in the interests of every one of us that

Potherthwaite transforms itself. It won't happen overnight. I look forward to the next years, together.'

There was loud applause, almost hysterical applause, dangerous applause, as if everything had been done already, as if dreams could be made real just by putting them into words.

Sally was overwhelmed with congratulations. There was excitement on all sides. It was heady stuff. Lots of people made offers of help. She was kissed by several people. Long Raincoat approached and she went blank and couldn't remember who he was or where she had met him. Luckily when he spoke he reminded her. 'Lots of people want to have a word with you,' he said, 'so I won't take up too much of your time – I learnt that on the taxis, as I told you on the footbridge – but I just wanted to say that I agree with everything you've said, everything, absolutely everything, and this is my phone number, and please ring me if you think there is anything I could do, anything at all I could do, and now I'll leave you in peace because I can see that there's lots of people dying to have a word with you, so I'll leave the field clear to them, just saying I mean it, I really do, any time, any time, I'm not one of those people who say things and don't mean it, any time, I really do mean it.' Linda Oughtibridge looked at her with a strange, pursed smile, and said nothing. The vicar gave her an awkward kiss, smiled broadly and looked very sad. Gunter Mulhausen gave her a stiff little bow, shook her hand and said, 'This will not go unnoticed in Schleswig-Holstein, I can assure you.' Arrangements were made, for those who wished, to go for a drink at the Dog and Duck. Sally explained to Rog and Sue that she would always acknowledge that the project had been born at the Weavers' Arms but that the whole town must have the chance to be equally involved. Councillor Frank Stratton shook hands with her in the most decorous manner and said, 'Very interesting. Lots to mull over.' Jill and Harry congratulated her enthusiastically and Harry said, 'Olive and Arnold will regret not coming.' Jill looked as if she didn't agree.

They swept off to the pub, Sally carried helplessly on a tidal wave of enthusiasm. It was heady stuff. Somewhere, deep down, she felt a tiny note of caution, but she wouldn't let it spoil her night, she felt so much love for all these people. The drink flowed, there were nibbles laid on by mine excited host – mine almost delirious host, in fact. She had done it. She had risen to the occasion. She wanted this to go on for ever. People were beginning to drift away, and she didn't want them to – that tiny feeling of distant fear returned, almost but not quite stilled by their enthusiastic words. She felt that, because this was her evening, she couldn't leave until everyone else had left.

Marigold bumped into her at the end of the evening and they found themselves walking away together.

'None of those bastards came,' said Marigold.

'Sorry?'

'I came here, bought them all drinks. David Fenton, thinks he's so handsome. Mick Webster from the travel agent's, he can disappear up his short weekend break from now on. I even invited that randy little tosser, Bill Etching. None of them came. Bastards. I've had men up to here. I'm starving. Are you?'

'There'll only be Indians open. Do you fancy a curry?'

'I love them.'

'I haven't had one since I met Barry.'

'Shall we?'

'Please.'

They hurried up High Street West like two excited schoolchildren, then turned right into Vernon Road.

Decisions, decisions. Should they go to the Old Bengal, the New Bengal or the Taj Mahal?

'I don't know any of them,' said Sally.

'The man in the New Bengal rushes out to persuade you to go in,' said Marigold.

'Horrid,' said Sally. 'Let's not go there then.'

'I often wonder what happened in their family to cause the rift,' said Marigold.

'I don't want anything to do with rifts tonight,' said Sally. 'Let's go to the Taj Mahal.'

'As good a reason as any.'

They walked past the Old Bengal. The head waiter of the New Bengal scuttled out of his restaurant, beaming.

'Plenty room. Very comfy. Very welcome,' he said. 'Lovely curry. Many balti. Very nice.'

They shook their heads, smiled in embarrassment, walked past his almost empty restaurant, and entered the Taj Mahal, which was not full but pleasantly busy. Drunk young men didn't frequent Indian restaurants late at night any more. They were able to drink late in pubs and then go on to clubs. There were four clubs at the end of Vernon Road. It was Potherthwaite's Reeperbahn.

The tables in the Taj Mahal were set in two long rows, one at either side of the long, thin restaurant. The music was soft and modern Indian and the paintings on the walls were vaguely modern too. When they were seated, and had surprised themselves by ordering large bottles of Cobra beer, Marigold commented on the head waiter of the New Bengal.

'It's so sad that he never realizes his mistake,' she said. 'It's so sad that in half the world the British descend from their cruise ships, are pestered by vendors, and so buy nothing. If only they were ignored like at home they'd empty the shops.'

'I wouldn't know,' said Sally. 'I've never been on a cruise. Barry didn't like them.'

'Having never been on one?'

'Absolutely.'

167

They began to talk about their husbands. Although they had said that they were starving, they hadn't even looked at their menus when the waiter came to take their order. What they were really hungry for, although they didn't realize it, was company and support.

The beer was cool and refreshing, and they sipped it with pleasure while they continued to talk. Marigold talked most, as was her wont. Besides, on the subject of men, she had more to talk about. She waxed lyrical and entertaining on the subject of her exes.

Malcolm Stent, an electrician, had been quite good-looking but obsessed with football and with nothing very electric in the way of sexual technique.

'I wore very sporty gear. I was still a working-class girl. I spent four long seasons supporting Charlton Athletic. Oh my God. That ground was not my happy valley. I should have walked out, but I didn't want to hurt him. Naive? I must have been the most naive person in Gravesend. He was knocking off a hairdresser in Dartford. He walked out on me. Ran off with the left full back of the Arsenal ladies' team. Or was it the right full back? I can't remember now. Anyway, she was a bitch and she couldn't head the ball for toffee. I went all respectable and safe, went for solid employment and regular money. I looked quite good . . .'

'I'll bet.'

'. . . and I got a job as PA to an international businessman. I discovered that I looked rather splendid in business garb.'

'I can quite believe it.'

'And then I met this Dane.'

The food arrived during Marigold's description of life with Henrik Larsen.

'He was one of our top contacts in Scandinavia. I went out with him, fell in love with him, went to bed with him, married him, went to Aarhus with him.'

She broke off to take a mouthful of curry.

'This food's delicious.'

'Mine too. Lovely.'

Marigold dipped a king prawn into the sauce and popped it into her mouth. Sally waited patiently.

'It turned out that there was something rotten in the state of Denmark and I had married it.'

'I'm really sorry,' said Sally.

Marigold smiled through her next mouthful, then continued.

'He had an open marriage, and I had open sandwiches.'

Sally laughed a 'I know you want me to laugh but I'm laughing in a way that shows that I sympathize totally with your misfortune' kind of laugh. She felt so sympathetic, so close to Marigold, such warmth for her that she was almost resenting the breaks for food.

'I decided I'd make sure *I* left *him* this time. I managed it by two and a half hours.'

'What?'

'I left after breakfast. He came back at lunchtime, took his things, left a note, didn't see the note I'd left. We both spent a fortune on hotels that night and the house stood there empty.'

Suddenly, as the memories came back, Marigold began to attack her food with angry enthusiasm, spearing each remaining prawn as if it was Henrik Larsen. Sally tried, meanwhile, to make an entertaining routine out of life with Barry Mottram.

'I didn't mind having to eat the boring food that was all he liked,' she said. 'That didn't take long. It was buying it and cooking it that I hated. It took so long, and it was so unchallenging. In the end I realized that he only really liked what his mother had cooked. I realized that I was a surrogate mother.'

'She's dead, is she?'

'Oh yes. He wouldn't have dared kill himself if she wasn't. And do you know, with all that cooking, in the last years he never once thanked me. Never ever.'

Sally mopped up the last of her sauce with her naan bread.

'That was really lovely,' she said. 'What a lot of pleasures I must have missed. I said to him once, "You never thank me for your food." He said, "I finish it, don't I? Isn't that praise enough?" I said, "No, it is not." He said, "Praise can be false, Sally. Praise can be fiction. An empty plate is a fact." He looked pleased with himself, as if he'd said something as witty as Oscar Wilde. Cheer me up, Marigold. Tell me how awful Timothy was.'

Marigold didn't take much persuading.

'He was cruel. Simple as that. He was physically cruel and he was mentally cruel. A friend – well, an acquaintance, I don't really have any friends except you – said that at least he wasn't unfaithful. That is not good news when a man is cruel, Sally. It means he's at home every sodding night.'

The waiter brought piping-hot towels, too hot to hold comfortably as they washed their hands.

'At least when Henrik was pursuing his Danish pastries I could have long hot baths and read romantic novels. Timothy was always there, and he was always cruel, except when we had visitors, and then he made up for it afterwards. The awful thing was that this time I didn't want to leave him. I didn't want to leave the flat. I wanted *him* to go. When he went off with Miss American Dental Floss or Miss Venezuelan Tits or whatever it was, I was glad. I was glad, Sally.'

The waiter tried to present them with dessert menus full of photographs of intensely coloured sweets. They shook their heads firmly.

'Just the bill, please,' said Sally.

'But, you know, this time it was harder than ever. Meeting people. Telling them. Admitting failure number three. My spirit is being very slow to come back.'

The bill arrived. They divided it into two without discussion. Instinctively, each knew that this was a moment of togetherness, of equality, of sharing. For either to have insisted or even offered to pay the lot would have been a social solecism. This was beautiful.

But Vernon Road was not beautiful. It was dark and cold and windy. The clubs were open, and, although it wasn't the weekend, youngsters were making their alcoholic ways to them in considerable numbers. Girls who were almost naked were shivering towards oblivion.

As they approached High Street West, Sally and Marigold's walking grew slower and slower, despite the cold. They could have ordered a taxi, but, if they had, the question of where they were going would have arisen too abruptly.

At the corner of Vernon Road and High Street West they stopped.

'You don't want to go back to that house on your own, do you?' asked Marigold.

'No.'

Sally's answer was a whisper.

'Come back with me. Have a liqueur. Stay the night. I have a spare room.'

'Thank you.'

They walked more briskly now, wanting comfort, wanting Marigold's flat, wanting Marigold's central heating, wanting Marigold's liqueurs.

Marigold drank Baileys. Sally chose Cointreau. They sat at either side of the log-effect fire, and stretched their legs out, like two old men in a club. They were tired, they needed to sleep, but they didn't want to be alone. They didn't want to break out of the warm cocoon of this sudden friendship.

This was true friendship. Only the fire, in this cosy confessional, was artificial. They sat there long into the night. They sipped their liqueurs, talking softly, and in the end they had that one too many.

Marigold confessed first, admitting that she was fearing the rest of her life, dreading the continuation of her inability to have a happy relationship with a man. 'Sometimes I wake up in the night,' she admitted, 'and see myself, in old age, talking to my budgie.'

Then it was Sally's turn, and she broke down altogether, told Marigold, with streams of tears, that she felt a complete failure, told her all about the suicide letter that Barry hadn't even sent to her, told her that the number of people who had come to the meeting, and the strength of their expectations, made her deeply uneasy, that her very triumph terrified her, told her that she couldn't go on with the Transition movement, she hadn't got it in her.

Marigold came over to her then, took her in her arms, and whispered, 'You have, you know,' and they hugged and kissed and waves of affection and love were transmitted between them. In this moment of pure friendship and shared vulnerability, they gave way to words that might not have been altogether wise. They swore undying friendship, love and support. They swore that they would never let any man come between them.

After that they at last felt so exhausted that they were ready to brave the solitude. Marigold showed Sally to the guest room, and within five minutes they were both asleep in their separate beds.

BOOK FOUR
Conrad

EIGHTEEN

The great cities of Italy

'There are so many great cities in Italy, and their beautiful historic centres are almost entirely unspoilt, but each city has a really individual character. The greatest of all has to be Venice. La Serenissima. The Most Serene. Isn't that a beautiful name? A city built on water. The main street is a canal, "The Grand Canal". We stood on the Rialto Bridge, looking down at a great bend in the canal, both sides lined with great palaces. The canal was a mass of boats, long crowded river buses, elegant gondolas, showy launches, stunted removal boats, laden delivery boats, and the bridge was crowded with tourists, of all ages from small children to great-grandparents, all staring in astonishment. "So many tourists," he moaned. I said nothing. I was just overjoyed to see so many people so happy in this rotten world. But I was blind. I never knew what a gulf there was between us. It seems so odd, looking back. You may ask why he went to such places.'

It didn't look as if Ellie had been intending to ask anything, let alone anything as personal as that. It was hard for Sally to know if Ellie was really interested. The plan seemed to be working, much to her surprise, but would it hold?

'He ticked the sights off, satisfied that he'd seen them. He was a great ticker off. Sights, Christmas cards, business tasks. Tick them off. The children, if they were out of line, tick them off too.'

Ellie, her mouth tiny between her huge cheeks, smiled as best she could. So did Ali and Oli, who were squashed into large chairs, one at either side of the bed.

'Florence, which the Italians call Firenze, is very different. More austere, more classical, less obviously romantic. It was the central figure in the Renaissance, the greatest art movement the world has ever known. It's a vast open-air museum, yet throbbing with life from elegant restaurants to nuns on Vespas.'

'I'd love to see a nun on a Vespa,' said Ellie.

'You will,' said Sally very seriously. 'I'll take you. I'll take all three of you to Italy.'

Her plan had always seemed like a long shot, because it depended not only on Ellie, but also on Ali and Oli. The plan came in two parts. The first part was that Sally would buy all their food, deliver it to them twice a week, with instructions for Ali and Oli to follow – simple cooking instructions, for none of the food was complicated, but also strict instructions on what to have when. It was as generous as a slimming diet could possibly be, but it would still leave the three sisters very, very hungry, and Ellie obviously much hungrier even than Ali and Oli.

The carrot (ha ha) that Sally dangled had seemed, when she first mentioned it, quite unfit for purpose. She would visit them regularly, at least twice a week in addition to her food deliveries, and she would talk to them about all the beautiful places that there were in this world, places that they would never see unless they followed the plan, places that she would take them to if they did follow the plan.

It was a big commitment, made in an emotional moment. In fact it was an absurd commitment. She simply wouldn't be able to take them everywhere. She felt that she must be honest with them about this. They weren't fools. But not now. Not yet. She would take them to as many places as she could, though, if they stuck to their commitment, but she would stick to it if they stuck to it.

An uneasy thought about money flashed through her mind like a sparrowhawk through a peaceful garden. How would she pay for these trips? How could she ever help Sam and Beth? How would she live?

She mustn't think about this now. Already she had paused for too long. But how could she start again, now that she had stopped? It wasn't easy to keep up her commentary, here in this overheated, crowded front room in Cadwallader Road. She felt awkward, self-conscious, a bit ridiculous. What could the Fazackerly sisters know of the Renaissance? How could they relate to it? Could it possibly inspire them?

Oli was winding herself up to ask a question. She was going all shy.

'It were going round cake factory yesterday that your speech t'other night were brill,' she said, and her great cheeks went slightly red. 'Carrie Husband said that her friend's mum thought it were fabulous.'

'Marvellous,' said Sally. 'Carrie Husband's friend's mum is just the sort of person we're hoping to attract.'

She spoke in all sincerity, but even as she said it she realized that this might sound very patronizing. But the Fazackerly sisters missed the subtext of 'we'll get the clever ones and the socially aware ones easily enough, but it's great to hear of ordinary working-class supporters' that Sally in her self-consciousness as a new leader of men had detected in herself.

She must plunge back into her theme, absurd though it was sounding.

'Milan is a different kettle of fish again.'

It wasn't going to work. That gear change had sounded horrid. Oh well, she just had to persist. She talked of the great Duomo, of Leonardo da Vinci, of the stylish galleries. She ploughed on.

'The Italians have many faults, but they have a natural sense of style in almost everything they do. And Milan has more style than anywhere else in Italy. It's the style capital of a stylish land. Ellie, the first time you walk through Potherthwaite, we will get you something really stylish to wear.'

'Italian?'

'If you want.'

The three girls exchanged looks. Sally didn't know what the looks meant. She made an inspired guess.

'You can all have something Italian.'

All three sisters beamed, and Sally's spirits rose. It seemed possible after all that they really wanted to work at this.

'How will we afford that?' asked Ali.

'From what you save on food. And on that question, ladies, I'm trusting you, you know. Tell me, tell me honestly, please, are you actually sticking completely to the rules?'

Oli went red again.

'I brought cakes back Tuesday.'

'We ate them,' said Ali.

'They didn't taste as nice as we remembered,' said Ellie.

'Too sweet,' said Ali.

'Ali gave me a right ticking off,' said Oli. 'I won't do it again.'

'Well done, Ali,' said Sally. 'And well done Oli for telling me. Marvellous. And too sweet, that's fantastic. Your tastes are changing already. Verona, with the *Romeo and Juliet* connection, and a huge great amphitheatre where they do opera in the open air on summer nights – just imagine it – is probably the most romantic city.'

'I wish I'd been able to come to your talk,' said Ellie. 'I told Ali and Oli they should go. I'd have been all right.'

It was going wrong. She had pitched it badly. She was almost sounding priggish.

'But Italy isn't just art,' she said. 'It's food and drink and mountains and lakes and ice cream and beaches and laughter and love.'

'What did you do afterwards?' asked Ali. Awe entered her voice. 'Did you go to a restaurant?' It had always been the great limit of her dreams – to go to a restaurant.

'One day I'll take you all to a restaurant in Italy,' said Sally. 'They have wonderful restaurants there.'

But the Fazackerly sisters were still not ready to return to Italy.

'Which restaurant did you go to?' asked Oli.

'We went to the pub first,' said Sally. 'The Dog and Duck.'

'You didn't!' exclaimed Oli. 'Glenda from Packaging goes there.'

'Don't sound so astonished,' said Sally. 'I'm not a creature from a different planet.'

God, what must they have thought of me all those years, she thought.

'Then Marigold and I went for a curry.'

'She's nice, Marigold. She called here.'

'Yes. Yes, she is. Very. Pisa . . .'

But her comment on Pisa never got off the ground. They were leaning towards other subjects now.

'So you still haven't sold?' asked Ellie.

'Um . . . well actually, yes, I think I have, yes. A man came round this morning, spent ages, loves the feel of it. He's going to make an offer.'

179

She was really concerned that she was going to blush. This was terrible. This was juvenile. This wasn't the stuff of leadership.

'Did you like him?'

They knew.

'I think it's nice when you can sell your house to somebody nice,' said Ellie.

'Well, he is nice,' said Sally. 'I'd be very happy thinking of him there, actually.'

'I mean, it doesn't make any difference, I don't suppose,' said Ali. 'I mean, you, like, get your money anyway, know what I mean . . .'

'. . . but it is nice – listen to me, *is* nice, what do I know, I've never owned a house let alone, like, sold it,' said Oli, 'but I think it would be, like, comforting to you if you sold it to me to think I were happy there. I'd like to think, like, that somebody else is happy there now.'

'What's his name?' asked Ellie, and there was something about the way she asked it.

They knew.

'Conrad,' she said, and she could feel herself blushing.

'O'oh! Conrad!' said Ellie, Ali and Oli in unison.

'But my personal favourite of all the Italian towns is Lucca,' said Sally.

NINETEEN

A thousand miles apart

Harry and Jill sat a few feet away from each other in the shade of a large cypress, unmistakably British in their floppy hats. They had easels in front of them, and from time to time they peered into the distance, trying to look as though they were observing the scene with deep, painterly vision. Eighteen other Brits sat close by, also with easels, also peering at the wonderful, biblical view. The sun shone on sharp, shapely hills. A castellated village looked white in the searing sun. The tall, slim cypresses looked as if they had been arranged on the hills by an artist with immaculate taste.

Yes, we may dwell on this scene, familiar to us as the background to a thousand religious paintings. We may pause to smile at the sight of twenty British hats, all with something of the absurd in them, dotted untidily around this magnificently ordered landscape. But let us be merciful, let us not peer too closely at what was being created on the fine paper so neatly arranged on Jill and Harry's easels.

When they arrived home – the next day in fact – as the forecast rain lashed the Pother Valley, their painting holiday would have become a week of triumph, of joy, a sacred memory. On the sixth day of peering at all this beauty and recreating almost none of it, the need to escape the sun had become a bore, the light had become blinding, the pain of sitting still for long periods had turned the hip hip hurrah of earlier days into thoughts of hip hip replacement.

In short, they had discovered that they had no talent. Well, none worth speaking about. They had discussed, as they packed to leave for Italy, how they would get their efforts home to be admired in the cul-de-sac, and entered for the annual arts festival that didn't yet exist but would soon be inaugurated by Sally. Only this reference to her proposed arts festival had reconciled Sally to Harry making the trip. 'You're my sergeant major,' she had reminded him. 'I think you need to start taking that role seriously, or resign.'

Harry and Jill needn't have worried about how they would get their paintings home. They were destined to become landfill on a Tuscan hill.

This was a great disappointment to Harry. He had not admitted it to anybody, least of all to himself, but this bald, bluff businessman yearned for spirituality and was too much of a realist to believe that he would find it in religion. Art had been his great hope. This week had been a massive reality check. He would bury his disappointment by throwing himself into his role as Sally's sergeant major.

But perhaps the week had been an even greater disappointment for Jill, who had suggested the holiday, whose early indifferent paintings had lacked, she had felt, only experience and instruction, and who had hoped that she might begin, this week in Tuscany, her transformation from amateur to professional, that it might be the beginning of a transition in her to mirror the Transition in Potherthwaite. And with Jill there was the added element of marital rivalry. Arnold's book might not be brilliant – no, let's face it, we've peered at page 537 and it isn't – but it's still a book, an achievement in the world of literature. She has always hoped that one day she might match his achievement – no, she's human, she has wished to *exceed* his achievement. Where were those hopes now, at the end of her sixth day of avoiding the sun in the hills of Italy?

Surely sexual attraction was a large part of the motive in arranging this trip? Well, a little, perhaps. Harry, like his daubs, was no oil painting, but he had a twinkle in his eyes and energy in his legs and a suggestion of virility that Arnold couldn't match. And Jill, she had worn shorts on all six days and nobody had thought her foolish, and of how many people in their early seventies could that be said? Even now, at this very moment, Harry, despairing of 'Morning Mist Outside Montepulciano', was admiring the exquisite slight fleshiness of her calves, the almost Italianate perfection of her ankles, the youthfulness still obstinately lingering in her shapely sun-burnished knees.

On six evenings they had eaten simply but well, and been free to have offal without incurring exclamations of disgust from their spouses. On six evenings they had drunk honest local wine. On six evenings they had walked up the stairs together. On six evenings they had stopped outside Jill's bedroom door – they came to that first – and had kissed on both cheeks. On six evenings their eyes had met. On six evenings the messages in those eyes had been inconclusive. On six evenings Harry had said 'Night night, Jill' and moved on towards his bedroom.

Now it was time to show their work to the tutor – his verbal dexterity in praising it without telling lies had to be admired – and to pack up their things. Their coach was waiting to take them back to their friendly three-star hotel. Nothing much would happen on the coach. We can safely move a thousand miles north.

Here, in the narrow valley between the inhospitable hills, the fitful sun of the last few days had disappeared. The sky was grey. The clouds over the hills at the head of the valley were pregnant with rain. Arnold and Olive had made much of the sunshine. 'It's lovely here too,' had been their refrain in phone calls and texts. They had been looking forward to saying 'Well it's been like this all week' with a barely hidden triumphant smirk. Now that was ruined. Bloody British climate.

Maybe the weather had something to do with what happened. We can't be sure. The definitive paper on '*Air pressure and its effect on the incidence of orgasms*' has yet to be written.

Arnold and Olive were preparing in their different ways for their last evening alone together, if one can be alone together. Arnold was in a world where rain was called 'precipitation' and orgasms were unmentionable. '*Thomas Grindley was Mayor for seventeen years. We can deduce from the fact that 80% of his orgasms happened on Thursdays that his marriage was not . . .*' You don't get that sort of thing in local-history books.

At the moment when Olive rang he was busy on chapter 107 – 'The Macmillan Administration. Had Potherthwaite Never Had it So Good?' He didn't like those two 'had's, but he wasn't agile enough to circumvent them. The conversation was brief. Olive knew better than to interrupt his thought processes for any length of time.

'Dinner at half past six.'

'Good.'

Olive was making a fine dinner to mark their last evening alone together. That, in itself, was a remarkable gesture – from Olive.

Reluctantly, Arnold rose from his MS – he hoped that stood for 'masterpiece', but he wasn't a fool and in his heart he knew it stood for 'manuscript' – and put a bottle of white wine in the fridge. He found himself choosing a remarkably good one, kept for a special occasion. Since he never had any special occasions, he had kept it for years. But he was using it that night. Strange.

At thirty-four minutes past six – absolute punctuality is a social solecism – Arnold rang Olive's doorbell. The first grim spots of rain were carried on to his glasses by the wind. He had trimmed his moustache. Olive didn't notice. Nor did she notice that the wine was a 1986 Chassagne-Montrachet. She wouldn't have commented if she had noticed. She knew nothing about wine, to Harry's chagrin.

Arnold drank his sherry on his own. Olive, over-reaching herself in the kitchen, was busy keeping chaos at bay. He realized that, like him with the wine, she had made a special effort with the sherry. It was indifferent, but not as indifferent as usual.

There was a slight delay. This resulted in his having a second glass. He said he only would if she did. She, in her nervousness, did.

The special meal that Olive produced consisted of roast chicken with sage-and-onion stuffing, bread sauce, cranberry sauce, chipolata sausages, roast potatoes, roast parsnips, purple-sprouting broccoli and carrots. Nothing could have pleased Arnold more. It looked wonderful.

At first they ate in comfortable silence. They had been brought up in the days before talking at mealtimes had been invented. The idea hadn't had a long life. It was disappearing fast. There were now very few mealtimes in many households. Millions of people didn't even have tables to eat at.

This was a truly peaceful moment, and there was nobody to spoil it, to say, 'I had a wonderful chicken dish with garlic and cumin in Salisbury,' or 'We must be the only country in the world that tries to make a great sauce out of bread.'

Then Olive told him of an incident that had occurred not much more than an hour ago. She had made her daily phone call to Harry, and Jill had answered. She had assured Olive that she was not in Harry's room – the call had been put through to the wrong room.

'It's unsettled me,' she said. 'I don't know whether to believe her.'

'Well, of course you can believe her,' said Arnold.

'How can you be so sure?'

If Olive hoped for a resounding character reference about Harry's reliability and morality and the depth of his unswerving love for her, she was to be disappointed.

'If she was in Harry's room she'd hardly have been stupid enough to answer the phone,' he said.

Olive had been a wonderfully efficient secretary to Harry all her life with him. How could she sometimes be so stupid? She blushed at her stupidity.

Arnold had dismissed the question of the wrong bedroom, but the conversation laid bare the fact that all week, at their less special lunches – they hadn't dared risk a dinner until now – there had been a third guest at the table. Suspicion.

Now that the subject had been hinted at, the floodgates were open.

'Do you think they have been . . . you know . . .?' asked Arnold.

Olive sighed and put down her knife and fork, as if what she was going to say was too important to be interrupted by any thought of food.

'I don't know,' she said. 'I've . . . He used to go away a lot of course, and . . . I was his secretary so of course I knew most things. I never . . . as far as I know he never . . . but I don't know. I didn't dare ask. I suppose, if I didn't know it . . . I wasn't the most beautiful woman in the world, Arnold.'

'No,' said Arnold naively, 'but you were pretty. I certainly thought so, that summer.'

'That summer in Cheltenham. Sounds like a film title.'

'No film in our story.'

'Could we . . . should we . . . have seconds?'

'Do you know, I think I will. It's my kind of food.'

A sudden burst of rain spattered against the windows like an over-obvious sound cue in a radio play. It made both of them think about sun-drenched Italy. Luckily neither of them thought about the fact that in Italy it was one hour later. Harry and Jill might be walking upstairs to bed at that very moment, their meal complete.

As indeed they were. Well, not exactly at that moment. They had just about completed their meal, and their conversation had been very different. At no stage did either of them wonder whether Arnold and Olive were up to anything. Neither of them believed that their spouses were ever up to anything any more. They were finishing their *affogato*. There was no one to say, 'Cold ice cream with hot coffee poured over it, what sort of pudding do you call that?' A few minutes later, Harry handed their waitress a very generous tip, wild words of international affection were uttered, and Harry and Jill walked slowly from the room.

Near the foot of the stairs they stopped to examine pamphlets about local attractions they hadn't had time to see and would now never see. Then Harry's hand reached across to Jill's far buttock, almost touched it, but retreated.

They walked slowly towards Jill's room. Usually at this moment they kissed, but that night she opened her bedroom door before they kissed. However, she didn't move towards her room and he had no idea whether she wanted to. All at the same time he felt a great desire for her body and he had a tender vision of Olive serving him a meal with a sad lack of confidence. Love flowed through him, and he couldn't have said who it was for. Or rather, he knew that it was for both of them but he had no idea in what proportions. He was hugging Jill and she seemed to have decided to hug him at exactly the same moment. Neither of them ventured a kiss that night. Perhaps they were both frightened of what it might lead to. Perhaps they were frightened of each other. Or perhaps, in their quiet ways, they just loved their dear old partners too much. It's difficult to tell from the outside; we are mysteries to each other from the day we are born.

Let us look at the facts, then. Harry gently moved away from the hug, and said, 'Night night, Jill.'

Jill moved away from the hug and said, 'Night night, Harry.'

Jill inserted her key card into her door, but didn't press it.

Harry walked slowly to his door, inserted his key card, but didn't press it.

They gave each other another look.

'Night night,' said Jill.

'Night night,' said Harry.

They pressed their key cards, opened their respective doors, went into their respective rooms, and closed the doors.

They opened their respective doors, and emerged into the corridor. They looked at each other with surprise.

They hung on their bedroom doors notices which stated 'Do Not Disturb' in Italian.

An appropriate ending, perhaps, to a scene mired in confusion and tension.

Except that it wasn't quite like that. Harry was the less cool of the two, and in the confusion of seeing Jill again when emotionally it was totally redundant to do so, he hung his notice the wrong way round.

The words on his notice were the Italian for 'Please Clean My Room'.

What would Dr Mallet, who wished his name was

Bronovsky, make of that? Not much, if his track record was anything to go by. But it does get us back to Potherthwaite.

Not a lot of time had elapsed since Olive served Arnold seconds, but by now they had finished their seconds and were well into their rhubarb crumble. A gap between courses was a sophisticated move to which Olive did not subscribe. Meals were for eating, finishing, and washing up.

On this particular evening the washing-up would not be done.

Maybe it was the drink that made Olive so direct. Maybe it was the drink that made her smile at Arnold with such affection. Maybe it was the drink that made her look at least thirty years younger to Arnold. But although they weren't habitual drinkers, they hadn't actually had all that much, and they had had it over a long period of time. More likely, perhaps, and certainly more charitable, to think that all their sudden affection and attraction for each other sprang from true feeling, in part from the feeling of what their life might have been like if they had been bolder and less inhibited in those bad old English days. Maybe too – we couldn't blame them, could we? Not entirely, anyway – they had been a little bit riled by the easy assumption of Harry and Jill that leaving them behind did not involve any emotional risk whatsoever.

'Come on,' said Olive.

Arnold didn't move a muscle or show any astonishment.

Olive went across to him, put her arms round his shoulders, and helped him out of his seat.

'Come on,' she repeated.

He made no real protest. His 'What about the washing-up?' was very weak. His heart wasn't in it.

Olive kept her arm round him, then leant across and kissed his cheek. Then she led him, quite forcefully, towards her bedroom. He was like a man who doesn't know whether it's heaven or the gallows he's being escorted to.

She closed the bedroom door gently behind them.

Olive and Arnold belonged to a generation that thought of sex as a very private matter. What went on behind the bedroom door was their concern and theirs only. For that reason, and also in respect for two people in their early seventies, we will go no further.

Except to say that Marigold Boyce-Willoughby, who was walking Kenneth for the Sparlings, told Sally that she passed number 9 in the cul-de-sac quite late, and heard a noise which suggested that Arnold Buss had not felt that he had been led to the gallows.

TWENTY

A long, hot summer

It was a long, hot summer, with the single exception that it wasn't hot. But it had, for Sally Mottram, all the character of a long, hot summer – slow, lazy, uneventful – even though it was wretchedly cold at times. There were a few fine days – we won't go mad and call them hot, but they were pleasantly warm – and there was one settled spell of more than a week. 'Lovely weather,' Sally commented to a man working at the edge of the allotments, as she passed. 'We'll pay for it,' he growled in true Potherthwaite fashion.

They did.

She had not expected to be still passing the allotments at that time, but the sale of 'The Larches' and, more important by far, the arrival of Conrad, who was planning to buy her house, proceeded more slowly than she had hoped. These days, as the town's unelected leader, it behove her to be democratic. She walked everywhere, setting an example of a low carbon footprint. Almost every day her walk took her to flats that she had been sent details of by the town's estate agents. She was planning, of course, to rent. She couldn't afford to buy. The estate agents' pictures surprised her. They were far from attractive, and she had always thought that they tried to present properties in their most favourable light. When she saw them, the properties also surprised her. The estate agents *had* presented them in their most favourable light.

On the Transition front, things were hanging fire too. It wasn't that nothing was being done. Plans were being made. Money was being sought. She soon realized that she was asking for money too soon. Inexperience again. Many people promised money 'when there's something to show for it', but it was difficult to have anything to show for it until you'd been given money. 'I move in vicious circles,' she told Marigold. Marigold touched her shoulder sympathetically. After their long confessional evening, they had been slightly tentative with each other, as if worried that they had gone too far, but they had now settled into a deep, stable affection, in which words were often not necessary at all.

Progress was made in one area. The tireless Harry persuaded more than two hundred people to devote a morning or afternoon every week to taking part in a clear-up campaign, the removal of litter from the town. Almost half the rubbish consisted of wrappings from McDonald's. People who ate there seemed to have an irresistible urge to rid themselves of the evidence of their meal as soon as possible.

Even this relatively small initiative created its problems. The clear-up inevitably produced a reaction against the project. Youths from the council estates, particularly the Baggit Estate, led by Luke Warburton, who thought volunteers were all snobby middle-class do-gooders, drove round at night throwing empty Carling cans, used condoms, Conservative Party newsletters and the remnants of yet more McDonald's dinners into the posher gardens of the town. A few of the volunteers gave up and others wanted to, but Sally fought on, assuring them that this was just a game and in the end the litter bugs would tire of it. Harry's bald head could be seen all round the town as he sought to catch them in the act. He proposed to set up teams of volunteers to chase and threaten them. He would have been happy to take on the job himself, even though he was in his seventies. Foiled in this ambition by Sally, he made a list of suspects and told her that he was happy to give the list to the police if that was what she wanted. It wasn't what she wanted. She told Harry that in her opinion that would be playing into their hands. They would run rings round the police. The best thing to do was the last thing they would want, which was to ignore them completely. That would solve the problem. She didn't doubt it.

She did doubt it, of course. She doubted it very much. But she couldn't say that.

She told Harry that she thought they needed to have a talk. She took him to the Dog and Duck. They sat in a corner. Harry was wary, on his guard, smouldering, awaiting rebuke. They talked for an hour. She asked him about his sailing, about his businesses, about his life. Not a word of rebuke did she utter. Harry entered the pub a frustrated rebel. He left a devoted puppy. Sally was almost disappointed how easy it was.

And all that long, indecisive summer she was looking for somewhere to live. She looked round flats so small that it was an exaggeration to say that she looked round them. She saw a flat, near the river, that had a clearly visible water line seven feet above all the carpets. It wouldn't have been much more obvious if there had been a plaque saying 'High water mark. Flood. 23 November 1978'. One flat smelt of stale cheese, although the fridge was empty. In the bedroom of the next she counted seventeen woodlice. At another, on what was laughingly described in the particulars as 'the patio', a rat gave her a defiant look before running off. The lawyers reported that at last there was progress with the sale of 'The

Larches'. It was what she had longed for, and now it terrified her.

To Sally's great relief her tactics over the litter just about worked, and it became possible to transfer the work of some of her volunteers to other, more positive projects. Restoration work was begun on the Playhouse – and, to prove that all this wasn't some middle-class takeover, to the children's playground in Boswell Road – and there were heavily publicized plans for teams of volunteers to repair the ravages of time at Warwick Road, the football ground, where Potherthwaite Athletic (optimism and self-delusion again) had finished the season seventh in the Evo-Stik League.

The real problem, however, was that the great council meeting at which they were to make their decision on the proposal for a second supermarket wouldn't take place until September, and everything hung on that. Slowly, largely in secret, Sally was planning a protest march, a huge protest march, to show the town's feelings a few days before the vote. If they could persuade the council to reject the plan, they could start on renovating the High Street with the knowledge that it would soon be pedestrianized; they could begin to design their new park, and the whole thing would lift off. A sculpture trail – was that too fantastic? What about Eric Sheepshank, on his rotting narrowboat, with his sculptor's block? He was there on the doorstep, waiting for inspiration. And there was Ben Wardle, that strange boy. She recalled the little column of stones he had built on the waste ground. It had grown, in Sally's memory, into an instinctively graceful tower, a work of naive genius, a harbinger of mature artistic mastery.

Another memory grew as well. Conrad grew. He grew taller. His brown eyes became more and more soulful and sparkly. His dark hair was rich and thick, with not a shade of grey. She didn't believe in love at first sight – that was

194

ridiculous – but she found that she had to believe in desire at first sight. She had planned to show him round the house as slowly as she could, but she hadn't needed to. He had lingered for almost two hours, accepting two cups of coffee. He had told her that his wife was dead. One night she had imagined him naked beside her, and she had willed herself not to desire the magnificent body that she had invented for him. But it had been no use. She ached for him, ached as she had never ached – she was in love, and to her horror she realized that she was in love for the first time, her first stab at an emotional life had never been the real thing. Now she longed for two contradictory happenings – her departure from this hollow home, and her building a home with the man she loved, who would be living in her hollow home. This love was absurd. Adult Sally, Sally the leader, Sally of the Transition movement, knew that. But Sally the woman, Sally the unfinished girl, Sally whose love life was going to have to be very busy if she was ever to equal even the average number of orgasms in this life of hers, felt sick with love and sick with herself.

The summer slid slowly past. There were further instances of graffiti appearing in inaccessible places on the walls of prominent buildings. A leader appeared in the *Chronicle* mocking the police's inability to catch a dyslexic young person, probably a girl, with the physical ability of a monkey. *'This monkey is making a monkey out of our police,'* it stated. Six days later, the words *'ILLIRITATE SCUM'* appeared right on top of the wall of the *Chronicle*'s office. There were also two more very strange burglaries. A painting was stolen from Councillor Stratton's apartment in Potherthwaite Hall, and a large pile of brochures on dealing with poverty disappeared from the Jobcentre. What was strange was that the following week the painting appeared on the wall of the Jobcentre, and the brochures on poverty turned up in the bidet in

Marian Stratton's bathroom. The police also had to inquire into the arrival of a traffic cone on the head of the statue of the first Mayor of Potherthwaite, Councillor Amos Marsden.

August was always the silly season. It was hard not to notice that people talked more of these mysteries than of the progress of Transition. The movement might have had its successes in Totnes and Worthing, in Lewes and Brixton and the Valley of the Lot in France, but it had met its match in Potherthwaite.

Disillusionment swept over Sally. She was no nearer to finding a flat. Without Marigold's support she would have crumbled. But she didn't crumble. She invited Frank Stratton, the town's most influential councillor, to lunch, to try to get him on her side in the battle to come. On the day she felt weak, and was on the point of cancelling when Marigold phoned and praised her to the skies. 'Two women against the town, Sally. Don't let me down.'

If she had cancelled the lunch, would any of the rest of the Potherthwaite story have happened?

She took the councillor to the Weavers' Arms. The pub was quiet, and she chose a dark corner table. Over the meal, she chatted aimlessly and left him to wonder why he was there. After the meal, very gently, as he sipped his large Armagnac, she told him. She didn't mention the protest march, but she did say that she was forming a committee to try to bring the Transition movement to bear on Potherthwaite, and that she would like a councillor on it, and that without falsehood – she wasn't one for buttering people up – he was far and away the best and most caring and most intelligent and most enlightened member of the council and she would like him on her committee. He didn't demur. Why should he? It was probably true.

'I'm sorry, Sally,' he said. 'I like you. You know that. I

admire you. I hope you know that too. But no, I couldn't accept, not before the council's decision. I know what you people want for the town. I understand. So if I go into the council chamber, on the night of the vote, with everyone knowing I am on your committee, how can it be a level playing field for me?'

'Is it a level playing field anyway?'

'Oh, Sally, don't be so suspicious. Why does everyone always think we're corrupt? This is Potherthwaite, not Palermo.'

'Is the supermarket bribing you?'

'No. In no way. They are offering, very generously, and they have no need to, to help fund the new road leading to the supermarket. That's not a bribe. That's sensible business.'

'Not a bribe?'

'No. We are not obligated to concur.'

'That's a good one, "not obligated to concur". It's a bribe.'

'Is your Armagnac not a bribe?'

'Frank! That's ungrateful.'

'I'm sorry. It is. Lovely stuff, incidentally.'

'Would you like another?'

'Thank you. It's not a bribe, Sally, we are free to vote against them.'

'OK, not a bribe, but not a level playing field either.'

'Well, perhaps not. Thank you very much for what you've promised for the football ground, incidentally.'

'Don't change the subject, Frank.'

Sue brought Councillor Stratton his double Armagnac. He gazed at it as if he hadn't touched strong drink for years.

'We're all behind a lot of what you talked about at the church hall, Sally,' said Councillor Stratton, raising his glass to her. 'We want to be your friends and colleagues.'

'But you won't vote against the supermarket?'

'I didn't say that.'

He took a sip of the Armagnac.

'Awesome stuff. I like you, Sally, and I'm going to say this, and mean it. If the vote was to be held at this moment in time, I would say "yes" to the supermarket, but Frank Stratton doesn't do closed minds and, if you all put a fantastic case to us, a case that in our moral responsibility to the town that democratically elected us we cannot resist, then I, and perhaps many others, will change our minds.'

Councillor Stratton's every word had sapped a little more of Sally's hope. The naivety of her suggestion that he join a committee appalled her. She wasn't up to this.

'I like you, as I said.' The words continued remorselessly. 'There isn't a person in this town who doesn't respect you for . . . how you've faced . . . what happened. So, I want you to know that what I'm about to say is not a threat.'

'Good.'

'If a single word about the supermarket's offer to share the cost of the road comes out, you won't stand a chance in this town.'

Her heart sank even further. She wasn't used to dealing with people like this. 'Thanks, Frank,' she said. 'I'm so glad that isn't a threat.'

'Good. We understand each other.'

Only too well.

Frank Stratton stood up. So did Sally.

'I'm just advising you, Sally,' he said, in a kindly voice, as to a naughty but well-meaning child. 'Don't get in out of your depth.'

He held out his hand, utterly unaware that, although she felt more tired than she could ever remember feeling, so tired that she had even thought of telephoning Judith to ask her to come north and give her some sisterly support, he had stiffened every sinew of her resolve in just seven words.

She longed to give his hand a really firm, hard shake, but she wanted Frank Stratton to misunderstand her words.

'Thank you, Frank,' she said. 'No, I won't get in out of my depth.'

'Good,' he said. 'That's good.'

He strode out of the pub, full of Armagnac and self-satisfaction.

'Do you know?' said Sally to Sue. 'I feel like a glass of champagne. Will you join me?'

TWENTY-ONE

Sally's dread

The flat was on the first floor of a concrete block of flats that would have disfigured Vatican Road if Vatican Road had not already consisted entirely of disfigurement. It was a narrow street that ran from Quays Approach between, and parallel to, Quays Wharf and High Street East. Nobody knew why it had been called Vatican Road. Arnold Buss, in 'A Complete History of Potherthwaite', which he regarded as definitive in the sense that there were no others, was no more helpful on the matter than he was on many other subjects. We will have to be satisfied with his words: *'We can only surmise that there was an ardent Catholic on the Conservative administration of Potherthwaite Council when the fields between the High Street and the Quays were built on in the 1870s.'*

The flat was what estate agents call 'compact' and the rest of us call 'tiny'. It had a kitchen/diner and a lounge. Let's be generous and call the lounge 'small' rather than 'tiny'. The walls had two clean bits where the previous occupant's two pictures had hung. The kitchen/diner was really a kitchen in which it was just feasible for two people to eat. There was one bedroom. The double bed was pushed against one wall. If she ever found a lover – unlikely, at the moment – one of them would have to crawl out of the bottom of the bed. There was no room for a bath in the bathroom. The prospectus spoke of *'a view over the canal'*. This was technically accurate. Sally could see the hills, which were over the canal. But in spirit it was an outrageous lie. She could see over the canal, but of the canal itself she got not a glimpse. It was hidden by the backs of the dilapidated old houses that lined Canal Wharf, which hadn't been a wharf since 1883.

Sally dreaded the moment when she would move in to this wretched place, which was simply the only clean accommodation that she could afford in the town. The prospect didn't help to make her feel optimistic. She knew now, beyond all doubt, that the Transition of Potherthwaite was dead in the silted water of the canal if the council didn't throw out the proposal for the second supermarket. Again, she blamed her inexperience in allowing herself to be cornered in this way, but in truth it's hard to see how she could have avoided it.

Every day she woke with dread, the dread of failure, the dread in particular that the protest march would be a flop, the fear that a dream would die. She carried that dread even into number 6 Cadwallader Road, where, as far as she could tell, Ellie, Ali and Oli were all sticking to the diet she created for them, all from independent shops of course, and she acknowledged to herself, rather ruefully, that the process of avoiding the supermarket was time consuming. Ali and Oli both looked detectably slimmer – just – and of course she couldn't very well ask to examine Ellie's vast rolls of fat.

She carried the dread around the streets as she walked and walked and cajoled people to join the march, when at last it came. She feared that she had started on this too soon, that people would be tired of the march by the time it happened, that she was doing too much, that her presence would soon become counterproductive – 'Oh God, here comes that supermarket woman. Get upstairs quick.'

But how could she just sit and worry? How could she behave in such a way that, when she failed, she would wish that she had done more? Some days she was certain she would fail. These were her good days, when she faced the failure bravely. Other days she was hopeful, almost confident. These were her bad days, when she was terrified that she was wrong.

She thought hard about each member of the council, men and women. In some instances she consulted people who knew them, their families and friends, trying to assess whether it would be effective to canvass them directly, or whether they would resent any attempt to change their minds. She felt weak, tired from the underlying stress which never went away as the long late-summer days slid slowly past. Most days she wished that she hadn't started this great venture. But on most days too she remembered Councillor Stratton's seven words, and her anger was fuelled.

At last, the day of completion on her house approached. Now she spent her time at home, packing, sorting, discarding, remembering. Should she keep anything of Barry's? Should she put a few things into storage or should she just ditch everything she didn't need? How much could she get into the little flat? Marigold came round to help. Her mixture of good nature, vitality and curiosity made her the perfect partner, though she might have just used the bin rather than saying, 'I presume you've no further use for three packets of condoms.'

Marigold came round on the day, and the two of them stood in front of the ugly little block of flats as the furniture

202

van arrived. Robson & Willow, Unequalled in the Pother Valley, had sent their smaller van, due to the difficulty of turning from Quays Approach into Vatican Road. Well, that was what Sally told people. The real reason was that she didn't need a larger van because she was bringing so little. Her furniture was far too bulky for her pathetic little flat, and Conrad, having left everything that reminded him of his wife and her death, had been happy to take it while he decided what kind of look he would want in his new house. Perhaps he was as attracted to her as she to him. Maybe he was keeping the furniture in case there came a day when she . . . stop dreaming, Sally.

Sally and Marigold stood just inside the flat, discussed where each object should go, and one or other of them escorted it to its destination. Half of Sally wished that nobody else was there to witness this sad scene. The other half knew that the scene would be even sadder without Marigold's presence and unfailing vitality. Besides, she didn't dare rebuff her second-in-command and best friend. She would need her soon.

Despite the meagre contents of the van, it was hard to find a place for every item in the flat. Everything seemed to grow in size as it passed through the cheap, glaringly white door. Eventually, somehow, a place of sorts was found for everything, the removal men were tipped, the job was done.

'I think I'll go,' said Marigold. 'I expect you'll want to be alone in your new home.'

When Marigold had gone, Sally looked longingly at her bottles of drink, which she had felt a bit ashamed of in front of the removal men, but then she went all English and made herself a cup of tea. She sat in her favourite armchair, one of the two she had brought, and tried to feel that she might be able to make a passable home here in this tiny place, even though the chair didn't really fit in. She felt amazingly exhausted.

Jill had suggested that she join the cul-de-sac gang that evening for the Early Bird supper at the Weavers'. She was glad she'd refused. She was too tired, and, more importantly, she might miss a call from Conrad. 'Feeling a bit lonely, don't know anyone here yet. Thought you might like to help me decide what to put where. You know the house and its little quirks.' As if he would. She hardly knew him. She had to get over these childish fantasies. Had Boedicea fantasized about men who looked wonderful in woad?

Besides, his move would be vast, it might even take two days. It was only mid-afternoon. £445,000 had slipped quietly into her bank account with no fuss. £398,000 had said, 'Hi there, can't stop, sorry. Bye.' The position was even worse than she had thought. Expenses come out of the woodwork when you move.

Well, at least she was free of debt. That was good, wasn't it?

Was it hell. She was terrified. She was a pauper.

She looked round her tiny flat and thought of Conrad sitting on her lawn with a gin and tonic, Conrad asleep in her bedroom, Conrad soaping himself in her bath.

She longed to phone Jill and change her mind about going to the Weavers'. She longed even more to open a bottle of wine.

She did neither.

She felt that there would be no comfort from the television set.

She heard the unmistakable noise of the beginning of an orgasm in the neighbouring flat. Oh God. Thin walls. Communal living. This was hell. She couldn't listen to that. She reached for the remote control to switch the television on, but the orgasm was over before she'd even found it. Ten minutes later she heard someone call at the flat, and she realized why the orgasm had been so brief. The man had been alone.

She heard him shut the door and there was the sound of loud, thoughtless footsteps hurtling down the stairs. She peered out of the window to see what he looked like. There were two men. She didn't know which one was the neighbour, but it didn't matter – they were both too young for her and too unkempt for her and in any case how could she have introduced herself? 'Hello. I'm your new neighbour. I heard you doing things earlier, which, well, let's just say they might be more fun with someone else rather than on your own'? Sally!

And still Conrad didn't ring. Every minute was the same. He didn't ring. She couldn't believe he didn't need to ask her something. 'Sorry to bother you, but where's the stop-cock?' Sally!

The next few days were agony for her. Conrad was in her old home, their eyes had met, she had thought that it had been an electric moment, and now there was nothing. There are not many sights more disturbing than a silent telephone, sitting there, immobile, not flashing, stopping you from speaking to the only person who matters to you. The vicar rang and she wanted to yell at him to get off the line. He carried good news – he would be at the march and would be bringing several people. 'I think the council should know the church isn't sitting on the fence on this one.' 'Excellent. That's so kind of you, Vicar, and so kind to let me know as well.' 'I think Linda Oughtibridge may have persuaded several of her knitting circle.' 'Wonderful, Vicar. Good old Linda.' 'Absolutely. No oil painting, sadly, but heart of gold.' And then when at last she could put the phone down, there was no red light to say there was a message. Why didn't he ring? Why should he ring? Yes, it had seemed like a rather significant glance between them as she'd shown him the bedroom, but had it been? Calm down. And then the phone did ring. She let it ring six times so as not to seem too eager. 'Hello!' I believe you have recently moved home. Our double glazing—' She banged the phone down. How did they know? She knew all about the world of phone tapping and secret spying. Were there any limits to it? Did President Obama know that she had moved home?

She shouldn't have banged the phone down. The man who'd phoned might know who she was, ring all his friends. 'You know that woman who's organizing the march. Snob. Only banged the bloody phone down on me. Tell people not to touch her with a bargepole.'

There were moments when she almost rang Conrad. She even began dialling once, but rang off hurriedly when she only had one more number to dial. How silly was that? There were so many things that she could so easily have said. 'I was just hoping that you weren't having any problems.' 'Just a courtesy call to see how you're settling in.' 'I just wondered if there were any tradesmen's details I could help you with.' But she knew why she'd rung off. She was frightened that she would discover immediately that he hadn't been thinking of her at all. 'Sorry, who are you? Oh, the lady who lived here. No, I've no problems, but thank you so much for ringing. Goodbye.'

She forced herself to be more adult, and then she realized that her worry about Conrad was the least of three worries, and worrying about him was her way of avoiding worrying about the other two – worrying about what the council would decide, and perhaps, sadly, worrying even more about how she was going to live on £47,000 with no job, for our society is structured in such a way that worrying about not having money is the greatest worry of all. How would she ever have anything left over for helping Sam and Beth when the inevitable crisis came? Bloody Barry.

And then he rang.

'Sally Mottram?'

She recognized his voice immediately.

The boiler's burst. I love you madly. Where do you keep that thing you unblock the sink with? The air was full of possible remarks before she'd even said yes, she was Sally Mottram.

'I wondered if you'd like to come out to dinner with me one night?'

TWENTY-TWO

Dinner for two

He picked her up in his bright red Audi.

'I thought we'd go out of town,' he said. 'I'm sure the town is crawling with your friends, and we don't want to be interrupted, do we?'

It was one of those infuriating English days when it rains until half past six and suddenly turns into a beautiful evening, but the air is too cold and the seats in the beer gardens are too wet to sit on, and there's no use for all the amazing beauty of the scene except to admire it. But how lovely it was to sit in an expensive car and get driven by an expert and considerate driver. The road twisted up on to the moors and the sudden sunshine took away all the bleakness. There was no wind. The monster windmills were thwarted. Bored sheep turned to look at the car. Sally noticed how Conrad slowed down when he was passing sheep that were close to the road. Aware of animals. Not a show-off. Promising.

He talked enough but not too much, and he talked about the scenes through which they were passing. No questions yet. No answers either. Sally's nerves were subsiding.

And yet . . . and yet . . . this was a scene she had imagined so much, longed for with such absurd intensity. Now, when it was happening, the intensity had gone. It was as if she was outside the scene, watching herself being driven over the rough inchoate summit of the moor and down towards another steep, spectacular valley, the first lights of the evening sparkling in some other town, a town that was eight miles from Potherthwaite but might just as well have been separated from it by the full range of the Himalayas.

Halfway down the hill, they came to a pub, the Shoulder of Mutton. It was a great stone place, its modest farmhouse heart buried among extensions and conservatories and annexes. The car park was the size of a cricket ground and it was almost full. More than half the cars were more expensive than Conrad Eltington's Audi.

'Not our kind of place, perhaps, but I'm told it's good,' said Conrad.

Sally noted his use of 'our' with a subdued thrill, but she was conscious that she still wasn't responding as if this was actually happening.

This was a dining pub. Nobody would come here just for a drink. It was buzzing with chatter, but the acoustics were so good that the buzz was muted, reassuring. The dining areas – there was nothing defined enough to be called a restaurant – were so well designed, the tables so placed, the alcoves so plentiful and spacious, the dividing walls between the alcoves so high, that every corner felt spacious and private.

The menu was vast.

'Ominously large menu,' said Conrad, 'but friends whose taste I trust have praised it.'

At least it wasn't one of those places that give the lady a menu with no prices on it. The prices were there, and they were high. The recession had passed the Shoulder of Mutton by.

Sally didn't try anything sophisticated or clever in her choice of aperitif. Good old G and T, ice and a slice.

'I'll wait for the wine,' said Conrad to the Lithuanian waitress. 'I'm driving.'

A first date is rarely without tension, but Sally had felt a sense of sudden relaxation, almost of exhilaration, the moment she had entered the pub. As she studied the menu, desperately trying not to give way under its weight of choices, she realized why. There was probably not a single person from Potherthwaite here. It was as if the Pother Valley was a secret place, unknown to the rest of the world. She needn't worry about offending any of these people. She needn't worry about what any of them would be doing next Saturday, the day of the march. She had gone abroad for the evening.

Yet she was not entirely free from tension. She was aware that she was feeling tense only because she was taking so many factors into consideration in making her choice. Not too cheap, as if afraid to spend his money. Not too expensive, as if she was greedy and grasping. No garlic (over-optimism?). Not such a large meal that she couldn't finish it. Not so small a meal that he'd think she didn't like food. She wanted to order the sort of meal that she thought that a man like him would want a woman like her to choose.

In the end, after weighing things up carefully, she chose, on sudden impulse, things she hadn't even considered. Later she couldn't remember what she had eaten.

Now that the ordering was over he leant across, looked her in the face, and smiled. He had a really nice smile. His eyes were even more brown than she had remembered, but his black hair was streaked with shades of grey, which she hadn't remembered. His nose was a little wide, and his mouth was businesslike.

'I've heard a bit of what you're doing,' he said. 'It seems to be the talk of the town.'

'Oh golly, what a responsibility,' she said. She would have

taken back the 'golly' if she could. It was a word she didn't think she had ever used before.

'Exactly. That's why I thought it would be nice for you to be taken out of Potherthwaite tonight.'

The evening was heavy with the faint sound of boxes being ticked.

The meal was surprisingly good. Conrad's contacts had been right. Their conversation was as smooth as the purring of the engine of his well-maintained Audi. He asked her about the march, and about the support that she might expect to receive.

'I can recruit a few people,' he said, with a smile. 'Three-line whip.'

This led naturally to her asking him what he did. He was an engineer in the water industry, a consultant in flood control.

'Very boring,' he said.

'To you, or to me? Or both?'

'Oh, to you. I love it, but I wouldn't expect you to be interested.'

'Because I'm a woman?'

'No, of course not. Because all people in general want from the water industry is water, enough of it and not too much.'

'Maybe I'm interested in a wide range of things.'

Their eyes met properly for the first time. Was he wondering if this remark carried sexual connotations? Had she intended it to carry sexual connotations? She wasn't sure herself.

IIer next remark rang out with first-date flatness.

'Is it your job that's brought you up north?'

It was. He'd been offered a better job, with better pay. He was very experienced in flood control.

She discovered that it was cancer that had taken his wife, four years ago. He was ready at last to build new life.

211

There are many moments in our lives when it is lucky, whatever we may think and however frustrating it may be, that we cannot see into other people's hearts and minds. It's even luckier that they can't see into ours. As Sally said her 'Oh, I'm so sorry' and her 'How sad!', her sympathy and distress at this news, real though they were, were being swamped by the joy of knowing how astonishingly available he was.

She tried to make her 'And do you have children?' seem like an innocent piece of fact-finding rather than a coded version of 'Do you have two monstrous, possessive, spoilt, grasping daughters who would make my life hell if we ever happened to marry?'

'No children, sadly. Magda had . . . internal problems.'

She hid her thoughts on that one too.

But, inevitably, the main subject of discussion was the house. Her house, now his. Why had he chosen it?

He said that it seemed a friendly house.

She thought of saying, but didn't, that she had once thought so too.

He said that it was the right size.

She thought of asking, but didn't, for what was it the right size? For a family with two children?

He heard the question that she hadn't asked, and replied to it without making it obvious. His brother had three small children. He needed something big enough for their visits.

He said that it had been reasonably priced.

She thought of commenting, but didn't, that this was not something she was overjoyed to hear.

He realized that perhaps he had not been entirely tactful, and said that he hadn't meant that it had been cheap. He had meant that it had been realistically priced.

He asked her questions about her childhood.

She told him that she had been the younger of two

212

daughters. Her father had been a GP and had died of a pulmonary embolism at the age of sixty-eight. Her mother had died in a plane crash at the age of seventy. She told him that she got on well with her sister in Devon but they weren't any closer socially than they were geographically, and that she was sad that her son and daughter also lived so far away, in Barnet and New Zealand. She had the self-awareness and the wit to realize, as she told him these facts, and in the way in which she was telling them, that she might as well have said, 'I too, Conrad, have remarkably little baggage.'

He drove her back over the dark, dark moors. Frozen by the dazzle of his headlights, the sheep were painted by Hockney. There were no other cars on this road. Separated by the cruel hills, Potherthwaite and the Shoulder of Mutton were on different planets.

A return journey after a first date is unlikely to be without a degree of uncertainty in the twenty-first century and particularly for someone who has not really lived in the twenty-first century yet. Will he ask me in? If he does, should I go in? Will I go in, which is a very different question? Will he kiss me on the cheek? Will he kiss me on the mouth? Will he kiss me on and in the mouth? Will he suggest another date? If he does, should I agree straight away? Will I agree straight away, which is a very different question? And why does it all depend on what he does, why am I not more proactive? Am I not really a modern woman at all?

Sally felt a degree of tension about these matters, and in this instance it was deepened by the fact of their dropping down into the Pother Valley, and into Potherthwaite, where every drawn curtain begged the question, will the people behind that curtain support me on the march?

Conrad drove his Audi smoothly down the almost deserted High Street West, through the almost deserted Market Place, down the even more deserted High Street East. Would all this ever be pedestrianized? He turned right into Quays Approach. Would the canal ever be cleared? He turned right again into Vatican Road. Sally's block of flats was not pretty, and the meanness of her new surroundings did shame her that night.

He got out of the car, came round to the passenger side, opened the door for her. She had waited for a moment to see if he was going to. To have pre-empted a polite gesture would have been a behavioural error.

He kissed her on both cheeks.

He said, 'We must do this again soon.'

Only then did he kiss her on the lips.

He kept his mouth closed and his tongue safely locked up.

She kept her mouth closed and her tongue safely locked up.

She walked to the door of the flats, unlocked them, turned to wave.

The Audi was already halfway down the road.

As she opened the door to her flat, in the unlovely hall, Sally wondered if it was healthy that such social and indeed sexual minutiae should be under examination by a forty-seven-year-old woman who might soon be a leader of men.

TWENTY-THREE

The march

Sally had spent the few days since her dinner with Conrad in a state of high anxiety. She had been to the doctor for sleeping pills and the Pother Health Centre for natural aids to relaxation. Rattling with pills, and stuffed with herbs, she had tottered through the days to the big event. She had longed for the day to come, and now it had, and of course she wished that it hadn't. She dreaded it.

But what disturbed her more than anything, more even than taking by the scruff of its neck the town in which she had lived as a quiet, rather shy, not very brave solicitor's wife for twenty-four years, and leading it in a campaign against that symbol of power in modern Britain, the supermarket, was the fact that Conrad hadn't phoned to ask her to dinner again.

She opened the curtains, and felt the same shock that she felt every morning. No longer did she look out over a well-tended garden, with finches and tits and magpies flying about with every appearance of joy. All she could see was the unimpressive mixture of offices and small shops on the northern side of Vatican Road. To the rear, over the badly maintained roofs of outhouses, were some scruffy back gardens, separated by dilapidated fencing from equally scruffy gardens at the backs of the houses on the neglected Quays. There was no way of smelling the weather, and she felt huge dismay at the thought that she might spend the rest of her life here. She shook her head several times, as if she believed that this negative attitude would drop out on to the threadbare carpet. She pulled herself together. She thought about the appalling conditions in which billions eked out an existence in much of the world. It didn't work. Now she felt full of guilt as well as dismay.

She went out – she had to feel the air. She took a brisk walk to the end of the road, turned right along Quays Approach, right again along the Quays, right yet again along a narrow ginnel that led back to Vatican Road, and a final right turn to her hateful block of flats.

She felt a little better after her walk. In fact, she took the walk twice more, before she forced herself to go back into her flat. It was a perfect morning. Perfect, that is, for a march. It was dry, a dry day in early September. There was very little sun, not enough to persuade anyone to lie half-naked on their lawn. There was the faintest of breezes, only just enough to make an occasional sail turn lazily on the giant windmills at the head of the valley.

The marchers were to gather in the park at half past one, ready to march at two. Marigold called round just after eleven, dressed entirely in green except for her boots. She laid out an attractive little lunch, also mainly green. 'Environmentally friendly,' she said excitedly, 'and my wearing only green is a statement of an ideal too.'

She had brought a bottle of vintage champagne, 'the last bottle from the Boyce-Willoughby family's wedding present' and they drank it together in that sad little room. The moment it was finished, the pit in Sally's stomach returned.

It was barely twelve when they finished their lunch and champagne. When Marigold suggested setting off to soak up the atmosphere, Sally said, 'What atmosphere?'

'Here we go, side by side, two true friends, two damsels in distress,' said Marigold.

In an impulse of affection Sally linked arms with Marigold as they marched to the end of the horrid road.

They turned left into Quays Approach and left again into High Street East. The traffic was crawling. The pollution was almost visible. In a few of the shops that weren't yet boarded up, the two women were puzzled to see staff busying themselves among the window displays.

They crossed the Market Place. No markets were held here any more. From the northern side of the square a road led up through the suburbs to the railway station.

Marigold indicated a few people who were moving towards the road.

'Quite a few people,' she said.

'Aren't they going to the station?' Sally asked.

'They're coming on the march, you idiot,' said Marigold. 'Sally, it's going to be huge.' She waved at some girls. 'Hello, girls,' she called out excitedly. 'Wave,' she told Sally.

Sally waved very uncertainly. The girls cheered.

'You see,' said Marigold.

Sally was beginning to see. And, ahead of her, she saw something that made her eyes widen in astonishment and set her at last into believing that something special might happen this day. Ali and Oli were struggling painfully up the road in front of them, Ali still just over eighteen stone, Oli twenty, which meant, since they were both four foot eleven, that they were still pretty fat. When Sally called out to them, they turned and gave her a thumbs-up and broad smiles.

'Ellie insisted we came,' said Ali, but it was exactly

217

twelve-thirty, and at that moment, right on cue, as planned, the Rackstraw and Potherthwaite Band struck up, rolling back the years in the steep, narrow valley, and causing old people to stop, and listen, and smile. Ali had to repeat herself. 'She, like, said she wouldn't never speak to us again if we didn't come and support you. She loves you,' she shouted.

There were a good few people coming out of the side streets and joining them, and there was over an hour still to go. These were mainly the older people, who remembered the little grocery stores of yore, when the smell of ground coffee wafted over the severe little town.

Baggit Park was to the left of the railway station, and the bandstand was at the top of the park, where the ground began to rise towards Baggit Moor. Sally stood and listened. For years she had disliked brass bands, but such was Barry's hatred of them that he had eventually driven her into the arms of admiration. It was only now that he was gone that she realized this. The band were playing for their lives, looking down towards the town as they did so. The seats around the bandstand were almost full, and a few people were standing and listening. 'Cherry Ripe' was followed by 'The Great Gate of Kiev'. Sally saw Jenny Hendrie, mother of the great soprano Arabella Kate Hendrie, standing smiling by this modest bandstand, and suddenly she realized that she was smiling at her husband. Arabella Kate's father Gordon was actually playing the euphonium in the band. That made her feel gloriously sentimental, and that was the moment that she cast off all doubt about the march.

Next she saw Sophie Partingon, the same Sophie who had defaced the church noticeboard, marching with friends and a large banner which stated *'Prostitutes Against A Second Supermarket'*.

The band swung into gentle jazz mode with 'Lazy Days', the crowd grew, it was a carnival. There was no food or drink, and nobody needed any. The air was their food, the music was their drink. The Revd Dominic Otley arrived, followed by a small group of his friends and worshippers, all smiling broadly. The Revd Otley began to jig, almost but not quite in time to 'Zadok the Priest', in the overenthusiastic way parsons do to show they're men of fun as well as God. He had no sense of rhythm whatsoever. The music was never the best part of a Revd Otley service. But today, in the park, his genial and inelegant fooling was charming rather than irritating.

Now another large banner was carried into the park. It stated 'Muslims Against Supermarkets'. The Muslim children were jumping up and down with excitement. 'Shenandoah' seemed wonderfully inappropriate.

Sally was delighted to see Jill and Harry, though she was a bit alarmed at the amount of time they were spending with each other. She wandered over to them and Harry said, 'We're so cross with Olive and Arnold. They're missing so much.'

A few police officers stood around, smiling. None smiled as much as Inspector Pellet. Getting on the side of the crowd had been an important part of those seminars on the Isle of Wight.

The sight of Inspector Pellet was a vivid reminder, to Sally, of the day that Barry hanged himself. To think of it here, now, at this lovely moment, was . . . barely disturbing at all. That was the past. She was looking to the future now.

A group of – were they yobbos, or were they villains, or were they just naughty boys? – sidled illegally into the park on their bicycles, looked at the scene, heard the music, laughed at its simplicity, but had enough sense to judge the mood of the town, did a few lukewarm wheelies, pretended that was all they had come to do, and rode off with front wheels in the air. Inspector Pellet watched, smiled, and congratulated himself on his laid-back approach to crowd control.

Sally saw more people whose presence gave her pleasure. Terence and Felicity Porchester, still stranded on their narrowboat. In two years, if things worked according to plan, they might be able to chug home.

Ben Wardle, that strange boy, arrived with his parents. A few minutes later, his friend Tricksy arrived, and he abandoned his parents. A few minutes after that he abandoned Tricksy too, went over to a large cage, and stared at it. Inside the cage there were a few moth-eaten marmots. After a few more minutes he took a piece of stiff paper from his pocket and began to draw the moth-eaten marmots.

There was a noticeable absence of professional people, but Marigold explained that the posh type wouldn't stand in a park listening to a brass band.

And where was Conrad? She longed to confide in Marigold about Conrad.

At two o'clock, with perfect timing, the band moved off, playing 'The Departure of the Queen of Sheba'. Behind the band went Sally and Marigold, side by side. More people were joining now that the march had actually started, but Sally felt that these latecomers had missed one of the best bits and was cross with Conrad for not being there.

They marched not through Georgia but along the dreary, unprepossessing Warwick Road, which curled round to reach the top of High Street West by the roundabout off which the allotments began. On the way they passed a little café, Beryl's Parlour, and Sally was amazed to see Linda Oughtibridge emerge from Beryl's Parlour with nine women almost as square as she was. They were, in geometric contradiction of their appearance, her knitting circle.

A few people in the allotments, mainly looking like lovable eccentrics, laid down their trowels and joined the march.

There were quite a few banners now, with mainly uninspired messages like *'No to the Second Supermarket'*.

The band's eclecticism continued. They were joyfully into 'Black-Eyed Susan' as they passed the end of Cadwallader Road. Sally thought not of Black-Eyed Susan but of Ellie whose eyes were almost completely hidden by rolls of fat. By the time they reached the cul-de-sac they were playing 'The Ash Grove' and Sally wondered if Arnold and Olive were peering out of the window to see what they were missing. And then, to the accompaniment of 'Lo! He comes with Clouds Descending', there came Conrad, not with clouds descending but with seven colleagues from flood control.

He wasn't quite as tall as she had thought, now that she saw him in full daylight. And he was slightly lined. Maybe he was a little older than she'd thought. Early fifties, perhaps. But all the more attractive for that. He waved, but didn't attempt to join the front of the march. He led his gang into the main body of the protest most tactfully, slid them in as it were.

People joined at every street corner. There was Kate Kavanagh from the Kosy Korner Kafé. Here was Jade Hunningbrooke, manageress of 'Hair Today, Gone Tomorrow'. Maurice Sibley, owner of the struggling wet fish shop, emerged from his thinly stocked premises carrying a large square placard with a brilliantly painted, slightly surreal fish and the words *'The Potherthwaite Aquarium. Prop M. Sibley'*. The placard was heavily ringed with black.

'Brill,' said Marigold.

'Bream, I think,' said Sally

'What?'

'The fish. Black bream, I think.'

'No, I meant, it's brill. The idea. Clever you.'

'It's not me. It's not my idea.'

'Well, who the hell's is it?'

Now Sally realized an extraordinary thing. All the independent shops in the High Street had their windows covered in black, and the manager or owner of every shop came out and joined the march, carrying a large banner with the name of their shop, and all the banners had slightly surreal representations of some aspect of their stock, and all were ringed with heavy black.

It had been done by some self-important clever clogs, and it had been done without even telling her, let alone consulting her. It was outrageous.

No, it was brilliant, stunning. It just might make all the difference. It wasn't outrageous at all. She had never called herself a leader, except in her thoughts. There was no power structure, she had no office or rank, so there was no way anybody had to consult her. Somebody had spent his or her time on this fantastic plan, in the aid of her cause. How could she be upset? And the paintings were bordering on genius.

As they passed the turning to the Dog and Duck, they were joined by those three faithful customers, Mick Webster from the travel agency 'Unravel Your Travel', that randy little tosser Bill Etching (but all were welcome on the march, however unspeakable), and David Fenton, now only the second-most attractive man in Potherthwaite, since the arrival of Conrad Eltington.

Sally was very surprised to see Matt Winkle, the manager of the supermarket, but, as he explained later, it was logical to oppose the introduction of a rival, and a rival with a more central site. She thought it unnecessarily combative of his unsmiling wife Nicola to watch the parade from the doorway of the deli, carrying a laden 'Potherthwaite Deli' shopping bag. Sally saw a woman approach Matt aggressively, and in the ten seconds of silence as the band finished one number and wound themselves up for the next, the indignant words 'went sodding bad before they sodding ripened' floated down High Street West. Nicola's marble face almost cracked into a smile.

Now Sally saw, to her pleasure, a few faces from Oxford Road, including the Hammonds, who, amazingly, were not in Tenerife, and Peter and Myfanwy Sparling with an excited if slightly overwhelmed Kenneth. Dr Ian Mallet was there too, unaccompanied by his wife due to her fear of crowds.

The marchers began to stream into the Market Place, still headed by the brass band, who were now into the 'The Arrival of the Queen of Sheba' some fifty-five minutes after her departure. There was already quite a crowd waiting, and more people were streaming in up High Street East. There were also, in the crowd, to Sally's knowledge, at least five councillors. That was promising, and on a Saturday too.

The crowd stood facing the Town Hall, which occupied more than half of the southern side of the square. It was an exuberant early Victorian affair, a fantasy of power in stone, heavy with gables and towers and turrets, mocked for its excesses and inconsistencies by students of architecture, and looking badly in need of maintenance.

Wide steps led up to the great doors with their peeling paint. Sally climbed as far as the fifth step, and turned to look down at the crowd. What a sight it was. Cars had been banned, to avoid trouble and damage, and every corner of the square was jammed with people. At the front of the great crowd stood all the independent shopkeepers, their black-lined placards resting on the ground in front of them like an impassable line of shields. Favoured customers of Lloyds and Barclays banks, warmly welcomed from one o'clock (the moment when mere mortals were less warmly excluded), were sipping champagne as they watched events from the double-glazed windows of the upper storeys. There hadn't been a crowd like this in Potherthwaite since VE Day, and perhaps not even then. And it was she who had done all this.

Above her, a few brave people appeared on the balcony, including the Leader of the Council, Councillor Stratton, three Heads of Departments, and His Honour the Mayor, who this year happened to be the popular window cleaner, Sid Haynes.

Sally was handed a loudhailer. An eerie silence fell. There was not a sound in the packed square.

To her amazement, she felt no nerves. The size of the crowd, and their marvellous discipline, gave her confidence.

'Thank you so much for coming,' she said. 'I am astounded and encouraged by your numbers, and by your conduct. Every one of us is here today to show our elected council-lors what we feel about the issue that they will be debating next week. We beg you, for the sake of our town, to turn down the proposal for a second supermarket on the waste ground next to the Potherthwaite Deli. I can see the deli's placard now, with a stunning, slightly surreal pork-and-apple pie upon it. I could eat that right now.'

Everyone could hear the confidence and passion in Sally's words. Everyone could see the pride she had in her adopted town. Only Sally knew that, on another level of conscious-ness, every word was also spoken to impress Conrad.

'You know the rest of what we ask. We ask for the planned new road to go straight on west instead of turning to service the supermarket. It would therefore become what we so sorely lack, a bypass, so that High Street East and High Street West can become pedestrianized, with motorized access to the Market Place only via its northern side. We could have asked for the Market Place to be pedestrianized in its entirety, but we are not unreasonable people. We are not asking for the moon, and we do not ask for all this to be done at once in these cash-strapped times. Nor have we any gripes with our existing supermarket. Supermarkets have their place, provided there are not too many of them. The one condition on which we will fight, is that the waste ground, that dreadful eyesore, becomes a small park in the centre of town. What an asset that could be.

'We for our part undertake to work our socks off to reverse the decline of this once great manufacturing town. We have all sorts of plans and we will work night and day to achieve them. One thought is a Sculpture Trail. Britain is waking up to the importance, and the financial importance at that, of the arts. Let Potherthwaite not be left behind. We also undertake to clean out the whole length of the Potherthwaite Arm of the canal through voluntary work, so that the Quays can be restored to their former glory. I personally would like to see the allotments extended and run as a cooperative, so that more and more of us can enjoy local fruit and vegetables. In one stroke we would reduce our carbon footprints and eat things that taste of something.

'I will argue no longer. The size of the crowd here today is the only argument we need. The people on the balcony have paid us the compliment of listening. Ladies and gentlemen of Potherthwaite, please pay them that compliment too.'

There was loud applause and cheering. Sally tried to spot Conrad among the throng, but couldn't. How could he not be impressed, though?

Now that she had finished speaking, Sally felt exhausted. The blood drained from her face. Marigold noticed, and hurried forward to support her and help her back down the steps. On her other side Jill came forward, and the two women held their leader firm.

The Mayor was handed a loudhailer, and he addressed the crowd.

'Bloody hell,' he said. 'This is a day. Haven't had a crowd like this since VE Day. I wasn't here then, mind. When I took job on I was told I was mainly ceremonial. So I'll leave Councillor Stratton to respond. Councillor Stratton.'

He passed the loudhailer on.

'I admit it. That were a grand speech. Persuasive,' said Councillor Stratton. 'I'm only one man on the council. I can make no promises on behalf of my fellow councillors. I have no idea how we'll vote. How could I have? But I do make this promise. We will consider what we have seen and heard today very carefully. You elected us. We won't forget that on Monday evening. We will consider your views, your strong views, with great respect. Thank you.'

Sally applauded loudly and gave a signal to the people around her to do the same. The last thing she wanted was for Councillor Stratton to feel slighted.

Suddenly the vicar jumped on to the steps. The communal groan of that great crowd was silent, but Sally felt it distinctly. Only last Sunday his sermon had come in at eighteen minutes and seventeen seconds. No one had got near enough to it to be paid out. It had been a rollover.

But his audience underestimated their spiritual leader on this occasion.

'I'll tell you why I'm here today,' he said. 'Because I want our town to have a human face.'

When they realized that he had finished, that his message had been of wonderful simplicity and brevity, the crowd cheered heartily. Never perhaps, in the history of the town, had a man been so cheered for shutting up.

And now, to everyone's astonishment, a young girl, aged about fifteen, slim as a mermaid, with scarlet streaks in her hair, rushed forward on to the steps and grabbed the loudhailer from the astonished clergyman.

'You won't know me,' she cried out in a surprisingly

226

strong voice, 'but you'll know my graffitis. I'm Lucy Basridge and I'm young and silly and dyslexic, but I'm not thick. So please hear me out.'

Sally buried her head in her hands, realized that this was not the thing to do, and looked up bravely. A murmuring of astonishment had been rumbling through the great crowd. Lucy Basridge waited calmly till it subsided. Now you could have heard a pigeon landing on the Town Hall.

'My life in this town is ahead of me. Don't take my town away from me. I love this town, me, and I love the little shops and the folk that run them and we all have a little natter, don't we, we do, and it's lovely, and that'll all get squeezed out if we have a great big supermarket bang in the middle, and they say it'll create jobs and it will but they don't say it'll destroy jobs too and of course it will. I'll make you a promise. If you vote to throw supermarket plan out I'll clean up all me graffitis. I will, I promise. Thank you for listening.'

There was a moment of utter silence, then the crowd burst into applause.

The march moved away, down High Street East. A small man with greasy hair and a large paunch hurried up to Sally and said, in a very cockney voice, 'That was impressive.'

'Thank you,' she said.

'That was well impressive.'

'Well, thank you very much.'

'I was well impressed.'

'Good. That's great.'

'I'm going to report back, and I'm going to tell the boss straight out, "Boss, I was impressed."'

He seemed to assume that Sally knew who his boss was, and she felt curiously unable to ask.

'And when I tell the boss I was impressed, I can tell you, lady, he'll be—'

'Impressed?'

'Got it in one. You have got it in one, lady. You have hit the nail well and truly on the bonce.'

He held out his hand. She shook it. His handshake was wet and clammy. He moved off so suddenly that she had no chance to say anything more. She hated wet, clammy handshakes. She wiped her hand surreptitiously on the back of her trousers, and with the gesture she dismissed all thoughts of this man.

The band led the march into Quays Approach. The plan was for a short final burst from the band, and then an orderly dispersal.

Sally didn't want to miss all that, but she was very shaky now, she was utterly exhausted, and the handshake had made her all the more conscious that her clothes were sweaty and unpleasant. She felt a huge need for a full change and a shower. By the time she came out, most of the crowds had disappeared. It didn't matter. Their spirit still lingered in the deserted streets, her triumph still warmed her blood. If only she could see Conrad. If only she hadn't had to break away. He might have been looking for her, to show off his friendship with her to his colleagues from the water industry.

She phoned Marigold on her mobile, and explained why she'd had to slip off. Marigold told her that she was in the Potherthwaite Arms.

Sally had never been in the Potherthwaite Arms, which had a reputation as being one of the town's less salubrious pubs. That early evening she hesitated outside, she felt suddenly shy, she hardly had the energy left to open the door.

Marigold's appearance in the pub had clearly been a bit of a sensation. She was sitting on a bar stool with her legs crossed as if she had been designed for just such a pose. She was surrounded by a gaggle of excited men. It was clear immediately that the vicar, sitting in a corner with Matt Winkle, couldn't take his eyes off the fleshy splendour of those crossed thighs as she perched on her bar stool in the simple little bar. Matt Winkle couldn't take his eyes off them either, but that was more to be expected in a supermarket manager than in a vicar.

Marigold gestured for Sally to join her at the bar, but she couldn't. That was Marigold's place, not hers. The vicar saw her hesitation and his chance. He hurried over, and bought Sally a glass of white wine, while also buying two pints of bitter and a large whisky chaser. Sally was surprised to find that the whisky chaser was for himself and not for Matt. Having been bought her drink, she felt obliged to join them, though they weren't highest on her list of people she'd like to spend the next hour with.

Warmed as she still was by the glory of the march, she wished she could just sit with a silly smile on her face, and perhaps accept a few compliments gracefully. She wanted to sit on a bar stool beside Marigold and perhaps be gloriously insalubrious for the rest of the evening. Instead she was sitting in a far corner with a vicar who was depressed because he couldn't hold a crowd the way she could and a supermarket manager who was still angry because his day had been spoilt by a very public verbal attack on the quality of his pears.

She decided to finish her drink rapidly, make her excuses, and leave the two men to their sorrows. But at that moment, Matt tossed back the remains of his drink with a grimace, stood up, said, 'I don't want Nicola attacking me as well,' and strode out of the pub. Not for the first time Sally regretted her good manners. There was no way she could abandon the vicar to solitude.

'Same again, Dominic?' she asked.

'Oh yes, please. Thank you.'

The vicar apologized when he saw that she'd bought him another large chaser.

'Didn't mean the chaser as well,' he said, but he poured it into the remains of his previous chaser just the same.

'I don't blame people for not coming to my services,' said the Revd Dominic Otley. 'I wouldn't come to my services if I was a member of my congregation. And I'll tell you why. I'm not inspiring. And I'll tell you why I'm not inspiring. It's because . . .'

But Sally didn't yet find out why the vicar wasn't inspiring. That treat would come much later.

She was rescued by Marigold.

'I forgot,' she called out. 'Ben Wardle was looking for you. He said he'd be up the allotments. He left his mobile number. He said it was important.'

She apologized to the vicar and said that she would have to go.

'Ben's sensitive,' she explained.

She saw his reply in his eyes. And I'm not? But he didn't say it. He said, 'Of course. He's young. He needs you.' She saw in his moist, milky eyes the words, And so do I, but he didn't utter them. She downed the rest of her wine in one gulp, and wished she hadn't.

The Revd Dominic Otley stood up. He swayed slightly, like a tower block in a gale.

'Congratulations for today, Sally,' he said sadly. 'A triumph.'

Then he kissed her on both cheeks.

The cool air of the street seemed lovely after the hot breath of the vicar's maudlin regrets.

Sally switched her mobile on, phoned Ben Wardle, and arranged to meet him in the Market Place. It was empty now, except for the people on that afternoon's voluntary clean-up roster, who were busy removing the detritus of the crowd.

'You've drawn the short straw,' she called out over the cobbles.

'A privilege, Mrs Mottram,' called back Linda Oughtibridge with a blush.

Praise from Linda Oughtibridge. Did life get any better than that? Her words fanned new life into the smouldering embers of Sally's joy.

She sat down on one of the benches, and looked around her. The great emptiness of the square spoke vividly of how full it had been so recently. The deserted balcony rang with fine words by the very fact of its silence.

Ben came running, stopped when he saw her, and walked slowly towards the bench where she was sitting. He looked down on her solemnly. He was embarrassed.

'I'm really sorry,' he said.

'Sorry?' she said. 'What are you sorry for?'

'For not telling you.'

'For not telling me what?'

'Oh, sorry, don't you know?'

'I don't know what it is I'm supposed not to know so how can I know whether I know it or not?'

Ben considered this.

'That's very true, actually,' he said. 'The placards.'

'The placards? What placards?'

'The ones I did. For the shops. With the little paintings and the black edging. I didn't know if you'd like them, so I just . . . did them.'

'You did those placards?'

'Yes. Sorry.'

'All of them?'

'Yes. Sorry.

'And did you do the paintings? The bream. The pork-and-apple pie. Those dancing greetings cards from "Send It With Kisses".'

231

'Yes. Sorry.'

'All of them?'

'Yes. Sorry.'

'You're not at all sorry actually, are you?'

'No. Sorry.'

Ben grinned. She had never seen him smile before. His smile was a window with a view into a secret and wonderful world.

'Nor am I. They were brilliant, Ben. Brilliant.'

'I know,' said Ben calmly.

'So why didn't you tell me you were doing them?'

'I didn't know if *you'd* know they were brilliant. You can't know, with art.'

Sally stood up, shook Ben's hand, and kissed him on both cheeks.

He looked very embarrassed. He struggled to find words. 'Cool,' he said.

Well, it would be unfair to expect you to be original with words as well as paint, thought Sally.

Ben walked away. He was getting tall. He was ceasing to be a child before her very eyes.

He turned round. He was smiling. He was excited, and in his excitement he became a child again.

'I'm well pleased you knew it was a bream,' he said.

'A black bream.'

'Cool.' He twisted his face into an expression of utter scorn. 'Dad thought it was a pollock.'

He walked away. The clear-up was finished, and when Ben had disappeared up High Street West, Sally had the whole scene of her triumph to herself.

She walked slowly across to the Town Hall, walked up to the fifth step, turned round, and looked across at the great crowd that was no longer there.

Slowly, very slowly, the faces and the placards faded.

Slowly, very slowly, now that there was not a single fan to revive them, the embers inside her faded.

Her sense of triumph had been pathetic. It had been sheer vanity. She had achieved nothing at all unless they won the vote.

The agony was going to go on. And on. And on.

Sally raised her shoulders, stiffened her back, and marched home alone.

TWENTY-FOUR

The waiting

The Weavers' Arms was fairly empty on a Monday, but even so, the new young waiter was so struck with nerves and stress that he spilt red wine all down Harry's trousers.

'It was the waiting that was the worst,' Sally said afterwards. 'Mind you, it was his first day at the pub.' It's an old joke, but under the circumstances it was irresistible.

Sally had found herself unable to face attending the diminutive public gallery in the council chamber to listen to the debate.

Marigold had decided to go.

'You're braver than me,' Sally told her.

'I'm not. You care more than me.'

'You care too.'

'I do. I care very much. But you, Sally. It's something else with you. It's life or death. To me it's as if you had one life, it didn't work, and you've sort of literally . . . I mean, I know it's not literally literally but it so almost is, it's like "I've reinvented myself and if this Sally Mottram doesn't work I don't see where the third one's coming from." Does that make sense?'

'Sort of, I suppose. I don't think it's healthy to think of oneself too much.'

'I'm frightened by how much you care, Sally.'

Sally had suggested to Harry, Jill, Olive and Arnold that they all go to the Weavers' for the Early Bird Special. Olive had turned the suggestion down on the grounds that her decision not to participate in the great Transition scheme rendered her an unfit companion on the night of the vote. Arnold, feeling trapped by Olive's decision, had with huge difficulty turned down a special offer for the first time in his life. So Sally, desperate to continue to cement the two marriages of her four pensioner friends, had found herself taking a pickaxe to the cement by escorting Jill and Harry to dinner.

And now she was almost too nervous to eat anything, and the clumsiness and lack of charm of the new waiter, poor boy, quite unsuited to the job, just piled the pressure on her nerves. Harry and Jill were nervous too. They were nervous for Sally, for Potherthwaite, and for themselves. Harry had after all been promised a very prominent role in the great adventure, and was, secretly, very thrilled indeed, and Jill, who gave the appearance of being at least half in love with him, was thrilled for him too. Neither of them could be said to be on what Harry called 'Top Nosh Mode'.

So here were three nervous people eating together in the pub where not long ago they had received a further discount because they were all badly bruised. It occurred to Sally, who was well aware of Harry and Jill's nervousness, that they might call this 'The Great Nerves Special' and ask for a further discount from the kindly Sue. Then they could ask for a further discount owing to the bad service from the desperate bespotted waiter, who would later cause Sue to change all the bread baskets because he had a rare allergy to wicker, and she didn't dare sack him in our litigious culture. Sally didn't mention these thoughts to Sue, of course, because Sue might have acted on them.

Their nervousness inhibited their conversation. Jill did try. She said, 'That woman over there is quite attractive, but all I can see is a great big polyp she had in her large intestine. That was what was so wonderful about that holiday in Italy. I didn't recognize anybody's backside for a whole week.' Nobody warmed to this theme, and the conversation fizzled out altogether. They ate in a silence broken only by their asides to the hopeless waiter. 'No, I'm the pork.' 'I did say, "Could I have chips instead of the dauphinoise potatoes?"' 'You've dribbled gravy on to my dessert spoon.'

The replacement spoon was never used. They never had any desserts. Arnold telephoned Harry to say that Olive had been taken ill, and was on her way to Potherthwaite District Hospital in an ambulance.

Jill drove Harry to the hospital as he was probably already over the limit. Sue brought Sally a large white wine on the house, and she didn't have the energy to demur. By now, though, she was a nervous wreck.

Nerves played a big part in the council chamber too. Marigold sat in the Visitors' Gallery, which was absolutely full. Councillor Stratton had to call for silence on more than one occasion. It had seemed to Marigold on the day of the march that the arguments for throwing out the supermarket's application were overwhelming. She didn't feel that now. In fact the very success of the march seemed to be used by some people as an argument for the application. We mustn't get carried away. We mustn't allow ourselves to be swayed by emotion. We are here to govern, not to dream. Many people couldn't afford the independent shops. The town was full of working-class people, not trendy foodies with their cupcakes.

The argument swung back and forth. One man proudly claimed to be working class to his boots and said that small shops cared about people, but supermarkets didn't. Another said that it was odd how people who weren't working class seemed to think they knew what working-class people wanted. A lady councillor put forward the idea that if everyone went to the independent shops they wouldn't have to be so expensive and people would be able to afford to use them. The shortest speech was from a man who said 'I'm from Guildford. Don't tell me about supermarkets', and sat down triumphantly, as if he thought he had just swung the meeting.

Back at the Weavers', Sally's nerves grew. It was proving a long meeting. Was that a good sign or a bad sign?

And back at the Town Hall, one speaker, tall, deathly pale, clutched his notes as if they were a handful of eels. His wife had written out his speech for him, and had added stage directions. In his fear he didn't realize this.

'I've been on the council for two years, and I've never dared speak,' he began in a tremulous voice. 'Slight pause. But tonight I have to. Slightly longer pause. This is the biggest choice this town has ever had to make. Bang side of chair with fist twice. Ever. The word is Transition. A longer word. Sorry a better word wait for laugh is Transformation. Look at our town. Raise voice and repeat slowly, Look at our town.'

All over the chamber people wished that they could look at their town. Anything was better than looking at each other. One sight of another face and they would have collapsed into laughter.

At this moment in her writing out of his speech, as it chanced, the councillor's loyal and loving wife had realized that she was going to be late for the school run. He had finished the job himself, and there were no more stage directions. His last words were uninterrupted.

'Nobody can deny that the town needs transformation. What is the best thing to transform it into? A place that is the same as everywhere else, or a place that is different from everywhere else, or better still, a place that can set the bar for other places to aspire to?'

There was even some applause at this. The speaker clutched his eels and sat down, a pink flush invading his deathly cheeks.

Soon after that, the voting began. It was done with a show of hands and from the start it was clear that it was going to be close. The tellers counted the raised hands three times to be quite sure. The tension in the room was almost visible. Marigold could scarcely breathe. It was as if their lives hung on the next thirty seconds.

At exactly the same moment, two people phoned Sally's mobile in the now almost empty Weavers' Arms. Jill must have rung just before Marigold, as she got through, and Marigold didn't.

Jill was phoning from the car park of the hospital. Olive had suffered a heart attack. It was hard to predict how serious it was. Harry was devastated. 'He loves her so much, Sally,' she said. 'I cried to see how much he loved her.' Olive was in bed, and comfortable. She was in the best place and other clichés. The trouble was that most people no longer believed that Potherthwaite District Hospital was the best place for anything. Dangerous enough if you were well. To be avoided at all costs if you were ill.

So Sally picked up Marigold's great message on her answer machine, which was a bit sad really, as it was such important news and such welcome news. The plans for the new supermarket had been thrown out by three votes. Marigold was going to the Potherthwaite Arms, her new favourite, to celebrate. 'See you there, sweetie, and congratulations.'

Sally paid Sue, kissed her, and set off towards the Potherthwaite Arms. Relief flooded through her. It was over. It was over at last. It was a moment when she could have truly rejoiced, but it seemed to her to be typical of her life that she couldn't do so, because of Olive's illness.

She regretted now that she hadn't been braver, hadn't witnessed the vote.

As she walked into the Market Place on her way to High Street East and the Potherthwaite Arms, she saw Councillor Stratton walking out of the Town Hall towards the George Hotel.

He came towards her, smiling broadly.

'Congratulations,' he said. 'Really well done.'

'Thank you.'

'It's a partnership now. We'll need to work together.'

'I hope so, Frank. I really do.'

'I told you we hadn't made up our minds. I told you we were prepared to listen.'

'You did indeed. Thanks, Frank.'

'I have an apology to make, Sally.'

'Oh?'

'Yes. I shouldn't have warned you not to get out of your depth.'

'Oh?'

'It was patronizing. You aren't out of your depth.'

'Thank you.'

'Apology accepted?'

'No need. I'm so glad you said it.'

'Glad? Glad, Sally? Why?'

'I was really losing faith in myself. I was about to give up. You made me just angry enough to carry on.'

Councillor Stratton's smile was distinctly sickly. Sally knew in that moment that he had voted for the supermarket. She knew in that moment that every word he was saying was insincere.

They shook hands, exchanged smiles that were also insincere, the insincerity in hers being forced into existence by the insincerity in his, and set off for two different palaces of liquid refreshment.

Despite two large glasses of free white wine from the ever generous Sue, Sally felt suddenly very sober.

She had thought that it was over. She had thought that if they won the vote it would be over. Over and over again she had thought that if they won the vote it would be over. They had won the vote, and it wasn't over. It would never be over. It was just beginning. It would always be just beginning. It was a thing called life. She was living it for the second time, and it wasn't getting any easier.

TWENTY-FIVE

A grand night in the hills

This time Conrad took a different road. After he had climbed out of the valley towards the invisible setting sun, he turned right instead of swinging left towards the Shoulder of Mutton. This road took him into higher hills, even more desolate moors. Lapwings flew wildly. Black grouse and buzzards stood on the posts that in winter would mark the depth of the snow. They flew up in irritation as the Audi approached.

The rain was even heavier up here, driving across the front of the car. They could feel the Audi juddering from the force of the wind. The sheep weren't even looking at them, they were cowering in any slight hollow they could find. Did they remember dancing with delight, gambolling gloriously under the bright sun, racing each other in the great novelty of existence, when they were lambs? They weren't dancing now. Did they say to themselves, in sheep-speak, 'I wouldn't have done all that rejoicing if I'd known what was to come'?

'This is how places like this are meant to be seen,' said Conrad.

The rain was so heavy that they could only see about fifty

yards ahead. Suddenly the isolated bulk of Aismaster Crag loomed up on the left. The pub cowered in its shelter like an exhausted sheep.

He took the car right to the door, stepped out into the storm, hurried round to the passenger side, opened an umbrella, then the passenger door. He held the umbrella open over her head as she ran for it. She was only in the open air for about two yards, and not one drop of rain fell on her. It was brilliantly done.

She stood in the shelter of a small porch, and watched him drive the car to the thinly populated car park. He got out of the car carrying his umbrella, but he didn't dare open it out there in the full force of the wind.

This was a man with perfect manners! Hadn't she fallen for men with manners before? Hadn't she concluded that she had no taste in men? Were his manners too good to be true? Should she be here?

Beneath the excitement of the moment, beneath the joy of the smell of food that was coming through the badly fitting front door of the pub, Marigold was scared. She had told Sally that she had no faith in men. They were all bastards. Was Conrad a bastard? What would Sally say if she could see them?

The Drovers' Arms was a much simpler place than the Shoulder of Mutton, but if they had gone to the Shoulder a waiter might have said, 'Good to see you again, sir,' and of course he didn't want that.

'Would you like a drink at the bar first, or would you like to go straight to your table?' asked the landlady.

'Marigold?' asked Conrad.

'Could we have one at the bar?'

'Perfect.'

Marigold was certain that if she'd said, 'Oh, let's go straight to our table,' he would still have said, 'Perfect.'

It was a lovely bar. Wooden floors, simple wooden tables, all different. Welcoming stools at the counter. A roaring fire.

'What would you like?'

'Would it be awfully unfeminine if I had a pint of beer?'

'I think it would be charming.'

She swung on to a bar stool before he had the chance to lead her to a table. Again she seemed like a lady who might have been built for bar stools. She rode them side-saddle, with her legs crossed. The legs were perhaps slightly too full to be described as perfect, but perfect is what most men had thought them.

Certainly Malcolm Stent, Henrik Larsen and Timothy Boyce-Willoughby had made no complaints.

She shouldn't have come.

The barman handed her the pint.

'My God, it's big,' she said.

'Aren't you a pint drinker?' asked Conrad. 'I assumed you were.'

'Good Lord, no. Martinis, darling. Negronis. Manhattans.'

'So why have you ordered a pint of bitter?'

'Because it's a pint-of-bitter sort of place. The Drovers' Arms. I thought it might be rather fun to sit here and think that maybe I'd just come in from a hard day's droving, gasping for a pint.' She took a careful sip. 'M'm, it's not bad actually.'

Why was she behaving like this? Because she wanted to test him? Because she didn't want him to see her real self? Because she wanted to hide how nervous she was? But wasn't it likely that she was actually showing him how nervous she was? Those brown eyes, they seemed so soft, but she suspected that they were as deep as a well. It was fine to flirt with seven men in the Potherthwaite Arms – by flirting with them all she avoided doing any real flirting with any of them. But this, this was dangerous. She had vowed that she would never again put herself in a position in which there was any risk whatsoever of falling in love.

She abandoned her pose and started to talk in a more down-to-earth fashion. But that was dangerous too. He was so easy to talk to. He behaved like a man who was truly charming and trustworthy, not a poser. But hadn't Timothy in particular seemed like that? Forget learning from experience. She felt that she knew less and less with experience. Timothy had been the worst. Was this man actually even worse? Was she destined to make worse and worse choices of men?

They talked casually about the nature of the Pennines, the unfortunate lives led by sheep, the difficulty pubs had in surviving in the modern era. They ordered at the bar, the food sounded delicious. She took her beer glass with her into the restaurant, which was quite small and simple and had a fantastic old dresser at one end, filled but not too filled with exquisite plates in blue and white.

He talked about his life, touching on his wife's cancer with a mixture of warmth and reticence. She found that she had to fight hard not to tell him the whole story of her three marriages. It was too soon.

The thought that it was too soon took her aback. It suggested a future together. For goodness' sake, this was a first date – she shouldn't be thinking of a future together.

She couldn't believe that she had accepted his invitation. By accepting it she had committed herself to agony. He really did seem so very, very nice.

They say that women are better at multitasking than men, and she certainly found it easy to think one thing while talking about another. This happened most spectacularly while she was actually saying, 'I am so grateful that I wasn't born a sheep.' There came into her mind a picture not of a sheep, but of Sally. She would seek Sally's advice. She would remember everything Conrad did, everything he said, his gestures, his looks, and she would ask her, 'Do you think I can trust this man?' Maybe – yes, why not? – she would suggest that the three of them went out together one day.

She felt better after that, until it occurred to her that if she could be having these thoughts while talking about something different, so perhaps could he. Perhaps he was thinking, 'I know just where I'll drive off the road, where nobody will see the car when the lights are switched off. I know exactly where I will ravish this beautiful woman.' A slight smile slipped out as she reflected on the absurdity of her being so egotistical as to think herself beautiful even in the middle of a fantasy of fear.

'What are you smiling at?' he asked with a smile.

The utter impossibility of telling him shocked her.

'I'm wondering what all those sheep are thinking about at this moment,' she improvised lamely.

'Marigold "Obsessed by Sheep" Boyce-Willoughby, do try to think of something else occasionally,' he said, but in a very pleasant way, not at all sarcastic.

They talked pleasantly of many subjects, so many subjects that Marigold feared she wouldn't remember any of them to tell to Sally.

They walked out of the delightful mixture of simplicity and sophistication that was the isolated Drovers' Arms into an astonishing sight. There wasn't a cloud in the sky. A crescent moon shone, and every star and every planet was clearly visible in the pure, unpolluted air.

Conrad drove back quite slowly. They were drinking in together this amazing scene. He pulled up at the side of the road and a stab of fear struck Marigold. He came round to the passenger side and opened her door. She told herself that she was safe, he was still on the main road. She told herself that if you had to fear every man you met, you were no longer living in a habitable world. She braced herself, undid her seat belt, stepped out. They stood together in the vastness. A few sheep bleated and then there was silence for ten billion miles. On this empty moor, hundreds of pairs of sheep's eyes reflected the light from the young, inexperienced moon, and from tired old stars long dead. They were silent, awed. She felt his faint touch on her shoulder, just one touch, gentle, not invasive. We are here, we are together, we are tiny, but we are safe. She hardly knew him, but she knew that she *could* love this man. The question was *should* she love this man?

And the sky – how could you look at the sky and wonder how there could possibly be a God? And the crescent moon – how can that too not lead to thoughts of people who worship different gods, and how can that not make your heart uneasy and make you wonder if this Transition you set your store by is enough, can be enough, can anything be enough? And that, when your imagination is heightened by the wine you have drunk, by the man you have drunk wine with, and by this scene that you are looking at beside the man with whom you have drunk the wine, how can that not lead you to think about innocence, and a world's lost innocence, and to wonder just for a moment, if it would be that bad to be a sheep?

There was nothing to say that could possibly follow that experience, and so, with rare good sense, they said nothing. Conrad drove her safely back to the cul-de-sac, kissed her on both cheeks but not on the lips, and said just two words.

'Goodnight, Marigold.'

TWENTY-SIX

Marigold seeks advice

'I'd like to take you out to dinner, Sally,' Marigold had said.

'That's very kind.'

'When I think where to go, there isn't anywhere really, is there? Not anywhere really good. Maybe that'll all change with the Transition.'

Sally had sighed.

'Feeling flat?' Marigold had asked.

'Yes, a bit.'

'Natural reaction to all the excitement.'

'I suppose.'

'Would you find the Weavers' awfully boring?'

'No. It's where it all started. If we can't kindle a bit of enthusiasm there, where can we?'

'True. And I don't mean the Early Bird. Later, with the full menu. Eight-thirty when it's quiet.'

'Great. That's very generous.'

'Not really. There's something I want to talk to you about. Something I want your advice on. I'm sure you can guess what.'

'Man trouble.'

'Well, not exactly, but yes.'

Join the club, Sally had thought.

And now here she was, five minutes late. She had been to see Olive at the hospital. She hadn't thought that Olive had looked good, she hadn't liked her colour. She'd been dozing, on and off.

'I've realized how much I love her,' Harry had said in a low voice, during one of Olive's moments of sleep.

'You realize how much you love someone when . . .' Sally had stopped. She had been on the point of saying, '. . . when you fear you might lose them.'

Harry had replied to her unspoken remark.

'It's not just here in the hospital,' he had said. 'It was in Montepulciano. I looked at Jill on the terrace with the vine-yards and the hills behind her, and she looked so wonderful in the sunshine. Bronzed, lovely legs, couldn't believe she was in her seventies. And I thought of Olive, always so anxious, so negative sometimes, and I wished she could laugh more, and risk more, and eat more, and drink more, but . . . I just longed to get home to her. And I think Jill felt the same about Arnold. It's so odd, because . . . I think we were both sorely tempted to go to bed together, but . . . when it was there on a plate . . . we both wanted to put our loyalty first.'

'That's fantastic.'

'And when I got back, I realized, yes, I've always loved her and I love her still.'

'So you told her?'

Harry had paused.

'Well, yes . . . I mean, not in those words, but . . . um . . . well, no.'

'Oh, Harry.'

Olive had woken up, had looked at them with tired eyes, had asked with a pale smile, 'And what have you two been nattering about?'

248

'Not much,' Harry had said.

'Sounds suspicious to me,' Olive had replied, and Sally had felt that she had to stay till Olive dozed off again.

'Tell her,' she had whispered, as she left.

'Sorry I'm late,' she said now, and she kissed Marigold on both cheeks.

'I've ordered a bottle of Tempranillo,' said Marigold. 'Hope that's all right.'

'Great.'

Sally talked about her visit to the hospital, and how she didn't like Olive's colour. Marigold grimaced. They discussed the success of the march. Sally told her how borne down she felt with the weight of all there was to do, and how concerned she was as to how they would pay for it all. They needed an action committee and she was proposing to send out leaflets to every house in Potherthwaite asking for volunteers to stand on the committee. There might be no volunteers, which would be awful. There might be eight, which would be great. There might be two hundred and thirty-three, which would be impossible. If there were more than ten volunteers they would have to have a vote. It might be simpler if initially she just chose a committee. If anybody was upset they could form other committees for other aspects of the work. The Canal Committee. The Quays Committee. The High Street Committee. The Park Committee. The Sculpture Trail Committee. The Committee Committee to create liaison between the committees. And of course a joint committee with the council.

'Let's start by just forming a committee between ourselves,' said Marigold. 'There has to be a start, Sally.'

'Yes. You're right. Everyone agrees on what we want, anyway. Will you chair it?'

'Me?'

'Yes. Why?'

'I'm not a chairing sort of person. I'm, like, tell me what to do and I'll either say yes or no. Why me, anyway, and above all, why not you?'

'Why not me? Because I don't want it to be a one-woman band. Why you? Because you're my best friend.'

'Aaah!'

They devoured the last morsels of their Parma ham and melon. The waitress, their friend now, took away their plates. Sally asked about her little boy. She glowed with pride as she told them how naughty he was.

'So,' said Sally when the waitress had gone. 'This problem.'

'It's not a problem as such,' said Marigold. 'On the face of it, it's great. A nice man asks me out, I go, I like him very much. I don't just like him, Sally. I fancy him. And I'm sitting there thinking, "I shouldn't be here," and he's like, "Have another glass," and I'm like, to myself, "I'd better not, it might be dangerous," and I hear myself saying, "Lovely. Thank you." I know what I'm like, Sally.'

Afterwards, thinking about the evening, Sally was surprised that she hadn't already guessed who it was. It was only after she had asked, 'What was he like?' and Marigold's reply had included the words 'very attractive' that the appalling possibility began to dawn. Very attractive. What other man in Potherthwaite did that description really fit? So, although it was a hammer blow, and very lucky that she hadn't any food in her mouth to choke over, it wasn't altogether a surprise when Marigold told her.

'I've just realized,' Marigold said. 'You'll know him, you'll have met him – he's the man who bought your house.'

'Conrad?'

'Yes. Conrad. What do you think of him?'

'I hardly know him.'

Sally was shocked to realize that this wasn't actually a lie. Her mouth was dry. She took a sip of water and tried to make the gesture look casual. She would have liked to gulp down three-quarters of a jug.

She had no idea how best to play this situation, so she played it carefully, revealing nothing about her relationship with the man, such as it was. This might make it all the harder for her ever to tell Marigold, but to commit herself now might be a worse mistake. Besides, as she wryly admitted to herself when she reflected on the evening (which she did for almost all of the night that followed), she longed to hear every word of what happened. Her thoughts at this moment were entirely with Marigold, with the awful way this monster had preyed upon her weakness with men – how could she blame Marigold, how could she call her naive when she also had been taken in? The deep friendship she had felt for Marigold during the long night of the liqueurs was as strong as ever at that moment. Conrad was entirely the villain of the piece. She felt almost as sorry for Marigold as she did for herself.

'So, tell me, what sort of an evening was it?' she asked very gently, careful not to sound too inquisitive.

Marigold launched herself on a detailed description, so vivid and thorough that when their main courses arrived – salmon for Marigold, lamb for Sally – Sally almost felt that they weren't real but were props for Marigold's story.

The Drovers'. She knew it, of course, after more than twenty years in Potherthwaite. A clever choice. The efficient Shoulder of Mutton for efficient Sally. The romantic Drovers' for romantic Marigold. This was a calculating man.

The bar stools made her smile to herself. She knew what Marigold was like with bar stools. But then Marigold said, 'You know what I'm like with bar stools,' and she admired Marigold's spontaneity and frankness. She contrasted Marigold's pint of beer with her careful ordering and gave herself a note to try hard to loosen up.

251

She began to feel slightly sick as she heard about their brief moment side by side on the moors. She was amused by Marigold's almost desperate search for decency in Conrad.

'He behaved impeccably. Didn't even touch me.'

No, he didn't need to, did he, with every sodding star and every puking planet and a crescent moon to seduce you with, she thought.

Marigold even described the goodnight kiss.

'No kiss on the mouth?'

'No.'

'Interesting.'

Marigold asked her what she thought. She just couldn't bring herself to say what she thought, that Conrad was a ruthless seducer of great charm and ability, and therefore utterly dangerous. She admitted to herself while she was taking a second dose of paracetamol at three-fifteen that sleepless night, that, lacking the kind of frankness and confidence that enabled Marigold to tell the tale of an evening in which a man might well turn out to have led her right up the garden path, it had been a failing in her that she had been unwilling to admit to the way she had been taken in on her trip to the Shoulder of Mutton.

'He sounds a bit smooth to me,' she said. 'A bit . . . suspiciously charming. But I wasn't there. You were.' Come on, Sally, no need to take refuge in the obvious. 'I really do advise extreme caution, darling.' She noted her use of 'darling' with surprise. It was so Marigold, and so not her. It wouldn't have slipped out if she had been being herself.

'You don't think I should refuse to see him again?'

That would be fatal. In absence he would become irresistible. That was easy to reply to.

'No, I don't.'

'Good. Thanks so much, Sally.'

'Thank you for a nice dinner.'

252

Sally walked home, through streets that still showed no sign of the effect of the Transition movement. So much had happened, yet so little had happened.

With every step that she took, she thought less of Marigold and more of herself. She had placed such hopes in Conrad. She realized a sad truth about herself. Her emotional life in the years with Barry had been so shrivelled that it had been as if she was beginning all over again, at forty-seven, with all the inexperience of youth. But she knew how hard life would be at forty-EIGHT, and she didn't know how, without the energy given by love, she would be able to face all the hard work and drudgery that now faced her. Dreams are fun. Making them real is hard work.

There was one message on her answerphone.

'Hello, Sally. This is Conrad. It's time we had another dinner. How about next Tuesday?'

TWENTY-SEVEN

A resounding whisper

Margaret Spreckley was fifty-one years old, tall, slim, with tactful breasts and almost no hips. She had freckled skin. She wasn't married, but there was said to be a Canadian in the offing, and she was not thought to be lesbian. She looked severe until she smiled. She didn't smile a lot. She wanted her smile to be effective when it came, and it came at important moments, and was indeed effective.

Her study looked less severe than her. There were cheerful paintings on the walls, as modern as they could be without losing the trust of the governors. The desk was modest. The chairs at either side of it did not look unduly confrontational. There were also two easy chairs, not wildly easy, but definitely not difficult. There was a rather fine Swiss teddy bear on top of the large bookcase. Unlike some headmistresses, Margaret Spreckley remembered having been a child. She didn't want the children to be overawed by her presence. She found out a lot by listening to what they said. If they said nothing, she would find out much less.

'Come in, Lucy,' she said, in a firm but soft voice.

Lucy Basridge wore a surly look that struck a false note, as if she was desperately trying to sulk, but failing.

The headmistress approached her, indicating that Lucy should sit in one of the easy chairs, and flashed that sudden smile.

Lucy's sulk looked uneasy, uncertain, taken aback by the smile. She sat uncomfortably. She was wearing her school uniform, but in a disorganized way that hinted at her disdain for it.

The headmistress sat on the other easy chair.

'Well now, Lucy,' she said. 'I heard about your speech at the Town Hall.'

Lucy didn't reply, but hunched herself into defensive mode, like a hedgehog hearing traffic.

'Well done.'

No smile this time. Margaret Spreckley was content to let the words do the work. Lucy frowned, and blushed slightly.

'It was a Saturday, so you didn't have to play truant, did you?'

Lucy tried not to say, 'No, miss', but failed rather humiliatingly.

'You play truant every now and then, do you, Lucy? Why?'

The headmistress could see Lucy plucking up her courage. It was strangely endearing.

'I get bored, Miss Spreckley. I'm sorry.'

'So am I. Very sorry. It's sad that we're failing you so badly – and so often!'

Margaret Spreckley smiled again. She could see that Lucy was wrestling with herself. She waited patiently.

'It's not that, Miss Spreckley.'

'I know. It's the world that's failing you, isn't it?'

Lucy's eyes widened. She narrowed them rapidly.

'Anyway, Lucy, from what I've been told of your speech it was really rather marvellous.'

Lucy blushed again, and shuffled in her chair.

'I really believed what I said,' she said.

'I know you did. Good for you. Now all these graffiti . . .'

'I don't do ones against individuals, Miss Spreckley. Ever.'

It was the headmistress's turn to try, not entirely success-fully, to hide her astonishment.

'No, you don't, do you?'

'I'm sorry I made spelling mistakes. It can't do the school good, that.'

'Maybe,' said the headmistress, in a curious tone, as if to a colleague and an equal, 'nobody will ever know that the graffitist was a pupil here. I might not tell anyone. As you say, bad for the school.'

Lucy Basridge smiled. It was a sheepish little smile, but never mind, it was a smile of sorts. She was remembering that she had broadcast her graffitist activities to the town through the tannoy.

'Besides, maybe we ought to have been able to do more for your dyslexia. It did rather reveal that it was you, though, didn't it? To me, anyway.'

'You knew!'

'I'm not stupid, Lucy.'

'Sorry.'

'It wasn't just the dyslexia, Lucy. It was the amazing athleticism.'

Lucy tried hard not to look proud.

'Do you miss the circus?'

'Terribly, miss.'

'I probably shouldn't say this, Lucy,' said the headmistress, 'but I'm going to. I don't want you to think that the world of authority is entirely full of closed minds. I rather admire your graffitist comments. Crude and exaggerated, but, yes, I . . . good targets. The strong, not the weak. And those burglaries, giving somebody else what you stole, and some-times rather amusingly too.'

Lucy was beyond speech at this point.

'Oh yes, I knew. Well, not knew. Guessed. Anyway, thank goodness the council voted against the supermarket. You said you'd give up the graffiti if they did, didn't you?'

'I didn't actually. I said I'd clean up the ones I've made. And I will. But I won't do any more, either. I promise.'

The headmistress had rather taken the fun out of it, with her approval, but she didn't say that.

'Good.'

'And I do try to keep my promises.'

'Good. I'm also pleased about the vote for a different reason. I don't like supermarkets either.'

'Good.'

The headmistress wanted to laugh at Lucy's saying 'Good', but it had been cheeky and she mustn't give too much.

'So, Lucy,' she said. 'The excitement's the thing, is it? The buzz?'

'Yeah. I like it. Yeah.'

'I think you're addicted to it, Lucy.'

Lucy thought about this.

'I suppose I am, yeah.'

'Now, shall I tell you what I think we should do?'

Lucy didn't reply. She realized that no reply was expected.

'I'm going to ask you to make me another promise in a minute, Lucy,' said the headmistress, 'and you've told me that you try to keep your promises. I am going to suggest that we – that's not just me but all your other teachers, and not just us but you as well – we'll work on this together. I am going to suggest that we make a big effort to find things for you to do, within the rules, that can bring you that same feeling of excitement, that same buzz, danger too, but danger of a different kind, danger as much of or more of the mind than the body, perhaps. I think with your athleticism and circus training you could and should do well at sports, and I'd welcome that, but that's not really what I'm talking about. I love the arts, Lucy. I do what I can to interest you all in them, and I would do more if our leaders of all persuasions had the sense and the character to support us more. I believe, Lucy, that ours is not much of a civilization if our education cannot provide for receptive young minds excitements from the arts to rival those of the circus. The promise I'm asking from you is not difficult. It's simply this. Will you do your best to try to find the excitement you crave and need from the activities that we take the trouble to put in your way?'

Lucy looked at her with an expression that wasn't at all promising. For a moment the headmistress was horrified and disappointed. Then she realized the explanation of the expression. Lucy was trying not to cry.

'I promise,' whispered Lucy, but it was a resounding whisper.

'Have you any questions, Lucy?' asked the headmistress.

Lucy remained silent.

'Ask something, Lucy. Please don't disappoint me.'

'If you knew everything, Miss Spreckley, why didn't you tell on me?'

'I wanted you to admit it of your own accord. I was confident you would. Run along now. I've work to do.'

Lucy went to the door of the study, opened it, turned briefly.

'Thank you,' she said.

'No. Thank *you*,' said Margaret Spreckley.

TWENTY-EIGHT

A glorious weekend

A glorious weekend burst upon the Pother Valley. Potherthwaite awoke to cloudless skies. There was barely a breath of wind. The weather forecast spoke of the possibility of the temperature touching twenty degrees. Twenty degrees, in Potherthwaite, in late October.

The sun shone brightly on the Quays, on what had until recently been the Canal Bookshop, on the rusting frontage of the Terminus Bist o, on the rusty tables outside the Quays Café, where a few brave souls were eating congealing breakfasts off cold plates. It was self-service. If you sat waiting to be served you would sit for ever. The waitress hadn't even the energy to come out to tell you that she wasn't coming out to serve you.

Sally strolled up on to the sharply curved footbridge that led to the other side of the canal, to the cracked and uneven towpath and the mean houses beyond. She looked down on the three trapped narrowboats. This morning, with courage sent from the sun, she filled the scene with happy people, lively dogs, lines of cafés with bright awnings, smooth waters, boats that moved.

She wandered back to the quayside. A thin, frail, elderly

man with bowed legs was precariously carrying a large tray laden with a huge fry-up, toast, butter, marmalade, condiments, brown sauce, tomato ketchup and a mug of tea. Behind him, his huge wife waddled with an even more piled tray. Sally watched, gripped by the drama. He just managed to plonk his tray on a table before he lost control of it. She lowered herself very slowly towards a chair, still clutching her tray. She lost control of the descent, and the tray crashed on to the table, slopping tea everywhere. Sally stood there until they had taken their first great mouthfuls of food that would already be almost cold. Between them on the iron top of the table was a dollop of bird shit. Neither of them took any notice of it. Over their heads was the natural canopy of a horse chestnut. One glorious orange leaf floated down on to their table. They didn't take any notice of that either.

Sally drifted past the sunken narrowboat, came to the trapped home of the Porchesters. Terence and Felicity were having breakfast in the cockpit – orange juice, strong coffee, toast and two boiled eggs each.

'This is the life,' called out Terence plummily.

'On a morning like this,' said Felicity.

'Come and join us,' said Terence.

'No, no,' said Sally. 'Enjoy your eggs.'

'From the deli,' said Terence proudly.

'Good man.'

Felicity, small and delicate as a bird, bashed the top of her egg violently. Terence, that bearded mountain of a man, picked the shell off the top of his egg with careful, delicate, scalded fingers. Sally would miss the Porchesters if – when – their boat was freed, and they chugged happily back to Oxford.

'We'll be there,' said Terence.

'Lending our muscle power,' said Felicity, who had no muscle power to lend.

Sally had arranged for a big clearing-up operation at the waste ground in High Street West from ten o'clock. This was a bit premature, as no decision had yet been made over the use of the site, but it was right in the centre of town and something had to be seen to be done if the excitement of the vote against the supermarket wasn't to die.

'Well, that's very good of you,' she said. 'It isn't even your town.'

'We wouldn't dream of not helping,' boomed Terence. 'You're our saviour, Sally. You're going to clear the canal and let us chug our way home.'

'We'd do anything for you,' said Felicity.

'Within reason,' said Terence, and he roared with laughter.

'Terence!' rebuked Felicity. 'You'll deafen the poor girl.'

'Always laugh at my own jokes,' said Terence. 'Somebody has to.'

Sally left them to their second eggs and meandered on towards the third narrowboat. Eric Sheepshank was lying full length on the roof, dressed only in his underpants. He clambered awkwardly to his feet. Twice in recent weeks he had lost his balance and tumbled into the foetid waters.

'I'm sorry I'm not decent,' he said. He lowered his voice, as if he was about to impart a really important secret. 'I've let myself go.'

'It's that I want to talk to you about, Eric,' said Sally. 'I've seen some of your early stuff.'

'Oh?'

He was a thin man with a huge paunch. He adjusted his pants nervously, as if he feared that he might show Sally a glimpse of something that would excite her.

'I'm not sure that I entirely believe this sculptor's block stuff,' said Sally.

'You and the world,' said Eric with a spurt of anger. 'Bloody writers. Prima donnas to a man. And woman. Got

261

stuck with their precious stories? It's not because they've got no imagination. Oh no, it's because of writer's block, that fungus of the imagination that sits there, waiting to strike the poor darlings. Cos writing a book's *so* difficult. Whereas all we ordinary folk do is shape a bit of stuff, so why should we have sculptor's block? Or painter's block. Or potter's block. Or butcher's block.'

She had made him angry. She had woken him up. Good.

'Eric, I fully accept the existence of sculptor's block, but you haven't tried the remedy for at least twenty years.'

She looked up at him, absurd and haggard and unshaven in his sadly inadequate grey overwashed underpants on the roof of his tilting boat in the late-autumn sunshine.

'Oh,' he said angrily. 'You know what the remedy is, do you, Mrs Bloody Couldn't Satisfy her Husband Clever Clogs?'

Sally went white. She shook with anger. She glared at him. There was a long silence. She suspected that he had gone pale behind his beard.

'I'm most terribly sorry, Sally,' he said. 'That was awful. That was inexcusable.'

'It's the drink, Eric,' said Sally. 'Cut it down, Eric, before you find you have to cut it out.'

Eric opened his mouth but said nothing. Sally could almost see the words appearing and being forced back. This was a matter too serious to discuss. He changed the subject back on to the safer ground of sculpture.

'So you think you have a remedy for sculptor's block, do you?'

'Yes, Eric.'

'And it is?'

'Sculpt.'

'What?'

'Work. Make things. Even if they don't come out very well at first.'

262

He shook his head, but not very firmly.

'You were good, really good. You can be again.'

This time he didn't even shake his head. He just stared. He looked as if he hadn't a thought in his head, but she knew that he had.

'You'll have heard of my plans, Eric,' she said. 'Well, I plan a Sculpture Trail and I want you to be in it. You can do it.'

'What would I make?'

'I wouldn't insult an artist of your potential by limiting his freedom. Eric, look at your life. Your boat is rotting. You are rotting. Your underpants are rotting. If you had a foreskin, that would be rotting too.'

She turned away. She didn't want him to see the astonishment on her face at what she had just found herself capable of saying. And she didn't need to look back at the astonishment on his face – she could imagine it.

She found herself accompanying the Porchesters up to the waste ground. As she went she looked at the scene with a mixture of dismay and hope – dismay at what it was, hope at what it might become. How the Market Place needed a few open-air cafés. In Potherthwaite the words 'Al Fresco' sounded like the name of a bandit.

The Revd Dominic Otley had volunteered to lead the clearing operation. Anything was better than worrying about tomorrow's sermon. Today, in his khaki shorts, he was all smiles; even his knobbly knees seemed to be smiling. Several of his declining band of faithful parishioners had come to support him. They were elderly and not capable of lifting heavy weights, but their spirit was admirable.

Marigold's knees were not knobbly, her shorts were very short and weren't khaki, and she wasn't capable of lifting heavy weights either. She went straight to a small broken square of York stone. Sally realized to her immense amusement that Marigold was only going to carry objects that did not detract from her elegance. She lived her life in the style of a woman who expected that she might be photographed at any moment. Sally's mocking thoughts about her dear friend were deeply affectionate, but she didn't want to talk to Marigold today; she didn't want any more conversations about Conrad until after her dinner with him. Yes, she had accepted his invitation made on her answerphone. She didn't know why, and she didn't know how she would play it, but there was nothing more to be said to Marigold about it until there were further developments. That did much to explain why she ended up lunching with . . .

But we anticipate. Shortly after ten o'clock, along came Ben, that strange – but was he really so strange? – boy. He carried a large canvas, attached to a pole like an estate agent's board. He wasn't tall, and he was decidedly thin, and he could only just manage to carry it.

He tried to stick the pole into the ground, which was still slightly wet after yesterday's rain, but it was also stony and he found it difficult.

'Let me, maestro,' said Terence Porchester. He pulled a large hammer from his rucksack, took the pole from Ben, found a suitable piece of ground, and hammered the canvas into it. Then he went round to the front of the canvas, which faced the High Street, and examined it.

'Brilliant,' he pronounced. 'The artist is embarrassed because he is not good at hammering things in, yet he has created a masterpiece. I am quite brilliant at hammering things in, but will never create a masterpiece. You've done it again, maestro. Congratulations.'

They all went round to the front to examine Ben's painting. It was of an extremely exhausted vicar, on his knees, holding a large stone up to the heavens rather feebly. From his mouth came a speech balloon: *'Oh Lord, help me.'*

Underneath the painting were the words: '*WE NEED YOUR HELP TOO. SATURDAY. 10–5.*' The painting of the vicar was brilliantly funny. Everyone laughed, particularly the vicar, though a few of his small flock looked a little uneasy at the mockery.

Sally put down her spade – with some relief – and led Ben away from the crowd.

'What are your plans, Ben?' she asked.

'Dunno. Might hang around the allotments with Tricksy. Don't know.'

'I actually meant, not what are you going to do today, but when you leave school.'

'Hang around the allotments with Tricksy, probably. No, sorry, Sally. I'll be serious. Go to art college.'

'Great. That's fantastic.'

'Dad's furious. He wants me to be an accountant.'

'I might have to have a word with your dad.'

'Oh Christ, no, Mrs Mottram. My dad's not a person you can have a word with.'

'Ben, do you think you could call me Sally?'

'Yeah, if you want me to . . . Sally. Cool!'

'Do you like your dad, Ben?'

'I dunno . . . Sally. I thought I did.' He thought for quite a moment. 'No. I never liked him. I loved him once, but . . . not now.'

'Oh. OK. Anyway, Ben, you're still going to art school?'

'Yes.'

'Good. I've been looking at the High Street, Ben, and it's—'

'Crap.'

'Yes. I was searching for the right word, but, well yes, crap, almost, but not quite, because it doesn't need to be. It's the shopfronts. They're—'

'Crap.'

He grinned. Sally had to laugh.

'Could you elaborate, Ben?'

'Certainly. They're ugly, garish, crude, aggressive and boastful. They compete with each other instead of complementing each other. The worse their products, the greater their conceit. Apart from that they're not too bad.'

'If I asked you – I only say "if", I'm not decided – if I asked you to . . . um . . . well, design matching shopfronts, matching but not identical shopfronts that would help to make this street beautiful, do you think you could do it?'

'Yes.'

'I just might ask you to, Ben.'

'Wow! Now that would be cool. Yeah, I think I . . .'

He stopped. He wasn't looking at her any more. Lucy Basridge was walking up the street. Sally could see him forcing his concentration back to the shopfronts.

'Yeah, that would be great,' he said.

'Terrific. Marvellous. Off you go now before she disappears.'

He looked at her in astonishment.

'Cool,' he said. 'Sally Mottram, you are one cool dude.'

'Go.'

He rushed off after Lucy, caught up with her just before she reached her house.

'Hello, Lucy,' he said.

'Well, hello you,' said Lucy.

'Hello.'

'Was that your painting?'

'Yep.'

'It's great.'

'Thanks.'

'You're clever.'

'Thanks. Fancy a . . .'

He couldn't think of anything to suggest.

'A what?'

'Dunno. Walk? Drink?'

'Neither if you can't decide which. I like my men to be masterful.'

This is a challenge, Ben. Rise to it.

She was going. Any second now she would be gone.

'Drink, then.'

'OK.'

It was as simple as that.

A drink was a good idea. The temperature had reached nineteen. The workers on the waste ground needed a drink too.

'It's a lovely day. We've done well. Break for lunch when you feel like it. It'll be hot this afternoon. Only come back if you want to. I will. You needn't,' intoned the vicar. He turned to Sally and in a much lower voice said, 'Come to lunch, Sally.' She, eager to escape Marigold until she'd had her dinner with Conrad on Tuesday, agreed immediately, failing to notice a dangerous urgency in the vicar's voice. They set off so fast that there was clear water between them and the waste ground before anyone noticed that they had gone.

'Brilliant,' he said. 'Well done. Um . . . I thought . . . um . . . I think I feel a bit too sweaty for the Weavers' if you know what I mean, Sally.'

'Yes, I do, Dominic.'

'You do? Are you feeling a bit too sweaty for the Weavers'?'

'Dominic, that is not at all the sort of thing you say to a lady.'

'I know. Small talk is my Achilles heel. Mother, a clever woman, once gave me some advice about the ministry that I never forgot. "Forget the Gospels, Dominic. Brush up your small talk, that's the way."'

'Um . . . yes.'

'What do you say to the Potherthwaite Arms?'

'I say, "Hello, Potherthwaite Arms."'

'What?'

'It was a joke – almost.'

'Ah. That's the Achilles heel on my other foot.'

They entered the pub. It was quiet at this early hour, on this lovely sunny day, apart from four men, two of them Muslims, playing dominoes together.

'Good morrow, ostler,' said the vicar, rendered somewhat fanciful by the morning's exertions and the sunshine and the fact that he had persuaded a lovely lady to visit the pub with him.

'You what?' said the barman.

'A large noggin for me,' said the vicar.

'A what?'

Some of the wind was knocked out of the vicar's sails.

'A pint of your best bitter,' he said rather more quietly. Sally plumped for a gin and tonic. 'Large, need I say?' said the vicar.

The barman gave the impression that he had needed to say it.

They ordered two ploughmans. 'Or should I call them ploughmen?' commented the vicar. The barman ignored the question totally. The vicar led Sally towards a corner. On their way he stopped to speak briefly to the dominoes players.

'Ah. Fives and twos. A great game.'

All four dominoes players stared at him.

'I sometimes think I don't have the common touch,' said the vicar to Sally as they moved on towards their table.

'It's just that the game's actually called fives and threes,' said Sally.

When they were seated, the Revd Dominic Otley leant forward and spoke very quietly. 'Little tip for you. For tomorrow. Seventeen minutes seventeen seconds.'

'What?'

'My estimate for tomorrow's sermon. Easy to remember. People bet on the length, you know. I do myself. Not myself, of course, in the sense of myself. Wouldn't do. I have what I believe is called a bookies' runner. Never won. Can't keep to my estimated time, you see.' He changed the tone of his voice into what he thought was an intimate one. 'Sally?'

Sally's heart began to race. Sadly for the vicar's chances, it raced with dread, not excitement.

'There's something I've been wanting to say to you for some time, Sally,' said the Revd Dominic Otley. 'I felt it needed a suitable pause after your dreadful tragedy. Tact, you know. A quality present in all the Otley family.' He began to breathe rather heavily. 'They all go on about the Boyce-Willoughby woman, and yes, she is beautiful, but you . . . you have a better beauty, a more discreet beauty.'

'Thank you, Dominic. What every woman wants to hear. Discreet beauty.'

The sarcasm escaped him entirely.

He put his great Bible-holding hand on her left knee. His breathing was getting harder. She removed his hand gently and placed it on his thigh in slow motion.

'Will you come to dinner with me on Tuesday?' he asked.

'Oh, Dominic, I can't. I'm having dinner on Tuesday.'

'With . . . a man?'

'The details of my social life are hardly your business, but yes, with a man.'

'Ah. Perhaps . . . Wednesday?'

'It's very kind of you, Dominic, but . . . at present my social life is somewhat in flux.'

'Flux?'

'Yes.'

'Somewhat?'

'Yes.'

'At present?'

'Yes.'

'That encourages me to think that the . . . um . . . "flux" may not be permanent. Maybe I have surprised you today. I shall make my feelings known later, when they will not be such a surprise.'

'Dominic, I wouldn't go to bed with you if I was the last woman in the Pother Valley and if you had inherited ten billion pounds, and I think that may very well go for every other woman in the Pother Valley and probably every female in the country including Polish and Portuguese immigrants, so I wouldn't waste your time with me or any other woman if I were you. Another noggin?'

But that was not what she said.

'Later, yes,' she said.

All afternoon the sun shone. The setting sun in the west that evening was most glorious to behold, but there was hardly anybody on the Quays to behold it, largely for the simple reason that there was nowhere for the beholders to sit down without ordering something from the café, and also because some seventy minutes before sunset it slid out of view behind the stark, sterile hills, and sunset comes early in late October.

And all day Sunday the sun shone too, but we have seen Potherthwaite in the sun and perhaps we should visit a couple of the places that the sun did not reach that day, for the sun never reaches everywhere in any town. We refer to the Intensive Care Unit of Potherthwaite District Hospital, and to the ground floor of number 6 Cadwallader Road.

Harry sat at Olive's bedside. Sunshine was streaming into the ward. On the bed, the sun didn't quite reach Harry's newspaper, with its proud headline of '*Warmer in Huddersfield than Marrakesh*'. Olive's eyes were closed, and she seemed to be asleep, but he knew that she wasn't. She opened her eyes just for a moment, gave him an anguished look.

'Harry?' she said in a faint voice.

He leant closer to her.

'Yes, my darling?'

'There's something I have to tell you.'

She closed her eyes and just for a moment he thought that she was dead.

'Harry?'

'I'm here.'

It dawned on him that she was plucking up her strength. She didn't have enough left to open her eyes and speak at the same time.

'Arnold and I met when we were students,' she whispered.

He had to lean even further forward.

'In Cheltenham. Harry, you're hurting.'

He realized that in his tension he was gripping her hand. He removed his hand hastily.

'Sorry. So sorry,' he said.

'We . . . were friends. Not lovers.'

'Ah.'

He wanted to ask her why she hadn't told him. He was so hurt that she hadn't told him. He wanted her to be fit and well again so they could talk it through.

'Harry?'

Was it his imagination or was the voice even weaker now? Was she dying?

'Yes, my darling.'

Don't leave me, Olive, not yet.

'It was while you were in Monte Cassino.'

It was absurd, at this moment, to correct her. But he did. Habit dies hard.

'Montepulciano.'

271

'Yes. We thought . . . we thought that you and Jill . . . we . . . anyway, we . . . we did it, Harry . . . Just once. Just once, Harry.'

He felt sick. It was so unfair of her to tell him this now, when there was no time to work through it, learn to cope with it, learn to accept it. What could he do but forgive her instantly? So unfair. But he stroked her hand, her old hand, her bony, veiny hand flecked with age spots. He stroked her hand very gently.

'Harry?'

The voice was going.

'Harry, I'm so sorry.'

He stroked her hand again. He couldn't speak. He could scarcely breathe.

'Just wanted to . . . wipe the . . .'

Those were her last words. He thought that she was dead. In a film she would have been. But then he saw that she was still breathing, her chest was still just moving.

He stumbled out of the room, tears cascading down his face. He reeled down the corridor as if he was drunk. The doors of the lift were opening and he stepped in before he realized that he didn't know why he needed to.

There was a man in the lift. A doctor.

'Are you all right?' the doctor asked with concern.

Harry knew that he would bitterly regret his anger, but he couldn't worry about that now.

'No, I'm not,' he said. 'It's all very well for her to wipe the fucking slate clean, but what about me?'

No sunshine ever lightened the gloom in the lift, but it promised every morning to flood Ellie's bed. Frustratingly, it never quite reached it. Not ever.

'It's just such a lovely scene,' Sally was saying. 'So beautiful, so serene. There's still a great deal of beauty in this world. I'll take you to see it.'

'What about your husband?' said Ellie.

'I don't have one any more, Ellie.'

'I know that, Mrs Mottram. I'm not stupid.'

'Ellie? I'm not a carer. I'm not a moral woman keen to satisfy my conscience by doing good works. I'm a friend who is passionate about this. Ellie, Ali, Oli, I will enjoy showing you these things even more than you'll enjoy them. Your joy will thrill me. So, please, no more Mrs Mottram. Mrs Mottram is gone. Call me Sally. If I ever have another husband, which is looking doubtful, he will have to accept that I have made you some commitments. Venice was my first commitment. Florence was the second. The Stockholm Archipelago is the third. When you are fit enough, Ellie, I will take you, and Ali and Oli of course, on a cruise to the Baltic, that great northern sea, where the air in summer is as clear as spring water, and the days are long.'

How could she promise those things when she was so strapped for cash? The thought slid into her mind like a burglar into a house. And she answered, to herself, How can I not? I know, in these moments in this house with my three obese friends, that the Transition of Potherthwaite will succeed, Ellie's great walk will succeed, and the generous heart of this new Potherthwaite will not allow me to renege upon my promise.

'We sailed up it in the early morning,' she continued. 'So few people got up early to see it. They pay all that money and they miss things because they can't be bothered to get out of bed, or rather, they can't be bothered to read up where they're going so they don't even know that it's something worth getting out of bed for. They're half alive, Ellie. Barry didn't bother to get out of bed. I tiptoed to the bathroom, put on my dressing gown, tiptoed back into the cabin, picked up the key, unlocked the door, slipped out. I thought that I half hoped to wake him but I realize now that I dreaded

273

waking him. I didn't want my husband beside me – isn't that awful?

'I stood at the bow and watched the ship slicing through the clear water. I suppose it was about six o'clock. There was still a touch of mist on the water, and there were islands everywhere, little islands covered in trees with rocky coasts and as you looked ahead you couldn't tell where the channel was, which islands you would pass to starboard and which to port, and dotted about the islands were houses, not crowding each other, pretty houses with clean simple lines and bright but never garish colours, and it went on and on and you dreamt of living there.'

Sally stopped for a moment. Nobody said a word. Ellie in her great bed which the sun never reached, Ali and Oli beside the bed in their large chairs – all three were silent. Sally realized that they weren't in Cadwallader Road at all. They were in the Stockholm Archipelago.

'We'd been going at least an hour, maybe more, and a little builder's boat came chugging towards us from the city, and I laughed out loud. I laughed because I'd thought of them arriving at some far-off island, settling to work and finding they'd brought the wrong-sized screws, and having to chug all the way back to Stockholm to change them. There was nobody there whom I wanted to share it with. When you're there, I will have someone to share it with, and, who knows, maybe a lovely husband to share it with as well.'

But not Conrad.

Tuesday loomed.

TWENTY-NINE

A difficult meal

This time Conrad took her towards the east, towards the gathering dark. It was a dull, stagnant evening. The clouds, the traffic and Sally's heart were heavy.

It was her birthday. She was forty-eight.

There were a few flecks of almost undetectable rain on the windscreen. Conrad gave the wipers one turn. There wasn't enough rain for them, and they screeched.

'We can go to the moon,' he said, 'but we can't make the perfect windscreen wiper.'

What a way to celebrate her birthday. A Chinese meal with an unscrupulous seducer.

Conrad looked at Sally as if he had suddenly noticed that everything wasn't right with her.

'Are you all right?' he asked.

She didn't want to tell him that it was her birthday. Nobody in Potherthwaite knew, not even the Indian restaurants. Barry had been so jealous of any sign of enjoyment in her that she had long ago given up any attempt at celebration.

'Yes. Fine. Why?'

'You seem very quiet.'

275

What could she talk about? Her three cards, too sad a sight even to put on the mantelpiece. One from Judith. Insincere? One from Sam and Beth. How she wished she could help them more. One from Alice and family. How lovely New Zealand has been looking this spring. No mention of an invitation.

She wished she was anywhere but in the Audi. She had no idea how to play the evening, but there was no point in challenging him now. She might at least get one more meal off the bastard.

'Not much to comment on really,' she said. 'It's not exactly an inspiring evening. It's not exactly an inspiring drive.'

'But worth it, I'm told,' said Conrad. 'My water people tell me it's the best Chinese restaurant for fifty miles.'

A cue. She grabbed it.

'How are you getting on with your water people?'

'Everything's fine. They're a nice bunch. I've just thought. I should have asked earlier. Do you like Chinese food?'

Yes, you should. But of course I know now that your perfect manners are just an act, a veneer, you conniving swine.

'To be honest, Conrad, I haven't had a Chinese meal for at least twenty-five years. Barry was not an adventurous eater.'

'Oh. Well. This'll be a bit of an adventure then.'

Not quite how I would have described it, Conrad.

'Yes. I'm looking forward to it.'

Liar.

The gaps between the small towns and villages in the Pother Valley were short, barely worth farming, and so they were barely farmed. There were a few disgruntled cows that had drawn the short straw. Sickly corn struggled to reach a height worth cutting. Elderly barns looked on the point of collapse. There was a dead badger at the side of the road.

The lights of 'Mr Kong' shone with spectacular vulgarity in the gathering gloom of this impatient evening. Once again, the cars in the car park made Conrad's Audi look very modest.

An extremely scrutable waiter greeted them with a broad smile and a warning of a dentist to be avoided at all costs. He led them into a vast, excessively bright room. Large groups of noisy people at circular tables were spinning their lazy Susans round, eating more than seemed possible, laughing more than seemed natural. Sally felt that if she confronted Conrad in this room he wouldn't hear a word that she was saying. Was this the point of his choice of restaurant? Did he suspect that she knew?

Seated at a table for two right at the far end of the room, Sally felt that she was drowning in fun. She stared at the enormous menu without comprehension. Her stomach tightened up at the sight of the endless lists of dishes.

'My friends didn't tell me it would be so noisy,' shouted Conrad.

'I beg your pardon?' she shouted.

'My friends didn't tell me it would be so noisy.'

'It is, isn't it?'

'I beg your pardon?'

'It is isn't it?'

'Yes. If you aren't used to Chinese food, shall I order?'

'Good . . . idea.'

'Is there anything you don't like?'

'Sorry. What?'

'Sorry. What?'

'That's what I said. "Sorry . . . What?"'

'Ah. I said, "Is there anything you don't like?"'

'Shark fin.'

'Right.'

A smiling waitress came to take their order and had no trouble hearing as Conrad rattled off a dismayingly large number of dishes. Well, it was all her fault. It was she who had thought that she might as well grab one more meal off the lecherous philanderer before she told him what she thought of him.

They were both silent after the waitress had gone. Sally felt an urgent need to speak.

'How are you finding the house?' she asked.

They discussed her old house with a pretence of vitality, and found that they had acclimatized themselves to the noise and could hear each other passably well if they just raised their voices a little.

Conrad leant forward and said, 'I'm sorry, Sally, this isn't going to work.'

'What isn't going to work?'

'I intended to wait till after the meal, but I just can't. Sally, I've . . . I'm afraid I've . . .' He looked round nervously, as if he really thought that people at neighbouring tables might be able to hear him above the din. 'I've met somebody.'

Sally's heart thudded dangerously. She was swept away by a tide of relief, but the tide had surged through a timberyard and had brought sharp shards of jealousy downstream with it, and soon there was nothing but shock and jealousy in her heart.

'Well, happy birthday, Sally' she thought.

But all she said was, 'Oh.'

'In fact, she's a friend of yours. Marigold Boyce-Willoughby.'

'Good Lord! Marigold!'

Why lie? Why commit herself to this charade? But she couldn't say, 'I know. She told me,' or he would say, 'Why did you come out with me if you knew?' and she would have to say, 'Because I thought you were a conniving two-timing tosspot and I was going to tear you to shreds in a very public and embarrassing scene once I'd eaten your expensive food and drunk your delicious wine.'

He was telling her how it had happened.

'After my dinner with you at the Shoulder of Mutton – what a lovely evening that was. You looked so beautiful, Sally, in that glorious sunset . . .'

'I'm good in sunsets. Everybody says so.'

She wished she hadn't said that. He looked as if he wished she hadn't said it too. He looked as if he thought that for her to show any evidence of hurt or bitterness was an affront to good manners.

'I enjoyed the whole evening enormously, Sally.'

Sally narrowly managed to avoid saying, 'So enormously that in the next few days you didn't ask me out again for fear you wouldn't be able to stand the excitement.'

'Then after the march I just ran into Marigold on the Quays . . .'

Sally just managed to avoid saying, 'How careless!'

'. . . and . . . well, a strange thing happened.'

Sally failed to avoid saying, 'You realized how much you preferred her to me and asked her to dinner.'

'Sally! No! Well, I mean, I did, I suppose, but not because I . . . well, I mean, I suppose in a way I must have done or . . .'

'When you dig a hole for yourself, don't carry on and fall into it, Conrad.'

Their starters arrived. Conrad had ordered far too much. Sally felt sick.

'Tuck in,' said Conrad.

Sally's attempts to tuck in were, frankly, pathetic, and Conrad didn't do much better.

Sally put her chopsticks down. At least three-quarters of the food remained uneaten.

'I'm really sorry that it's turned out like this,' said Conrad.

'Do you know, so am I,' said Sally.

THIRTY

Sally confronts her soul

In the morning the clouds had lifted, but Sally's heart hadn't. She was furious with Marigold for stealing Conrad from her. She was furious with Conrad for dumping her, and for the huge miscalculation he had made in the way that he told her about it. She was furious with Barry for having killed himself, thus forcing her into this ridiculous business of leading the ˙Transition movement in Potherthwaite, and having such debts that she was condemned to live in this wretched flat. She was furious with Potherthwaite for having become such an abject place that she had persuaded herself to attempt to save it. She was furious with the kettle for being so slow – you bought British out of the goodness of your heart and look what you landed yourself with. She was furious with herself for having thought that the most effective way of dealing with Conrad was to accept an expensive dinner from him and then throw it, metaphorically speaking, in his face. She was furious with herself for not having realized that there was even the smallest chance that Conrad was actually an all-right guy. She was furious with herself for not having bigger breasts. She was furious with Marigold for having such big breasts. She was furious with Marigold for claiming to be completely disillusioned with men and then tempting them with her soft, fleshy legs on every bar stool from Land's End to John o'Groats. She was furious with her toothbrush for being such a silly shape. In short, she was furious.

She had to get out of Potherthwaite. She had to escape the valley. She had to walk. She had to punish her body. She would walk, and walk, and walk, walk out of the valley, walk over the hills, walk into the setting sun, walk through the dark night, under that absurd plethora of stars, under dead stars, past dead sheep, until she fell, until she herself was dead. They'd all be sorry then.

She finished her meagre breakfast, filled three empty water bottles with three litres of tap water – perhaps she might change her mind about dying at some later stage – put on walking clothes and boots, took up her rucksack, walked out of her hated flat, locked the door, strode along Vatican Road, turned left into Quays Approach, left again into High Street East, passed the Potherthwaite Arms – one good thing if she did manage to die would be that she would never need to set eyes upon the Revd Dominic Otley again in her life – walked through the Market Place, scene of that great afternoon which she now understood to have been a false dawn, crossed the river where the two bipolar mallard were having a mad moment, walked past the waste ground, the hole in the heart of Potherthwaite, looked in on it and saw how little impact the great clean-up on Saturday had achieved, entered the Potherthwaite Deli – there were no other customers, the bloody place didn't deserve a deli – bought three sandwiches and a slice of apple tart – it would be stupid to decide not to die and then die after all because you'd got nothing to eat – walked out of the deli just as Nicola Winkle walked in – did the bloody woman live there? – and walked on past the cul-de-sac, where Marigold would even now be fucking her lover, past Cadwallader Road, where she was going to let Ellie down really badly, past the Rose and Crown, which was still boarded up, past the turning for Oxford Road, where Conrad was even now fucking his lover – no, even bloody Marigold couldn't be fucked by the same man in two different places at the same time – on on on past the allotments and there at the end of the valley, on the left, was the supermarket, and the cars were pouring in – people who had been on the march were busy betraying their principles, the town didn't deserve to be saved, she had wasted all her time and energy.

The road began to rise now, up up up into the bare hills, up up up to the five hairpin bends. The sun was breaking through, the ground was still wet from the night's rain, the moors were steaming as they dried, Sally's world smelt like a laundry. On on on she went, round the first hairpin bend. 'I'm going round the bend,' she cried to an inquisitive sheep. 'That's what I'm doing. I'm going round the bend.'

The sheep ran away. I'd run away if a madwoman shouted at me, she told herself.

She found that with her articulation of the thought that she was going round the bend, she started to cease going round the bend. By the time she went round the second bend she looked back on the morning and realized that she really had been going round the bend.

She took a long draught of water. Already there wasn't much left in the first bottle. She decided not to take any more water until she reached the third bend, and not to eat any of her sandwiches until she had got to the top. She also vowed not to look back until she had reached the top.

She wasn't angry any more. Strangely, that disappointed

283

her. And it also made her very tired. The anger had been fuelling her walk, moving her legs for her.

It was more than an hour later before she reached the top. She was hot and extremely weary. She sank on to the ground. Sheep watched her cautiously. She took a draught of water from the second bottle.

After about half an hour, for quite a few minutes of which she had actually been asleep, she pulled herself to her feet. To her left were the vast windmills of the wind farm. Three of them weren't turning even though there was a steady breeze up here. Above her, three buzzards circled slowly on the thermals. Behind her, the inhospitable moors stretched to infinity. In front of her, in the valley, Potherthwaite looked tiny.

Sally had realized, deep down, as she passed the end of Cadwallader Road, that she would not abandon the town and the Transition movement. She was hating herself for her jealous feelings towards Marigold. How much more would she hate herself if she failed Ellie? After she had eaten she would walk down to the town and call on her and describe a boat trip on the Rhine.

She had seen many women fall prey to jealousy and had always felt that it demeaned them, so she had been very shocked to find herself giving way to such thoughts over the long wretched night. But how could she stop her feelings? She couldn't cut them off like a gangrenous leg.

She munched her hummus-and-red-pepper sandwich slowly. She didn't feel hungry. The memory of all that Chinese food still haunted her. The look of contempt in the waitress's eyes as she removed the vast amount they hadn't managed to eat still taunted her.

She tried logic. Marigold didn't know that she had been out with Conrad. Marigold was a sexy woman. She hadn't asked to be. She might not even have wanted to be. It had hardly been of great benefit to her. She had suffered three broken marriages. Her assertion that it had all been the fault of the men might have been an exaggeration – there were cupboards full of shoes to testify that Marigold wasn't blameless – but Sally had known Timothy Boyce-Willoughby and any woman who had been married to him needed sympathy. And her brain examining. No, find generosity in your heart, Sally. You can't do this Potherthwaite stuff without generosity in your heart. Marigold didn't know that you had been out with Conrad. Concentrate on that. Marigold, damn her, was blameless.

Marigold was her best friend. They had sworn undying love. They had sworn that no man would ever come between them. What sort of a woman was she if those words were empty? What sort of a woman was she if she hated her best friend? But she didn't hate her best friend. She wanted to hate her best friend, but she couldn't. In fact, she wanted both to hate her and not to hate her at the same time.

She sought refuge in an easier debate. Should she eat her second sandwich now or save it for the walk down? She couldn't decide on this issue either. She looked down on the town, the church, the Market Place, Oxford Road, 'The Larches'.

She began the long walk down, the walk to Marigold, the walk towards Conrad. She still hadn't made her mind up about the sandwich, but it was already too late to eat it before she started, so it had already decided for itself.

Instead of the sandwich she chewed over the situation as she walked. She couldn't absolve herself of all blame for the fact that her dinner with Conrad hadn't led on to romance. She had been tense, stiff, insufficiently amusing. The pub had been efficient, attractive, professional, courteous. It had lacked only heart. And she, she had been much the same.

Marigold was right for Conrad, more right than her. She had no reason to complain. Marigold was her friend. She needed her.

Conrad had never given her, in word or deed, any kind of promise. If Marigold could bring herself to trust him, she might find happiness at last.

This morning Sally had felt herself capable of abandoning this town, of reneging on all her promises to it. What sort of a woman did that make her?

Well, not too bad, because she had found that she couldn't. But to even be capable of thinking it, that was enough to disqualify her from any thoughts of condemning Marigold.

She was very tired now, and walking more and more slowly. 'Bit of a wasted day? Every day's like that for us,' said the body language of the sheep. She had finished her water, but the air was getting cooler. There were few cars, and none of them stopped for her. Even if she had thumbed them, none of them would have stopped. The days of trust were over.

It was early evening, and getting dark, by the time she reached the floor of the valley. She telephoned Marigold. Yes, she was in. Yes, she would like to see her. Lovely.

She walked to the supermarket. It was like every supermarket everywhere. She saw Matt Winkle talking to a woman whom she didn't know. She waited for him to be free, so that he could advise her about champagne.

But his conversation went on and on. His voice was rising. She could hear his words clearly now. 'Madam, I didn't grow them, I didn't pick them, I didn't store them, I didn't put a notice on them stating they were ripe and ready to eat, I accept that they weren't, I offer you two more packs of inedible peaches or double your money back, plus I will pay all your dental bills for the next five years and I apologize, but I am sorry, I have to go, I'm off to Italy to buy peaches which I will bring back in my car and ripen in my garden specially for you, see you Tuesday, goodbye.'

He walked over to Sally.

'I've had enough,' he said.

'So I see.'

'I'm losing my marbles and my wife. She says she can't live with me any more.'

'Oh, Matt. Poor Matt.'

'So how can I help you, Sally?'

'Do you have a good bottle of champagne, chilled?'

'Certainly do. Peace offering?'

'Something like that.'

'This is nice. Not too sharp. Nice and biscuity. Have it on the house.'

'No, Matt, please.'

'Yes, Sally, please. Nice to see your face, brought me back to sanity.'

'Are things really bad with Nicola?'

'Not good. I'm not liveable with.'

'Oh, Matt, be careful.'

'Yep.'

'Thanks.'

'Pleasure.'

She hardly found the energy to walk on, but she did. She limped past the turning to Oxford Road. She told herself that it wouldn't have worked, living there with Conrad. She told herself that it wouldn't have worked, living anywhere with Conrad.

She didn't quite believe herself.

She paused at Cadwallader Road. How could she have even thought of turning her back on Ellie?

She was too tired to recreate the castles of the Rhine today.

287

She turned into the cul-de-sac. Number 9 looked empty. Well, it would be. Olive hadn't died, but she had been in a coma since Sunday. Harry spent all his days at her side, stroking her hand and trying to forgive her.

Marigold waved from an upstairs window. The door opened as she approached it. Her heart was racing. She handed Marigold the champagne. Marigold kissed her and asked to what she owed this treat?

'I bring good news,' said Sally bravely.

She apologized for being in walking clothes.

Marigold said, 'You look good in anything. That's what I envy about you.'

Marigold conjured up nibbles as if she had known that she was going to be brought a bottle of vintage champagne. They didn't sit in the chairs where they had drunk deep from Baileys, Cointreau and friendship. Sally was very relieved by this. They sat on the window seat above the dimly lit cul-de-sac, a little table in front of them with the vintage champagne in vintage flutes, and the nibbles stylishly arrayed on tiny Japanese plates.

'So what's this good news?' Marigold asked.

Sally told her of her dinner with Conrad, her feelings for Conrad, her reaction to Marigold's tale about *her* dinner with Conrad, and about her second dinner with Conrad last night.

'So the good news is that I think you can trust him. I think he's proved he's a good man.'

'Aren't you jealous?' asked Marigold.

'Why should I be?' said Sally. 'I've got my own lover boy chasing me.'

'Ooh! Who's he?'

'No less a person than the vicar of this parish.'

Marigold hooted and then suddenly stopped.

'Don't say you mean it,' she said.

'I do.'

'Oh God.'

'Not much help there.'

'Are you really serious?'

'I'm serious that he's chasing me. He can't run fast enough though.'

Marigold laughed.

'Can you imagine it?' said Sally. '"For what I am about to receive may nobody ever give thanks."'

They giggled and laughed and Marigold refilled their glasses.

Sally raised hers.

'To you, Marigold,' she said. 'I hope that you will find the courage to trust in Conrad and that the two of you will have a long and happy life together.'

'Do you really mean that, Sally?'

Sally smiled.

'Of course I don't, you idiot. But I hope if I say it often enough I may mean it one day.'

'Oh, Sally.'

Marigold went over to her and hugged her solemnly.

'I think you will meet a wonderful man very, very soon,' she said.

BOOK FIVE

Transition

THIRTY-ONE

An emissary with a wet handshake

It was the handshake that Sally remembered. If she'd been asked to describe his face, she wouldn't have had a clue. She had forgotten the paunch. She had forgotten that he looked more like a pregnant man than any man she had ever seen. She had forgotten the long strands of his oily hair. She wasn't sure if he had shown her his lopsided smile. Well, she had only met him once, on the day of the great march, as she left the crowded Market Place, and a whole winter had passed since then.

It had been a dispiriting winter, wet and wild, and with desperately little to show for it. True, work on the bypass had begun, but it had ground to a halt in the mud. True, the clearance of the Potherthwaite Arm of the Rackstraw and Sladfield Canal had begun. Five and a quarter miles makes a fairly pitiful canal, but five and a quarter miles turned out to be a hell of a distance to clear. There was so little to show for it, and so much to do, and only the hardiest and the most loyal persisted.

She was walking through the Market Place again, on a cool day in late spring. There were no crowds now. She was dreaming of how it would look when it was pedestrianized, when the whole of the High Street was pedestrianized, when her dreams had become reality. At the moment, there was nothing to be done but to dream. Sally was feeling very small that morning. Her dreams seemed absurd.

Now the thing that she had dreaded since she had seen him limping into the square from High Street East was happening. He was holding out his hand.

'We meet again, clever lady,' he said.

She shook the proffered hand. In her excessive need for good manners she didn't want to hurt his feelings by making the handshake too brief, in case he was aware of its unpleasant dampness. So she overcompensated and held his hand for just a moment longer than was necessary, as if to say, 'Don't worry, strange man. I at least don't find your handshake repulsive.'

But she did. A tremor of revulsion passed through her.

'You recall our first meeting?' he asked.

Who could forget him?

'I do. The march was just leaving the square. The band was playing. You said nice things.'

'I said them, lady, because I meant them. You were impressive. I wished to leave you in no doubt about that.'

'You succeeded.'

'Good. You may recall that I told you that when I reported that I had found you impressive, the boss would be impressed.'

'I do recall it.'

'I told him, and he was impressed.'

'That's good news.'

'He was more than impressed. He was *very* impressed. I have to tell you, lovely lady, that he is not often impressed, and very rarely is he deeply impressed, but when I described the march to him, your speech, your charisma, your beauty – oh, yes, you are beautiful, Mrs Sally Mottram – I told him how you and . . . um . . . your partner . . .'

'Marigold Boyce-Willoughby.' Paradoxically, Marigold had irritated Sally that winter by seeming to proceed so slowly with her romance. It was one thing to have lost Conrad, but to have lost him to a woman who could do so little about it because her nerve had gone, that was painful. Sally had to work hard to prevent a touch of lingering iciness from creeping into her voice as she spoke the name.

'Correct. The two of you, at the head of that march – I told him that if you were to smile at the glaciers of the Arctic, the global warming that we all fear would become an avalanche.'

Sally just managed to say, 'You're very kind,' without laughing.

'I can tell you, lovely lady, that—'

'He was impressed?'

'You have got it in one. As ever, you have hit the nail on the proverbial.' He lowered his voice. 'I was impressed by how impressed he was. In fact, I don't think I have ever seen him so impressed.'

They were walking slowly up High Street West now, though neither of them could have said why.

'This is all very nice,' said Sally, 'but I have to say that I haven't the faintest idea who you are.'

'Oh, my goodness me. How remiss of me. You are walking, lady, with none other than Leonard Tiptree, more widely known to his friends and associates as Lennie.'

'Well, it's very good to meet you, Lennie, if I also may call you so.'

She realized her mistake even as she said it. Out came the hand. Once again, she shook it with every appearance of enthusiasm.

'How do you do, Lennie,' she said.

'How do you do, Mrs . . . or may I call you Sally?'

'Certainly, Lennie.'

'Thank you, Sally.'

'Lennie?'

'Yes, Sally?'

'I feel a fool.'

'You? Never.'

'I've let you go on and on. It was egotism. I was just thrilled to hear that you and your boss both found me impressive.'

'Oh, we did. Very impressive.'

'Yes, but – and thank you – but I should have said that I haven't the faintest idea who your boss is. I have no idea why you're here.'

'You have no idea why I'm here? Well, stone the pigeons as we used to say where I come from. Not many crows in Stoke Newington. I am so sorry. Stupid me. I am *so* sorry. That is *so* stupid. I come from none other than Sir Norman Oldfield himself. Don't tell me you haven't heard of Sir Norman Oldfield.'

'Of course I have.'

'He's one of the ten richest men in the *Sunday Times* list.'

'Yes, I know.'

'He was born in modest circumstances here in Potherthwaite.'

'Oh, I know. There's a plaque.'

'I know. Last time I was here I took a peep. I said to myself, "Lennie Tiptree, you little thought when your teacher said you'll never amount to anything – bastards, teachers, oops, excuse my French, but they are – you little thought that one day you would be emissary to the great Sir Norman Oldfield.'

'Emissary?'

'Sir Norman is allergic to people. I am his go-between. I prefer the word "emissary". A harmless piece of conceit, perhaps. I was sent here to find out whether I found you—'

'Impressive.'

'Once again you're too quick for me. The only reason I have not been back here sooner is that Sir Norman winters abroad. He has a house in Bermuda. But he had barely returned home, and he was speaking of you. Sally Mottram, you are about to have the most important conversation of your young life.'

'Young?'

'To me. Your enthusiasm for your cause has brought the bloom of youth to your lovely cheeks. Our talk may take some time.'

'Why am I not surprised?'

'Is there somewhere where we may sit, take a latte and perhaps a toasted teacake?'

'There is, on the next corner.'

They walked past the end of the cul-de-sac. Sally dreaded that she might run into Marigold. She didn't want to introduce her to Lennie, and then snub her by going off to talk to him alone, and she certainly didn't want Marigold to be present at the most important conversation of her 'young' life. Besides, there were bar stools at the Kosy Korner Kafé. She didn't want to witness Lennie Tiptree's admiration of Marigold's legs.

They sat in a far korner, as far as possible from the kounter. Sally ordered a kappuccino and a kream kake, Lennie a latte and a toasted teakake. Lennie told Kate Kavanagh, 'I'm never happier than with butter on my chin, me.' When Kate had gone, they began their konversation.

'So you're an emissary,' said Sally.

'I'm all sorts of things. I'm a factotum. I'm an enabler. I'm a communicator. I'm a major-duomo, or is that an Italian cathedral? I am the world for a man who has withdrawn from it. He sent me to Potherthwaite with specific instructions to watch you at work and return to him with my view on whether you were imp—'

'—ressive, yes.'

'Precisely. To cut a long story short, I told him you were. Very. He said he would like to meet you. Now that is extraordinary. If you don't know him, you can't begin to imagine how extraordinary that is. He does not meet people. He makes Howard Hughes seem like a socialite. He thinks everyone is planning to infect him. He lives in a large house outside Marlow, with a spectacular view of the Thames. Views give him little pleasure. We were standing by the window one day, talking, he was giving me his instructions, I ventured to say, "It's a lovely view. Why don't you look at it?", and he said, "I looked at it yesterday. It'll be the same. It never bloody changes." Sir Norman, Sally, is not a happy man. Nor is he known for his generosity. That's what makes this all the more extraordinary.'

'All this?'

'He wants to give you a great deal of money.'

Sally's heart was racing. Hope surged through her.

'Good Lord.'

'Don't say things like that to him. "Good Lord." "Oh God." Anathema. I mean it. An-bleeding-athema.'

'He doesn't believe in God?'

'He believes in him and he hates him. He gave him all this money and took away all the qualities that he might have needed to enjoy it. Now, Sir Norman could have written to you – not by computer, he hates computers – but he prefers to send me. He likes to be paradoxical, does Sir Norman, if you ask me, so, hating the personal touch himself, he uses it, via his henchmen, in all his dealings.'

'So, you're a henchman as well?'

'I like to think I'm his senior henchman. Not that I'm quite sure what a henchman is, but, if I am one, I like to think I'm the senior one. So, I came up to Potherthwaite, wanted to take you off guard, to see if you really are as impressive as I thought. Got your address – everybody knows you, as I knew they would – went to your flat, you weren't in. You were out.'

'Sorry.'

'No. Not your fault. Can't blame you. You weren't expecting me. So, went to the Market Place, saw you. End of story. Do you know, I think I fancy another toasted teacake.' Suddenly he roared, 'Butter on the chin. Butter on the chin, eh?'

Several people looked round. Sally's smile reassured them that she wasn't being attacked by a lunatic. Lennie ordered another latte and another toasted teakake. Sally just had a glass of tap water. Lennie waited until they had been served before resuming his tale.

'Now,' he said at last, 'please don't let what I say make you feel nervous, but I must give you a few hints, because if you play your cards right you will be given a great deal of money and all your problems will be solved at a stroke. At, lovely Sally Mottram, a stroke. Now, you will be sent train tickets for this coming Saturday. If you aren't free, change your arrangements – Sir Norman hates cancellations. You will be met at the station, not by me—'

'I should think not. You'll be too busy being an emissary, a henchman, a factotum, an enabler, a communicator and a major-duomo, which I'm sure you're quite capable of even though you're right, it is an Italian cathedral.'

Lennie Tiptree showed no sign of amusement at this, but said, 'Sally Mottram, you are a card. Right. You will dine that night with Sir Norman, in the morning you will be served breakfast on your own – Sir Norman doesn't do breakfast, he hates breakfast – you will have an early Sunday lunch with Sir Norman, very traditional, and a chauffeur will then take you back to the station to catch what I'm afraid will be the first of at least three trains. You will, I fervently hope, leave with the offer of a small fortune. Take as little luggage as possible. Sir Norman hates luggage. He once booked on a ship to America, saw all the luggage and refused to go. Oh, and make sure you have gloves.'

'Gloves, why?'

'For shaking hands. Sir Norman will not touch a naked hand. Even with me, after all these years, he won't touch my naked hand.'

I wish I had some gloves today, thought Sally.

'Oh, and one more thing. Don't mention Market Harborough.'

'What?'

'Sir Norman cannot abide references to Market Harborough.'

'Why?'

'Haven't the faintest idea. No idea. Nobody has. Maybe something bad happened there once. But a Canadian financier once happened to say, over the brandy, that his aunt lived in Market Harborough, and he was thrown out at eleven minutes past midnight.'

'Good Lord.'

'And don't say "Good Lord".'

'Oh, sorry. Oh God, this . . . Oh my God! Oh, this is going to be difficult. Thank goodness I've never been to Market Harborough though.'

'Don't tell him!'

'I don't think I can do this.'

'You can. You can, Sally. You can walk it. You have to. You have to, Sally. Remember only one other thing. Be yourself at all times. Be true to yourself. Only that will work. Any questions?'

'Well, just one, I suppose. Why is he doing all this?'

'Ah. Now that, lovely lady, is a question. That most definitely *is* a question.'

'Is there an answer?'

'I have a theory. I am sure you will be able to reach the same answer as me. Clever lady, clever impressive Sally, what is the answer? Take your time.'

Sally took a sip of water, and thought.

'Um . . .'

'Yes?'

'Um . . . is it because he loves Potherthwaite?'

'I think so, but that is only half the answer.'

'The other half being the answer to the question, "Why does he love Potherthwaite?"'

'Precisely. And why *does* he love Potherthwaite?'

'Um . . .'

'Yes?'

'Because . . . could it be because . . . this is so sad, Lennie . . . it was the last place in which he was happy?'

'Exactly . . . and yes, it is sad, Sally. Well done. You see, you can do it. For you it will be what my dear mother in Stoke Newington used to call a doodle. Impressive? The word itself is not impressive enough to describe you.'

'Thank you.'

'Good luck, Sally.'

He held out his hand. Sally shook it. They both allowed their hands to remain clasped just a moment longer than was necessary.

Their eyes met. Sally had no idea what he was thinking, and he, she suspected, had no idea what she was thinking.

It was disturbing.

THIRTY-TWO

A life of luxury

Sir Norman's Rolls-Royce purred almost silently through the thick beech woods of the Chiltern Hills. Overhead, red kite circled slowly in their perpetual search for carrion. Sally's nerves were as taut as the strings of a violin. In her stomach, tiny creatures were churning cream into butter. This visit, this taste of unimagined luxury, was in fact yet another hurdle, her greatest hurdle yet. Each hurdle overcome was a relief. Each hurdle seemed like the last hurdle, but by now Sally believed that there was no last hurdle, there would be hurdles for her till the day of her death. This, however, might well be the greatest hurdle. Money in large quantities was promised, if she passed this test.

The Rolls-Royce turned off on to a side road, climbed steadily through the great trees. There was an occasional brief glimpse of the Thames far below, alive with boats on this sunny Saturday afternoon. On the left were the thick, dark, daunting woods. On the right they passed discreet drives that led to big houses built to impress and then carefully hidden, behind thick hedges, from all the people who might have been impressed, had they been able to catch a glimpse of them.

No house name stood at the beginning of Sir Norman Oldfield's drive. This was a discreet world. Postmen in Buckinghamshire were not expected to suffer from Alzheimer's.

The gates to the property opened slowly, solemnly, silently at the chauffeur's touch. The drive was long, and passed through more woods, thinned out and less foreboding. Then the house stood before Sally. Its centre was Georgian, red-brick, with regular windows. It was immense. One end of the house turned suddenly French, with a large round turret. The other end favoured Italy, with a tall square tower. None of it was old.

A maid, smart and formal in black and white, led Sally up a wide staircase, past rows of indifferent Italianate land-scapes. Behind them, a manservant in morning dress carried her tiny suitcase. The maid led her along a corridor studded with oak chests, opened a door, and stood aside to let Sally enter her suite. The male servant followed, carrying the case as if contemptuous of its wheels. He placed the case upon a receptacle for cases. It was large enough to have held four such cases side by side.

'Tea will be served in the drawing room in thirty minutes,' said the maid. It was a command, not a suggestion. 'Sir Norman will join you there for a pair of teeth at six-thirty.' Afterwards, Sally was quite proud that she hadn't shown any astonishment in the twenty seconds that it took for her to realize that the maid had said 'an aperitif'.

It was clear that the thirty minutes allowed her before tea, a period of time to be taken far more seriously than 'half an hour' would have been, was to enable her to change her clothes, soiled from sitting in seats sometimes occupied by the working classes, on three trains. She hadn't brought enough changes of clothes to be able to make one now. Damn Lennie Tiptree and his advice.

She stood at the window and looked out on a fantasy of terraces and fountains. Water spouted from the mouths of gods and goddesses and fat Cupids. Far below, the Thames meandered gently, as if reluctant to reach London and its crowds.

The drawing room looked as if the people chosen to actually present their proud possessions on *The Antiques Roadshow* had been allowed to store them there. There was too much of everything, it was all valuable, very little of it matched. There were too many old chairs, too many old sofas, too many chaise longues. It looked like a care home for the former staff of Sotheby's.

Sally sipped her Lady Grey tea. There were even cucumber sandwiches, as if new money was parodying the traditions of old money. She felt uncomfortable, but also, it has to be admitted, rather excited. She became aware that she might enjoy a third life, a life of luxury, if chance permitted.

Back in her suite, she faced a forest of aids to cleanliness, glamour and fragrance. Lennie had seemed to preach the doctrine of simplicity, but Sally had never seen a bathroom furnished with less simplicity. She decided to ignore Lennie's advice. How could she be herself here? What was her self, between Sally the lawyer's wife, Sally the leader of men, and Sally who dreamt of luxury?

She had never before walked down a staircase smelling so sweet, and looking so good, and feeling so awful.

The eighteenth-century clock in the twentieth-century hall struck six-thirty as she descended the last step. With perfect synchronization Sir Norman appeared from the doorway of the room opposite the drawing room. He was wearing gloves. Sally wondered suddenly whether Lennie had been leading her up the garden proverbial over the gloves, but she put on a pair and solemnly shook hands with her host.

'Good girl,' said Sir Norman, in a voice that still contained traces of Potherthwaite, and he led her into the drawing room with a smile.

He was shorter than she had expected, slim, even slight. He was wearing smart, well-fitting trousers, an expensive shirt, and a neat jacket. His clothes avoided his lack of colour sense by having almost no colour at all. His face, too, was pleasant without leaving any vivid memory. He had no need to show even a vestige of power. His money did that for him.

She took off her gloves as discreetly as she could.

'What would you like to drink, Sally?' enquired Sir Norman.

She was appalled to hear herself saying, 'What are you having?' It's the most infuriating of all replies. She felt obliged to continue, to make amends, even though it might be frightfully unwise, and her riches might go up in smoke right at the start. 'I don't know why I said that,' she said. 'I find it a most irritating remark. I'd like a sherry, please.'

'I have a nutty oloroso that has quite a stern dryness under the easy promise of its lush surface,' said Sir Norman.

'Good . . .' She was on the verge of saying 'Good Lord'. That would never do. God, this was difficult. 'Good. That sounds really good.'

'Does it? Sounds like cobblers to me. That's my wine merchant talking.'

'Oh.' This was just too difficult. She felt tempted to say, 'I once had a marvellous sherry in Market Harborough. Oh shit. Sorry. Shall I ring for the chauffeur or will you?' But no, she must struggle on. She owed it to Ben, and Ellie, and old Uncle Harry Patterson and all.

'I don't do alcohol. I get no pleasure from it,' said Sir Norman.

'I'm afraid I rather like it.'

'Don't ever be afraid,' said Sir Norman.

He handed her the sherry. She was disappointed that its proportions didn't match those of the house.

It tasted wonderful.

'It's wonderful,' she said.

He nodded, as if to say, 'Of course.'

She felt that she might have committed another gaffe. Everything would be delicious, so to comment on it would be superfluous.

'It's so good of you to come,' he said.

'It's so good of you to invite me.'

Oh God. Oh no!

'Tiptree was most impressed by you.'

'Well, yes, he gave me that impression.'

'A strange man, but I'd be lost without him. He's street-wise. I'm not. I last saw a street in nineteen ninety-seven. Would you like another sherry?'

She toyed with being polite. Luckily she overcame the temptation. 'Be yourself.' She was slightly shocked to find that being herself involved simply longing for another sherry.

'I'd love one.'

'Good.'

It was the first time she had sensed a touch of pleasure in his voice.

'I expect Tiptree has outlined the plan,' said Sir Norman, as he handed her the second sherry. 'But let me elaborate.'

Sally was very pleased, as she sipped her second sensational glass, to let Sir Norman elaborate.

'We will dine shortly, and over dinner you can tell me your plans for Potherthwaite, for this Transition of Potherthwaite, in detail. I want to know everything. Every single thing. I made my way in the world very swiftly, Sally. I loved money, and I understood it, and I was lucky. It was

306

natural to leave Potherthwaite behind, to discard it as beneath me. If that sounds arrogant it's because it was. I now regret it. I had feelings when I lived in Potherthwaite. I renounced these feelings. Some of the things I did in business, though never quite illegal, could not have been done if I'd had feelings. Now I have no feelings, and I miss them. Would you try to rekindle those feelings for me, Sally, over dinner this evening?'

'I would love to.' She had an uneasy feeling that she was not being proactive enough. She asked a question now, knowing that there was a risk that it might be unwise. 'May I ask, do you still love money and understand it?'

'That's a good question, Sally Mottram. And like all good questions, it's hard to answer. I think I understand it as well as ever, but I am fifty-four and that might be an illusion. I think I don't love it any more, but that too might be an illusion. I suppose, Sally, that I no longer think it's enough, so perhaps now I only like it rather than love it. Oh, and I hate it too, but then I think you always hate the things you love. I hate this house, for instance. You find it hideous?'

'I have to say I don't much like it.'

'You're finding the tenor of the conversation just a little dangerous, are you not? Let's move back to safer ground. The schedule. We will finish dinner . . . let's say, nine o'clock. Ish. I don't think we'll be able to drag it out much beyond that, with the best will in the world. I don't do long evenings. I will retire to my room, and you may use the drawing room or retire to your room. In the morning you will have breakfast in this room – it will be served in the buffet style – and then at ten-thirty Lung will bring you to the far office, which is entirely private. Nobody is allowed in under any circumstances – it is actually quite a privilege that I will see you there . . .'

'Thank you, Sir Norman.'

'My pleasure. I will then put to you my proposals for giving you the financial support you so need, and of course I hope you will agree. Please don't say, "I'm sure I will." You won't know till I tell you. You'll either be thrilled or disappointed. This should not take terribly long, and, if it's a nice morning tomorrow – the weathermen promise rain, so it should be lovely, I am nothing if not a cynic – you might want to wander on the terraces. Somebody should. All those statues, nobody ever visiting them, how depressing, go to it, Sally, step out and admire. And then at twelve-fifteen we will meet for an early luncheon, which will be medium-rare roast beef with all the trimmings, horseradish not mustard – I insist on that, even though I can barely taste either – and then Cattermole will deliver you safely to Maidenhead station, where you will begin a Sunday-evening journey of quite horrid complexity and boredom. How does that all sound to you?'

'It sounds very good, sir, except for the journey.'

And so that was what happened. They had dinner in the large dining room, which was the opposite of the drawing room, being rather too stark for Sally's taste. Sally ate smoked salmon, lamb cutlets with Reform sauce, and syllabub. Sir Norman ate scrambled eggs on toast. Sally drank Meursault and Pomerol. Sir Norman drank water. Sally told Sir Norman all her plans for Potherthwaite, all about the march, all about the plans for the Quays, the High Street East and West, and the waste ground, and the shopfronts, and the Sculpture Trail, and even broached for the first time a rather wild idea that had been suggested to her by reports in the newspapers about ideas in more exotic places than Potherthwaite, places like Buenos Aires and Rio de Janeiro, in which the houses in run-down neighbourhoods had been painted with wild, colourful murals. Perhaps the same could be done in the Baggit Estate, all undistinguished council houses in neat rows, where the likes of Ben and Tricksy, with the collaboration of the locals, would paint the walls with vivid murals.

Sir Norman remained largely silent, listening and nodding, and making just the occasional remark. Sally actually had the feeling that on a couple of occasions he was quite moved. At one moment she saw, she thought, a wetness in his eyes. He retired at twenty to ten, saying that he had not been up this late for many a long day. He told her to feel free to finish the wine. It was tempting – she might never drink such good stuff again – but she resisted the temptation. She had been a lawyer's wife for too long to throw off the manners of the middle classes entirely. She mustn't take advantage. It wouldn't be seemly. Too much was at stake.

She found it difficult to sleep. The tension of the day had been exhausting, but tension is not good for sleep, and there was just too much on her mind. Also, the silence kept her awake.

But with the aid of a couple of paracetamol, she did eventually fall into a sound sleep. In the morning she felt a bit like a prisoner condemned to die at ten-thirty. She did not manage a hearty breakfast. Lung came to her at twenty-five past ten. He was tall and pale. He led her along corridors and up staircases and eventually knocked on a door.

'Gloves,' he reminded her.

'Oh yes, thank you.'

'Come in, Sally,' called out Sir Norman. He sounded cheerful and Sally felt a terrible spasm of hope.

'I shan't come in,' said Lung. 'It is not allowed.'

He held the door open for her.

'Good luck,' he whispered unexpectedly. It was kind of him, but it made her feel worse.

'Thank you, Lung,' she whispered.

The far office was entirely round and Sally realized that they were in the great turret at the French end of the house.

Sir Normal sat behind a seventeenth-century walnut desk. He smiled, not unkindly. They shook gloves.

'I'll get straight down to it,' he said. 'No beating about the proverbial. What I am proposing to do, Sally, entirely unconditionally except for a few bits and bobs, is to offer to pay the council for the full cost of building the bypass.'

Relief hit Sally like the warmth from the opened door of a hot oven.

'That's incredibly generous of you, Sir Norman,' she said.

'I haven't finished. Tiptree told me something of your personal situation, of the mess your husband left. I'm deeply sorry. Deeply sorry.'

'Thank you.'

'You need money. You need a job. But, if you had a job, you wouldn't have the time for the Transition movement.'

'That is true.'

'You need what is in effect a salary, though for tax purposes of course it will not be called that.'

'Oh, Sir Norman, in my position I will have to avoid even the smallest hint of impropriety. I need the support of the townsfolk.'

'That is also true. All right, perhaps we had better call it a salary. For the same reason I do not want your personal remuneration to seem excessive. Fifty thousand pounds a year.'

'That's very generous of you too, Sir Norman.'

'I haven't finished. I want the townsfolk, those who can afford it, to contribute, either personally or through a programme of events. I will match, pound for pound, any monies raised.'

'Again, Sir Norman, I'm deeply grateful.'

Sally was a little shocked to find herself disappointed that Sir Norman didn't say 'I haven't finished' for a fourth time. How swiftly we can become greedy.

'Well, thank you very much, Sir Norman,' she said. 'Um . . . you did say you were making this offer . . . I think your words were something like "entirely unconditionally, except for a few bits and bobs".'

'Word perfect! Silly phrase, really, "bits and bobs".'

'Could you tell me what . . . um . . . I mean, this is all wonderfully generous, I don't want to seem to be quibbling over small trifles . . . could you tell me exactly what these bits and bobs are?'

'Of course. Just three really. Two are for the council. The money for the bypass is given on condition that they use the money they would have spent on the bypass entirely on other Transition projects.'

'Thank you.'

'The second is that what I am doing must receive no publicity. I know these councils. At the drop of a hat they'll be calling the bypass "Sir Norman Oldfield Boulevard".'

'I will make that clear to them.'

'Thank you. And the third condition is for you. You will have to marry me. See you at lunch, twelve-fifteen.'

THIRTY-THREE

A *hard decision*

Sally walked slowly along the towpath on the following Tuesday morning. It was a cool, cloudy day, with barely a hint of the approaching summer in the keen wind. She waved across the cut to Terence and Felicity Porchester. He was sluicing down their narrowboat. She was sitting in the cockpit, out of the wind, knitting a sweater for next winter. They brought a steady kind of love to Potherthwaite, a love that Felicity might have knitted herself, so snugly did it sit upon them, so perfectly did it fit. To come and be stranded in this silted backwater could have destroyed their marriage, but the disastrous decision to explore the Potherthwaite Arm had been a joint one, and they had quietly settled down together to make the best of it. Their love, reflected Sally, might not be a thing of passion (though it might!) but it was seamless, it was warming, it was another sweater for next winter. She didn't envy them for it – she had jealousy only for Marigold, and less and less even for her. She hadn't ever really loved Barry, and for many years he hadn't loved her at all, if indeed he ever had. Conrad had found her attractive, but he hadn't fallen for her. She thought back over her life since Barry's death. It was awful, but the only man she would find it remotely interesting to see again was the odiferous and unshaven driver of a ramshackle lorry, and that only because she felt guilty that she hadn't thanked him, in effect, for not raping her. She felt now that it had been absurd of her to have thought this worthy of thanks. It was more likely, given the state of her that night, that the thought of any kind of physical contact would have been revolting to him. Even to think about this man was to emphasize to herself how bleak the sexual side of her life had become. Would it be so very awful, under these circumstances, to marry Sir Norman?

'We're counting the days,' called out Felicity cheerfully, cutting right through Sally's melancholy thoughts. 'Pity we don't know how many days we have to count.'

If she married Sir Norman, work could begin very soon. If she didn't, it might take years. How could she disappoint them? Could she face them if she disappointed them?

Here was Eric Sheepshank, dressed in dirty but no longer distressing denims. He no longer loitered on deck in his underpants. Newcomers to the area would have to ask, if they were interested in whether he still had a foreskin or not.

'I'm looking at an old shed beyond the allotments,' he called out to her. 'Might be just right for a workshop. Sculptor's block? What sculptor's block?'

He locked his cabin with two different keys. Suddenly, in the chaos, there were things that he cherished and needed to protect. If she didn't marry Sir Norman, what were the chances for the Sculpture Trail? She told herself that she had to do it. It wouldn't be such a very unpleasant thing. She would live in luxury for the rest of her life. She would be rich. She would commute to Potherthwaite three days a week till the work was done, so she wouldn't be trapped. She might even . . . well, no, she mustn't think of that. Sir

313

Norman had laid out, over the medium-rare roast beef, all the details of how the arrangement might work. He would trust her. He would keep her. He would feed her shopping habits as extravagantly as she desired. He would be kind to her, as he was to all his staff. He had told her, as he speared a small sliver of roast parsnip and looked at it on the fork, that she would be able to enjoy roast parsnips every Sunday for the rest of her life. Maybe, who knows, the parsnip had turned his thoughts to another small, narrow object, because at that moment he had lowered his voice, as if he hadn't even wanted the Yorkshire pudding to hear, to confess to her that he had now been impotent for seven years and eighty-two days. She had wondered, but hadn't dared to ask, what had happened, two thousand, six hundred and thirty-nine days ago, to cause this sudden incapacity. Perhaps it had been in Market Harborough. Whatever it was, it meant that he would not, as he put it, make any demands. 'So why do I want a wife? You may well ask,' he had said, just as she was thinking it. 'Because I am lonely,' he had said, over the sticky toffee pudding. 'So lonely, Sally.' 'I hardly think you love me,' she had said, 'so surely you can find someone else?' 'People like you don't grow on trees,' he had said, and she had felt surprisingly touched by this strange compliment.

'Think it over,' he had said. 'Take your time. I will give you . . .' He had paused, working out, it seemed, what would be a fair deadline for this unusual proposal. '. . . a month.'

She was two days into that month, and she had not yet made a decision. She would be set up to live for her whole life with a kindly and generous man, and she would be able to bring the dreams of her many friends in Potherthwaite to a swift reality. To turn him down was to risk losing all that, to risk the Porchesters being stranded at the Quays till death, to risk the return of sculptor's block to a disillusioned

314

Eric. And all for what? The chance of love? The chance of that great rarity, perfect love? There had been no sign of it so far. Why should it ever be different? She wasn't made like the Marigolds of this world. She wasn't made for passion.

She had broken the journey at Barnet. 'Beth has made a few little tweaks to her lasagne since you last came,' Sam had said. 'See if you can spot them.' She hadn't been able to identify them. Beth had been delighted. 'I've fooled your mother, Sam,' she had boasted. She had gone to bed early. At the door she had paused, and a look of shy pride had passed across her face. 'The little one has to have its sleep too,' she had said, with a blush.

'You mean . . .?' Sally had begun.

'Yes,' Sam had said. 'We're expecting.'

'Well, congratulations,' Sally had said.

'Thank you,' Beth and Sam had said in unison.

Sally had gone over to Beth and kissed her. Beth had blushed again.

'So you don't know its sex?' Sally had asked.

'No,' Beth had said. 'I hate calling it "it", but it's a small price to pay for the excitement of the uncertainty.'

When Beth had gone to bed, Sally had tried to talk to Sam about the baby, and their life together, but he had wanted to talk about her. 'Something's on your mind, Mum. I know you. You can't fool me,' he had said, and the utter impossibility of marrying Sir Norman had swept over her, and with it had come anger that he should even contemplate making her marry him as a condition of giving her money, and she also couldn't conceive of a moment when she would have the courage to tell them, and Beth would have been thrown into such a panic by the news, and would have said, 'He'll be used to fine meals. I'd never dare serve him my lasagne,' and she would have burst into tears and might even have lost the baby, so that next morning, when she had left Barnet, Sally had felt that it was utterly impossible even to think of such an absurd proposition.

But the moment she was back home, surrounded by the people who were living for the Transition, Sally had felt that it was perhaps not such an absurd proposition after all. Certainly it would make the financial situation infinitely more hopeful at the stroke of a pen in a registrar's book.

And now, this windy Tuesday, it was as if all the arguments for marrying Sir Norman were presenting themselves to her. Another strong argument for marrying him had spotted her and waved. This argument was a stooping sort of argument, an ungainly kind of argument, a knobbly-kneed kind of argument, the sort of argument that clings to a person, maybe even stalks them.

The Revd Dominic Otley bounded over the bridge at the Quays, and approached her like an over-optimistic kangaroo.

'Sally, what a pleasant surprise, what a joyous culmination for my walk.'

Sally suspected that he had been following her, but she didn't mention this.

'You have travelled, you have returned, all your financial problems are solved,' boomed the vicar.

'I beg your pardon, Dominic?'

How could he possibly have heard about Sir Norman's offer?

'Sixteen minutes, forty-three seconds.'

'What?'

'My sermon, on Sunday. Sixteen minutes, forty-three seconds. And who is this week's lucky winner? None other than our unofficial leader, our unrivalled inspiration, Mrs Sally Mottram. Rumour has it that you've won eighty-six pounds. Eighty-six smackers, Sally. Wouldn't care to take a lonely vicar out to lunch, don't suppose? No. Bad form. Let me take you – that feat deserves celebrating. Sixteen minutes, forty-three seconds exactly. Nineteen seconds longer than I'd calculated. Flung in a little extra quip about the Venerable Bede, you see. Fault of mine. Lets me down week after week. Could be subliminally deliberate, who knows? So, how about it, Sally? Lunch?'

'I'm sorry, Dominic,' she said. 'I'd love to, but I can't.'

The Revd Dominic Otley subsided like a pricked balloon. Sally hated the sight of it, hated the power she had over this man, and thought, 'If I marry Sir Norman, I'll never need to tell such a whopping great lie to the vicar again.'

'Well,' she said, 'enjoy the rest of your walk.'

The vicar was now unable to admit that he wasn't actually on a walk, he *had* been following her, he had heard where she was from Eric, and had hurried after her. Now he had to walk on, along the hated towpath, to the silted winding hole that marked the end of the cut.

Sally walked back over the bridge, and up High Street East. She was walking through the town, but seeing nothing. The enormity of the decision she had to make was the only thing that registered in her brain.

A burst of sunlight flooded the Market Place and shone fiercely on Harry's bald head. He was walking very slowly up High Street East ahead of her. She hurried after him.

'Hello, Harry,' she called.

He turned. The top of his head was glistening in the sunshine, and the sweat was running down into his eyes. His usually cheerful bluff, round face looked drawn, longer and paler and puffy round the eyes.

'Well,' he said. 'She's gone.'

'Oh, Harry.'

'Yep.'

Olive had lain in a coma for several months, watched over day after day by Harry. Some days she hadn't moved at all. Other days she'd had tiny convulsions. Just occasionally, a

317

groan had come from far away. But she had been there, and now suddenly she wasn't there any more, and it was almost more than Harry could bear.

'You look as though you could do with a drink,' said Sally.

'Do you know, I could. The Dog and Duck opens at eleven. Shall we?'

They did. Sally had a red wine. Harry had a half of bitter and a large malt whisky. There were no other customers yet. The pub smelt of carbolic.

'She never regained consciousness,' said Harry. 'Sunday she made a noise. I thought it was going to be a word – I was terrified she'd say something nasty, but it was just a cough. That's odd, isn't it? I mean, why should I think she'd say something nasty?'

'Tension, probably.'

'They'd been friends as students.'

'What?'

'Olive and Arnold. In Cheltenham.'

'Good Lord.'

'Never told us. Why didn't they tell us, Sally?'

'Embarrassment?'

'No need. Nothing even happened. Not properly. Not in Cheltenham.'

'What?'

'It was when Jill and I were in Montepulciwhatsit. People always thought I was Jack the Lad. Something about my face, and being bald, and being up for . . . you know . . . the sailing . . . the painting course . . . but I'm not. Jill, she was bronzed in the sun . . . in Montethingummybobiano. One evening . . . it wouldn't have taken much . . . but, well, we didn't, in the end. I loved Olive too much. I think Jill probably loved Arnold too much. They . . . the quiet ones . . . the sly ones . . . would you believe it? Only once . . . I forgave her, of course . . . I mean . . . once . . . it's hardly a hanging offence . . . but why did she have to tell me? Why did she have to tell me, Sally? I needn't ever have known. I wouldn't ever have guessed.'

'She thought . . . tidy things up, get things straight?'

'Try to make peace with her maker. Lessen her chances of going to hell. How could she believe those things, Sally? How could she believe all that? But she obviously did.'

'It beats me, Harry.'

'But she obviously did. Look how desperately she hung on. I wish she hadn't have told me. I do. I wish she hadn't have told me. I do, Sally. I never told a soul all these months. I watched her, day after day, sleeping, and I felt cross with her for not waking up, so we could have it out, make our peace. Now I know we never will, I have to tell someone, have to try to get it off my chest, clear it away so I can grieve properly. Sorry to burden you.'

'Don't worry, Harry. I understand.'

'Same again?'

'I think if we're going to get maudlin, maybe we'd better stop.'

'You're probably right. Thanks, Sally . . . for this . . . and everything.'

'Not a problem, Harry.'

Although they had decided not to have another drink, neither of them wanted to go. They sat in companionable silence for several minutes.

'Do you think, Sally, that if folk could see how their marriages ended – the pain, the loss – they'd still get married?' asked Harry eventually.

'Yes, I think most of them would.'

'Yeah. I do too.'

These thoughts might have led to a reason for not marrying Sir Norman, in Sally's endless quest for a decision. Avoid marriage. Avoid the loss and the pain.

But they didn't. They led Sally to the conclusion that a marriage of practicality, of convenience, might be the best way. Not to feel enough love to ever feel pain. An even keel.

Harry was a sailor. Harry got quickly bored, on ships, when the keels were even.

Did Sally want an even keel?

There were certainly worse things.

She bought herself a couple of wraps in the deli, clambered into the waste ground, sat on a stone far out of sight from the road. It wasn't really warm enough to sit out, but she welcomed the chill and the shivers, they were suitable accompaniments to the absurdity of the decision she was being forced to make.

And as she sat there, she had a most unworthy thought. If she married Sir Norman, would she not become Lady Oldfield? If so, what a massive one in the eye for her dear sister Judith. Totnes Schnotnes, I live high above the Thames Valley with my shining knight.

Then she thought back to her visit to Sam and Beth. While she was there she had seen Sir Norman's suggestion as absurd, but it would enable her to help them with their lurking money problems. God, it was difficult. The more she thought, the less she knew. Then she went slowly up High Street West to Cadwallader Road where Ali let her in to number 6. Ali and Oli sat in chairs at either side of the bed – they were both certainly looking quite a bit slimmer, Sally thought, but that might have been just the effect of hope. She was amazed, and thrilled, that they appeared to be sticking to their diet, day after day after day.

She talked of the Rhine, the great hills through which it had carved its route, the endless healthy vineyards covering the high, steep slopes, castle after spectacular castle to be admired without fear in one of the lengthiest periods of peace Europe had ever enjoyed due to an institution which was otherwise derided on all sides. She talked of the small towns and villages on the route, the winding banks of the great river, the old, timbered houses, the ramparts, the defences, the towers, the beauty that the warlike history of the Continent had created and left as our heritage. She talked of the thrill of the long passenger boats with their fine restaurants and succulent white wines, their finely cooked trout, their sparkling sunny beer. She spoke of the other ships, the great barges, and of the railway lines at both sides of the river, with express trains to all sorts of destinations north and south, and everyone on the boats being conscious of this great movement of people, of sharing their wonder at the magnificence of the scenery, and she told how, unlike in the great cities, the immense amount of traffic was exciting, it was thrilling to be part of all this, as one day they would be, when they would laugh at how small the boundaries of their lives had been, as she took them through the Rhine Gorge and perhaps on to the mighty cathedral of Speyer and the gentler beauties of Strasbourg. And they drank it all in and relished it, because they believed what Sally told them, that Ellie would walk again, and that they would sit on a Rhine steamer and eat Wiener schnitzels with clean consciences.

And Sally, as she talked to them, realized that she had made her decision. At first it seemed like a relief, but this feeling didn't last. It came with an ever increasing terror that she might be making the wrong decision, but that, of course, is the nature of decisions.

She kissed each of the three girls on both cheeks. Ali led her to the door. She walked slowly through the town, slowly across the Market Place, and on every step of the way she thought of how Sir Norman's money might speed the town's transformation. She stopped at a stationer's – you've guessed it, 'The Potherthwaite Stationer's' – and bought their most

321

expensive writing paper, with matching envelopes, for Sir Norman Oldfield was a billionaire and she wasn't going to have her writing paper ridiculed in the Thames Valley.

She turned right into Quays Approach, right again into Vatican Road. She opened the mean communal door, climbed the tacky communal stairs, unlocked her thin, shoddy, deformed door, and entered her tiny flat, and there, she thought, thought again, decided that she had been right in her decision, and wrote her reply to Sir Norman Oldfield on writing paper destined for a far finer house.

THIRTY-FOUR

An unfinished manuscript

Under the stewardship of Walter 'Wally' Frond, one of the Fronds of Willis & Frond, 'Potherthwaite's Premier Store', the Chronicle was a truly, and indeed solely, local weekly newspaper. The Suez Crisis held the capital in a ferment, with pitched battles of an intensity and hostility rarely seen on the streets of this isle of reason and moderation, but—

Jill entered the stuffy study, with its walls covered in bookshelves that contained rows and rows of great classic novels and history books. She was aware that every single book on those shelves was better than her dear husband's 'A Complete History of Potherthwaite', but Arnold wasn't, so it didn't really matter.

'I've made some tea,' she said.

Arnold's expression was that of a Tolstoy being interrupted by Mrs Tolstoy with a buttered muffin just as he was pushing Anna Karenina under a train. Then he recovered himself, smiled as sweetly as he could, and said, 'Bring it in here, darling, will you? Thanks.'

'I want you to take a break. You're overdoing it.'

'I am not overdoing it, and I do not want to take a break.

London is in a ferment, Jill. I want to set the Suez Crisis to rest. Then I'll take a break.'

Jill sighed.

'You'll make yourself ill,' she said.

'I will not make myself ill,' he insisted. 'I will not make myself ill, Jill.'

'Stubborn old fool,' she muttered.

'I heard that,' he said.

'You were meant to.'

She closed the door carefully as she left. She would be back in less than a minute, but he couldn't write a word with the door open. It was one of his many little kinks.

—not a word of the Crisis reached the pages of the Chronicle. *Were the pros and cons of Sir Anthony Eden's actions hotly debated in the town's pubs, which still numbered twenty-two at the time, or was Potherthwaite, protected and imprisoned in its steep valley, a more parochial place even than it is today? We will never—*

The door opened. Arnold stopped writing, even though there was only one word left in the sentence. His writing was a private business, not to be witnessed even by his dear wife. In truth, this practice was more an affectation than an obsession. If he just sat there, his whole being taut with interruption, she would leave more quickly, and, much as he loved her, he always longed for her to leave when he was writing.

'Your tea, darling.'

'Thank you, darling.'

'Arnold, I must speak.'

'Must you, Jill? Well, all right then. Speak.'

'I know you're upset about Olive. We all are. But you mustn't let yourself get obsessed about it.'

'You know, Jill, it's ironic. I think you are beginning to

get obsessed by the idea that I am obsessed. I am not obsessed. I have seen our dear new friend die, and, yes, I find I was fonder of her than I realized. We had time together, you know – we were thrust together, you might even say – when you and Harry went gallivanting together.'

'We didn't gallivant, Arnold. I helped him bring his boat home, and we tried to keep our minds active by learning new skills. It's odd. "Gallivant" sounded wrong to me, though it must be a word if "gallivanting" is.'

'It's perfectly correct grammatically, Jill. Now please let me be. Thank you very much for the tea, which looks lovely and is very welcome, but, now, please, leave the room.'

Jill was as near to storming out as she would ever be. She came as near to slamming his study door as she would ever dare, for this was a door to and from an author's place of inspiration, and therefore to be treated with extreme respect.

—know. While researching this passage, in fact, I came upon a short paragraph that says more to me about the true spirit of my native town than any political debate or council issue. It appeared under the headline, 'Unusual Leg of Lamb at W.I. Talk!'

Jill entered the room again. Arnold's deep sigh was more dramatic than anything in his huge tome.

'There's no need to sigh, Arnold,' she said. 'Sighing is not pleasant.'

'Jill,' he said, 'let's have this out. I have just seen our dear friend die, and I would be a strange man if that didn't lead me to think of my own mortality. Who will finish this book if I snuff it? Who? I have to catch up, and I am not catching up, and now there is the prospect of this stupid Translation business—'

'You know it's Transition. You get it wrong deliberately. You're a stubborn old ex-teacher and you'll kill yourself.'

'May I finish my sentence? Thank you. Most kind of you. —with this stupid Transformation business and that Sally Mottram creature out of whose admittedly curvaceous backside you seem to think the sun shines, I am going to fall further and further behind unless I am allowed to continue uninterrupted. All right?'

'I came to tell you that I'm going round to see Harry, see how he's coping, see if he needs anything. So you'll have no interruptions for at least the next few minutes. I love you, Arnold.'

'Well, I love you too, obviously, of course I do, but I must get on.'

'You've time for a quick kiss.'

'Well . . . yes, of course.'

Jill bent down towards his face. He grabbed her shoulders and reached for her lips. They kissed.

'Don't go on too long,' she said.

'Not too long, no. I won't.'

She gave him a loving smile. He smiled back, but it was a rushed sort of smile. The kiss had been good but it was over, every fibre of his being was stretched, poised, eager to create more and more words, she could see it all and she couldn't stop it.

She left the room as quietly as she could, shut the door with slow, precise care.

There was an unusual presentation at this month's meeting of the W.I. in the Railway Rooms on Tuesday, when Mrs Victoria Penrose of the Halifax W.I. gave a demonstration on the subject of 'How to Bone a Shoulder of Lamb'. She had to admit, with embarrassment, that she had forgotten to bring the shoulder of lamb. However, a cushion was found, and stood in very successfully for the missing shoulder. 'It didn't affect our understanding of the process one little bit,' commented W.I. member Annie Bramble.

Arnold smiled at this little absurdity. Suddenly, he felt gripped by the most intense pain. He . . . he couldn't move. He . . .

The smile was still on his face when they found him.

THIRTY-FIVE

An envelope of distinction

Sally noticed the envelope straight away. All the letters at the unlovely block of flats were sorted by the postman into the eight occupancies, and delivered one flat at a time but into the same big wire box, so that the occupants had to sort their own ones out all over again. Sally didn't want to stand out as a person of superior organizational ability by suggesting that this absurd state of affairs should be improved. So there the envelope was, in a confusion of brown threats from HM Revenue & Customs and eight crumpled copies of the menu of a new Indian takeaway. There it sat, not askew like most of the other envelopes, but level, neat, holding itself apart from the rabble. This envelope spoke of a large house, of a neat hand, of a clear mind. Sally knew immediately that it was from Sir Norman Oldfield.

She was surprised to see the envelope. It had only been three days since she had posted her letter to him, and this promptness seemed beyond the current capabilities of the British postal service.

The human brain is a marvellous thing. It has such capacity for thinking of several things at the same time. Who, looking at Sally carefully rescuing her envelope from its impersonal companions, could have thought that she was in a ferment of anxiety about its contents, while also reflecting anxiously on the wisdom of her letter to him, and all this overlaid with the memory of last night, Arnold's death, Jill shaken and shattered, Harry not knowing how or indeed whether to try to console her, the vicar desperately mouthing words of consolation?

Even as she lifted the envelope, Sally was thinking that she had seen the Revd Dominic Otley at his very best. In this moment of professional responsibility he had managed to convey to her, with the slightest of gestures, that tonight he would not embarrass her with any reference to his feelings for her. He had talked to Jill and Harry without pomposity and with, she felt, genuine shock and sorrow at their loss of their respective spouses to a heart attack and the consequences of a severe stroke within a few days of each other.

Harry, too, had shown how much more sensitive a soul he was than his bluff exterior suggested. With the very slightest look towards Jill, accompanied by a mixture of warning and reassurance in his usually boyish eyes, he had managed to indicate to Sally that Jill didn't know of Arnold's past friendship with Olive or of their one act of unfaithfulness.

Harry's social dilemma had been obvious, and all the more touching because he had been trying so hard not to make it obvious. His dilemma had been that he had wished to console Jill, had wished to mingle his grief with hers in the natural warmth of two friends who have both suffered a huge loss, but he was also aware that Potherthwaite society, if Baroness Thatcher was wrong and such a thing existed, would be thinking that now the field would be clear – after a decent interval of course, this wasn't London – for the two more adventurous of the four pensioners to get together. By calling round to Jill's house he had put himself into her space, and he'd had an uneasy feeling that he shouldn't be there. Sally had seen all this, had done what she could to keep the conversation from also dying. Everyone had thought, and no one had said, that it was ironic that the two who had feared death had died, and the two who had ignored it were still in rude health for their age. Sally had tried, as she made her departure, to hint to the Revd Dominic Otley that she respected his performance, without reinstating in his breast any hopes that he might one day have her for his wife. It had been, she had reflected as she had trudged slowly up the bare unfriendly stairs to her flat, a singularly exhausting evening.

When she'd got home, she had opened a bottle of red wine – how shocked Barry would have been, if there was an afterlife, to see how much she drank these days – and had reread the copy she had taken of her letter to Sir Norman.

Dear Sir Norman,

Thank you so much for the lovely visit I made to your home last weekend, and for the impeccable hospitality you offered me, which included quite the best sherry I have ever drunk.

Thank you also for the generous financial offers that you made, and which I really do appreciate. As you can imagine, the condition that you imposed, that I must agree to marry you, has been uppermost in my thoughts. You gave me a month to make up my mind. It was such an extraordinary offer that I thought I might need more than a month, but in fact I came to my decision within three days, hence this letter.

I can imagine that some women might feel offended at an offer of marriage being tied in with a financial offer in that way, but I want to assure you that I did not. I was surprised, shocked even, but I want you to know that my main feelings are of gratitude that you feel you could lead a pleasant life with me, and of sympathy for you in that all your wealth has clearly not made you happy. Loneliness is a terrible thing, as I know only too well, having experienced a great deal of it recently.

I have realized that in my life with my late husband I did not once achieve a true moment of spontaneous physical joy. More important, I did not once wake up in the morning and think that I was blessed to find myself beside a man who could make me feel happier than any man on earth.

It is very likely that I never will, that I am giving up the chance of a perfectly happy life for a dream. No. If I could accept the word 'dream' as a description of my ambition, I would accept your offer. I don't believe in dreams. But the word that comes to mind is not 'dream', but 'hope'. Had you put your offer of marriage to me in such a way that there was even a faint hope of our relationship growing beyond our expectations, then maybe I would have accepted it, but you didn't. You made it clear that to accept your offer was to accept the conditions that came with your offer, and give up all thoughts of true love. I am too selfish, and perhaps too foolish, to give up all hope of that.

I bear you no ill feelings. I am flattered that you feel able to make me such an offer, and I am very conscious that in my old age I may find that my decision will seem like a great mistake. I also feel that, in a world with all the problems that we are trying in our little way to redress, I may be quite wrong to place my romantic and perhaps deluded hope above all other interests and responsibilities. I do not turn you down because I believe it is right to do so. I turn you down because I find I can't not.

With all best wishes,
Yours sincerely,
Sally Mottram

She looked at Sir Norman's envelope, and suddenly she didn't want to open it. It looked so virginal, so neat, with its smooth solid paper, and its subtle lavender tone. The handwriting was very neat too. It gave away no secrets, except for the revealing fact that it was carefully created not to give away any secrets. She slit it open gently, slowly, carefully, as if it was a sentient being.

It was a beautiful envelope. It also smelt of lavender. It deserved respect. As she opened it the scent of lavender grew stronger. Gripped with tension though she was, Sally also felt that this moment was an elegiac tribute to a past form of communication. She knew what Sir Norman's letter would not say. It would not say, *'Hi, Sally. Got your note, sad but I understand. Hope to see u again one day. N xx.'*

My Dear Sally, she read.

Thank you so much for your marvellous letter. After he had first met you, Tiptree told me, with a fervour that impressed me, how impressed he was by you, and your letter simply confirms what an impressive person you are. I little thought, when I put that outrageous condition on my offer of money, that you would take it so calmly.

As I told you, I have not the capability for physical love, nor do I have the temperament or the warmth or the intensity necessary for deep affection and true friendship. My palate is not subtle enough or strong enough to appreciate great food, and I have no desire for alcohol because I would hate to lose control. I have neither the fine ear for great music nor eyes sharp enough and distinguishing enough to understand and enjoy great visual art. Only one pleasure is truly available to me from all the wealth I have amassed, and that is the joy of power. I made that suggestion of marriage so that I could feel my power over you. I cannot tell you how much I enjoyed the look of astonishment on your face, before your amazing middle-class manners swept it into the dustbin.

In the days between your departure and the arrival of your letter I relished the thought of the agonies of indecision you would be going through, all that temptation, all that cost, your sense of duty to others clashing violently with your search for personal pleasure. I imagined your sleepless nights, your frenzied walks along the canal bank, and I felt a real sense of excitement that at least verged upon the sexual. I have to admit, though, that the thrill of this was not as great as I had hoped, maybe age is beginning to affect me. I gave you a month in the hope that you would twist yourself into despair for four whole weeks. I am not, as I seem, a kindly if rather dull and unemotional man. I am wicked. I am cruel.

However, dear Sally, there are limits to my cruelty. I didn't mean it. I was teasing you. I can give you sleepless nights. I could not consider destroying a life. The offer remains open in full – the cost of the bypass, a salary of £50,000, and I will match any money raised by the people of Potherthwaite. My emissary, Tiptree, will come to meet you and the council representatives and I hope you will all very soon have an agreement and be able to shake hands on it.

Oh dear.

I also hope that you will meet a man who will make you very happy.

Sally, I never dreamt that in the end you would accept my proposition, but there was one moment in the reading of your letter when I thought that maybe you were going to. I feared that I was being hoist with my own petard, and I was terrified. I realize that this must sound abominably rude, but I want you to know that, if I was to be hoist, there is not in the whole world a petard that I would as much like to be hoist with as you. I would have gone through with the

333

marriage, of course, a promise is a promise, but I don't know how I could have borne the constant proximity even of a petard as lovely as you.

I cannot endure the company of my fellow men for very long. I become claustrophobic. I need space. I give most men an hour, Tiptree ten minutes. But you, Sally, I invite you to come here to stay occasionally – very occasionally! – to try a new sherry, to enjoy poached wild salmon or roast red deer and watch me eating scrambled eggs, and to lunch with me next day. Roast parsnips every six months – how does that sound to you?

I will make you one more promise. I will attempt – I cannot guarantee that I will succeed – to pluck up enough courage to come to my beloved birthplace for the great ceremony which you told me you plan to hold when you celebrate the completion of your main work. I would love to be there, dear petard.

You have something in you, Sally, that is rare. You will create a miracle in the transformation of Potherthwaite. You will make Ellie walk again. You may, also, rescue my heart from the dead. I do not say that you are some kind of god, I do not believe in gods, but you are a very special person.

With very best wishes and with the nearest I have ever been to, and the nearest I will ever get to, love,

Your friend,

Norman

THIRTY-SIX

Public and private changes

Now that Sir Norman had made his offer, work at last could begin in earnest. Lennie Tiptree came up to the town, met council officials, signed an agreement, handed over an initial cheque. Councillor Frank Stratton, Lennie and Sally had lunch at the Weavers' Arms. They lingered a little too long over their celebratory Calvados and suddenly there was a risk of Lennie missing his train. In the haste and confusion Sally managed to avoid a final handshake with him. A small thing, but to her it felt like an omen of good luck, a harbinger of joy.

She bounced to the Market Place as if the roads were made of rubber. Even the sight of Linda Oughtibridge, waddling painfully towards her across the cobbles with heavy shopping bags in both arms, failed to dent her ecstasy.

Linda Oughtibridge came straight up to Sally, put both her bags down on the cobbles, and said, 'Oh, Mrs Mottram.' She panted breathlessly, then braced herself to speak again. 'Oh, Mrs Mottram.'

'What on earth's the matter, Mrs Oughtibridge?' asked Sally. 'Painful feet?'

'A verruca,' panted Linda.

On this happy, Calvados-fuelled afternoon, Sally had no wish to say 'Oh dear' to Linda Oughtibridge, yet again, but what else could she say?

'Oh dear.'

'I have a history of verrucas.'

'You must lend it to me some time. I love a good book.' How this new Sally, riding on a tide of triumph and frivolity, wished she could say that. But she didn't of course. She said, 'Oh dear.'

'Can you help me? You're so clever,' wailed Linda Oughtibridge.

'Well, yes,' said Sally. 'I mean, not personally, but I know a very good chiropodist.'

'It's not the verruca,' said Linda Oughtibridge.

'Not the verruca?'

'No. It's hubby.'

'Hubby?'

'He went to Canada. He has cousins there.'

'Nice for him.'

'He isn't coming back.'

One look at Linda Oughtibridge's face stopped Sally's thought of 'I'm not surprised' in its tracks.

'Oh dear,' she said. 'Oh, I'm so sorry.'

She didn't want to listen to tales of woe this afternoon of all afternoons, but what choice had she? She took the poor woman to the Market Café for a cup of good old English tea.

'It's funny you should mention a chiropodist,' said Linda. 'Well, not funny. Odd. Funny peculiar, not funny ha-ha. *She's* a chiropodist.'

'She?' asked Sally, slow on the uptake because she wasn't really listening.

'The woman he's run off with, in Canada,' said Linda Oughtibridge rather sharply, and Sally, still in her bubble of happiness and frivolity, thought, 'You could go and drag him back and have your verruca done at the same time,' while saying, 'Oh, Linda, I'm so very sorry.'

'I've prayed to God,' said Linda. 'Nothing. I've worshipped him twice every Sunday and not committed even one small sin in fifty years and what do I get back, the first time I ask him for anything? Nothing.'

Sally heard herself making noises, heard the kindliness and concern in her voice, knew that Linda Oughtibridge would say, 'What a nice woman Sally Mottram is. She'll always make time for you,' and all the time she was making time she was nursing the secret joy of her day like a hot-water bottle in her stomach.

That warm feeling stayed with Sally later in the day when her path crossed that of the Revd Dominic Otley.

'I'm so glad I've run into you,' he said. 'I want to apologize.'

They found themselves walking down towards the Quays, although neither of them had decided to do so.

'I apologize for making such a nuisance of myself,' he said. 'I've been thinking a lot about it and I've realized that there is no chance for me. You're a bit out of my league, to be honest.'

'Oh, Dominic,' she said. 'Don't think that.'

'Oh, but I do.'

Sally looked round the dilapidated, almost derelict scene. It no longer looked sad to her. In her mind it was already transformed.

The Revd Dominic Otley appeared to be looking at the scene too, but when he spoke it was to continue his theme.

'I have . . . how can I put it . . . I have fought my yearnings for you. I have taken myself in hand.' He seemed fortunately unaware of the implication that a less naive person might put into this remark, and particularly fortunately

337

unaware that one of those less naive persons, in this her second life, was Sally Mottram.

'Well, thank you, Vicar,' said Sally. She had got what she wanted and she should have stopped, like a good salesman on getting an order. But her kindness led her on, and she said, 'I thought you were very good at Jill's the other day, and at the two funerals.'

'Really?' he said. 'Oh, how kind.' As he spoke, he wandered into the Quays Café, the only establishment that was still active in the Quays. 'The cup that cheers?' he asked, and without waiting for a reply, ordered a pot of tea for two. The last thing Sally wanted was more tea.

The vicar put on his confessional face. Sally's heart sank. What was coming?

'I feel awful, you know,' he began, 'every time I don my vicar's voice. I can just hear my words coming out more and more hollow.'

'They don't sound hollow, I do assure you.'

'Dear Linda Oughtibridge has hit a marital cliff.'

'Yes, she was telling me.'

'She is seeking consolation in the Lord, and finding none. I have felt myself so inadequate in consoling her.'

'If the Lord can't help her, why should you feel bad about your failure?'

'Yes, but he doesn't exist. I do.'

Sally's jaw dropped.

'You don't believe in God?'

'Haven't for . . . oh, I don't know . . . twenty years? Feels like thirty. Every week, Sally, the same words, hollower and hollower. Having bets on the length of my own sermons and not feeling any guilt. Awful.'

'Why don't you resign?'

'What would I tell people? I am *not* going to invent some ghastly sexual misdemeanour. Besides, who would believe me, and who could I say I'd done it with? We have no choirboys. Mrs Oughtibridge?' He let this prospect hang in the air. 'Unless you . . .'

'No, Dominic. No. We've been there. Sorry.'

'No. Quite. Well, there you are, you see. More tea?'

'No, thank you.'

'Jolly good.'

The vicar poured Sally another cup.

'Dominic, couldn't you just say you've lost your faith?'

'No.'

'Oh?'

The Revd Dominic Otley leant forward and lowered his voice. His breath smelt of biscuits.

'There are twenty-six people in this town who look to me and my church to buttress their faith. One or two are close to death. Some are lonely and only have me and God to help them. They are my flock. My tiny flock, my diminishing flock, but my flock. They need me. I can never tell them that I no longer believe. I'm trapped, Sally.'

Sally felt her arm moving towards him to comfort him. That would never do. She managed to stop it just in time. But she knew that he had noticed. She knew that she couldn't blink without his noticing. She liked the vicar more at that moment than she had ever done. She must be careful.

The thought occurred to her that maybe he needed his flock as much as they needed him.

'Maybe I also need them,' he said. 'Oh, Sally, it's so good to talk to you. If I promise to be a very good boy and behave like a vicar, can we have lunch together some time?'

'Maybe not lunch, Dominic. Maybe a cup of coffee.'

He sighed. It was clear that his defeat of his yearnings had not been as thorough as he had thought, and Sally, being a woman, couldn't help feeling rather glad about that.

'Would you be able to do something for me?' she asked.

'Perhaps,' he replied cautiously.

'Would you rustle up some of those fabulous helpers of yours, so that we can start on clearing the canal?'

'Yes. Yes, of course. A pleasure. A privilege. Anything for you. As always. With joy.'

Yes, don't overdo it.

It crossed Sally's mind that in her new role she would always be seeking to turn the conversation towards what people could do for her. If she wasn't very careful, people would realize this and be on their guard. Oh Lord, here comes the Transition person.

One of the people she no longer had to worry about was Councillor Frank Stratton, stationer supreme. Now that she had inspired the gift of so much money from Sir Norman Oldfield, Sally had become, at the stroke of a pen, his golden girl. At the very next council meeting, the route for the bypass was passed. At the following month's meeting, the plan for a park on the waste ground was voted in with one abstention and no votes against. There was always at least one abstention on Potherthwaite Council. Councillor Farsley, a retired doctor, had sat on the council for forty-three years, having realized that if he never voted for or against anything he would survive a lifetime without making enemies.

Sally was satisfied with these victories. She had the sense not to be too greedy. The idea of painting all the houses on the Baggit Estate would need to wait until other schemes had proved themselves, until all the councillors except Councillor Farsley had cottoned on to the fact that art could inspire, and art could pay.

Work resumed on the bypass, and with greater urgency, and at weekends more and more volunteers began the long task of clearing the canal. Sally spoke to all the shopkeepers in both High Street West and High Street East, attempting to recruit them to a common style of shopfront. Most agreed that, if all agreed, they would agree. Some agreed that they would agree even if they didn't quite all agree, but others felt that it was pointless to agree if they didn't quite all agree. In the end they all agreed that it would be better to wait until nearer the time of the pedestrianization of the street. Sally believed that at that time excitement would grow and at the last minute everyone would jump on the bandwagon.

Not everything went so smoothly, though. Beth lost her baby, neither she nor Sam coped very well, and Sally found herself making regular lasagne-filled visits to Barnet to help, quite successfully, to cement a relationship on which she was not actually all that keen. Twenty minutes after she had returned from one of these visits, Ben Wardle called on her at her tiny flat, which was piled with packing cases. She was about to move. With her salary she could afford to rent a flat, still quite small but no longer tiny, in one of the rather tatty but characterful old late Georgian warehouses on the Quays, where she would in fact look out directly on to Terence and Felicity's narrowboat.

Ben was very nervous. Sally offered him a coffee, and he asked for a mug rather than the cup and saucer that Sally normally gave him. As he took his mug it dawned on her why he had chosen it. His hands were shaking so much that the cup would have rattled noisily in its saucer.

'So what's the problem, Ben?' she asked gently.

'I've been accepted by Wimbledon College of Art.'

'Well, that's marvellous, Ben,' she said. 'That's great news. Oh, I'm so pleased for you.'

'Yes, but . . . Oh, and thanks. Thanks very much, Sally, but . . .' He hesitated.

'Hasn't that got a great name, particularly for sculpture?'

'Yes, it has, but . . .'

341

'Well, that's a great achievement, Ben. No, really, congratulations.'

'Thanks, Sally. I want to say . . . I need to say . . . I couldn't have done it without you.'

'Of course you could.'

'No!' He almost shouted it. 'No, you did it. You gave me the confidence. I was still scared, but . . . not as scared as I would have been if I hadn't met you. If I hadn't met you I might never even have thought about it. But . . .'

'Don't think like that, Ben. You're going and you'll be brilliant. You really will. Don't be nervous.'

'I'm not nervous. Well, I am, but not about that.'

'So why are you nervous?'

'I feel dreadful about this, but I'm not going to have time to do the shopfronts. That's a great way to repay you, isn't it?'

He had to hold his right hand firm with his left hand in order to get the coffee to his mouth.

'Ben! You mustn't be upset about that. You've got your life now.'

'That worries me about college, Sally. I won't be doing it *for* anybody. I'll just be doing it for myself. I think I might feel there isn't any point to it.'

'You mustn't feel like that. Art is for oneself.'

'It shouldn't be.'

'Well, it doesn't have to be when you've got your degree.'

'*If* I get my degree.'

'Don't think like that, Ben.'

Ben took another sip of coffee, with less difficulty this time. He was looking disappointed, and with that look he suddenly seemed much younger than eighteen.

'I thought you'd be disappointed,' he said. 'About the shopfronts.'

'I am disappointed,' said Sally. 'I'm very disappointed.'

342

'You don't look disappointed.'

'I'm hiding it. That's what grown-ups do.'

'I think it's a pity to hide things.'

'Well, maybe it is. Ben, I think your shopfront ideas would have been wonderful, but it's your life and I understand it and I'm just going to have to find somebody else.'

'You won't.'

'What?'

'There isn't anybody else. Not in Potherthwaite. Lots of people could do some of it, but nobody could do all of it, except me. I've heard about that idea about painting the Baggit Estate – cool, great, that'll be fine, anyone can do that, same with the Sculpture Trail – but the shopfronts, they're, like, in my head, so how can they be in anybody else's heads as well? It's as if Picasso had said, "Sorry, I haven't time to do *Guernica*, get somebody else." Not that I'm, like, comparing me with Picasso.'

'Good. I'm glad of that. So, Wimbledon, eh? Do you think you'll miss Potherthwaite?'

'Dunno.'

'Do you . . . see much of . . .?'

'Lucy?'

'Yes. I remember that day when you went off after her. You looked so good together.'

Ben looked very uncomfortable, very young, very vulnerable.

'Yeah. Didn't work out.'

'Oh dear. That's a shame.'

'Yeah. Yeah, it was.'

'I really thought you two might—'

'I don't want to talk about it any more, Mrs Mottram.'

Ben's use of the words 'Mrs Mottram' hit Sally like a sack of coal. In that moment she knew a terrible thing. She wished Ben was her son, not Sam.

Ben was right about one thing. Sally hunted for a replacement to do the shopfronts. There wasn't anybody. And she realized something else. The town was in transition, but so were the love lives of the people in it. We have seen the blow suffered by Linda Oughtibridge. We have seen the Revd Dominic Otley going at least halfway to conquering his yearnings for Sally. We have also heard, from none other than the man himself, that Matt Winkle's marriage was not going terribly well. Sally had now learnt that things had gone from bad to worse. He had been having a burgeoning affair with Jade Hunningbrooke, manageress of 'Hair Today, Gone Tomorrow'. Jade was thin and tall, with almost no bust, but she had a voracious mouth, mischievous eyes and legs that went on for ever. One evening, slightly the worse for wear on drink and drugs, he had told her that his wife Nicola was a very sound sleeper, and they had entered upon a little bet for no less than £20. She would win if she could throw an object at Matt's bedroom window, waking him but not Nicola. The following evening, even more the worse for drink and drugs, she had lobbed a nectarine very gently at the Winkles' bedroom window. The window had shattered. The nectarine had been as hard as a new cricket ball. It hadn't helped when she had told Matt that she had bought it, advertised as *Juicy and ready to eat*, at his supermarket. Nicola had run out of the house, screaming. Jade had said, 'Come on, Matt, there's something here that really is juicy and ready to eat.' Matt had not appreciated the humour at that moment. Jade had been, rather like the name of her business, here today and gone tomorrow, but so had Nicola, and, in his more sober moments, Matt was devastated.

Who does this leave among our new friends? Harry and Jill. Marigold and Conrad. Ellie. And of course Sally herself. Were their lives in transition too?

Sally, post-Conrad, had given up on all thoughts of

transition for herself. All her energies were to be devoted to the Transition of Potherthwaite.

Ellie's life could hardly be said to be in transition. There was no change in her situation, by definition. She was stuck in the front room of number 6 Cadwallader Road. Yet in a way she was in the biggest transition of all. When she could walk again, as she would if she could stick to her new regime, her life would be utterly transformed.

Harry and Jill had suddenly found themselves bereaved within a matter of days. The whole town knew that they had brought Harry's yawl home together. The whole town knew that they had been on a painting course in Montepulciano together. The whole town assumed that they would now feel free to go to bed together. The facts that in truth Harry's only lapse had been the secret one of having had to cope with and defeat a very healthy erection in the corridor of their hotel in Montepulciano after a day in the sun and humiliation from the principles of perspective, while Olive and Arnold had gone to bed together in the cul-de-sac without even a pretence of resistance, were not known to anybody except Harry. Even Jill didn't know.

Each's garden gave access to the other's. It was a situation to dream of. And why should they not go to bed together, when everybody in the town except themselves knew that they were? Well, they didn't. They were inhibited by the very obviousness of the situation, by the freedom of opportunity, by the apparent inevitability of the action. And they were inhibited even more by their love for their dead spouses. Jill missed Arnold's lovable pomposity, which had not seemed truly lovable until he died. All the obsessive little rituals of the writer, and particularly of the untalented writer, were suddenly endearing. Harry missed Olive's cooking and the inexhaustible opportunities for criticism that it afforded. He missed her social awkwardness, and all the fidgety, jittery movements of her tense, worried body.

Harry thought that Jill must be expecting him to pounce, shower her with passionate kisses, remove her summer dress and kiss those smooth, bare, burnished legs that no woman in her seventies had a right to have, and that very few men in their seventies would be able to resist.

Jill thought that Harry must be waiting for her to tease him, to tempt him, to seduce him with a thousand little subtleties.

They played Scrabble four times a week, twice in his house, twice in hers. He beat her more than she beat him, which embarrassed her in her role as a writer's widow. At the end of the evenings they kissed each other on both cheeks. Once a week they went to the Weavers' Arms together. On the other two evenings they sat at home on their own and watched programmes they had recorded. Harry watched sport and series about serial killers. Jill watched series about serial killers and cookery and travel programmes. They no longer went away together. The longest trips they made together were to the canal, to help with the slow, painful clearance of the silt, the removal of rusted bicycles and shining, indestructible old lavatory bowls; disintegrating condoms and Tampaxes; the carcasses of poisoned rabbits, badgers and fish; a statue of an owl; a child's hand; and a great mass of sodden paper which Inspector Pellet identified as being, mysteriously, thirty-three copies of the same volume of the *Macropaedia Britannica*, the volume that went from 'Excretion' to 'Geometry'.

Conrad introduced Marigold to the rather regimented charms of the Shoulder of Mutton and took her back to the classier, more individual attractions of the Drovers' Arms, where the bar stools swivelled so easily. They went, with a party of his friends from flood control and their spouses, to the Chinese restaurant. They talked about sex, food, drink, sex, flood control and sex. Marigold was a little concerned to hear that Potherthwaite was due a major flood. She was even more concerned to notice how deftly Conrad changed the subject at this point. A huge amount of food swivelled on the lazy Susan, and a lot of seriously indifferent wine was drunk. As they got into their car, she commented that it was not encouraging that the most senior of all the flood controllers had seemed utterly incapable of controlling the flood of his conversation. Conrad laughed, said how wonderful it was to be with a woman who was both beautiful and witty, and, gently, with perfect timing, just as he said 'beautiful and witty', placed his left hand very gently on her beautiful, witty right thigh. She let it stay there for a moment, then gently removed it, but she squeezed it very slightly as she did so. Her heart was racing. She had known that she couldn't just accept dinners for ever. She had known that the moment would come when she would have to brace herself for the possibility of another commitment to a man. She had known that there were only two explanations for the slow pace of his seduction. Either he didn't want her enough, or he wanted her so much that he couldn't let impetuosity frighten her. If it was the latter, he was doing too good a job.

'Come back to "The Larches" for a nightcap,' he said. 'See what I've done with Sally's old place.'

She tried to speak, couldn't find the air, swallowed desperately, only just stifling what would have been one of the worst-timed burps in the history of romance. She wished she hadn't drunk so much.

'Only a nightcap,' said Marigold.

'Of course.'

Marigold didn't like what he'd done to the house, or rather, what he hadn't done. He'd had nearly a year, but he seemed to have just plonked his furniture down. Sally's sitting room had become Conrad's lounge. Most of Sally's furniture had gone, replaced by a bulky three-piece suite, an elderly Lloyd Loom chair and an inappropriately elegant Pembroke table. On the table were two mounted photographs, one of a much younger Conrad receiving a medal from an elderly man, and one of an older but still young Conrad in full morning dress beside his rather short, slightly plump, toothily smiling wife Magda, who looked quite attractive despite these defects, but not as attractive as Marigold. There were no decorations, no flowers, no paintings on the walls, just ghostly spaces where Sally's paintings had once been. It was a room waiting for a woman. Was she that woman?

His choice of drinks lacked anything unusual. Wine, beer, whisky, gin, vodka. She opted for a vodka and tonic. Wine would have been safer, but the wine in the Chinese restaurant had not put her in the mood for more. It had left a gentle but dangerous burn of acid in her throat.

As she waited for him to return with her drink, her mind raced. Would the vodka be of seducer's strength? Why had he not produced any friends from his old life? It was good news that his wife hadn't been as pretty as her, but why hadn't she? Was he not as good a catch as she had thought? Why were there no pictures? She had vowed never to marry again, never to trust a man again, never to be hurt again. What was she doing here?

The vodka was reassuringly, disappointingly weak. He walked towards a cavernous settee; she veered off to sit in an equally bulky chair. It was a suite for giants. The room felt cold, although the evening was reasonably warm. She shivered slightly and he put the flame-effect fire on with his remote control. The brief reference to Potherthwaite's floods was nagging at her, and it wasn't helping her to feel romantic. A few minutes ago she had been worrying that they might go too fast. Now she was worrying that they might not go at all. The evening was dying, and that definitely wasn't in the plan. She wished that she was sitting with him on the settee, so that she could just touch him. But to move over to join him would be too obvious a tactic.

He offered her another drink and she felt that to refuse would be to risk never being invited again. It was as if the whole potential relationship was sliding away. She accepted, came with him to the kitchen to watch him make it, sat beside him on the settee on their return. She asked him questions about his wife. He said that Magda had never had a day's illness before the cancer struck. She used this moment to put her arm round him. They sat with their arms round each other, but almost motionless. She longed for the same thing as she dreaded, which was for him to kiss her fiercely. He didn't. She yawned theatrically.

'I should be going,' she said.

She stood up rather abruptly.

He kissed her, but not fiercely.

'I'll drive you home,' he said. 'I'm sure I'm not over the limit.'

He drove her home. She was glad the evening was over, but she longed to see him again. That was ridiculous. This wasn't going to work.

He switched the engine off.

'Thank you,' he said.

'No, thank *you*,' she said.

'I'm inspecting the town's flood-relief plans tomorrow morning,' he said. 'Sally's going to be there.'

'Ah.'

Marigold was quite pleased with her 'ah'. She felt that it had been completely devoid of meaning.

'I think it would be rather nice if you were there,' he said. 'After all . . .'

349

He stopped. She realized that she had no idea how he would have continued, if he hadn't stopped. 'After all, you're really her second-in-command, aren't you?' 'After all, if I'm there alone with Sally people will talk.' 'After all, I'm hoping that before too long you're going to be my wife.'

It had been an evening half cool, half warm, which had ended in a room with no decorations or charm, with unimaginative, careful, rather weak alcoholic drinks and a complete absence of nibbles. It had been a meeting between a woman who was frightened of the man going too quickly and frightened of him going too slowly, and a man who seemed so conscious of the significance of his movements that he didn't make any real movements at all. Had it been a good evening? Had it been a bad evening? Had it been a successful evening? Would there be another evening? If so, would it go better or would it go worse?

She had no idea.

THIRTY-SEVEN

Flood control

Next day, she met Sally and Conrad as arranged. Conrad was accompanied by a senior colleague, Stanley Willink, a tall and grizzled man with a hooked nose and penetrating eyes.

A persistent rain was falling, and all four carried golf umbrellas. They walked up the main road towards the head of the valley. As they walked, Marigold referred to the conversation of the previous evening, in the Chinese restaurant. She asked for more information about the Potherthwaite floods. Conrad and Stanley exchanged a look, then Stanley spoke.

'There have been occasional devastating floods in Potherthwaite throughout known history,' said Stanley. 'Strangely, the last three have occurred at intervals of thirty-five years.'

They were passing the allotments now. The allotments were deserted on this grey, inhospitable morning. Under Sally's inspiration, would they one day soon be brought back to teeming life?

'And how long ago was the last flood?' Marigold asked.

Conrad and Stanley exchanged another look. Stanley's

look indicated that he felt that Conrad should answer this question.

'Thirty-four years,' said Conrad.

They were walking past the supermarket and its attendant car parks.

'Don't look so worried,' said Stanley Willink. 'There can be no significance to the thirty-five-year gaps. Weather doesn't work like that. In the nineteenth century, the gaps between floods were forty-two years, eleven years and twenty-eight years.' He paused. 'Nevertheless,' he added.

'Precisely,' said Conrad.

They had reached the head of the valley. They stood in silence for a moment, looking at the river. Here the Pother came hurling itself thunderously down off the hills, spray flying, foam leaping, as the young stream learnt to play, found energy, surged ecstatically from rock to rock, became aggressive, and flung itself with angry spoilt impotence against the long wall of the supermarket car park. Its failure to destroy this wall seemed to sober it, teach it something of the bitterness of life. It became a little calmer, a little slower, a little wiser. At the moment the water here was barely halfway up the banks. On went the river, past the back of the allotments, almost straight now, slightly dull in truth. Now, suddenly middle-aged, it would flow, slowly, serenely, through the western outskirts of the town. Now it would set its course to the east-north-east, away from the southern range of moors. Beyond its right bank a road of houses, scheduled for demolition, separated it from the end of the Potherthwaite Arm of the Rackstraw and Sladfield Canal. Down in the town it would seem to pose no threat. Here, at the foot of the hills, they could all sense its potential power.

'Nevertheless,' said Stanley, 'we are taking no chances. In flood-control circles our friend Conrad here has long been marked out as something rather special.'

Conrad looked at the two ladies and grimaced with mock embarrassment.

'He has ideas,' continued Stanley, 'and I'm glad to say that we have decided to put him in sole charge of what we must now call the Potherthwaite Flood Control Plan.'

'Or, as I prefer to call it, the Potherthwaite Flood Avoidance Plan,' said Conrad.

'This has nothing to do with any significance in any period of years since the last flood. It could happen any time. It may not happen for another twenty years. It might happen tomorrow,' said Stanley.

'Oh Lord,' said Marigold, and Conrad threw Stanley a reproving look.

Stanley Willink led the small group round the back of the supermarket, following the course of the river. On their left now were the allotments, and then the riverside path became the scruffy little street with its houses scheduled for demolition.

'Is there any particular reason why these houses are scheduled for demolition?' asked Sally.

Conrad and Stanley exchanged another look. It seemed that this one was Stanley's turn.

'Under Conrad's master plan,' said Stanley, 'these are the only houses whose safety from flooding he cannot guarantee. Isn't that right, Conrad?'

'Yes, that's right,' said Conrad. 'Besides, they're just simply in the way.'

He led them round the back of the condemned houses towards the Potherthwaite Arm of the Rackstraw and Sladfield Canal. The Potherthwaite Arm, five and a quarter miles of badly maintained, absurdly narrow canal, was not a jewel in the crown of the British canal system, but nothing about it was less elegant than its end, which was just a stagnant dribble in a featureless marsh. Stanley halted at the edge of the marsh. A shy heron, disturbed by their approach, flew off with slow, resigned flaps of its great grey wings.

'Any comments?' Stanley asked Conrad Eltington. 'Any reason why you've brought us on this walk today, and disturbed that lovely heron?'

Conrad nodded.

'Ladies?' he said. 'Any ideas?'

Sally guessed the answer. It wasn't exactly rocket science, but in a sudden surge of affection for Marigold she said nothing. She wanted her friend to have a chance to shine in Conrad's eyes.

And Marigold, in the remorseless light rain, with the legs that had graced a hundred bar stools now encased in wellington boots, on the edge of an unattractive marsh from which the only lovely thing, a heron, had been driven away by their approach, suddenly felt it extremely important that she should impress Conrad.

'You're going to build a channel from the river to the canal,' she said, 'and I suppose some sort of sluice gate that you can open to divert the water. Once the canal is cleared, it'll take a lot of extra water, which can be released down-stream into the water meadows if there's a threat of the river breaking its banks. Sort of thing.'

Conrad tried to hide how pleased he was by her reply, but his childish delight seeped through and its childishness revealed to her that he was much more fond of her than he had shown last night.

But all he said was, 'Just so.'

They walked on. A lone red kite circled above them as their four multicoloured golf umbrellas moved slowly across the marsh to the point where, on the southern end of the canal, the towpath began. As they walked on, the dribble of water grew. Stanley Willink explained to Sally and Marigold that the water for the canal came via underground pipes laid in early Victorian times to catch the waters pouring down off the southern moors.

Conrad indicated where the sluice gates would be, where the course of the relief cut would lead. Now the canal became more like a large pond, or even a small lake. This was the famous winding hole, scooped out to provide a turning circle for the narrowboats. Here, when the clearance of the canal was completed, Terence and Felicity Porchester would turn in readiness for their journey back to the mooring that they hadn't been able to reach for what was now ten years. Conrad explained where the necessary reinforcements to the banks of the winding hole would go. Sally knew that all this should give her a feeling of reassurance, but it didn't. The scale of the works revealed to her the scale of the threat, and, if it didn't work, the scale of the damage to all her plans. Her eyes met Marigold's, and she knew that her friend was thinking the same thing. This little river could destroy all their great work. This little river could wreck the Transition of Potherthwaite.

Beyond the winding hole, the canal proper began, with the towpath on the southern side, and a dirt track to the north. They passed the spot at which they would soon have been going under the new bridge, if the plan for the second supermarket had not been thrown out. Here the track became a road, flanked by old houses in bad repair, two of them empty and threatened with demolition.

Behind them, and below the level of the canal, stood the Canal Basin, that tiny, dark, cobbled square, its old houses looking down with Victorian disapproval on the prostitutes parading their wares below them.

They carried on along the towpath towards the Quays, with the dark grey slates of the town shining in the rain on the other side of the cut. There was Sally's new flat, which occupied the whole first floor of a three-storey converted late Georgian warehouse. How characterful it looked, but how badly the window frames needed painting. In front of it, Terence Porchester was lying on the roof of his narrowboat, his great frame overhanging the edge, his thick arms stretching out to reach the sliver of deck that ran round the side of the boat. Felicity was crouched down on the roof behind him, holding his legs with ferocious concentration. One slip from her, and he'd be in the drink, and not the kind of drink that he liked.

He waved cheerfully, a dangerous act.

'Don't wave,' shouted Felicity urgently.

'Got to, darling. Friends,' said Terence. A thought struck him. 'Don't *you* bloody wave. Mending a leak,' he told the four walkers. 'Wretched climate. Be a nice place, this, if it wasn't for the rain. Fancy a glass of bubbly, cheer yourselves up?'

'Thanks,' said Conrad, 'but another time. We're working.'

'Bad luck,' boomed Terence.

After they had finished their reconnaissance, Conrad and Stanley took Sally and Margaret to lunch at the Weavers'. It was clear to both Sally and Stanley that today Conrad and Marigold were getting on significantly well. It was also clear to both Sally and Stanley that nothing whatsoever was going on between Sally and Stanley.

At the end of the meal, when the others ordered coffee, Sally said that she must go. 'The Transition won't happen on its own,' was her passing shot.

She wanted a coffee, to gee her up, but not with the others. She wandered to the place that she suddenly realized was her favourite haunt in town – the warm, reliable, blessedly ordinary Kosy Korner Kafé.

Lucy Basridge was sitting with a Diet Coke at a quiet table towards the back of the café. She was reading a book. Like her, it was very slim. She seemed to Sally to have changed, though. She looked more solid. She looked as if she had matured in the eleven months since she had spoken out during the march. She still had her ring and her stud, but her hair was its natural gold again. Sally was surprised to find how keen she was to speak to her. She hoped Lucy would become Ben's girlfriend. He needed a girlfriend. That was the only subject in the whole world on which she agreed with Ben's father.

She took her coffee – goodness, how she needed the thrust the double espresso would give her – and walked slowly towards Lucy's table.

'Hello,' she said. 'It's Lucy, isn't it?'

Lucy looked up. Sally knew immediately that she had been reading the book properly, with concentration, and wasn't happy to be interrupted. She knew too that it had been a bit crass to interrupt.

'Yeah.'

'I'm Sally Mottram.'

'Yeah, I know.'

Sally had experienced conversations that had started better than this.

'I'm a friend of Ben's,' she said. It came out sounding like a piece of code, with a hidden meaning.

'Yeah, I know.'

Despite all her good intentions, seeing Conrad and Marigold, in the flesh, getting on so well over lunch had made Sally feel isolated and lonely, and now she heard herself saying rather to her horror, 'Do you mind if I join you?' It was wrong, she was interrupting, but she just did not want to sit on her own, the only element not kosy in this Kosy Korner. How could Lucy have said, 'Yes. I do'? But Lucy said, 'No. Of course not,' and Sally couldn't say, 'Thanks, but I've changed my mind.'

Now that she was sitting there, she felt that it would look odd not to speak.

'What are you reading?'

'A play.'

'Ah.'

There was a silence between them that went on just slightly too long.

'Good,' said Sally. 'That's good.'

How patronizing was that?

'Is it good?'

This was terrible. How old are you, Sally?

'I've just started it.'

'Oh. And now I'm stopping you getting on with it.'

'It's all right. My concentration's broken now anyway.'

Shit.

'Sorry.'

'No, it doesn't matter. I've gotta split anyway.'

Sally wondered if Lucy was playing truant. She didn't look as if she was, but you never knew.

'Miss Spreckley told me to choose some plays from the library and read some in my study lesson.'

Lucy had answered Sally's thought. Was she a mind reader?

'She wants me to direct a play.'

'That's great. That's fantastic.'

'Yeah.'

Lucy stood up. She was taller than Sally had thought. What was she now? Sixteen?

'I really do have to split,' she said.

It was now or never.

'I gathered from Ben that things hadn't worked out too well . . . you know . . . between you.'

'Oh. Maybe.' Lucy didn't say 'So what?' but her eyes did. And she was entitled to. What business was it of Sally's? What on earth was she doing?

'No. It's just that I saw you together. I'm very friendly with Ben – I like him a lot, I think he's very talented, and . . .'

Sally could think of no way to end her sentence, but she had to say something.

'Maybe you could do a play for me, for the festival,' she said.

'What festival?'

'The Potherthwaite Festival.'

'I didn't know there was a Potherthwaite Festival.'

'There wasn't. There will be.'

'Cool. Yeah, maybe. Cool. I really do have to split.'

Sally hardly saw Lucy move. One minute she was there, the next minute she wasn't. Sally felt about a hundred and thirty-six years old. Her wish that Ben was her son had shocked her, and now what was she doing? Trying to find a suitable partner for him. Not only behaving as if she was his mother, but as if she was his interfering cow of a mother at that. Sam and Beth were her concern. And Alice. When the Transition had been fully set in place she'd step away from it and begin to look after her own family. She should never have started it.

If only Sam and Beth lived nearer. If only Alice wasn't at the other side of the world.

Oh, come back, Alice. Please.

THIRTY-EIGHT

The remorseless passage of time

Autumn slid slowly, inexorably, painfully into winter. It does. Short days in a dark valley. The weather grew colder. It does. But the onset of this winter felt very different from the last one, to Sally. It would be wrong to exaggerate the number of people who were actively involved in Transition activities. Some people used wild words like 'half the town'. But, as winter's grip hardened, Sally had expected that the number of helpers would drop off, as in the previous year. Not so. In fact to her amazement the reverse happened. To a man, and woman, the active helpers refused to be beaten, in a Pennine town, by a mere winter, and other people, noting the indomitability of the helpers, were driven by guilt, or shame, or pride, or sheer good nature, to join in. The bypass would soon be completed. Stretches of the canal were clear. The whole thing had gathered momentum.

A competition for the design of the park was held, and it was won by a quiet and apparently unambitious young man in the council's Parks and Gardens department. Sally had actually met him when she had tried to persuade Barry to get Mottram & Caldwell to sponsor a roundabout. Barry had told her that Tom Caldwell had no vision and thought it a waste of money. After Barry's death she had discovered that he had never even told Tom. Many and often trivial were her moments of disillusionment. The young man was called Fred Burns and perhaps he wasn't as unambitious as everyone thought. He changed his name to Frederick J. Burns, resigned from the council, and set himself up as a bespoke landscape designer. Volunteers began to prepare the ground for his vision. Others, perhaps fearing a two-tier Potherthwaite, worked on improvements to Baggit Park.

The council reopened the Royalty Suite at the back of the Town Hall. Here prominent citizens held dinners to raise money for the Transition cause. They couldn't hold an exhibition of live dodos, but they could rescue the dinner dance from extinction. With every little lift in the public mood, more money was raised. Raffles were generously supported. Even on the Baggit Estate, the Hugh Gaitskell Memorial Hall became the seat of a monthly horse-racing evening. And Sir Norman, as promised, matched every penny. A committee was set up to decide what to do with the money. It was independent of the council though with one councillor from each major party on the committee. Largely due to Sally's excellent man-management skills and even better woman-management skills, the committee worked well. A subcommittee of the committee was set up and it surveyed all public buildings in the town, allocating money from the fund for their renovation by the town's craftsmen. Sally deliberately let slip by accident on Radio Pother that she would suggest a memorial of thanks to all craftsmen or craftswomen who had helped under this scheme. Once they knew this, every craftsman and craftswoman in the town volunteered.

The thing to be in this newly environmentally conscious town was a provider of solar panels. Suddenly they became a status symbol, and within months more than half the houses in Oxford Road had them.

Another great environmental scheme was the recycling of urine. Special devices were installed in the town's public conveniences, enabling the urine to be siphoned off, treated, stored, and used to fertilize what arable land there was. Several pubs joined in. The Dog and Duck put up a board which announced, electronically, its gallonage. Currently it stands at 893. Drinkers will cheer when it flicks to 894. When it reaches 900, all hell will break loose, and there will be a free fish-and-chip supper for the lucky urinator. At the bottom of the board were the chalked words: *'British Urine – British Measures – No Litres Here'*. The town's buses – repainted green, of course – carried the simple slogan: *'Pee For Potherthwaite'*. One night five buses were deformed with the added words: *'And Shit For Sheffield'*. Luke Warburton, the prime suspect, produced dated photographs that showed him in Amsterdam on a stag night that weekend, but who can believe any photograph in the digital age? The more he proved he hadn't been there, the more people believed he had. Lucy, of course, was also suspected. She grew really angry when accused, shouting that she always kept her promises, and in the end most people believed her. But in fact nobody worried too much about this very mild obscenity, and the *Chronicle*, without mentioning the potentially offensive word, even went so far as to state that, if the one recycling project was sound, why not go for the other one as well? Food was expensive. Why not put a bit back with the end product?

Several towns, notably Totnes in Devon and Lewes in East Sussex, had created their own banknotes, and now Potherthwaite followed suit. The alliteration in the words 'Potherthwaite Pound' proved effective, and lots of shops agreed to participate in the scheme. People who used these shops knew that the shop observed the principles of the movement, sold only food that was healthily and humanely produced, and supported the local economy whenever possible. Another competition was held to decide the design of the notes, and it was won by a lady interior designer who lived in the loveliest of all the old houses on the Quays, for her colourful representation of a semi-mythical, semi-historic Saxon do-gooder called Povver the Magnanimous, whose name was said to be the original source of the names of the river, the valley and the town.

As the winter drew to its end, Sir Norman returned from Bermuda rather earlier than usual, and Sally visited him as planned, drank two glasses of the most marvellous manzanilla, enjoyed her roast red deer while Sir Norman tucked into his scrambled eggs, told him every detail of every initiative, and felt that her visit had been a success when her plate at Sunday lunch contained not one, but two individual Yorkshire puddings.

Not only that, but when she left he actually came to the front steps, stood there in the biting wind and spoke at some length.

'Tiptree is not a man suited to social life,' he said. 'Put it this way. If I needed an emissary to represent me at some royal event, I would not choose him. In fact he is eminently suited to hermitude, if there is such a word, and if there isn't it should be invented specially for him. I do respect his judgement, however, so when I sent him to Potherthwaite to vet you – oh dear oh dear, how awful that sounds – and he informed me that you had impressed him, his statement impressed me more than somewhat. In casual moments over my scrambled eggs during my solitary dinners I wondered just how impressive you must be to have impressed him so. I invited you here and found you to be even more impressive than I had dared to hope.'

'Thank you.'

'And now, this weekend, as you've revealed to me the progress of your great work, I have found you more impressive than ever.'

'Well, thank you.'

A few days later, Sally had a visit from Ben Wardle. His complexion was ashen, he had black bags under his eyes, he looked too thin, but at least he wasn't shaking.

'Can I come in?' he asked.

'Ben, of course. You never need to ask.'

'Sorry, you do at college, people might be humping, lot of it about.'

'Sadly, you're safe here. You have entered a no-humping area.'

She offered him a drink. He asked for a Diet Coke.

'Not alcohol?'

'Not at the moment, thanks. I've left all that.'

'What do you mean?'

'I've left uni.'

'What? Sacked? Sent down?'

'No. No, not sacked at all. They begged me to stay.'

'Then why, Ben? Why?'

'I can't cope with leaving uni owing forty thousand pounds. It terrifies me, Sally.'

He looked so intense. His left leg was working, the way young people's legs often did. It was sad to see how many young people's legs drummed nervously beneath pub and café tables.

'I understand,' said Sally. 'I think it's terrible that young people face such stress.'

'Lots of older people hate students and burden them with debt and still expect them to grow up to clear up the messes that they themselves have made of the world. Don't call this a civilized country.'

'I agree the debt is awful,' she said gently, 'but I don't believe you'll have any problem in paying it off. I believe you have a very real talent, Ben.'

'So do I,' he said. 'That's not my problem. Does that sound awful?'

'No. You're brave to say it, not just think it.'

'I've been immersed in art, Sally. I've seen people with talent making money and people with no talent not making money, but I've also seen people with talent making no money and people with no talent making heaps of money. Art, like, has no rules any more, and lots of people have no taste, and fashion is almost everything, so I can't say as a serious artist trying to have integrity that I will ever be able to pay off my debts. Don't try to persuade me to go back. I won't. Am I still on for the High Street job?'

'If you want to be. That would be fantastic.'

'Cool. Sally?'

He went slightly pink.

'Yes, Ben?'

'My dad thinks what I've done is cowardly.'

'It could be called that. It could equally be called brave. It isn't either. It's what it is.'

'I can't live with him. He's a pig.'

'Oh dear. Oh, Ben.'

'Ever since I've taken up art, gone to London, he's been hateful.'

'He's jealous.'

'Of me?'

'Oh yes, Ben. Of you.'

'Bloody hell. Sally?'

'Yes, Ben?'

'Can I live with you?'

'Oh, Ben. Oh, Ben.'

'I've been thinking.'

'I know you have.'

She walked over, and sat beside him on the settee.

'I'm young for my age. I think I still need a mother.'

Sally took hold of his hand, kissed it very gently.

'You have a mother,' she said.

'Yeah, she's not bad, but Dad comes with her.'

Sally was tempted. So tempted. It was her dream. But it wasn't right. His parents had feelings. They might stir up controversy. There might even be accusations that she had stolen him. These days you never knew.

Besides, he needed to learn to stand on his own two feet, free himself from his mother, not lean on more mothers.

And it would get in the way of her work.

And he didn't drink. At their meals she would feel that she was setting him a bad example.

Each sip of wine would taste of guilt as well as grape.

But it was hard, hard not to seize him for her own.

She forced herself to be very definite.

'I'm sorry, Ben. I'm afraid it's not possible.'

He was hurt.

'Much as I might want it.'

He didn't believe her.

Shortly afterwards, Eric Sheepshank suggested a place, up near Baggit Park, that he had looked at as a possible studio before making his final choice, and it suited Ben well, so he rented it, and he was happy to sleep on a camp bed surrounded by his creations. The two artists worked in solitude a few doors away from each other for long hours, and just occasionally, in the rare moments when the muse failed them both at the same time, went down to the Dog and Duck, sat in a corner, and talked art for hours and hours.

The days lengthened. They do. Sally introduced a badge for people who supported and helped Potherthwaite in Transition, or Transition Town Potherthwaite, as the creators of the movement dubbed it. Large numbers of people wore this with pride, and were delighted to feel a connection with Brixton, and Tooting, and Los Angeles, and Brasilia, and all the other places that were working towards the salvation of the planet in a myriad little ways. The badge provided benefits, local buses gave 20p off. It provided obligations. When wearing the badge, people in public places (and in their homes if the family decided it so) had to observe what Sally called Football Free Fridays. Millions of people in Britain talk about football almost all day almost every day. Under Sally's scheme they were not allowed to do so on Fridays, and were fined if they did. The money went to the cause, and Sir Norman, hating anything that was as popular as football, contributed the same amount to this as well. To Sally's surprise, the Baggit Arms took this up big time, trapping the unwary and fining them with relish. 'I've had a great evening,' Luke Warburton said once. 'Didn't mention football all evening.' 'You just have,' said his sister. 'That's 20p.'

The bypass grew longer at amazing speed, with Sir Norman's money behind it. Ellie could not yet be weighed, but she felt that she was on track. Harry and Jill continued to play Scrabble and go to the Weavers' Arms once a week. Marigold led a varied life, having sex with Conrad in her home in the cul-de-sac, having sex with Conrad in Sally's old home, and having sex with Conrad in nice hotels in the Lake District, which he charged against tax on grounds of urgent research into flood control. Every time they met, Marigold braced herself to find the courage to agree to brave a fourth marriage, to be ready and decisive when he popped the question. It was galling that he never did.

Harry and Jill were still not having sex anywhere, but one unusually warm evening, on their return from the Weavers' Arms, Harry suggested a nightcap in the garden. It's not often, in Potherthwaite, that it's warm enough to sit in the garden as dusk falls, but on that spring evening there was the first faint smell of summer. Soon his and Jill's arms were round each other and soon after that they were no longer taking advantage of the warm evening, they were standing by Harry's bed and taking their clothes off. Jill pulled back the duvet and flung herself on to the bed, lying on her back and smiling. Harry could not believe that a woman in her seventies could look so beautiful. As he clambered on top of her he saw the photograph of his wedding day that he still kept on the bedside table. He longed to turn the picture round, hide from himself how pretty Olive had been before anxiety had carved lines in her lovely face. He couldn't do that, but he couldn't stand that photograph's hope and certainty. It was over before it began. They dressed in what seemed to Harry to be the loudest silence he had ever heard.

'I'm so sorry,' he said as he led her out of the room. 'Are you upset?'

'Why do you think I've never suggested doing it in my house?' said Jill. She gave a gentle, sad smile, kissed him on one cheek, and stepped back into the cool warmth of a black, perfect night.

And now the nights *were* perfect. Summer came. It does. Occasionally. Even to Potherthwaite. Everything burgeoned. Flowers. Trees. Works of art. Eric Sheepshank presented Sally with three massive pieces for the Sculpture Trail. He was no Henry Moore, but there was a rugged strength about them, a rippling vitality that held an echo of the town's industrial heritage.

'They're lovely,' she said.

He hugged her and kissed her, then stood back in confusion that he had let her see his feelings.

Potherthwaite steamed in the wonderful, golden, stifling heat. Mornings were exquisite. The air was cool and virginal, as if this was the first day of existence. Sally took to having a kroissant and a koffee outside at the Kosy Korner Kafé. One day, Matt Winkle walked past, power-walking with a grimace on his face, thinner and paler than ever.

'Matt,' she called out.

It took him twenty yards to register that she had spoken, and to stop. He left all his energy on that spot, and walked back wearily.

'Sally!' he said. 'Why do you never come to my supermarket?'

'You know why,' she said. 'I can't be hypocritical.'

'But you're the only person in this town I want to see. Fuck all the others.'

'Matt! Language!'

'I don't mean it literally. I mean, the exact opposite, of course. Sally . . .?'

'No, Matt.'

'Why not?'

'Don't force me to say negative things, Matt. Sit down. Have a kroissant.'

'I haven't time. The bitches will be queuing with their unripe avocados. "Oh, isn't it hot," the fat cows will be saying, the same fat, stupid cows who complained cos there wasn't a summer last year.'

'Matt, please, relax.'

'I'm off. If ever you . . . oh well . . . nice to see you as always, Sally.'

She stood up. She didn't want to, but she couldn't avoid it. She let him kiss her.

He walked off, quite slowly at first, then gathering pace, pistons working, a high-speed train on the verge of coming off the rails.

The temperature rose. It does. Occasionally. Even in Potherthwaite.

Now the glistening bald head of Sergeant Major Harry Patterson was everywhere, noting the work being done on the canal, noting the names of the brave souls who were sweltering for their town, cajoling, encouraging, the sweat on his bald head shaming people into one extra effort. But, for all his efforts, the heat did slow the work down, and Sally knew that every day from now until the festival date next summer, she would be anxious about their progress.

And then the long, lingering, lovely evenings came. They do. Even in Potherthwaite. A cool little breeze from the east gently feathered the sweat off the tired pavements, and breathed new life into lovers and into clearers of canals.

The council held an open evening to enable the townsfolk to have a first look at their new park. At the front, there were two formal, elegant parterres, with areas marked out by posts. Next year these would be, in the words of the shy Fred Burns, who was halfway on his journey to becoming the not-so-shy Frederick J. Burns, 'awash with flowers'. Then there was a huge pile of stones. Next year this would be a terrace. Its fountains would be, in the words of Frederick J. Burns, 'literally flowing with colour'. Did he mean 'water', people wondered.

Beyond the terrace, 'French sophistication gives way to good old Pennine honesty', in the words of Frederick J. Burns, who was growing less shy with every minute. 'He'll earn a sodding billion with that J' was the overheard opinion of the most bitter and twisted of all Potherthwaite's traffic wardens. Here, at the back of the park, there would be an informal look, with lawns, areas for sitting and picnicking.

On one of those memorable evenings, Lucy called round at Sally's house on the Quays. The girl who had performed in a circus at five years of age, and had jumped from the wall of the police station on to a magnolia, and, even more precariously, from the magnolia back on to the wall, looked really nervous now.

'I've come to apologize, Mrs Mottram,' she said. 'I was rude to you that time we met in the café.'

'Not very rude, Lucy, and you were very young. And it's very nice of you to apologize.'

'Not really. I'm only doing it because I want something from you.'

'Oh. And what do you want from me, Lucy?'

'Advice.'

'Shall we have a drink?' said Sally. 'Would you like a glass of wine?'

'Oh, that would be great.'

Sally opened a bottle of white wine. They stood by the window, looking out over the Quays as the sun approached the moors.

'This is the Viognier grape,' said Sally. 'I'd like your opinion on it.'

'I'm seventeen, Mrs Mottram.'

'Please call me Sally, Lucy.'

'Cool.'

Lucy took a sip and drank it carefully.

'It's nice.'

'I thought you'd like it.'

Sally sat on the settee and patted the place beside her. Lucy sat.

'So,' said Sally, 'what do you want my advice on?'

'Ben.'

'Oh.'

'He . . . I shouldn't be telling you this. He'd hate it if he knew. We . . . quite a while ago . . . we . . . he bedded me. Well, more I bedded him really.'

'As you do.'

'As you do.'

371

'No. As *you* do.'

'What?'

'I didn't. Not in my day. Not at your age.'

'I suppose not. But . . . you know . . . Sally . . .' Lucy smiled at her success in calling Sally Sally, then went very serious again. 'Guys today . . . young guys . . . they're all supposed to be brill in the sack. Know what I mean?'

'Yes, Lucy, I know what you mean.'

'But . . . I shouldn't be telling you . . .'

'He couldn't manage it?'

'Well, not . . . you know . . . not really.'

'Yes, I do know.'

Sally realized that the memory of Barry that flashed through her mind at this moment was the first time she had thought of him for many weeks.

'I mean, he . . .'

'Shall we leave it there, Lucy?'

'He was so ashamed. So embarrassed. He's terrified of me now. You know how nervous he can be. He's not like other boys. That's what I like about him, Sally. So, I wondered, can you help?'

'Maybe I can, Lucy. I do have a kind of idea. Maybe I can. Will you leave it with me?'

'You won't tell him I told you, will you?'

'Lucy!'

'Sorry.'

'When are you going to do that play, Lucy?'

'I've done it.'

'What?'

'I did it a few weeks ago.'

'And you didn't tell me?'

'No. Why?'

'I'd have come.'

'You wouldn't.'

'I would. I'd have definitely come.'

'Wow!'

'How did it go?'

Lucy suddenly looked very serious.

'I wasn't satisfied, but I learnt a lot.'

She sounded so unexpectedly adult that Sally only just managed to keep a tremor of amusement out of her voice as she said, 'Marvellous.'

'Sally?'

Sally felt a frisson of excitement at something in Lucy's tone, but Lucy's next remark took her completely by surprise.

'Can I come and live with you?'

Sally's mouth opened in astonishment.

'I can't believe this,' she said. 'Ben asked me that.'

'Really? Oh, could we both come? That would be wicked.'

'It would be wicked, yes. Wicked of me. You both have parents.'

'I don't. Not really.'

'Are you prepared to tell me what happened with your parents, Lucy?'

'They split up. They had a row. Very nasty.'

'How old were you?'

'Ten. They had this argument. I was terrified.'

'I'm not surprised. It can't be nice hearing your parents saying horrid things to each other when you're ten.'

'It wasn't so much what they said. It was where they said it.'

'Where did they say it?'

'On the trapeze.'

'Oh my God.'

'Mum fell, broke her leg. Never performed again. Took me with her. Dad stayed. It turned out she'd been longing to leave. She hated the circus. She hated the treatment of the animals. She hated that she was losing her nerve.

I understand all that now, but I mean really, honestly, Sally, from the circus to selling envelopes in bloody Stratton's.'

'How do you get on with your parents?'

'Mum looks after me. She doesn't love me. She drinks.'

Sally cringed inwardly at the adult phrase that Lucy used. 'She drinks.'

'I haven't seen Dad since we left. He's never even sent a fucking Christmas card.'

'Oh, Lucy.'

'I'm sorry, Sally. I shouldn't have said that word.'

'I think you can be forgiven under the circumstances. That's awful.'

'I know. How can a dad do a thing like that?'

'I don't know, Lucy. I don't know.'

To have Ben and Lucy with her. To meet their friends. To watch their abilities develop. Oh, Sally, Sally, if only you could.

'More wine, Lucy?'

'No thanks, Sally. I see my mum using it as a crutch every night.'

On another of those memorable evenings, Ben led Sally silently through the velvet dusk, led her slowly, excitedly to his studio. He opened the door with shy pride. There, on three walls, was a painting of the prettiest high street she had ever seen. She gazed at it in wonder. Every window was different, but every window had clean, clear lines. The colour of the paintwork in every shop was a variant of the colour of its neighbours, so that the whole of High Street East had become a slow, subtle journey through the spectrum, and High Street West presented the same journey in reverse. The names of the various premises were in a lovely hand, subtly varied, and for every building there was a glorious little painting – a fish, a cupcake, a delicious dessert, a dress, a tie, a foaming pint, a worried accountant. For William Hill's, for instance, there was a little dramatic scene – an exultant punter, a weeping bookmaker.

'It is itself, in its entirety, a Work of Art,' he said. 'It is, in its entirety, an Installation.'

She was so overawed by it that she found him unapproachable at that moment. She wanted to hug him, but couldn't.

'Show it to Lucy,' she said.

'Would she be interested?'

'Would she?? She loves you, Ben.'

Ben looked at her in astonishment.

'Don't tell her you've shown it to me. Tell her she's the first person you've shown it to. You've saved it for her.'

'Are you suggesting I tell her a complete lie?'

'You bet I am.'

Three days later, shy, shaking and embarrassed, Ben plucked up his courage and asked Lucy out. Men often arouse women by showing them something rather special. It isn't usually a high street, but on this occasion it was. And it worked. Lucy was very excited, and Ben, seeing Lucy's excitement, was very proud, and in his pride Ben had no problem. He got it up, up up and beyond.

The following week, armed with photographs of Ben's High Street, Sally made her summer visit to the great house above Marlow. The sherry was Tio Pepe. Her main course at dinner was poached Thames salmon with lemon mayonnaise. Sir Norman plumped for scrambled eggs. At lunch next day Sally told Sir Norman that she really did think that the parsnips were the best yet.

After their lunch, Sally showed him Ben's designs for the High Street, and he did something that he had never done before. He walked with her over the gravel towards the Rolls-Royce, and there he kissed her on both cheeks.

On the train home Sally thought of all the men who had kissed her in this her second life. Sir Norman Oldfield, Ben Wardle, Harry Patterson, Arnold Buss, Conrad Eltington, Stanley Willink, Matt Winkle, Eric Sheepshank, Councillor Frank Stratton, The Revd Dominic Otley and Terence Porchester.

Would she ever be kissed by a man whose kisses she could return, and then return again, and then return once more, in secret and in public, with affection and with love?

THIRTY-NINE

Before the deluge

'It was a long, long drive up the Pan-American Highway. That sounds impressive, doesn't it? But it was just a two-lane road, with no central reservation, dusty, dry, passing through long, low villages of simple, one-storey cottages, their pastel paintwork made pale by the sun and darkened by the dirt from the road. Night came fast, and now the road's course was identified by the progress of the lorries – more than ships of the desert, these were cruise liners of the desert, their rigging studded with multicoloured lights, bravely defiant against a colourless world.'

Sally was enjoying herself. She had come to love telling tales of her travels to Ellie, Ali and Oli. She had long ago stopped promising to take them to the places she was describing. She had already promised them Venice, Florence, the Stockholm Archipelago and the Rhine. To promise more would be to render her promises meaningless.

'At every town, at every stop, schoolchildren hurried on to the bus, selling limes, oranges and pancakes. As the long night wore on, the children ceased to be the ones who were up long past their bedtime and became the ones who had struggled from their beds long before their breakfast time, all to earn a tiny sum of extra money for their families, all to keep starvation at bay.'

Ali, Ellie and Oli forgot the limitations of their own lives and sympathized with these poor children, whose weariness would quite prevent them from taking in the next day's lessons at school.

'The rickety old bus turned right, and began to emit a bad-tempered growl as it started its approach to the foothills of the mighty Andes. The bus's elderly snarl deepened as it began to climb. Now the light tiptoed into the world like a careful burglar intent on stealing the darkness. The bus was passing through paddy fields, shockingly fertile below the rocky hills, and studded with ibis, standing in the shallow water, still as statues, white as ghosts in the milky, misty morning.'

Ali, Ellie and Oli were with Sally in that creaking old bus. They could see the ibis. They envied her this spectacular journey. Little did they know that she had never even been to Peru. She had only learnt of this journey from a very dreary aunt of Barry's, in letters written in a much less picturesque style. She had entirely run out of inspiring places that she herself had actually seen. These talks were now involving quite a bit of research.

'The valley narrowed and steepened. Now there was no more room for the rice, no more moisture in a barren world. The ibis gave way to eagles and vultures and even the occasional condor as the bus twisted perilously up the narrow road, round the steep bends, over the wonky bridges.'

Suddenly Sally faltered. The weather forecast suggested that a storm was coming, the first storm of the winter, and that it was going to be huge and destructive. Despite the scepticism of Conrad and Stanley, the thirty-five-year gap was proving significant once again. The Potherthwaite Flood Avoidance Scheme was in place. Conrad seemed calm and confident. Everyone trusted him. Everyone believed in him. But Sally had never had a huge belief in experts, and, much as she admired Conrad, much as she felt that he deserved Marigold and she deserved him, there had to be just a bit of doubt in the judgement of a man who had rejected the opportunity of being loved by her. And Conrad's judgement and ability were now of huge importance, for Sally had just realized that, if the flood was as catastrophic as the doommongers predicted, Ellie might be drowned in her bed.

She must continue her tale. Her three obese friends were looking at her with slight alarm. She must quash that.

'Up up up went the creaky bus. Up up up went the dusty road. And then it crested the top of the mountain.' She didn't think it had actually – Barry's aunt's bus had crossed the great range somewhat below the summit – but this was dramatic licence. The trouble was, she didn't feel dramatic any more.

'And there was the huge sweep of the valley, stretching all the way to the horizon.'

She knew that the valley, and indeed the horizon, had been distinctly anticlimactic. Her purple passage had become a mauve plain. It was so much more tiring talking of places she hadn't been to, and having to pretend that she had. It seemed to her that the need for lies never stopped.

She left number 6 Cadwallader Road as soon as she decently could, and walked slowly home. As she crossed the river, she looked down at its slow, peaceful, only slightly dirty water and wondered just what violence it could be capable of. The bipolar mallard looked listless, disillusioned. They were going to have a rude awakening. As she crossed the Market Place she passed Luke Warburton going the other way. He looked listless and disillusioned too. Would he have a rude awakening? She smiled at him warmly, and this confused him so much that he couldn't summon up any facial expression in reply, so he just walked past blankly, kicked a loose stone angrily and tried valiantly to hide that he had hurt his foot.

She also found Councillor Frank Stratton walking towards her.

'All set for the storm?' she asked.

'Southerners!' he replied. 'Wimps! Journalists! Scaremongers! BBC! Poofters!' He nodded twice, in satisfaction at his intellectual demolition of more than half the British nation.

Sally walked on. His complacency did nothing to calm the unease she felt. Winter had arrived. This was the third winter since she had taken on her great task. They were interruptions. They slowed things down. And they were so long, here among the hills. This had to be a busy and productive one, if they were to meet their target for the festival next year. If it started with destruction, damage . . . if Ellie . . . without Ellie everything would collapse. She feared equally for Ellie and for High Street East, at the bottom of which the first twelve shopfronts had already been installed, all the shopkeepers having miraculously been persuaded to sign up for the new frontages.

In the morning she telephoned her doctor and asked if there was any way Ellie could be moved or if facilities could be on hand to move her if the situation demanded it. 'She is,' Sally said, 'a bit of a special case.'

'She is,' said her doctor very gently, 'in that of all the people in my practice who have special needs and serious health problems she more than anyone has brought it on herself. I have people with terminal cancer. I have cripples who can't walk. Ellie eats too much. It hardly compares.'

'Ate too much.'

'All right. Ate too much. I admire what you're doing, but I cannot consider any way in which the health service can give her special help. Try the hospital if you like, but I'd be amazed if their attitude was any different.'

Sally didn't try the hospital. She accepted the doctor's argument.

Each day, the forecast grew worse. Even Conrad was worried, as he went through every aspect of his plans every evening, checking the calculations of likely water flow down the river and the extent to which this could be relieved by diverting water down the canal. The weather was calm, the wind light, the sky pale with streaky high cloud. It was as if the elements were teasing them.

The high cloud was just thick enough to keep the nights dark. Nobody saw the lone figure who worked every night on his special project, his obsession. His energy was prodigious. The energy of madmen often is. And this man, now, was almost certainly mad. Normality had failed him. Normality had been contemptuous of him. When normality is contemptuous of a person, surely he has the right to lose his sanity? Every evening, towards dusk, this man prepared.

Every evening, towards dusk, in his position closer to the town centre, Conrad checked his plans yet again. And every evening, soon after dusk, the TV channels spoke of the intensification of the storm, the closeness of the isobars, the estimates of the level of that long word for rain, precipitation, which seems to be used as if the pain of the thing can be eased by being spread across so many letters.

Two days before the expected arrival of the storm, Sally was walking through the darkened town, down Cadwallader Road to the Canal Basin and the canal. She was in some of the most vulnerable parts of the town. People don't usually walk through towns thinking about their likely vulnerability in times of flood. Sally had lived in the town for more than a quarter of a century without realizing that the whole place had, with only minor variations, a tilt to the south and east. If the river overflowed, its waters would run down the High Street to the east and down the streets that led to the canal. The canal had been built at a slightly higher level than the surrounding town, in order to save on the number of locks that were needed when it rose to join the Rackstraw and Sladfield Canal at Pother Junction. It occurred to Sally now that the use of the canal to ease pressure on the river was intrinsically very risky. She telephoned Conrad, prefacing her concern with the words, 'I know this is a bit late, but . . .' He reassured her that he had taken all this into account and it was true that these factors limited the amount of water he could divert. The sluice eased the threat but did not eliminate it. It would all be down to judgement on the day. If the waters exceeded a certain force and volume, they were powerless. She did not feel reassured by this.

Everywhere there were sandbags, unbroken rows of sandbags outside every house and shop, layers of sandbags tightly packed along the banks of the river and canal, spare sandbags stored ready for emergencies. Some people said sandbags were virtually useless, their presence was largely cosmetic, psychological. Sally didn't know, but she was reassured to see them.

It was a town in waiting. Nobody was about, not a drinker, not a prostitute.

Then she heard footsteps, men's footsteps. Three tall young men became visible as they passed a dim street light, and Sally recognized them. They were Luke Warburton, Johnny Blackstock and Digger Llewellyn. Three of the Baggit Boys. There was no reason to suspect them of anything in particular at that moment, they just looked like three young men searching for a purpose in life and not finding it in the Canal Basin. But they had a reputation, and they were dressed in black, matching the night, and it's never reassuring for a woman to be faced with men who dress to match the night, and who have a reputation.

Sally didn't lack courage but it takes a special kind of courage to face up to men in black and still be able to think calmly, and afterwards, she wasn't at all certain that she *had* thought calmly. She had been more disturbed than she would admit by Conrad's frankness about the danger. She felt terrified for Ellie, for Ben's High Street, for the whole Transition project. In the dictionary there are two definitions of the word 'brainwave' – an electrical impulse of the brain, and a brilliant idea. Down there by the canal on a black cloudy night, Sally had an electrical impulse of the brain, but had she also had a brilliant idea?

She remembered seeing Luke recently in the Market Place, and she felt that she knew the right approach to him.

'Hello, Luke,' she said warmly, even enthusiastically.

Again, the surprise stopped him in his tracks.

'You what?' he said.

'This is serendipity,' she said.

'You what?' he said.

'I wonder if you and your lads could do something for me?'

In the dimness on the edge of the pool of dirty yellow light from the street lamp she couldn't see whether there was pride in his face at her assumption that he was the leader, but she suspected that there was.

'Me?' he said at last.

'You. All of you.'

She told them of Ellie's predicament.

'I want you to help me,' she said.

'Us?'

'You.'

'Fu— Oh, sorry, Mrs Mottram. What do you want us to do?'

'I wondered if you and your lads could go round to Ellie's house when the storm arrives and stand by to move her upstairs if it looks as if it'll be flooded.'

'Fu— Oh, sorry, Mrs Mottram, but . . . you mean you trust us?'

'Not altogether, Luke. If you came to do odd jobs for me I wouldn't leave a hundred pounds on the kitchen table. I'd lock up my lawnmower too. But I trust you absolutely and totally to do your best for a fellow human being in an emergency.'

'Fu— Oh, sorry, Mrs Mottram,' said Luke Warburton.

FORTY

The deluge

The day of the predicted flood dawned dry. The wind howled. The people who remembered the last flood all remembered it suspiciously well. Some who had lived through the last two floods remembered them equally well, even though almost all of them had been children at the time of the one seventy years ago. Arnie Blenkinsop, safe in the Paradise Old People's Home in Abattoir Rise, claimed to remember the last three floods, but if he had been five at the time of the third one back he would now be a hundred and ten, so his memories were not taken too seriously. But all these people were suddenly experts, and on the buses and in the cafés and the shops and the post office and the old people's homes and the benefit office they reassured the younger people. There was too much wind. It hadn't been windy in any of the great floods. Wind moved the clouds on, swept them to Holland. The weathermen were panicking as usual. The council had been recklessly prodigal with sandbags. 'One of the councillors has a contract with a sandbag producer, you mark my words.' And as for the *Chronicle* – sensationalists to a man. And woman.

The rain began just after a quarter past nine, and it was gentle, piddling little stuff. Old men went out in it without umbrellas, though that might have been at least in part because the wind would have turned their umbrellas inside out within seconds. But hadn't they told everyone that the threat had been exaggerated? Rain had been rain in the old days.

Down on the Quays, the owners of the three narrowboats stood and waited, boathooks at the ready. All three boats had been tied with extra ropes, all three were riding the gale well. But you don't take chances with boats. Terence and Felicity Porchester stood at the ready, Eric Sheepshank stood at the ready, Harry and Jill stood at the ready.

Harry and Jill? What were they doing there?

Harry's idea, late in the long night after he had failed to make love to Jill, had been to buy the third of the narrowboats, the ruined one, the sunken one. Restoration had been a big job. The boat had been raised, lifted out of the water, taken to a boatyard more than fifty miles away; its bodywork had been repaired, and it had been brought back and lowered carefully into its place near the bridge. Work had begun on the interior. Before the great day of the canal's reopening, Harry and Jill planned to be living in their new home, and there, freed from associations with Arnold and Olive, they would become lovers at last.

Very gradually, so gradually that nobody really noticed it, the rain grew heavier. Very gradually, so gradually that nobody really noticed it, the wind dropped lighter. The threat from the gale was so reduced that the five boat-owners, Harry and Jill, Terence and Felicity, and Eric, went for a lunchtime drink at the Potherthwaite Arms. They felt a bit special, drinking with the landlubbers. 'Look at them,' commented old Bomber Hartley, who really could remember in detail two of the great floods. 'Look at them poncing in their waterproofs. You'd think they'd just crossed the Atlantic in a rowing boat, not walked from their narrowboats that never leave the Quays.'

After their quick lunch, the five mariners walked out of the pub into much heavier rain, but even then, the rain was so steady, so uniform, so uneventful that it was difficult to take it too seriously, although Conrad knew that eight hours of this would begin to cause major problems.

All afternoon it rained. The clouds thickened. An eerie premature mauve dusk bathed the town. Dusk comes early in winter, earlier in the north than in the south, and it comes even earlier on cloudy, wet days. By four o'clock it was as dark as sin, and with the darkness came yet heavier rain, as if the storm had been biding its time, hoping people wouldn't notice, in the dark, that it had raised its game, hoping to catch them unawares, hoping to break through the river banks while they had their tea. But it overdid it. One sudden burst of rain was so strong people took up a last mouthful and rushed out while still chewing to see if the sandbags were holding. They were holding, but all was not well in Conrad's mind. The river was rising more swiftly than he would have expected, more swiftly than it should be according to his calculations. That meant that the rain was heavier on the inhospitable tops, running off the drenched moors into the feeder streams, crashing from the feeder streams into the swelling, excited river. Thirty-five years of indolence, of waiting, of gathering strength. This was its moment.

Now, in the buses and commuter trains and cafés and pubs, the optimists, who believed the threat had all been exaggerated, were well and truly routed. Now it was the turn of the pessimists, who had known all along that the threat had been underestimated, the council couldn't run a piss-up in a brewery, there was a criminal shortage of sandbags, Potherthwaite had learnt nothing from history and had been caught with its trousers down yet again.

Many of the people who were now accusing the council of complacency were the same ones who had earlier accused it of panicking. But let us not despair of human nature. Large numbers of people were not debating these matters, because they had no time to do so. They were ready, waiting, to act, to help, to save. Several of them stood with short-wave radios, ready to exchange the latest situations and make the swiftest and most accurate decisions.

If you have not stood around for hours, in the dark, on a wet night in a Pennine town, you will find it very hard to picture just how wet it was that night. Think of standing for five hours in the shower fully clothed with the cold water on maximum and you may just be beginning to get there.

All over the town, people, anxious to help, anxious to be seen to help, were placing unnecessary sandbags on top of sandbags. At danger points in the town and in the Pother Valley beyond the town there were drenched people trying to keep their short-wave radios dry. In the kitchen of number 6 Cadwallader Road, six young men from the Baggit Estate were playing poker while waiting to be called to rescue Ellie from the front room. On the rising river the bipolar mallard were in skittish mood. Down at the Quays, some twenty or so boys and young men came down with extra boathooks, ready for the moment when the placid canal suddenly became a river after the sluice gates had been opened. These young men were also from the Baggit Estate, and had been sent by Luke Warburton. Since Sally had shown her trust in him the estate had been transformed. Flood Protection had become the New Hooliganism.

The waters continued to rise, frighteningly so now. The river was almost brim full and running fast. Luke and his young men could barely concentrate on their poker, Conrad had his hand on the mechanism for opening the sluice. Marigold brought him a bottle filled with whisky and water, a flask full of hot tea, and a supply of cream buns. He had a weakness for cream buns.

And what of the man who had worked so feverishly, so obsessively, all on his own, night after dark night, on his secret project? Up at the supermarket the last customers had left, and Matt Winkle, abandoned by his wife, abandoned by Jade Hunningbrooke, abandoned by the world, locked all the doors. Ten minutes later, when the last of the cars had left the sodden car park, he opened the great doors at the back, where the delivery lorries came. It was time to implement his plan.

Back in the town, the water was hurling itself against the tops of the river banks, overlapping here and there against the walls of sandbags. Just in time Conrad opened half the great sluice gates. Water, released like sheep from a pen, poured down the sluice, rushed across the winding hole and formed quite a wave as it was funnelled into the narrow canal.

The wave came rushing down the canal, sailing over the still waters as if they were solid. It surged past the Canal Basin, sped on towards the boats like the Severn Bore. It crashed into them, sending their bows out towards the centre of the cut. The mooring ropes stretched and moaned but did not break. The boats, able to swing no further, hurtled back towards the quayside. Their owners and some of Luke's recruits from the Baggit Estate fended them off valiantly with their boathooks, preventing damaging collision with the merciless stone of the Quays. Now, after the first impact of that wall of water, the boats rode the unaccustomed tide more happily. Except for Harry and Jill's. Water began to slip into the cabin of their new home, slowly at first, then a little faster as the leak grew worse. Harry and Jill cried out, and people ran to their rescue. Terence and Felicity Porchester left their boat to chance and the elements, and hurried over with bowls. Teams of balers scooped up the water, passed the full bowls through the companion-hatch, but the gap in the planks was widening, and it was hard, hard work to keep up with the rising water.

They had barely started when Sally contacted them on the short-wave radio. She was coordinating matters from the middle of the bridge where the river was thundering under High Street West. She could just as easily have done it from home, but she was a commander who felt the need to be seen to be as wet as her troops. Her crackling message told of a crisis at the Canal Basin. The sandbags were barely holding.

Jill and Harry shouted to their helpers to abandon their boat and go to the Canal Basin. Terence and Felicity Porchester and Eric Sheepshank abandoned their boats too. A crowd of Baggit Boys followed them. All was chaos. There was a slight bend in the cut near the Canal Basin and the water was hitting the side at an angle and was not able to flow away fast enough, so the level was rising over the canal itself and hitting the sandbags piled above the canal bank, and threatening the stability of the sandbags.

Conrad opened the sluice gates still further, now that the waters had almost stabilized on the canal. As more and more of the diverted water began to pour along the canal, the level of the river began to fall back very slightly.

Ben rushed to the Canal Basin. What a crowd there was. Harry and Jill, Terence and Felicity, Eric, the vicar, Linda Oughtibridge, several large Baggit Boys, and little slight Lucy. Love surged through him like an echo of the wave that had swept down the canal.

People were pressing their weight against the sandbags, some of which were threatening to slide out of their flimsy, soaking wall. Other people were fetching more sandbags. People were getting in each other's way, and there was panic and confusion everywhere, despite busy, bald Harry's frantic commands.

Sally's radio burst into crackling life again. There was also a crisis on the river, right under where Sally was standing on the High Street West bridge. Ben grabbed hold of Lucy and took her off in that direction. Harry began to divide people between the two crises, shouting the names as if on the parade ground at Catterick Camp. And still the torrential, relentless rain continued. Everyone was soaked. Everything was soaked.

His urgency, his joy, his insanity, gave huge strength to Matt Winkle. The force of the river here was huge, this really was a torrent. He couldn't see the banks. He walked the length of the short canal that he had dug, and as he approached the river he was in at least a foot of water. He had placed a wooden barrier across the end of his canal, and it had held. He had made it too well, too strong, and now he had to remove it. He was bending down, standing in more than a foot of water, pulling with all his might. The barrier came up suddenly and he fell backwards, still holding on, and crashed down on to it. The barrier was now a raft. The water at the side of his little canal took his raft, with him on it, into the ditch that he had dug, which was filling with water pouring in from the river. He was white-water rafting on the raft he had built in the canal he had dug, the Matt Winkle Overflow Canal linking the River Pother and the supermarket in a miracle of modern science. He was ecstatic.

His ride was short and exciting. The raft tossed and turned like an angry bronco. At the end of his short canal, it hit the edge of the lorry park. Matt jumped. Little helpless Matt. Callow, sallow Matt. Supermarket man but not Superman.

Suddenly he *was* Superman. He jumped over the edge of the concreted lorry park, landed inelegantly on the concrete, but he just managed to stay on his feet. He had built two rudimentary walls of sandbags leading across the lorry park from the end of his canal to the big delivery doors at the back of the supermarket. He ran along them, waving insanely to non-existent crowds cheering the finish of his biathlon. He ran into the supermarket with the first of the water. Now he could have hurried through, opened one of the front doors, and slipped away. But he didn't. He couldn't. He was mesmerized. He was ecstatic. He was orgasmic. He was mighty. He was God.

Back in the town, Sally radioed through and put Luke and his boys on Red Alert. 'Red Alert,' she said. 'Standby Positions.' 'Red Alert Operating. Men at Standby Positions,' radioed Luke excitedly, breathlessly. Sally couldn't see the scene in number 6, but she could imagine it – six strong Baggit Boys standing proudly, three at each side of the bed, their hands out ready to dive under Ellie's back at the call to action, Ellie smiling bravely if a little fearfully, Ali and Oli on tenterhooks.

Despite the sterling efforts of the helpers at the Canal Basin, the sandbag wall was leaking. But it hadn't yet collapsed. Leaks didn't matter. Collapse did. And, at the newer crisis point, underneath the High Street bridge, the collapse of the river bank was distinctly possible. A small portion was on the point of breaking away. It was being shored up with sandbags, but not fast enough. The water was only trickling as yet, but the trickle was getting wider. Access was difficult. The bridge was held up on iron columns drilled into brick foundations. Behind these columns, deep in darkness, the water was banging against earth and sandbags. The sandbags weren't holding. People were fetching more, but they couldn't squeeze through under the bridge and have room to stand and place the sandbags in the correct positions. Lucy, slim and agile as an eel, with the balance of a trapeze artiste, was just what was needed.

The bags were sodden and heavy. Ben could hardly carry them, but only he was slim enough to get through and throw the bags as gently as he could to Lucy. Their work rate was prodigious. They were winning the fight. After all, this was a girl who at the age of seven had balanced on a rubber ball and caught live fish in her mouth. The gap was narrowing fast. But then, when the job was almost done, Lucy reached out one more time, and slipped. She was in the water, tossed against one of the iron columns, she was away, downstream, carried on the roaring torrent, far beyond the bridge, with the remorseless waters pushing her towards the hard containing wall of the churchyard and its graves.

Ben's heart-rending cry of 'Lucy!' was swept away by the screaming wind, and then he hurled himself headlong into the angry water. He'd been swept to the middle of the swirling river before he even remembered that he could barely swim two struggling lengths of the municipal baths. He could see Lucy far ahead, still managing in her magnificent athleticism to swim in the choppy waters. And then he began to sink.

But a third person had seen Ben's jump, and now this person – a man, surely, from the bulk of his body – also flung himself into the torrent. Watchers on the bank could see that this man, whom they couldn't recognize in the dark, was a strong swimmer, and before they could even think what to do he had been taken far down the river, and was swimming frenziedly, forcing himself away from the wall of the cemetery, which would crush him to death if he gave it the chance.

'No point in following,' shouted Harry. 'Nothing we can do. Save the town. Get those sandbags. Plug the gap.'

Lucy, swimming for her life, heard none of this over the

wailing of the wind. Ben was barely conscious.

The third swimmer couldn't see Ben in the night's darkness. There was no chance. No chance at all.

Behind him, unbeknown to him, young men and women from the Baggit Estate continued their heroic battle against the waters.

Far upstream, unaware of any of this, Matt Winkle was a happy man. He had climbed a stepladder and was surveying the huge customer area from the top of it, laughing maniacally as the waters rose. The amount of water was amazing – he hadn't been aware till now how huge his temple of Mammon was. He was five foot eleven and couldn't swim. God, he was enjoying this. The water rose remorselessly over bags of unripe, tasteless, artificially ripened fruit. Pears that would go bad before they ripened, nectarines with the texture of mush, stony-hearted avocados, peaches that had never even smelt the sun – water pouring over them, and the blatantly dishonest notices carried away on the flood, *'Ripe and ready to eat'*, *'Juicy and full of summer promise'*, *'Crisp and orchard-fresh'*. How he roared as they were carried away by the waters. Up yours, Mrs Walton, with your endless complaints. Up yours, Miss Mountford, with your delusions of style. He judged that there were at least eight feet of water everywhere. How he laughed. He was happier than he had been since he'd ceased to be an ambitious, hopeful youth. What a way to die, watching the destruction of his hated supermarket.

Sally too had no knowledge of the drama on the river, even though it was happening so close to her. She was concentrating on Operation Ellie. 'Red Alert Activated. Operation Ellie, Action,' she called out urgently on her radio. 'Red Alert Activated. Operation Ellie Activated,' cried Luke Warburton ecstatically.

Luke and his five helpers slowly raised Ellie's mighty body, ready for the journey upstairs. Slowly, with infinite care, they approached the door out of the front room with their mighty cargo. Three of the young men went slowly backwards through the door into the corridor that led to the stairs. They walked backwards over towards the far wall of the corridor, beginning to turn Ellie's front half slowly towards the left. In the room they were pushing her great nether regions to the right, hoping against hope that they would be able to get her through – she wasn't a bendy bus. Luckily, although fat, she wasn't tall. They just made it. They were breathing hard. They looked at the stairs, and the sharp corner on the stairs, and wondered how they could ever get her up the stairs.

The unidentified swimmer could see only the foaming, tossing water of the River Pother. He felt in his heart that Ben must have drowned. But there were lights on the quay in front of the great lines of the old mills, and suddenly where a ray from one of the lights struck the water he saw a body hurled into the air like a dead dolphin. But the body was not dead – it was flailing its arms, though to no avail, and it was sucked under the surface again. Frantically the would-be rescuer swam on, though his arms were seizing up. He dived towards the spot where Ben – it had to be Ben – had disappeared, though by this time he wasn't certain if it was the right spot. But then he felt him. He opened his arms and grabbed at Ben's body. The water tried to tear Ben away, but he hung on. He was in pain. His heart was bursting. He was having a heart attack. He was dying. But he pushed on, pushed Ben upwards, upwards, upwards, their faces were suddenly above the water, Ben was still alive, they weren't far from the quay, on the edge of the quay men were waiting to help, urging them on, he pushed on through swords of pain, he was there, the men were bending down and reaching out to pull them ashore, someone cried, 'We've got him,' and he let go of Ben. He was falling now, falling back, too weak to push himself any more, hands were grabbing him, pulling him upwards, but at the same time he was falling, falling into his grave. The darkness crept over him, covered him, now he was unconscious, now he was dead.

Several strong men lifted him over the cobbles and then lowered him gently to the ground. The gentleness seemed unnecessary. He wasn't breathing.

Lucy, who had swum entirely single-mindedly, with no knowledge of the mayhem behind her, looked aghast at the choking, coughing Ben, and the lifeless body of the Revd Dominic Otley. Paramedics hurried towards the inert vicar, but a very square woman hurried faster than any of them, charging past the shattered Lucy, the vomiting Ben, the calm, measured paramedics.

'Let me through,' cried Linda Oughtibridge. 'Let me through. I'm going to give him mouth-to-mouth resuscitation.'

The vicar suddenly coughed violently, and a great stream of river water and a small shoal of tiny perch emerged from his mouth.

'That won't be necessary,' said one of the paramedics.

'I don't care. I'm going to give it anyway,' cried Linda Oughtibridge.

Luke Warburton and his gang never did lift Ellie up the stairs, and Matt Winkle didn't die. To his huge disappointment, the water level stopped rising. The river stopped rising too, and so did the canal. Conrad was the first to realize why. No more heavy rain was falling on the sodden moors. It had started earlier in the hills, and it had stopped earlier in the hills. It didn't matter that it was still raining in Potherthwaite, that was no danger. It had stopped where the streams fed the river.

The front three of the six Baggit Boys were just stepping

backwards on to the alarmingly narrow stairs when their radio crackled and there was Sally's voice.

'Sally to Luke. End of Red Alert. Beginning of Yellow Alert. Abort mission. Remain at action stations. Over,' she said.

'Luke to Sally. Thank the fuck for that. Over,' said Luke Warburton.

The Baggit Boys slowly manoeuvred Ellie back into the front room and into bed. Now, the rain was slackening off in the town as well, in fact it had almost stopped. Conrad announced that the weathermen had told him that there would be no more rain.

Nobody left their posts for another hour. Conrad thanked everyone over the short-wave radio, and explained that since they were so close to the source of the river, the water level would start to drop quite soon, and quite rapidly.

The emergency was over. Miraculously, although water did escape, it was not in amounts that threatened more than minor damage. Miraculously, Lucy, Ben and the vicar suffered no more than bruising. Miraculously, the town had survived with only three casualties. Linda Oughtibridge lost an earring, Digger Llewellyn broke one of Ali's very best teacups, and Harry and Jill's narrowboat, sacrificed for the greater need, sank back into the silt at the bottom of the Potherthwaite Arm of the Rackstraw and Sladfield Canal.

FORTY-ONE
After the deluge

By the time they got into the pubs it was past closing time, but none of them had dared to close that night, and any policeman who had arrested anybody for drunkenness would never have felt it safe to set foot in the town again. There were, of course – there always are – a few catastrophiles who felt cheated of disaster. People who see everything in sexual terms find it difficult to cope with anything that doesn't end in a climax. But these people kept a very low profile in Potherthwaite that long, noisy night.

Sally's celebrations began at the stuffy old George Hotel, in the Market Place. She knew that she must start there, or she would never get there, and it wouldn't do to offend the town's premier hotel. She had been an intermittent regular there in her first life. Barry, a lawyer to his fingertips, would never have gone into any of the other pubs.

In the George many people shook her hand, including Barry's partner, Tom Caldwell, and Councillor Stratton, who pumped her hand, kissed her, and said, 'I always knew you had it in you.'

Tricksy's father Alan bought her a drink, said it was sad

that Tricksy and Ben were no longer friends, 'but that's youngsters for you'.

'That's youngsters for you,' agreed Sally, without really having any idea what she was agreeing with.

Alan told her that Tricksy had left university to go round the world with a potter from Finland on the back of the potter's motorbike.

She managed to edge towards the door, and quietly slipped out into the square. The hum of conversation from councillors, lawyers and estate agents faded. The wind had dropped, and a moon that looked as if it had been painted by Atkinson Grimshaw was casting eerie reflections in the puddles. Half of Sally longed for sleep. The other half would talk and drink all night in its relief.

Her next stop was the Baggit Arms, up the hill, beyond Baggit Park, quite a step, but she had to go there. The Baggit Boys, now that they were on her side, must be kept on her side.

The Baggit Arms was packed with noisy revellers. She entered to a most boisterous welcome. Luke Warburton offered her a drink, and she opted for a pint of bitter. This was a PR exercise, and she might as well go the whole hog.

She didn't mention her plan to paint the boring stucco of the estate's houses with fascinating, fabulous paintings. She would keep this suggestion on hold until the dullest, greyest days of February, when the spirit of the flood would need a boost. The leaders in the very separate community of the estate had been deeply touched by the trust invested in them, by the sense of responsibility that their tasks had brought out. For this generation in this sort of estate, the choice was between extremely dreary safe jobs, unemployment, or a really quite high risk of death in wars for causes that they would find it very difficult to take up with enthusiasm. It was a desperate choice. But here at least they could take their share of responsibility in the successful Transition of the town. What a glorious thing is responsibility. Anyone who has seen children taking part in youth theatre will have noticed it. However small their role, they are responsible to the whole team. They grow under it, they thrive under it. And afterwards, when there is nothing to follow it, they lose it. Potherthwaite must not lose the Baggit Estate. Sally's visit to the Baggit Arms was no sinecure, but a moment of real hope for the town, and for her. She drained the last of her pint to loud acclaim. It was so easy to win popularity that she felt a little ashamed.

She wished Luke goodnight and he said an astonishing thing. He said, 'Thank you, Sally. You've given me summat great, you. You've given me a second life, you have.' Then he kissed her, with touching awkwardness. She reflected, as she added him to the list of men who had kissed her, that in her first life she had hardly been kissed at all. Oh, Sally, Sally, she told herself, for quarter of a century of adult life you weren't kissable. She shuddered.

It felt like the middle of the night when she entered the Weavers' Arms. Well, she had to call in there, it was where it had all started. The Weavers' was quieter. In its heart it wasn't a pub at all. It was a restaurant. Sue was doing her best, but Rog looked out of place behind the bar.

She caught sight of Marigold and Conrad, deep in conversation in an alcove at the back. Instinct told her that this was a very bad moment to interrupt. Instinct was right.

Conrad had made a triumphant entry into the town centre, congratulated by everyone as they buzzed from one pub to another. The pub was extremely proud of being the place where the Transition movement in Potherthwaite really began, and it seemed the natural place in which to pop the question.

Yes, Conrad was going to pop the question, the question

400

for which Marigold longed. He was skilled socially, it was easy work for him to accept congratulations, slip out of conversations without causing offence, and find himself in the furthest, quietest, darkest corner of the pub. Something about the determined, single-minded way he did it led Marigold to expect the suggestion at last.

'I've grown to feel happier and happier with you, Marigold,' he began, just as Sally entered the pub. She had been so right in her belief that it would be a bad moment to interrupt, and we may reflect, now that we have paused, that because Conrad is such a private man we cannot know whether he had experienced doubts himself about marrying again, and about marrying a woman with such a bad track record in the marital department. He was one of those men who never quite let you know them. Nevertheless, when he said, in his straightforward flood controller's English, 'Marigold, will you marry me?' it struck her with sudden panic that all she really knew about him was that he had a big willy and a passion for cream buns. Where was the joy that she had rehearsed? She felt her genitals tightening. She hardly had enough air to breathe, let alone reply. Her mouth was dry, so dry that she had to sip her drink, although she felt it to be a very ill-timed gesture. She forced herself to look into his eyes, hoping for reassurance. What she found was hope, fear, vulnerability she had never imagined. She closed her eyes. Her body sank, and the world rotated, as it did when she'd had too much to drink. She must speak. She remembered what Sally had said. Sally had said that you couldn't live your life fearing and mistrusting half the human race. Sally thought she would be safe with him. She adored Sally. Sally would be so thrilled to hear her happy news, so she just had to have happy news to tell her. 'Yes, please,' she said at last. 'Oh, Conrad, yes.'

Sally watched them while accepting yet another free drink,

401

this time, as so often, from Sue. At last she decided that it was time to make her way to them.

'Oh, darling,' said Marigold. 'Oh, darling, darling Sally, Conrad and I are engaged.'

Sally didn't attempt to pretend to be surprised. 'I'm so pleased for you both,' she said. If you put in a line all the people who have said, 'I'm so pleased for you both,' while meaning, 'That's my chance gone for a Burton, then,' you'd have something not far smaller than the Great Wall of China, but in that pub, in that moment, Sally discovered that at last she really did mean it with all her heart. She hugged Marigold, and hugged her again, and hugged her a third time for luck, and said, 'I'm so happy I could cry.' Conrad just smiled, smiled and smiled and smiled. And then yawned. 'Sorry,' he said. 'I'm pooped. I'm whacked.'

Marigold added a third fact to her knowledge of Conrad. He had a big willy, a passion for cream buns and he would never use a word like 'knackered'.

Sally left them to it, and moved back out into the square. She felt a sudden surge of happiness. In overcoming her jealousy of Marigold she had won a victory, she had won her freedom; she had an overwhelming feeling that one day, perhaps even this evening, she would meet a man she could love, and who could love her.

She contemplated going home to bed, but then she thought that she would drop in at the Potherthwaite Arms, if it was still open. Well, she had to really. She had almost become a regular there. She owed them a visit. She wasn't the sort of woman who avoided a pub because it had a reputation for being slightly insalubrious.

There was a sense of unconsummated joy about the pub that night. Its motor was missing. People had been doing their best to live up to the joy they should be feeling, but it wasn't quite the same without Marigold, without her legs curved voluptuously round her bar stool, and there were only a few customers left.

But then who should follow her in but the Revd Dominic Otley and Linda Oughtibridge? Linda was smiling as she had never smiled before, a smile full of joy, a smile utterly free from hidden meanings. He looked bashful. A small cheer broke out from the remaining drinkers. The vicar looked like an embarrassed boy who couldn't admit that he was ecstatic.

'The doctor wanted to keep me in hospital,' he said. 'For observation. I wasn't having that. "Young man," I said. "I have waited all my life to become a hero. I'm not going to miss a minute of it. I want the whole town to observe me, not just you."'

There was another cheer. The landlord bought him a pint of bitter and a large whisky.

'I didn't know you were such a good swimmer, Dominic,' said Sally.

'Olympic triallist,' said Dominic shyly.

'Why do you never talk about it?'

'It was a long time ago, and it's got nothing to do with anything.'

Oh, Dominic Dominic, thought Sally. It may have nothing to do with anything, but people would have looked at you with more respect for every day of the rest of your life, if they'd known.

Sally proposed a toast to Dominic, raised her glass to him, and set off towards the door. At that very moment, in came Harry and Jill, on their way back from a final inspection of the boat that had so nearly become their love nest.

'I'm so sorry about—' began Sally.

'No apologies, please,' said Harry. 'The lovely Jill, your dear friend, has eased the pain of the evening by agreeing to become my wife.'

'Oh, I'm so thrilled,' said Sally, and she kissed them both. 'Will you . . . um . . .?'

'Probably,' said Jill.

'Definitely,' said Harry.

'Definitely probably,' said Jill.

Sally, realizing how drunk they were, abandoned any further questions.

'Onwards and . . .' began Jill. She threw her arms up in the air with such a lurch of enthusiasm that she knocked herself off her feet and fell to the floor.

'Onwards and downwards,' said Harry.

Sally finished her drink, and set off, as she thought, for bed. But instead of turning right, she found that she had turned left. She didn't want to go to bed. She didn't want this night to end. Ever.

Besides, if she went to all the pubs that she had frequented, except the Dog and Duck, that would be rather insensitive.

At the last moment she almost didn't go in. She knew that she'd already had too much to drink.

But she had not yet seen Ben or Lucy, and she did so want to share a corner of this blessed night with them. And also, even more importantly, she still had a feeling that, on this happy and exciting night, she might meet the man of her dreams. It was an absurd thought, fanciful, romantic, deeply sentimental, but if she went straight home to bed she would never know if she had missed the greatest chance of her life.

He was sitting on his own, as if he had deliberately moved away from the few remaining revellers. He was staring moodily into his glass of beer, and the expression on his face suggested that he was regarding it as half-empty, rather than half-full.

His face lit up at the sight of Sally.

'Sally!' he said. 'What'll you have? What's it to be?'

Could she really face more white wine? But a switch to spirits would be fatal.

'A small white wine, please, Eric,' she said.

Eric bought the wine, she joined him at his table, and they clinked glasses.

'A penny for them,' he said.

'What?'

'Your thoughts. Your expression is enigmatic. You look like the *Mona Lisa*, though much larger, of course.'

She knew what he meant, but it hadn't come out sounding tactful. Very little of what Eric Sheepshank said came out sounding tactful. She was almost tempted to tell him what she *had* been thinking, which was that it seemed typical of her life that she should have an irrational feeling that she was going to meet the man of her dreams, and then she should meet a man with no foreskin, which didn't matter, but also with no warmth and no charm, which did.

'Oh, nothing much,' she said lamely, leaving him feeling very suspicious.

'On your own?' asked Eric Sheepshank, talented sculptor and stater of the obvious.

'Yes. On my own.'

'What's wrong with people?'

'What?'

'Lovely woman like you. On your own. What's wrong with people? Got to do something about that.'

'What do you suggest we do about it?'

'I suggest that I take you back to my boat, which entirely due to you is actually pleasant enough to invite a woman like you, a lovely woman like you, on to – because women, you know, they deserve, they need, particularly lovely women, and particularly particularly lovely women, and you are particularly lovely . . . lost my thread a bit.'

'On to the boat.'

'Ah yes. Absolutely. For a nightcap.'

'I couldn't drink any more.'

'No, no. Never drink. No drink on board. Gave it up. At the suggestion of a very lovely woman, who has helped save my life, which is why, seeing her on her own, which is disgraceful, I wish to see her not on her own, on this very night, having a little nightcap, which I don't have, because of her, which is bad luck really. Shame.'

'Yes, it is a shame, Eric.'

'I drink here. It's what it's for. Because it's a pub, and that's what they're for. But I don't have any at home. That's what did the damage, you see. Too easy. Drink now, only in the pub. Had one or two tonight. In the pub. Here, in fact. Thought I might see Ben. No Ben. Growing up, you see. Growing up fast. Nudge nudge. Would it be all right, do you think, to buy you a nightcap, here, and take it back to the boat, because, you see, on your own, lovely woman like you, I don't like to see it.'

'It's a lovely thought,' said Sally, 'but I'm tired, I'm going home.'

She wanted to kiss him, because it suddenly seemed to her that he was the only other person in Potherthwaite on that great night who was alone. He had once kissed her when she praised his sculptures, but for her to instigate a kiss was beyond possibility. That beard. It looked as if the bits were from the same egg as last time she'd seen it. It didn't seem likely that he would spill egg on his beard, clear it up, and then spill an identical amount of egg on the same bit of his beard. The odds were against it.

She stood up abruptly, called out, 'Goodnight, everyone,' to the almost empty pub, and set off for the Quays, and her first-floor flat. The rain had stopped, the clouds had gone, the stars were shining, and as the cold air hit her she began to feel very drunk. By the time she got to the bottom of High Street East she had to stop and rest herself against a shop window to prevent herself fainting. She longed for a man's arm to support her.

The shop was one of Ben's. It was beautiful. She set off again. Ben's shops looked lovely. The whole street would look lovely. She had achieved amazing things. She wished she wasn't alone, but it didn't matter. Well, it would be nice not to be alone.

She negotiated Quays Approach very carefully. The moon was shining on the canal. The waters were still again. She had a shock as she saw Harry and Jill's re-sunken boat. She wanted to cry, and now it mattered very much that she had no shoulder to cry on.

How quiet it all seemed after the storm. The Porchesters' boat looked so sweet in the moonlight, so warm and welcoming. A mellow light shone in the cabin. She tried to walk the last yards to her flat quietly.

'On your own? Won't do. Come in and have a noggin,' called out Terence Porchester cheerfully.

Sally had two more drinks – 'Cointreau isn't really a drink, Sally, not a serious drink, eh, Felicity?' before, at twenty-five past four, she finally stumbled to her front door, supported on her left by the great bulk of Terence Porchester, and on her right by the tiny form of Felicity Porchester.

She went into her bedroom very carefully, and soon she was in bed and fast asleep.

Potherthwaite slept. Jill Buss could hear Harry's snores from the neighbouring house and hoped he wouldn't drink the way he had tonight when, if ever, they were in bed together in their narrowboat. Conrad and Marigold slept together in deep contentment. Matt Winkle fell fast asleep, most precariously, on his stomach, on the tiny top step of his ladder, his hands dangling in front of him and his feet behind, just inches from the top of his very own great lake. The early shift found him there. He no longer looked like a god. Gods don't cry.

And Ben and Lucy? Ben felt humiliated by the fiasco of his rescue attempt, which had led to the need for him to be rescued. Lucy was thrilled by his demonstration of love and courage, and pointed out that, if he hadn't failed, the Revd Dominic Otley would have been denied his act of heroism. Lucy led him to a most perfect spot for their lovemaking, there in his cosy studio, beside his lovely miniature scale model of the High Street. And there, with their feet outside the Potherthwaite Deli, and their faces beside the Kosy Korner Kafé, they celebrated most energetically the fact that neither of them had drowned.

BOOK SIX

The Last Day

Of course it wasn't actually the last day. There didn't need ever to be a last day, that was the joy of it.

FORTY-TWO

Morning

What a lot of wasted daylight there is on summer mornings. The political parties could agree in five minutes to give us an extra hour's daylight on summer evenings, perhaps even two extra hours. But no party would benefit, only the nation, so it is of no interest to them.

It was barely five o'clock when Sally awoke from a restless sleep, but already the sun was making its appearance in the lower valley.

It was the first day of the first ever Potherthwaite Festival. More than half a year had passed since the battle against the deluge, and it had passed too quickly. The last few days had been manic, and Sally was certain that something major had been forgotten. She was on the point of leaping anxiously out of bed, but she restrained herself, controlled her anxiety with reflections on what a great day this was, and how she owed it to herself to enjoy it, and levered herself gently and calmly out of the left-hand side of the bed. Intelligent, rational woman though she was, she felt that she might ruin the whole day if she got out on the right-hand side.

She drew the curtains on a stunning scene. There wasn't a cloud in the sky. There was barely a breath of wind. There

411

were just the faintest ripples on the water. There were now almost twenty narrowboats moored along the quay. There was barely a space left between the bridge and the winding hole, and it was only a week since the canal had been officially reopened.

The morning didn't fool her. It was one of those great British mornings, when you laid the table for breakfast in the garden, only to find the first cloud, fluffy and innocent, forming itself as you brought out the cushions for the chairs. A larger cloud, with a hint of darkness at its centre, drifted slowly over as you laid out the marmalade and honey. A spiteful little wind waited for you. A larger cloud, distinctly threatening, drifted over as you hovered uncertainly in the doorway with the bacon and eggs. This was the wind's cue. 'Piss off, you pampered people,' whispered the wind. You took the whole lot indoors, and dreamt of Corfu as you ate it.

Sally felt sad that only she was witnessing this stunning scene. There was no sign of life from Terence and Felicity Porchester on this their last day in Potherthwaite. There was no sign of life from Eric Sheepshank on the day his sculptures in the Sculpture Trail would be admired by local and visitor alike. Someone that day would no doubt call him the Henry Moore of Potherthwaite. (Someone did. It was Eric himself.) And there was no sign of life from Harry and Jill. They had sued the boatyard for the inadequate work that had caused the boat to sink on the night of the flood, they had been helped by many people, notably the Porchesters, and they had repaired the boat and were living in her, watched over, they chose to feel, by Olive and Arnold with a generosity that they had never quite been able to manage in life itself.

Sally showered, dressed, made herself look as lovely as befitted the Queen of the Day, and walked out into the pure air of morning. This air came from the Pennines. It had to be breathed with care. Too much of it would overload the lungs.

She walked slowly past Eric's boat, slowly past Harry and Jill's boat where, she guessed from the smiles on their faces in recent days, they would be in deep post-coital slumber. She didn't begrudge them this. In any case, for the moment she wanted to be alone. For the moment, as Queen of the Day, she was pleased to wander among her subjects unencumbered.

She walked slowly on to the little hump-backed bridge. Here, this evening, the lovely Arabella Kate Hendrie, the Pride of Potherthwaite, the Yorkshire Callas, would sing.

Sally stood with her back to the sun, and drank in the scene. To her right, along the wide quay, there were tables and chairs outside the restored Terminus Bistro, outside the reopened Canal Bookshop with the added words 'and Café', outside the new, gently trendy Navigation Inn and outside the reincarnation of the Quays Café as the Sir Norman Oldfield Tea Room, renamed in tribute to the town's benefactor, against his wishes, but, to his joy, not remotely trendy.

Sir Norman had told her that he would try to find the courage to come to the town that afternoon, but he was promising nothing. 'If I do come, I will be accompanied by your old friend, Lennie Tiptree.' There is, Sally had thought on hearing that news, no such thing as a complete utopia.

On the left, on the towpath side, temporary seating had been erected. Everything was ready, waiting. And still the sun shone, wasting itself on all this emptiness. It was a huge thrill to Sally that she had this great scene to herself, but at the same time it gave her a sharp sense of frustration.

She walked along Canal Approach, past the turning on to Vatican Road, where as always she looked at the mean block of flats where she had lived, and gave a little private thank-you to Sir Norman.

And there, spread before her, was High Street East, with its new shopfronts, its fresh paint, its gleaming readiness for custom. Some of the buildings were still the product of sixties budget architecture, but Ben's masterly design helped to obscure this and drew them all into a communal elegance, a retail event, a shoppers' paradise. There were days when the pedestrian strollers in High Street East and High Street West gave the town the feel of a small Italian town. There were three new restaurants here too, one Italian, one Indian, one vegetarian, none of them part of chains. And only two of the shops were still empty. Everyone wanted to be part of Ben's High Street.

Poor Ben. He was most upset, deeply upset. His beloved Lucy would not be with him on his great day, when his graceful sculptures, quite large but light as froth, would be a sensation on the Sculpture Trail, where they would outclass Eric's efforts, making them look cumbersome and clumsy, in many people's eyes, though Sally would defend the contrast as being the most essential element in the success of the trail.

What a problem Lucy had faced. Her father, Lionel Basridge, had written to her after five years of total silence and neglect.

My darling Lucy,

How can I write those words when I've completely nelgected you for five years? How could I not even have sent you cards at Christmas? I was so angry sweetheart for your mum going and taking you and with you for going but I realize now you were too young to blame. You've inherited so much of me – my athelticism, my courage, even my dylsexia. Your teacher wrote me that you are a wonderful girl and produced a play wich was very good and I felt so proud of you and I cried and cried and was so sorry I was so uncaring. You have a good life and are acamedic and are well out of the circus wich is not for the modern life. But I am having a big party for my fitfieth birthday with all the circus and I would like you to come and be my Guest of Honour, my darling.

The date of the party – Sod's Law in all its glory – was today. Lucy had set off to catch the 6.22 from Potherthwaite. Ben had found it extremely hard to accept that a man who hadn't even sent Lucy Christmas cards should take precedence over the day when at least two prominent art agents were expected to be in the town to see his sculpture and his High Street. She had said that they would have a whole life together, the High Street was permanent, he would see the art experts unencumbered, and her father would never have another fiftieth birthday and it was an honour to be invited to be guest of honour and if she missed the chance she might spend the rest of her life without a father. Also, it might hurt her mother and make her mother care about her a bit more. Ben understood with his old head, but failed to understand with his young heart. She had promised to keep in contact with text messages.

Sally walked into the still-deserted Market Place, the southern third of which was now pedestrianized to link up with High Street East and High Street West. Use of cars in the town had declined by 47 per cent in one year. A service of free small buses had been introduced a month ago to take people from the outlying districts into the Market Place, and a further reduction in car use was expected.

Over there on the north side, in the charmless rooms of the George Hotel, her sister Judith would be sleeping as soundly as the hotel's elderly water pipes and bad sound insulation permitted. She had thanked Sally for her offer of accommodation, but had said that she couldn't cope with staying with people any more.

Sam and Beth, who was pregnant again, had also opted not to stay with Sally. They'd combined the visit with a little holiday, and had rented a simple cottage on the moors, silent except for the cries of the lapwing and the grouse. When this great day was over, she would have time to work on their relationship. She had been shocked to hear of Lucy's mother's lack of love. Was she so very much better?

She turned right and walked past the side wall of the George. The gentle slope led to the upper part of the town, the railway station, Baggit Park, and the Baggit Estate. The gates to the park were locked overnight, and it was not yet quite six o'clock in the morning, but she could see four of the sculptures on the Trail, including a massive one by Eric and a slender, twisting, sadly elegant entwined couple by Ben. It looked so light that the wind might knock it down, but it had taken two strong men to carry it.

She wandered round the once dreary streets of the estate. Now the walls were covered with paintings, bright, sometimes gaudy. The idea for a whole housing estate with house-to-house murals had come from articles that she had read about the Dutch architects Jeroen Koolhaas and Dre Urhahn, who had turned estates in the poorest parts of ghettos in Rio de Janeiro, North Philadelphia and other places into amazing works of art. Sally had taken a different line, which had grown out of her direct experiences in Potherthwaite. She hadn't wanted to create a lovely little upmarket centre in a surrounding desert. She had realized that to impose any artist's dream upon the estate would be to at best divide opinion and at worst foster resentment and destruction. The residents must create their own dreams. They would just have to live with the consequences. She had only imposed one condition. Nothing must be painted

416

for a month, giving them the chance to debate what they wanted, rule out what they didn't want, make their own rules. They made three rules. No depiction of sex with children or violence with children. And no bad weather. There were enough of those three things in the outside world. Sally had cried with pride when they told her these rules.

And now, the real sun shone on a thousand painted suns. There was a lot of bare flesh, mostly attractive flesh. A more attractive race of people lived on the walls of Mural Land than in the houses behind them. Some people, including a particularly sensitive post girl, took exception to a huge penis on the southern wall of number 53 Prospect Close, but Sally pointed out that among the great chalk figures crafted in ancient times on the hills of England and preserved as great art there was the Long Man of Somewhere or Other, immortalized in our culture due solely to his vast chalk plonker. Millie Rathbone, a delicate old lady who lived opposite, did complain about it, but on being told that she didn't need to look at it, had said, 'What? I look at it at least three times every day,' so her complaint wasn't taken too seriously.

There were snakes, dragons, tigers, exotic birds, vast feasts, succulent breasts, sandy beaches, impressive viaducts, noble towers, fast cars, muscled footballers, well-known pop stars, beautiful yachts, scenes from a better, greater, idealized Potherthwaite, and all under blue skies and a shining sun.

By the time Sally had feasted on all these wonders the park was open, and she walked through it, past the bandstand, the small lake, the cages of exotic birds, and, gloriously, ten new sculptures, three by Ben, three by Eric, the others by artists from other Pennine towns.

She felt tired, and slightly weak. She'd had no breakfast. So she sat in the sun, by the lake, watching the birds, trying to spot the sixteen varieties of duck which were listed on a board at the lakeside. A few joggers were about now, and

417

some dog walkers, and a man who rode to work on a unicycle.

Sally moved on, down to the roundabout where the pedestrianized High Street met the old through road, with Oxford Road branching off to the right. Here she saw a sight that astonished her. A large furniture van was coming slowly down Oxford Road towards the roundabout. Her mouth opened in surprise. It was uncanny. It was the same van that she had seen bringing Harry and Olive's furniture, on the day that Barry had killed himself, on the day her first life had died. '*Barnard's Removals. Serving Chichester and the World*'. Its appearance led Sally into a host of brief, vivid memories, of Olive and her worries, of Arnold with his unfinished book, of Ben as an awkward young boy on the waste ground, of Johnny Blackstock destroying Ben's column of stones.

The van manoeuvred slowly round the roundabout, and Sally saw that in its wake was a car that she recognized but couldn't place. The driver wound the window down and called out, 'See what you've done to me.'

It was Dr Mallet, the psychiatrist.

'I beg your pardon?' said Sally.

'Everyone's happy. I can't make a living here any more. I'm having to go south, where they're bored and rich and guilty.'

There was a low moan from the back of the car.

'It's all right, Diana,' said Dr Mallet soothingly. 'Everything's all right.' He turned back to Sally. 'Car sick already, and we're still in Potherthwaite. Well, I'll be on my way. Sorry for what I said. I like you. You're one of the better ones.'

'Thank you,' said Sally dryly. 'I'll put that on my gravestone. "Here lies Sally Mottram. She was one of the better ones." Well, good luck down south, Dr Mallet.'

'Bronovsky,' said Dr Mallet.

'What?'

'I'm changing my name to Bronovsky. I should have done it years ago.'

Dr Bronovsky – let us give him his wish on this fine and happy morning – moved off round the roundabout. A man was approaching the roundabout from the allotments, wheeling a barrow full of lovely vegetables. Dr Bronovsky wound down the window, shouted, 'Bastard!', closed the window and accelerated angrily up the new bypass, which was called Pennine Way. The council had wanted to call it Sir Norman Oldfield Boulevard, but Sally had known that, while Sir Norman would accept the use of his name for the tea room, and secretly be pleased because it was his kind of place, he would never want a road named after him, and she had fought successfully against it. Users of the original Pennine Way objected, but it's easier for councils to upset large numbers of ramblers than one billionaire.

The man with the barrow was Matt Winkle, who had been busy on his allotments since half past five. He had three adjoining allotments, and tried, every day, to have some fresh vegetables for his shop, 'Matt's Market'. He placed these in a special corner, labelled *Today's Allotment from my Allotment*. The allotments were all in use now, and busy. The town had adopted another Transition idea called 'Gardenshare', whose name was self-explanatory and which was helping towards their ultimate aim of a self-sufficient town.

'Morning, Sally.'

'Morning, Matt.'

They kissed on both cheeks. Matt's cheeks had colour in them, now that he saw fresh air every day.

'What was all that about?' asked Sally, as they walked slowly along High Street West, past the refurbished and reopened Rose and Crown.

'He's angry with me because I've stopped going to him. I told him I was cured. He told me I was only NHS cured. I don't feel that, Sally. I feel utterly cured. You can't go to a shrink when you're cured, can you?'

'Of course you can't. You mustn't feel guilty about that.'

'I got cross in the Dog and Duck and called him a shrink. He went berserk. He said, "I am not a shrink. I am a psychiatrist. I have sixteen letters after my name. Sixteen. And you call me a shrink. How many letters have you got after your name? Three. FSM. Failed Supermarket Manager."'

'Oh dear. Poor old Dr . . . Bronovsky,' said Sally.

The supermarket company had dismissed Matt and threatened to sue him for the loss of revenue and the cost of the repairs caused by his actions. He had told them that he had built his little canal to help save the town, and that his actions had indeed done just enough to prevent a major catastrophe. He was a saviour, not a wrecker. Conrad had sent the supermarket's owners a letter in which he calculated that the amount of water diverted from the river and the canal might have been just sufficient, if not diverted, to have caused the banks of the cut at Canal Basin and the river under the bridge across High Street West to burst, thereby creating incalculable damage, or rather, damage that he would happily calculate. They should offer Matt a generous redundancy package, which would be good publicity. They should not sue, which would be very bad publicity. Matt had used his redundancy payment to buy a nice little property in the High Street, and achieve his ambition, to be the greenest greengrocer in the grocery world.

They had reached the corner of Cadwallader Road.

'I have to pay a call here,' she said.

She kissed him impulsively, out of sheer affection. He tried to kiss her on the lips. She turned away.

He blushed.

The Kosy Korner Kafé was open, and before she made her call, Sally had breakfast. After all, she had been out walking for two and a half hours. She had two poached eggs with hollandaise sauce on a muffin.

Matt's attempt to kiss her on the lips had disturbed her. Well, no. It was more true to say that her refusal to let him kiss her on the lips had disturbed her. He was nice, he was gentle, he was ethically sound on vegetables, his carrots were awesome, his broccoli was sprouting more purple than any north of Watford, he had colour in his cheeks, he was in no way repulsive to look at, and she was all alone on this, her great day. But no, she had already decided that it was a virtue that she was on her own today. Tomorrow now . . . no. Sadly, nice happy Matt would not be the man of her dreams even tomorrow.

As she finished her delicious eggs, she forced herself to think of a subject other than men. She thought about the supermarket. It had been repaired. It had reopened. But in the brief period of its closure very few people had missed it, and they were growing to love their refurbished High Street, their ripe fruit, their fresh vegetables, their ability to buy two potatoes when they didn't want a bag of twenty-four, their meat that contained no horse, their fish that, in the words of 'Prop M. Sibley' on his board outside the wet fish shop, contained no seahorse. Sally hoped that the supermarket would cut their losses and leave, that the area would become an arts centre. It might never happen, but it was a nice story to dream of.

She paid for her breakfast and set off down Cadwallader Road to number 6. On the pavement opposite, a small group of people were sitting on folded chairs. She walked across to them and asked them what they were doing there.

'We're waiting to see her,' said one of them.

'See her? See who?'

421

'The very fat person. We've read about her. We're waiting to see her. See how she does. Cheer her on.'

'You'll have to wait hours.'

'We know that. We don't mind waiting. We like waiting. We waited six hours for Mrs Thatcher's funeral. All night for the Centre Court. There's no point if you just walk in, is there?'

'But don't you get bored?'

'No. We get chatting. You meet some very nice people in queues.'

'Nothing much'll happen, you know. It's not like Wimbledon or Mrs T's funeral.'

'We know that. We waited nine hours for the Olympic torch. This feller, like, walked past with it. That were it, know what I mean? It were great.'

'Oh. Well. Right.'

The woman's husband, who had said nothing, spoke for the first time.

'I like the clapping,' he said. 'Clapping some bugger that's done summat. Makes me feel good about life. And your Ellie, she's done wonders, hasn't she? Course she has.'

'Course she has,' echoed his wife.

'Well, enjoy yourselves,' said Sally.

'We will,' the onlookers chorused.

Sally knocked on the door. After quite a long pause, Ali opened it.

'I hope I'm not too early,' said Sally.

'No. Come in, Mrs Mottram. Ellie's still in bed, but she's having her breakfast.'

Ali led Sally into the front room. Oli was sitting by the bed, watching Ellie eat a small bowl of Fruit 'n Fibre.

'Good morning, Mrs Mottram,' said Ellie. 'They didn't want to get me up too early, so that I'd get all nervous hanging around.'

422

'That makes sense. But I do wish you'd call me Sally.'

'I'll call you Sally when I've done me walk,' said Ellie. 'When I've earned it. When I feel I'm worthy to be your friend.'

'Oh, Ellie, you shouldn't feel like that,' said Sally.

'Oh, but I should,' said Ellie, 'and I do.'

'Ladies,' said Sally. 'I've . . . um . . . something I've got to tell you. There's some people outside.'

'What sort of people?' asked Ali.

'They were opposite when you answered the door,' said Sally. 'Tourists. With folding chairs.'

'Oh aye, I saw them. Who are they?'

'They're the audience.'

'What audience?'

'Ellie's audience. They've come to see you walk, Ellie. To cheer you on.'

Oli went to the window, moved to draw back the curtain.

'Don't let them see us peeping,' cried out Ellie. 'We have us pride. Don't let them see us peeping.'

Oli peeped out very carefully.

'Whar are they like?' asked Ellie.

'They're just, like, people,' said Oli.

'They've come to see me?' asked Ellie in disbelief.

'Yes.'

'Stood standing there just to see me?'

'Well, they have chairs.'

'Still . . . long wait. And just to see me!'

'Wonderful. That's great, is that. That's amazing. All to see little . . . well, no, not so little . . .' The three Fazackerly sisters laughed.

'Just to see Ellie Fazackerly from Potherthwaite. Eh up, that's fantastic, is that.'

'You don't mind?' asked Sally.

'Why should I mind? Hey, I'll be on telly. I will, won't I?'

'You may.'

Sally dug into her handbag and produced an envelope.

'I've got something to show you three ladies,' she said.

'A present?' asked Oli eagerly.

'I suppose so. Ladies, your tickets.'

She handed a ticket to each of the three.

They examined them in bewilderment.

'What's a dampshiffart?' asked Ellie. 'Sounds horrible.'

'Hope I don't have to clean up after it,' said Ali.

'No, no. It's German. It means a boat journey. These, ladies, are three tickets for a journey down the beautiful Rhine Gorge by boat.'

'The one you told us about with all them castles?' said Ellie.

'That's right. It's dated next year, in August. And I'm coming with you as promised. Our first holiday. Amsterdam to Basel, on the Rhine by boat. Holland, Germany, France and Switzerland. Four countries.'

'Bloody hell,' said Oli.

'That's Ellie's next targct,' said Sally.

'Bloody hell,' said Ellie. 'But you should of got five tickets.'

'Why?' asked Ali.

'One for her feller,' said Ellie.

'She hasn't got a feller,' said Oli.

'No, but she bloody should have,' said Ellie. 'If I was a feller, which I'm not, and if I wasn't so fat, which I am, I'd shag her summat rotten.'

The Fazackerly sisters shook with laughter. All three insisted on kissing Sally, and then she took her leave. As she closed the door on number 6 Cadwallader Road, she waved to the little crowd on the opposite pavement, and all seven waved back.

Seven? The crowd was growing!

The first clouds, small and as yet unthreatening, were

bubbling up in the atmosphere. These were the most unfair of clouds. They didn't come floating in over the horizon. They formed out of the air itself, right overhead.

Ellie's remark had affected Sally. She was trying not to think of the nagging loneliness hidden far below, but always there. It wasn't the day for it.

As she turned the corner into High Street West, she caught sight of Ben admiring his handiwork. He blushed. She would miss it when, if ever, his blushing days were over.

'You must be so proud.'

'Oh, I am.'

'You've nothing to worry about with your career. Nothing.'

'I don't think it's quite like that, Sally. I look at my work and I think, "I don't believe Rembrandt was any better than this at my age." I shouldn't say that, should I?'

'Well, possibly it might be better just to think it.'

'But what people don't understand is, it doesn't give me any right to say I'll ever produce anything as good again. Even produce anything good at all again ever. It's a knack. Came to me, might just as easily go from me. I've not heard anything from Lucy, Sally. She said she'd text.'

'It's early, Ben. It's not much past nine o'clock.'

'True. Oh, thanks, Sally. I'm just being silly. There's a surprise.'

Sally wandered on, past the turning into the cul-de-sac. It looked much as normal, but to her it was a forlorn, desolate place. Olive and Arnold were dead, Jill and Harry had moved to their boat, Marigold was living with Conrad in *her* old house. She had felt that she was all alone many times in recent months, but now she felt it more sharply than ever. Today, on her great day, she had wanted to be alone. This sudden ache was absurd.

FORTY-THREE

Afternoon

Bang on twelve, Sally entered 'La Piccola', on High Street East. The blue sky was by now almost entirely hidden by cloud. There were just two small patches of blue, darker than the morning blue, valiantly hanging on, but doomed. The whole street was throbbing with its normal Saturday-morning buzz. The shops were crowded. The police were everywhere, smiling as they put up barriers to hold back the crowds. Already, people were three deep along the route. The route! How that would fill Ellie with pride. Thirty-six years unnoticed, and now she had a route.

The sight of Inspector Pellet and PC Cartwright transported Sally back to that dreadful evening on which she had discovered Barry at the top of the stairs. It didn't make a good prelude to the next hour and a quarter. She was having something that many people have regularly, but that she hadn't experienced since the week of Barry's funeral. She was having a family lunch. It wasn't a large gathering, just Judith, Sam, Beth and her. Alice had been unable to make the trip from New Zealand. 'It's such a long way,' she had wailed, as she always did, as if its location had been a secret withheld from her until she had arrived there. But Sally missed Alice so much. In Alice she could see something of herself. In Sam, she could only see Barry. A warmer Barry. A kinder Barry. But still Barry. Beth was pregnant. Very pregnant. All women who have babies get pregnant, but some get more pregnant than others. Beth had been pregnant when Sally had visited her after her first meeting with Sir Norman, when she had just had that most upsetting offer of marriage. When Beth lost the baby, she had believed that this was her fault, that because she hadn't wanted to know the baby's sex, and had therefore been forced to refer to it as 'it', it had never become a real person. This time she knew the sex. It was a girl. No, she was a girl. They were going to call her Desiree, because they had desired her so much. Oh dear.

There was conversation, but it was hard work. It didn't flow. Alcohol might have helped, but that didn't flow either. Sam was driving, Beth was pregnant, Judith didn't think the wine list was good enough and Sally had to keep a very clear head.

Sally couldn't believe that Beth and Sam both chose lasagne, their staple dish at home, but she was too wise to comment. In fact she didn't need to. Sam commented for her. 'We find we pick up some great hints for our lasagne, eating it in restaurants,' he said.

Judith ordered a veal cutlet, and salad. She finished neither. She went through life eating the bare minimum that would sustain her through eighteen holes of golf.

Nerves were making Sally extremely hungry. She had a rare fillet steak with pepper sauce.

Over the coffee, Beth showed them three little children's books that she had bought that morning for the time when she would teach Desiree to read.

'What age would that be at?' enquired Judith dryly. 'Eleven months?'

427

Careful, Judith, said Sally's eyebrows.

Well, honestly, replied Judith's.

Sally was delighted when the meal was finished. She insisted on paying, which she did very proudly with Potherthwaite Pounds. Judith protested with the first real vitality she had shown, but didn't put up much of a fight. Sam, after a low whisper from Beth, tried to insist that they pay their share, but his generosity collapsed at the first resistance it met.

The joy that Sally felt on leaving the restaurant troubled her for a moment. She had no lover, and scarcely a family. But then she was swept into the day's events. The sight of the crowds, four and five deep now, astonished her. The presence of the television cameras thrilled her. A few spears of rain came in on the westerly wind. Nobody minded. It was expected. It was Potherthwaite.

There was a stir among the crowd, and applause and a bit of cheering, as Sally arrived at number 6. Ali opened the door for her but stood shyly out of sight of the crowd. Ellie was up and dressed and waiting in the kitchen. She was wearing an enormous pair of beige trousers which, amazingly, were slightly too big. She had lost a little more weight than had been anticipated. She was still hugely obese, substantially fatter still than Ali and Oli had been at their peak, but perhaps not quite as much as Sally had expected. Ali and Oli no longer looked obese. They looked like two normal lazy women who ate too much and would need to watch their weight. They were wearing new dresses, Italian, as had been promised. They looked so proud.

At exactly two o'clock, Ellie came out of her front door sideways. A great cheer went up. She looked at the crowd in astonishment, and raised her fat arm and great podgy hand in acknowledgement. She was beaming from ear to ear, and from ear to ear was still quite a long way. Ali and

Oli, both carrying umbrellas, stood at either side of her, smiling shyly.

They set off at a very slow pace, Ellie moving her legs in short, awkward shuffles. They were too heavy still to actually be raised. Ali and Oli supported her, one on each side. Behind them, at a discreet distance, her doctor accompanied them.

The cheering grew in intensity as the party reached High Street West and turned right. Ellie's great mouth opened in astonishment as she took in the beauty of Ben's design. She had heard all about it, of course, but the reality took the breath away.

Past Matt's Market they went; past the new dress shop, Velvet and Verve; past Hopkinson's Game Emporium, the specialist butcher's; past Lidyard & Penfold, the most expensive of the town's three independent grocers; past the wet fish shop; past the dry fish shop; past the Potherthwaite Deli; past the crowds standing around the colourful parterres in Central Park – a slow, slow shuffle. Behind them came four mounted police officers, two men and two women, and then there were eight police officers on foot. All the police officers were smiling self-consciously.

The little procession moved slowly over the river. Sally was disappointed that there was no sign of the bipolar mallard – it was wretched of them not to be there on the town's great day. But even this view had changed since the project had begun. As the river swung to the right behind the churchyard and the car park of the George Hotel, a very brief shaft of sunlight lit up the row of cranes that had been brought in for the transformation of the town's great mills into desirable but not huge apartments.

Now Ellie came in sight of the crowds in the Market Place. The loudest cheer of all went up at this point and there, standing on the crowded balcony of the Town Hall, were all the town's leading public figures, crammed together, and all smiling and applauding. Sally thought that perhaps they should not have allowed car parking that day, but if they hadn't she wouldn't have seen the lorry.

A spatter of rain sailed in on the wind. Ali and Oli opened their umbrellas in unison. The rain stopped. Ali and Oli closed their umbrellas. The crowd laughed. Then the rain began again. Ali and Oli opened their umbrellas. There was even more laughter. The rain stopped again. Ali and Oli closed their umbrellas again. There was loud and prolonged applause at this very British little pantomime. Sally didn't think she had ever seen so many smiles, and a huge feeling of joy swept through her. She had never believed that it would be like this. She had created all this, with a great deal of help from some wonderful people. Now at last she felt the full glory of the day and her part in it. Loneliness was banished. She was utterly happy.

A small settee had been placed in the square in front of the Town Hall. Nobody was quite sure how broad Ellie would be, and a chair might not have been wide enough. Ali and Oli led Ellie towards the settee and lowered her gently on to it. It sagged, but it did not split, and there was renewed applause at this successful manoeuvre, at this triumph for British furniture. Make the most of it, folks, thought Sally. Applause will never be so easily achieved again.

Her heart didn't even sink when she realized that Councillor Frank Stratton was going to speak. He was handed a microphone and he moved forward to the front of the balcony. Silence fell rapidly. This was not only the largest crowd the town had ever seen, it was the most obedient.

'This is a great day for Potherthwaite, for you, the people of Potherthwaite. The achievement is yours, and that in particular of one wonderful woman, Sally Mottram,' said Councillor Stratton.

A great cheer broke out. Sally felt obliged to acknowledge it, with a mixture of joy and embarrassment. She was frightened that she might burst into tears. She turned her eyes away from the balcony, from Ellie, from the crowds. She found herself looking at the lorry again. Something about it puzzled her.

'Your council, and its officers, have done very little except – which is quite important – that we have let it all happen,' continued Councillor Stratton. 'We take no more credit than that, so I'd like to pass you over now to the lady of the hour, Sally Mottram.'

Sally was thrilled by Councillor Stratton's unexpected grace and modesty. Thrilled, but also shocked. She wasn't ready for this.

A loudhailer was produced for her. Clearly all this had been prepared, and she hadn't been told for fear that she would be overcome with nerves.

'I'm not the lady of the hour,' she said. 'I've done what I've done and I'm proud of it. I couldn't have done it without my second-in-command, Marigold Boyce-Willoughby.'

There was more applause, not huge because nobody really knew what Marigold had actually done, but not feeble either, because everybody liked her.

'. . . or without my wonderful young artist, who has given us our magnificent, quite unique High Street, Ben Wardle.'

There was huge applause. Ben, who was bright pink, jumped up and down a couple of times to make himself visible, then slid hurriedly back into the crowd.

'. . . or that great man of Potherthwaite, that most successful of all Potherthwaitians, our great benefactor, Sir Norman Oldfield.'

Again, there was applause, not as much as for Ben and Sally, but still a decent hand, although there was no sign of the man himself.

431

'Finally, I must mention Luke Warburton and his gang, the Baggit Boys.'

There was loud cheering again.

'They showed their true colours on the night of the storm and have been wonderful ever since, and I love their estate, even the naughty bits.'

There was laughter as well as applause at that.

'But as much as anyone, I thank you, the people of Potherthwaite. Go on, give yourselves a clap.'

The people of Potherthwaite gave themselves an almighty clap.

'And now,' said Sally. 'I call upon the real lady of the hour, Miss Ellie Fazackerly.'

She handed the loudhailer to Ellie.

'I won't get up,' said Ellie. 'I can't.'

There was laughter and applause at this. It was true. Laughter and applause would never be so easily gained as this afternoon.

'Thank you, Mrs Mottram,' continued Ellie. 'You've been wonderful. She's been me helper, me saviour, has Mrs Mottram, and she wants me to treat her as a friend and call her Sally, and I've told her I won't do this till I've finished me walk, but will I finish it, cos by heck, I'll tell you, it looks a long way. Ee, this is an amazing day, and don't town look lovely? Thank you, everybody. It's funny, i'n't it? I'm famous cos I'm fat and whar am I doing about it, I'm slimming, so I'll not be fat no more so I'll not be famous no more, will I? Listen. I tell you . . . there's nowt funny in being fat. It's horrid. I'm smiling cos I can walk . . . just . . . bur I'm not smiling inside cos I'm still fat. If whar I've done today helps other people to get less fat, I'll be happy. I will. I can do it, you can do it. So thank you, Mrs Mottram, and thank you Ali and Oli, best sisters I could have had, love you, love you a lot, so come on then, sod all this sitting, let's finish job.'

Ali, Oli and the doctor helped to raise Ellie slowly from the settee. The members of the band, who had slipped in on their right while everybody was listening to the speeches, struck up and set off, very very slowly, with their great favourite, 'The Departure of the Queen of Sheba'. It had never seemed as appropriate as on this day. Behind them Ellie, Ali and Oli resumed their walk, with Sally just behind them, and the doctor keeping a watchful eye in the rear.

Just as the band began to march through Georgia – their repertoire was not huge – Sally remembered where she had seen the lorry before. In Devon, near the sea. It had been battered and caked in mud. It was still battered, but it was gleaming. What on earth was it doing here?

They were moving out of the square into High Street East now. It had always been the poor relation, but not any more. It was quite the equal of High Street West. Sally caught sight of Ben, waved at him, raised her eyebrows to ask him how he was doing. He shook his head, grimaced, and spread his arms in a gesture of puzzlement. He looked distraught. A cold fear shuddered its way through Sally's heart.

Beside the band there walked a very pretty young woman, tall and slender, with rich brown hair and bright blue eyes. She was looking proudly at the band, her lips were moving to the unsung words of the tune. Sally recognized her as Arabella Kate Hendrie, the Yorkshire Callas. Sally saw her exchange a grin with her father Gordon – the woman who had conquered La Scala smiling in joy and equality at her dad playing the euphonium in the Rackstraw and Potherthwaite Brass Band.

She caught sight of Marigold and Conrad among the crowd. Marigold was behaving very peculiarly. She looked solemn and pompous for a moment, then raised both hands with the fingers and thumbs outstretched, then raised one hand with four fingers outstretched but the thumb hidden.

Then she talked and laughed with Conrad and then both Marigold and Conrad looked very stiff and severe and pompous and serious and then they both raised both hands with the fingers and thumbs outstretched and then one hand with the fingers outstretched but the thumb hidden. Sally looked utterly bewildered and they obviously thought this was the funniest thing they had ever seen, and then they did the whole strange mime again, but this time Conrad went on to mime putting a ring on Marigold's finger, pointed at Sally and mimed raising a glass. Then he mimed making energetic and really rather specific love to Marigold, and she hit him gently for being so naughty. They were in hysterics. Sally felt such a fool. What did it all mean?

Work it out, Sally. The ring mime must have meant marriage. Had they fixed the date? Ah. Those fingers. Count them. Both hands. Include the thumbs? Yes, because they held the thumbs up very clearly. So that's five plus five plus four. The fourteenth. But what the fourteenth? Which month? What had all that pomposity and solemnity been about?

July? August? September? Summer surely? August probably. Ah. Au-gust. The word meant pompous and solemn and all that stuff. A wise and august man. It was so Marigold to tell her in charades. And it was so not Conrad. Easy to see who was going to wear the trousers in that marriage.

She nodded wildly and blew them kisses. They blew kisses back. She didn't feel jealous, didn't feel jealous at all, she felt happy for them, she felt warm and generous and it didn't matter at all that she had nobody, and almost as if it was her reward for not minding having nobody, for enjoying other people's happiness above her own, there he was. He was tall, weather-beaten, his whole face was slightly twisted to the right, he was smart in a sheepskin jacket and pale trousers; it was hard to recognize him but she knew it was

434

him, the man from the lorry, the man from that night, the man who hadn't tried to rape her. She didn't know why he was there, but there must be some reason, some small coincidence. It wasn't particularly significant, but she had hoped to meet him again one day, though she had long forgotten this, but it would be nice to see him again, so she showed that she had seen him, and she pointed to the right to indicate that she would be going down Canal Approach to the Quays, and he nodded, and he looked pleased, and that was that.

The band turned right on to Quays Approach, which became the Great Gate of Kiev. Ahead of them, at the bottom of High Street East, now free of cars, a permanent street market had been established, and even the stallholders had come forward to wave and cheer. Here there were stalls with Indian specialities, and Muslim specialities, and Polish specialities, and Jewish specialities, and it was strange because the town both worried itself to death about immigration and queued to buy the produce on those stalls.

Ellie was getting exhausted. She was barely able to even shuffle now, and moving more slowly than ever. She turned to ask the doctor if everything was all right; he nodded and mimed for her to take it even more slowly. So slow was her progress now that tension swept through the crowd. Almost imperceptibly the procession inched towards the Quays. Ali and Oli were anxious. Sally was anxious. Everybody was anxious. Would Ellie make it?

Who knew just how much pain Ellie went through on that last stretch? The doctor perhaps. But she made it.

The Quays were awash with people. The Sir Norman Oldfield Tea Room, the Terminus Bistro, the Canal Bookshop and Café, the Navigation Inn, they were all heaving. There wasn't a spare seat on the temporary stand at the towpath side of the canal.

435

And there, standing to welcome Ellie, smiling perhaps the shyest of all the smiles on that day of smiles, was the small, insignificant figure of Sir Norman Oldfield.

Ali and Oli steered Ellie to another large settee, into which she collapsed.

'You made it, Ellie,' said Sally.

'I made it, Sally,' said Ellie.

Sally turned to Sir Norman, gestured to him to come forward to meet Ellie. He shook his head violently, gave Ellie a thumbs-up, and walked slowly away. Sally followed him, and he turned to her and kissed her on both cheeks.

'You made it, Sir Norman,' said Sally.

'People are just as awful as I'd remembered,' said Sir Norman, 'but I may as well stay now I'm here.'

Lennie Tiptree disentangled himself from the throng and came towards her.

'It's the lady herself,' he enthused. 'It's the lady herself in all her glory.'

Sally held out her hand tremulously.

'No, no, we're beyond the 'andshake. We're well beyond the 'andshake. You're my friend, you are.'

Sally's relief at avoiding the handshake didn't last long. The same thin sheen of damp covered the whole of Lennie Tiptree's cheek as he kissed her.

'Lovely,' he said. 'Lovely as ever. Neater, tighter little arse than what I ever saw in Stoke Newington.'

'Tiptree!' said Sir Norman, scandalized. 'Where's your style? Where's your breeding?'

'Never 'ad no style, Sir Norm,' said Lennie Tiptree with a wicked grin. 'Never 'ad no bleeding breeding. Left 'em in the Old Kent Road.'

Ben came rushing towards Sally like a frightened partridge chick.

'No message from her, Sally,' he said. 'Nothing.'

'There'll be some explanation.'

'Yes. She's heard the call of the circus. She's staying.'

'She can't. I need her.'

Her headmistress, Margaret Spreckley, had been true to her word. People just occasionally are. She had got Lucy to write a play and it was a clever play for an eighteen-year-old, a tale of two versions of Potherthwaite's future, one utopian, the other dystopian. Never again would ignorant people think Lucy stupid because of her dyslexia. She was starring in it too, and it was opening in the Festival on Thursday. Yes, they needed her back. And she would come back. Faith.

'She'll be back, Ben. Have faith. Faith, Ben. Very important. Not in God. In people.'

'Some people.'

'Yes. Including Lucy, Ben.'

There was a black cloud overhead and suddenly it was as if it tipped and all the rain fell out. A wall of rain, a deluge, pinging off the pavements, soaking the crowd. Hard for Ben and Sally not to see it as a bad omen.

Ali's umbrella became entangled with Oli's so Ellie got soaked. People ran undercover, where there was cover, but most people just got soaked.

Sally turned to run and there in front of her was the man from the lorry, and the rain was a bad omen no longer.

He was just standing there in the rain, motionless, smiling. She found herself smiling too. They stood there in the deluge. He kissed her very gently on the mouth.

'Hello again,' he said.

'Hello again,' she whispered.

Everyone else had run for shelter. They stood, motionless, holding each other tight, alone on the quay from which everyone had fled. There was no point in their moving now. They were as wet as they would ever be.

The rain stopped as suddenly as it had begun. The lucky people who had found cover started to walk out again, but all the seats were soaking so nobody could sit down.

The sky lightened, and then suddenly the sun burst through, the clouds moved away, there was quite a patch of blue sky. And the sun was hot. This was a summer sun. Everything steamed. The ground steamed. Sally steamed. The man from the lorry steamed. Ellie steamed. Oli and Ali steamed. More than a thousand wet coats steamed. They were standing in steam, surrounded by steam, in a steaming world. Only Ellie sat. There was no point in her standing. Her settee was still dry, protected by her vast bulk.

'I didn't expect our meeting to be quite as dramatic as this,' said the man from the lorry.

'Amazing,' said Sally. 'Amazing. Well, I'm Sally Mottram.'

'Yes, I know,' he said. 'I'm John Forrester.'

'The man with the lorry.'

'The man with the lorry indeed.'

'I saw your lorry parked in the square.'

'It isn't my lorry.'

'Sorry?'

'It isn't my lorry.'

'It isn't your lorry?'

'No. Sorry.'

Did ever a love affair start with such a ridiculous conversation? Yet Sally never doubted, not for a moment, that this was a love affair. Nevertheless, they needed to move on from the lorry.

'Oh,' she said. 'Well, anyway, this is a very nice coincidence.'

'Not at all.'

'Not nice?'

'Not a coincidence. Sally, that night, when I gave you that lift, the memory stuck with me.'

'Yes, and with me.'

'I never saw a woman look so scared, so sad, so spent.'

'Oh my God.'

'I never saw – excuse my frankness – I never saw a pretty woman look so awful. You looked as if you'd seen death approaching.'

'I had. I really had.'

He took her hand, and squeezed it very gently.

'I longed to touch you,' he said, 'but I think you'd have fallen to pieces if I had.'

'I think I would.'

'I think you thought I was the South Hams rapist.'

'The what? The South what?'

'The South Hams is what they call that area of Devon.'

'Ah.'

'I called on your sister. Judith. No joy there.'

'She isn't brimming with it.'

'She refused to give me any information about you.'

'Just protecting me, I expect.'

'Maybe. Maybe not. Anyway, not long ago, I came upon a photo of you, in a magazine article about the Transition of Potherthwaite.'

'Oh yes. I think I know the one.'

'Very good. Good photo.'

'It wasn't the worst, no.'

'I googled Potherthwaite. I found out about the festival. I knew then where I could find you. Here, today. The lorry's my brother's. He's a farmer. I was helping him that night. I was . . . well, I was saving his farm for him, I suppose. He was ill. Depression. Lots of farmers suffer from depression.'

'Oh, John, I'm sorry. That's horrid.'

It was the first time she had called him by name and even in that moment of sympathy a corner of her brain noticed

439

how that strong, plain name suited him, and how easily it
sat on her.

'Is he . . . um . . .?'

'He's much better now.'

'Oh, good.'

'Hard times. I borrowed his lorry. Parked it in the square
so that you'd see it. Wondered if you'd recognize it. He
thought *I* was mad.'

'Why did you do that?'

'I don't really know. I just did it. For a bit of a lark, I
suppose. A childish touch. Maybe a bit of romance. Maybe
a touch of superstition too. And . . . I don't know . . . an
exorcism of that night's fear, if that isn't a bit fanciful for a
farmer.'

'A farmer?'

'Yes, I'm a farmer too. Just.'

'What do you mean – "just"?'

'I'm purely arable, no animal smells, very little mud, and
I've got big. It's big business.'

'Still a farmer, though.'

'As I say, "just". I'm trying to sell up. I'm tired of it. I
fancy a challenge. I fancy . . . changes to my life, Sally. In
all sorts of ways.'

'Ah.'

Their eyes met so briefly that Sally wondered if they really
had.

'You're as beautiful as I had imagined that night. Many
men will think so. Many men will fancy you. Luckily for
me, there is something about you that – I hope this doesn't
upset you, I rather like it – something that holds people
back.'

'Oh God!'

'No, no. It's not bad. It's good. You have . . . what should
I call it? Reserve? Dignity? Class? I guess it makes it difficult

440

for lesser men to approach you as the warm, sexy person you are. But I know you better. I have seen you terrified. You hold no fears for me. Do your duties take you away from me, or shall we watch the fun together?'

'The fun?'

'All this.'

'Of course. How stupid. I'd sort of forgotten where we were.'

'Oh, had you? How marvellous.'

'I would love us to watch the fun together, John.'

Sally looked round and was surprised to see that she and John were standing in a little space on the crowded quay, standing so intensely together that nobody had dared to intrude on their space. She was amazed to see that so many people, people that she knew, were all looking at her. Terence and Felicity Porchester, as they made their final preparations for departure, had smiles so broad there shouldn't have been room for them on a narrowboat. Marigold and Conrad, and Ellie and Ali and Oli, and Lennie Tiptree and Sir Norman, and Sam and Beth and Judith, were smiling too, although the smiles of Judith, and of Sam and Beth, held an unflattering element of surprise. Miss Margaret Spreckley, Lucy's headmistress, was reputed to have a Canadian in the offing, and there he was, sitting right next to her, handsome and tall and as Canadian as a tree, and they were smiling too. And there beside them was the Revd Dominic Otley. His smile had a touch of wistfulness about it, but the smile of his wife, the former Linda Oughtibridge, most assuredly did not.

FORTY-FOUR

Evening

The clouds disappeared. They didn't move on to plague other Pennine towns. They just melted away. It was still very warm in the sunshine, and the sun seemed to shine that evening into every corner of the Potherthwaite Quays. All traces of the downpour had disappeared. It was hard to believe that it had ever happened.

It had been Sally's suggestion that Sir Norman Oldfield should introduce Arabella Kate Hendrie to the crowd. He had been reluctant.

'Supposing I make you a solemn promise never to ask any favour of any kind of you ever again?' she had said.

'I suppose I can't say no,' he had replied.

The crowd sat expectantly. Now Sir Norman walked up on to the little hump-backed bridge, went to the microphone that had been set up for Arabella Kate. There was loud applause. He held up his hand to stem it.

'Ladies and gentlemen,' he said, and most of the people in the crowd were astonished to hear the nervousness and uncertainty in the voice of this billionaire. 'Ladies and gentlemen, I am told that I am the most famous living Potherthwaitian man.'

There was yet more applause on this day of applause. Sally wondered where the shy heron was; how confused he would be by the day's happenings if he had not long gone.

'So who better than me, I suppose, to introduce the person who is without doubt the most famous living Potherthwaitian woman? I refer of course to the lovely young lady who has been dubbed the Yorkshire Callas. Tomorrow she will be reopening our once beloved theatre in company with Opera North. Today she is the Callas of the Canal. How lucky, how privileged we are, to be here today. Is she more famous than me? I don't know. I don't care. Fame isn't important. Where have all the clouds gone this evening? Nowhere. They've just disappeared. Fame's like that.'

Sally was amused by the fact that, here in his native town, the flat Pennine tones were flatter than they had been in his mansion above Marlow.

'Fame's nowt. Money's nowt. I'm realizing that today, and, by gum, it hurts. I asked which of us was the more famous. Ladies and gentlemen, if I were to ask you which of us, me or our guest tonight, has brought the most pleasure into the world, well, it's not even a question worth asking. And that hurts too. But tonight is not a night for hurt, so I am ready, here tonight, to open my mind to beauty in a way I haven't done nearly enough. The next hour will be a privilege. Ladies and gentlemen, I give you Arabella Kate Hendrie, the Yorkshire Callas.'

The wind had dropped entirely. There was a flat calm on the surface of the canal. The acoustics were perfect. The voice that had charmed La Scala rang out over the glassy waters. Its purity set Sally's flesh tingling. Its liquid softness pierced her heart. There was tragedy and hope, pity and despair, love and passion in that voice. The glory of 'Queen of the Night', from Mozart's *Magic Flute*, sailed into that pale blue evening sky. Heron, heron, come back, you will never

443

have heard anything as lovely as this, and you will never hear anything as lovely again. Jenny and Gordon Hendrie felt that they might pass out from the emotion.

At the end of the aria, the applause was tremendous. Opera lovers clapped, opera haters clapped, people who had never heard opera before in their lives clapped. The beautiful and the ugly, the thin and the obese, they all clapped. Sally caught sight of Linda Oughtibridge that was, and even she looked almost lovely.

Now Arabella Kate Hendrie paid homage to her name as 'The Yorkshire Callas'. Now, boldly, exultantly, triumphantly, she sang some of Maria Callas's most famous arias. Somehow, she made them her own but gave no impression that she was boasting. She sang in tribute to Callas, in tribute to opera, in tribute to art, in tribute to Potherthwaite, in tribute, ultimately, to life itself. 'Una Voce Poco Fa' from *The Barber of Seville* was followed by 'O Mio Babbino Caro' from *Gianni Schicchi*. Alone on the bridge, her perfectly proportioned face lit up by the evening sun as it slanted in from the north-west, Arabella sang so beautifully that Sally felt sad for the composers of the music, sad that they were dead this night.

Even in her exultation Sally was ruefully conscious that her ear was not subtle enough to deserve this treat. If it was, she would not have had space to reflect at this moment. But reflect she did. She reflected on Barry's legacy, that she could never be fully confident of what was going on in another person's head. She found herself wondering whether the rapture on Linda Otley's face was genuine or assumed. Judith's face was a mask. She was motionless. She might have been a portrait entitled 'Society Lady in the Act of Admiring Great Music'. Above all, she wondered about John Forrester, who seemed to be rapt in the music in a way that she couldn't be, yet also utterly at one with her. They were holding hands, and she had the strangest feeling that the music was flowing through his fingers into hers. But he was a farmer. Did he really actually fully appreciate the music? Could he? And did he know that she was unable to give herself to it as she would wish?

And then, at last, Arabella Kate Hendrie took her over, possessed her in the most lovely and unpossessive way. She was singing 'Dei Tuoi Figli La Madre', from *Medea*, and Sally was suddenly captured by the beauty of it. Quite soon after that, the performance was over. It had been an hour, and it had passed in minutes, yet it had also been a lifetime. For just a few seconds at the end of the performance, there was the loudest silence Sally had ever heard. She felt John's gnarled farmer's fingers press hers ever so slightly. Now applause burst out over the Potherthwaite Quays. People claimed later to have heard a faint echo of it as far away as Heckmondwike. The Mayor, who was now Councillor Maurice Sibley, found himself doing something that he could never have dreamt of when he told his careers officer that he wanted to run a wet fish shop when he grew up. He climbed a hump-backed canal bridge and presented a magnificent bouquet to one of the greatest divas of our times.

It was as if people couldn't face the ending of the applause. It was as if people dreaded their return to reality. And yet, Sally felt that they needn't dread it, that there would be a little extra element of magic in them for the rest of their lives.

At last the applause did stop. Sally didn't want to speak. Any words would spoil the moment. How she feared that John Forrester would say something. But he didn't.

The return to reality was a difficult gear change, but now Terence and Felicity Porchester came to the evening's rescue. Terence was casting off. Felicity was at the helm. The Porchesters were returning home, and everyone was cheering again. 'Wish Me Luck As You Wave Me Goodbye', sung by half a town, represented quite a drop in musical sophistication, but at that moment it was wonderfully moving.

The Porchesters chugged out of sight, towards the winding hole. A few people began to move off, the temporary stand was emptying – people feel foolish staying on in a temporary stand – but the Sir Norman Oldfield Tea Room, the Terminus Bistro, the Canal Bookshop and Café and the Navigation Inn were still doing tremendous business. Also, quite a lot of people were hanging on to wave again to Terence and Felicity Porchester, who were now gently chugging back, having successfully turned in the unsilted winding hole. Sally could see that they were both crying. They had their arms round each other. Sally saw the look that passed between them, and then she was crying too. All the day's emotion came flooding out. John saw it and understood, and he began to cry too – oh God, oh miracle, he understood and he didn't mind being seen to cry.

Terence and Felicity exchanged a few words now, and then they slowed down, and the bows of their narrowboat began to turn in towards their old berth. There was another great roar now, a roar to send frightened herons migrating to Holland. Everyone in the crowd understood something of the language of the world of boats. Terence and Felicity hadn't stopped because they felt they might need one more pint of milk. They were stopping because they had found that they couldn't leave their new friends after so many years. And Potherthwaite, delightfully flattered, was welcoming them home.

Now it was time to say goodbye to Ellie, Ali and Oli. They were being taken home in a bus adapted for the disabled, though Ali and Oli could have managed the walk back with ease.

'I can't believe what I've seen today,' Ellie told Sally.

Sally was almost too moved to reply, but John, who had heard all about the Fazackerly sisters by then, saved the day.

'See you next year on the Rhine,' he said.

The Fazackerly sisters took in the implications of this remark quite slowly, and then beamed broadly – even Ali and Oli were, after all, still slightly broad.

'I told you you should of got five tickets,' said Ellie.

Sam and Beth said goodbye, slipped away. The parting between Beth and Judith was a desperately polite affair, brimming with insincerity and invitations from and to people who with luck would never see each other again in their lives.

Judith, though, surprised Sally, stayed on, took them to the Navigation Inn, bought them a bottle of champagne, laughed at what she had taken John for on that terrifying night. When he went to get another bottle, Judith said, 'I like him, Sal, but I realized today how special you are, and you hardly know him. Be careful, won't you?'

'No,' said Sally.

'What?'

'No, I won't.'

'Won't what?'

'Be careful.'

'What?'

'I'll throw myself at him.'

'Sally!'

'For over twenty years I didn't know what Barry was thinking. I don't think Marigold has a clue what Conrad is thinking, and she's accepting him as her fourth husband. I don't know what you're thinking now. Are you telling me to be careful because you love me and don't want me hurt or because you're jealous and don't want me happy? I don't know. What I do know is what I want. I want you and me

447

to be closer, better sisters. I want to marry John if he asks me and be a farmer's wife or a whatever-he-does-next's wife. I don't know how he votes, what he loves, what he hates, which side of the bed he likes to sleep on, what time he goes to bed, what time he gets up, whether he likes the windows open, whether his farmhouse is lovely or horrid, whether he will stay there anyway, whether he believes in God, how clever he is, how brave he is. I'll find out and it'll be fun or indeed it may not but let's not start by thinking it won't be and here he is, give me a lovely hug and kiss, my darling darling Judith, and oh God, I'm going to cry. Hello, darling man, I'm so happy, here I am crying again.'

The sun, trapped in its orbit, began to say goodbye, whether it wanted to or not. It soon disappeared entirely behind the hills, a loss that Potherthwaite would feel every evening, for ever. Now it began to get cold. It was time to leave, but it had been a great day, and there were smiles on every face but one.

Oh, could there not for just one evening be a smile on everybody's face? Was that too much to ask?

Ben was walking towards them along Quays Wharf. He didn't look like a great artist. He looked like a twelve-year-old on the verge of tears.

Sally felt ashamed that in the excitement she had forgotten all about him. And of course with his worry, her worry returned. The school play was very precious to her. Lucy wouldn't let her down. Would she? Not even for the call of the circus.

'Oh, Ben,' she said, 'you look so sad. No news?'

'No news.'

Sally explained the story of Ben and Lucy to John and Judith.

'I've told myself she loves me,' said Ben. 'I've told myself to have faith. But it's hard. He is her father after all. And

448

the circus is very exciting. And she did so love it.' He stopped, overcome by the possibility.

'I thought your High Street was marvellous,' said John desperately.

'Thank you. So did two agents and a gallery owner. I could be rich. I don't want to be rich without Lucy.'

'Haven't you tried her?'

'Yes. She isn't answering.'

'Why isn't she answering? What's happened?'

'Calm down,' said Sally. 'We all know Lucy. She'll be back.'

She met Judith's eyes and she knew that Judith was remembering what she'd said a few minutes ago. We can never really know anybody.

Suddenly Ben went very tense. His father was approaching the canal, and, in a typically unimaginative way, he was approaching down Canal Approach.

Ben stood up, stared at his father fearfully.

'I've been looking for you,' said his father, waving his mobile phone.

'Well, now you've found him,' said Sally. 'Have you heard anything?'

'I've been to the cricket,' said Ben's father, relishing the moment, revelling in his brief stardom. 'I don't believe in all this Transition stuff, and I don't like opera.'

'Never mind that,' said John. 'Is Lucy all right?'

She left her phone on the train, so she used her great-uncle's. It hadn't got your name, and she must have remembered your number wrong because it told her there was no such number, but it had mine because her great-uncle and I used to . . .'

Everyone's patience with Ben's father snapped at the same moment.

'Never mind her great-uncle,' said Judith angrily. 'What did she say?'

'Don't all get on at me.'

'What did she say?' shouted Judith. Sally had never seen her sister like this.

'Just thirteen words. Unlucky for someone.'

'We don't care how many sodding words,' screamed John. 'What were they?'

'Not very literate, I'm afraid,' said Ben's father with a smirk. 'Bad spelling error.'

'What were they?' shouted Ben, Sally, John and Judith in unison.

Ben's father realized that there was no more fun to be dredged out of the situation.

'"Please tell Ben I'll see him tomorrow. Tell him I'm missing him tebrilly."'